A WISH TOO DARK AND KIND

M.L. BLACKBIRD

Annmarie, I hope
you'll enjoy reading
it as much as I loved
writing it

Published by Little Blackbird LLC (www.mylittleblackbird.com)

ISBN 978-1-7370192-0-6 (e-book)

ISBN 978-1-7370192-1-3 (paperback)

ISBN 978-1-7370192-2-0 (hardcover)

This book is a work of fiction. Any references to historical events, real people, or real places are used fictitiously. Other names, characters, places, and events are products of the author's imagination, and any resemblance to actual events or places or persons, living or dead, is entirely coincidental.

For any inquiries regarding this book, please e-mail:
info@mylittleblackbird.com

Cover illustration and design by Xavier Comas.

Chapter illustration by Valentina Ferro.

Edited by Fiona McLaren (developmental), and Tim Marquitz (copy/line).

Proofread by Jonathan Oliver, Katherine Stephen, and Sandra Ogle.

Author photo by Rossella Di Pietro.

To Valentina, for teaching me there are important things that cannot be measured.

To my family and friends, for all the books, movies, and games.

To Po, for all the cuddles and purrs.

S.E.C. 1316:2011:117

What dwells in man I already knew. Now I learnt what is not given him. It is not given to man to know his own needs . . . but I still did not know all. I did not know what men live by.

—LEV TOLSTOY, "WHAT MEN LIVE BY"

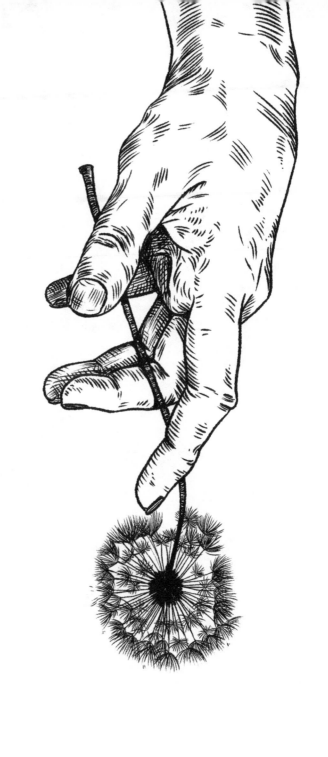

THE PROPHET AND THE NUN

Evidence N-0112 to the investigation I-7242
Arnaud Demeure's handwritten note
Scribbled on an ancient text—the title translates as "A weapon that
pierced the heavens"

A ring,
A vow,
The soul of an angel.

Only two men are fit to use. One who has lost the will to live,
and one who has given himself to death.

The young sister ran through the silent city while the prophet
waited for her to arrive. The old man knew she would come; he
had seen her already. Hidden by the shadow of an old staircase,
eyes fixed on the door, he tried not to get distracted by the creatures in his vision.

Thousands of them, maybe millions, all crammed within glass walls.

The youngest sat at the center of the glass prison. It was taller than the tallest mountain. It was quiet amid the frenzy of its brothers. Its head so high it saw beyond the ceiling of its prison, straight into the realm of the Eldest Lords. Light leaked from underneath its shaking, half-closed eyelids. It peeked into the future.

As the prophet watched them, the creatures stared at him from far away. He could see them, yet his mind could not make full sense of their shapes, only of a few features. A crowd of wings, fangs, stingers, and every piece of every animal he could think of, and some he had never seen, crawling on each other while human parts pushed their way through. The tall one, its eyes closed, hummed over and over.

"We are so close. It won't be long."

The others followed its chanting and moved back and forth in front of the glass holding them prisoners, just like animals expecting a bite of their prey.

The prophet almost missed the nun's arrival. She ran up the stairs, hesitating as she put one foot on the first step.

Unseen, the prophet followed.

From the roof, he tasted the entire city. A forest of concrete and metal spreading in every direction, so much so that nothing existed if not within it. The sun blinded him, shining in white and gold. Dawn was a miracle. He stood still, in awe of the most magnificent city, and he almost forgot he had followed someone.

But there she was, the young sister, standing close to the balustrade, her arms raised to the sky, her shape dark against the sunlight.

The tall metallic tower pierced the sky and stabbed the sun, just like an arrow. The star bled, scattering its light all over the town.

White particles fell from the sky. Snow perhaps, or dust, he could not say. He dared to look up. The sky had turned dark despite the sun shining in it, light still leaking over the city.

In the cold air, no sound but the wind.

Nothing else made a noise. No sound of cars or their horns. No talking or music playing, no chirping of birds.

The prophet stood transfixed.

Cars were still on the asphalt, their lights on. Some stuck in place, some coasting along the streets. Many had slid, hitting nearby objects. Tombstones in an old graveyard, they lay against each other, against lampposts, or sat on the sidewalks.

Men and women, asleep, still clung to their steering wheels. Their heads blasted out of the windshields or hung from the windows. Hundreds and hundreds of bodies covered the sidewalks and the streets. More must have been resting within the buildings, unmoving, untouched.

Here and there, white, black, and red stains, each tens of meters long, covered the streets—flocks of birds caught in whatever happened.

Nobody moved, nobody talked, everyone rested in this cemetery, testimony of a dark miracle.

The world had moved on. The city, now empty, stayed behind.

Paris was dead, and the Great Ones were free.

Preface to the investigation I-7242
Letter, John Ricart Wilhelm to Horace Hastings (Interim Headmaster
of the School of Winchester)

Sir, I have taken the liberty to send this to your personal address, as I am not sure I can trust anyone else on the matter. I have drafted and sent it, ensuring others, even the councilors, could not intercept the missive. In it, you will find everything pertaining to the Paris Paranatural Occurrence and the related investigation (I-7242).

After our investigation of Demeure's palace, we believe there is a connection between the events in Paris, the sudden disappearance of the headmaster, and the potential death of Councilor Dryden. We also suspect the headmaster and most of the council have been in contact with Mr. Demeure for the past few centuries. I have collected all the evidence in the packet accompanying this letter. It contains Mr. Demeure's memoir, notes, scraps, voice recordings, and photographs relating to the guests.

Whatever magick-related event has happened, it has dissipated already. Our agents in the area claim they have observed an increase in telluric pressure beyond Schwarzschild level. Assuming this information is true, we did not find remnants of a Schwarzschild box, and it would be a first for one to appear and disappear in such a short time.

What we found is concerning, though. We have discovered traces of fights and, at the time of writing, three dead bodies: two women, one beheaded, the other killed by what seems a rib piercing her skull, and one man who had gone through full turning before dying from an unknown cause. We suspect at least another one dead, incinerated. The analysis of the ashes will confirm.

Councilor Dryden might have encountered a similar fate. We have not found her body, but we found a bowl of blood, confirmed to be hers, and marks suggesting she performed some kind of ritual.

I will send an update as soon as my agents complete the sweep at the guests' addresses (you can find the locations in the notes I sent over).

THE WITCH OF WINCHESTER

Evidence L-0354 to the investigation I-7242
Letter, Tylanus Spencer to the Eminent Gwrtheyrn Blake (Headmaster
of the School of Winchester)
2 March 1549

It was bound to happen.

The servants carried the bodies to me immediately after the fact, but there was no hope to save them. Cracked skulls, burns all over, dislocated elbows, and broken knees. Bryce's back had been snapped in half, and by the time the man reached my rooms, he had bled out enough that nothing, not even magick, could save him. Katrina was already dead. They are Drydens, so it will cost me many favors to keep this quiet.

It is not hard to see, eminent headmaster, that the child is out of control. She is showing the traits of the monsters she got her blood from. She is restless, does not trust any of her tutors, and still refuses to learn our language. But she is powerful indeed. Such a gift I have never seen. The servants report she lifted Bryce and Katrina Dryden, accomplished wizards of their own, using only her mind, burned their skin using pure tellur as heat, and threw them flying against the walls with such sheer force it cracked the stones.

This is power the School cannot leave uncollected. We need to grow and use it.

I have an idea that might allow us to harness the child while also solving the situation she has created with the Dryden family. A spell of my devising, but seeing now how strong she has become, I will need the council's support.

I will be back at Penrose in two days. We can discuss the details then.

Councilor Tylanus Spencer

The moment Alex stepped onto the small stage at the helm of the class, a murmuring chatter spread across the students.

"Silence," Alex hissed and snapped her fingers. Everyone stopped talking and stared. "Not yet the time to show your true colors. The reason you are here," Alex said, stepping forward, "is we have selected you as the most gifted among your peers in the great families."

She was one or two years older than the teenagers in front of her, or at least so it must have seemed to them. Her body, crystalized in an unchanging youth by the secret magick of the School, might have made them doubt her authority, but she was sure she had enough attitude and presence to stop any of their rebellious thoughts. For sure, she had been already more effective than Professor Corbyn, who stood next to her; a greasy old man who had lectured for decades but had, nonetheless, failed any attempt to halt the kids' chatter.

"I came here to welcome you to your new school, your new life, and your new family. The School of Winchester is one of the few institutions of its kind, hailed as the most honored among this few.

"What characterizes us," Alex said, pacing from one side to the other, "what makes us special, is our continued pursuit of knowledge. Where others lingered on the teachings of the ancients, we have pushed the boundaries. Therefore, today should be the happiest day of your life. The day you start a new one."

Alex paused and breathed in. The house smelled like daisies, as it always did for her, but only for her. She glanced out of the window, and there it was, a beautiful garden nobody else could ever see. There, bushes and trees, masterfully shaped as animals, formed a labyrinth where only she could walk. Alex looked at the kids again. She had seen so many coming and going over the years, and the thought the house would never be such a caring mother to them as it had been to her clung to her stomach. But their puzzled faces made her realize she had been silent for far too long.

"Now, what are we going to teach you?" She cleared her throat and signaled to her assistant: Ricart, a man with fiery red hair, so tall and slim it looked as if someone had stretched him. He had a frowning expression persistently stuck on his face, of which Alex suspected herself to be the cause.

Ricart, who had stood waiting near the door, rushed out, followed by Corbyn.

"We are going to teach you how to change reality in your favor. The noble role all humans and us, the pinnacle of humanity, play every single day. This is what we learn, what we discover, and what we apply."

The men brought four candles, each on its own identical golden pedestal, and placed them on the desk between Alex and the class. The same four unextinguishable candles she had enchanted when she was still a pupil herself. They had seen as many kids come and go as she had.

"As some of you might already know, this reality is nothing but an agreement between the parts that compose it. Physics, chemistry, and mathematics result from this agreement. At first —" Alex stopped as a man rushed into the room.

Sweat ran down his forehead and his blond hair stuck to his skin. His desert boots, brown trousers, and wide green jacket over a striped T-shirt made him look like something between a hipster and a soldier.

The girls in the class giggled at one another.

The man panted, bent with his hand on his thighs. "Grand Inspector Dryden," he said, taking a deep breath. "We need your help at the containment quarters. A creature has escaped."

Alex opened her mouth to speak, but before she could do so, her assistant roared. "How dare you? It's Councilor Dryden, you fool! Don't you have someone else who can help you?"

The audience chuckled, but Alex glared at her assistant with such bitterness he froze in place. "Kids," she said without taking her eyes off Ricart, "I give you back to Professor Corbyn, who actually has something to teach you and has been eyeing me for stealing time from his lesson. I promise I'll stop by before the end." Then she glanced at the black-haired man next to her assistant. "Professor Corbyn, make sure you show them the basics with the candles."

The professor, still standing in front of the entrance door, waved both hands and mouthed something that read like *"I would never . . ."*

Alex ignored him. "You," she said, now talking to the man in desert boots, "lead the way."

The man nodded and rushed out of the room. Alex and her assistant followed.

"There is no need to run," Alex said flatly as the man, who had run ahead, turned to look at where she was.

"But, Councilor," the man in desert boots said, stopping, "if that thing escapes the house—"

"What's your name, young man?" Alex asked, interrupting him.

"Thomas Blake."

"And have you solved the house, Thomas Blake?"

Thomas swallowed without speaking and glanced away from her. "No, Councilor Dryden, I haven't."

"What are the rules of Penrose House for someone who hasn't solved it?"

Thomas stared at her and spoke, his voice shaking, with the cadence of one repeating something learned by heart. "A condition to leave the house is to solve it by learning how to navigate the currents of its tellur. The house forbids pupils from performing magick unsupervised. They must not run, stare straight through glass and mirrors, or draw on any surface of the house. If they open a door, should they find a corridor behind it, they should close it and reopen it until the room they expect appears. Ignore any creature, humans included, that appears in such corridors. Pupils must not turn right in the main hallway over five times in a day. Should a portrait or poster appear hanging on a wall of their dormitories, they must not remove it, nor look behind it. Should they not respect these guidelines, the council takes no responsibilities of the consequences the house might cast on them."

"Good," Alex said, smiled, and took to strolling again. "Now, as we walk, tell me about this creature."

"We couldn't see it," Thomas said. As he continued, he kept upping the pace, gaining a few steps on Alex and Ricard, then stopping until they caught up. "But there was a loud buzz, and all the wizards in the lab ended up killed, cut into pieces by an invisible sword. Only one assistant was alive when I left but badly wounded."

"Invisible and buzzing," she said. "And it killed the wizards before the assistants? I might know what it is. Stop." Alex stood still and counted to five.

The other two stared at her.

"Turn around now," Alex said as she finished counting and spun on her heels.

As she did, she found a wooden double door a few inches from her nose. *"Containment Rooms"* had been engraved on the top of the door's stone arch. A metallic sign attached to the side of the door read, *"Warning: authorized personnel only. Any creature you might see with your peripheral vision is likely an illusion. We store the real ones in the cells."*

Alex shrugged. "Not true anymore." She was about to open the door, but she turned back to the others. "Ricart, off you go. Fetch me a tea. I'll meet you back at Professor Corbyn's classroom." She glanced at Thomas. "You should wait outside while I sort this one out. It's dangerous in there, and, in any case, it shouldn't take me long."

Ricart didn't wait for her to repeat herself, and by the time she was mid-sentence, he was already leaving.

"I'll come in with you, Councilor," said Thomas.

As he spoke, Ricart stumbled and muttered a curse.

"You won't," Alex said, and she glared at Thomas. "There is no need for you to get back in and risk your life after who knows how you managed to escape."

"I can't sit out here while she . . . my colleague is in there."

Alex sighed. "Okay, we are wasting more time arguing. You can come in but stay out of my way, and don't even think unless I tell you so."

The hall of the containment area was like she remembered. A large circular room acted as a hub for the real containment sectors. No more, no less than labyrinth-like dungeons, where the School stored any specimen (animal, human, or parahuman) that piqued its interest. The headmaster had hence arranged the space as a laboratory to support the experiments on parahumanity and immortality. Since then, it had always worked as one of the most respected institutions within the School of Winchester, having produced paper after paper for decades and promoted many council members from within its ranks.

Two hospital beds sat empty at the center of the room, enveloped in pieces of electronics attached to cables that sprouted from the ceiling above them. Some old-looking tables ran along the walls, covered in whirring and puffing lab instruments. Portraits of illustrious former members of the laboratory decorated its walls. In one glance, Alex found a picture of herself hanging between the two doors leading to the dungeons —*"Alexandra Emilia Dryden, Councilor"* was engraved at the bottom of the frame. They had received the memo. She would have a hard time being just Alex anywhere she would go.

All normal, if not for the two dead wizards. One, a woman, had fallen facedown a few inches from the beds, both her hands cut away and nowhere to be seen. Another, a man, sat against one of the doors. His decapitated head rested on his lap. A young woman, blonde and fair who, judging from her clothes, was an assistant, was alive but pale as a corpse. She had crawled under one bed and was curled up like a ball. She hadn't seen Alex and Thomas come in.

"That your girlfriend?" Alex asked Thomas, pointing at the woman. "Kinda obvious, but fits your type of hero. What's her name?"

Thomas swallowed hard. "Ariel . . . She . . . You think that thing is still here? You know what it is?"

"Yes, to both. Those two were experienced wizards, and they

likely tried to use their sight but didn't see it. This, and that it cuts everything in its way, tells me it's a fully turned fae. Nasty beasts, invisible even to people with the sight, eyes all over, and two pairs of claws as sharp as razors. We are in luck as it can't see us either."

"But it did," Thomas said. "It followed them around the lab as they tried to escape."

"That's because they moved. If you stay still, you'll be safe. It can't see you, and it can't hear you either. It just follows the flicker of light as we move."

"So, what do we do?"

"Easy," Alex said, and carefully took off the robe she was wearing on top of her mundane clothes. "We bait it out." She threw the robe in the air.

A loud buzz filled the air, as if thousands of insects had flown in.

"There you are," Alex said, and she opened her mind's eye. With it open, she had the sight, and she could see the network, the mesh of tellur and its translucent floating strands that connected everything with everything else.

Alex was ready to cast a spell, but before she could, Ariel, having noticed them, and probably believing Alex's distraction would offer her a cover, rushed out of her hideout. But as she did, the buzzing noise shifted in her direction.

"No," the young man yelled, and raced toward his girlfriend. As he did so, the strands of tellur around him shook, and a single wave traversed them, running away from him.

"Don't! You foolish child," Alex said. "Don't do magick without a plan."

The network of tellur vibrated as Thomas reached Ariel and hugged her tight. A moment later, a splash of green sticky liquid drowned them both, and a pair of enormous claws, severed from the fae, fell from thin air. The beast shrieked so loud it covered its own buzzing.

The strands of tellur moved again. This time, a wave traversed them toward the young man.

"Newbie," Alex called, "handle your dissonance!"

It was too late, and Thomas too slow to react. The wave reached him and, again, a spatter of liquid, red this time, covered both him and his companion. His own right arm vaporized.

Thomas's screams roared so loud they rivaled the buzzing and shrieking of the fae.

Alex hurried. She focused on the network in front of her and the place where she heard the noise coming from, above the other two. Once again, the strands pulsed, this time with her at the center.

Another loud shriek, and the creature fell out of thin air, now visible. It smashed against the floor in front of the couple, cracking it as if someone had smacked a huge invisible hammer on the monster. All that remained was a mess of wings, eyes, and claws curled together.

Alex had no time to celebrate as the network already throbbed once again around her. She focused on the wave of tellur that moved in her direction through the strands. Under her watch, the wave changed direction and flew toward Thomas, who sat, ghostly white, on the ground, one arm around Ariel's shoulders. As it hit him, the wound on his shoulder burst into a bright flame that died out in an instant.

"It's done," Alex said, exhaling, "it's done." Then, looking at Thomas lying in Ariel's arms, Alex's face burned, and her heart beat hard again. "I told you not to move," she yelled at the man, pointing a finger at him. "Teaches you a lesson not to disobey me!"

But Thomas didn't react. He had lost consciousness. Alex found Ariel's watery blue eyes staring at her the same way they looked at the beast dead on the floor.

She glanced at the crushed body of the fae too, and was

reminded that for most wizards she was closer to the specimens than she was to them. She might be an improved version, a better parahuman, and the School made sure to stress that being turned immortal should be considered the highest honor, but after all, she still was a parahuman. Just a receptacle for the bundle of instincts that boiled within her soul.

Maybe one day she'd lose control, turning finally into a beast like the fae she had just killed. The odd sense of peace coming from this thought left a dull feeling in her stomach.

"I told him not to move," Alex said, but to Ariel this time, slowly, almost soothingly.

"Councilor," said Ariel, her voice cracking, "can't you help him?"

"I did," Alex said, checking that the man was still breathing. "I cauterized his wound. The healers will get to fix the rest in a couple of days. We'll just have to wait for them to arrive."

Once Alex reached the classroom, Ricart was outside with her tea in his hands. She ignored him, distracted as she was by Professor Corbyn's long-winded discourse on the magick principles of will, energy, form, and dissonance. He had already lighted three of the four candles, and since Alex knew that lesson by heart—as she had taught it for decades—she also knew what came next.

But Corbyn went on for minutes on a rant so obscure even Alex struggled to understand. On and on he went about the divine waters and the Lord of Shards, the Thelema and the Kia.

Alex watched the man talking in disbelief. He was such a quack. How could someone speak like that in this century? Her blood pumped into her ears at the thought Corbyn would indoctrinate the children with his religious misrepresentation of something as natural as magick. It was only quantum physics, a network, and a basic reapplication of Newton's third law. No need for divine waters and mills of God.

Corbyn glanced at the door and nodded at her. "You have also seen that, to impress your will on the collective agreement, you must use a form, a shape, that helps you focus on the outcome you desire. We used our voice and a wave of our hands. Now, I want to show you how an expert wizard can do the same by just focusing on the shape of the desire in their mind. Councilor," he said, "would you lend a hand?"

Of course he would ask her. Corbyn, the quack he was, could never do formless magick.

Alex stepped into the classroom without taking her eyes off the professor.

Corbyn jumped, startled, as the last candle caught fire, burning so high and bright it looked more like a torch. An instant later, the other three flared too. An icy breeze traversed the room and frosted the glass of its windows.

"Magnificent!" Corbyn said. "A round of applause for the councilor and her perfect demonstration."

Alex waved one hand, stopping the kids before they could obey. "Can I have my tea, please?" she said, gesturing to Ricart.

The assistant rushed into the room and almost tumbled, but delivered the cup of tea safely in her hands.

She took it quickly and sipped the tea. As she did so, her face contorted in disgust. "Cold, as usual," she said. As she spoke, the fire on all the candles extinguished and their tips were covered in frost. The cup in her hand fumed. She took another sip, and a smile escaped from her.

"Magick in reverse, and using the dissonance to the wizard's advantage," said Corbyn. "This, right here, is the mark of a great wizard. We should be grateful to the councilor for being so generous to show us. Now," he continued, "any questions before we let the councilor go?"

The kids glanced at each other hesitantly, and no one spoke.

"Well then," Corbyn began, but a girl raised one hand.

"Sure," he said, pointing in her direction.

"I just wanted to ask . . . well . . . Father says you are immortal. Is it true?"

The other students looked at each other again.

Ricart, who had been leaning against the wall looking at his own shoes for the previous few minutes, jumped up as if about to run to put himself between the student and Alex.

The witch just offered a faint smile. "What is your name, dear?" she asked.

"Maggy . . . Margareth Owen, Councilor Dryden."

"Owen," Alex repeated. "Daughter of Jonah and Lilian?"

"Yes, I am," said the girl, sitting with her back now rigid against her chair.

"Your father is a good man, but he overvalues me," Alex said. "I'm not immortal. Hard to kill, maybe. Unless someone puts some effort into it, I won't die of age, no. But I can still die, for sure."

The kids exchanged even more puzzled looks and whispered.

"Immortality is an honor only a selected few of our pupils receive," said Corbyn. "The greatest achievement of the School, I might say."

"Any other questions?" Alex asked.

Many hands rose among the students. She smiled. "Anything not related to me or the likelihood of my departure from this world?"

The same hands went slowly down.

"Excellent!" she said, nodding, and glanced at Corbyn.

"Class," Corbyn said. He took a book from his desk drawer and showed it to the class.

On its leather cover, three figures were etched—a crescent moon, a long-legged bird, and a dog-faced baboon. Alongside the three figures, also carved on the leather, stood four words:

knowledge, wisdom, intelligence, and valor. Alex recognized that book. She had studied it herself as a young pupil.

"Take your copies of *Mercurius ter Maximus' De Natura Absconditus* from the library as you walk to your dorm," Corbyn continued. "But before you go, stand up to thank Councilor Dryden for visiting us."

The class stood. She nodded at them before disappearing through the door, followed by her assistant, who had gathered the candles and the tea she had left behind.

Alex had reached her office at last. With Ricart gone for a while, she would enjoy some time alone. She already savored the silence of the room and the relaxing idea of an armchair against her back, thus took her seat, threw the glasses and heavy robe on a nearby chair, dropped her feet on the desk, and hard-pressed her eyes, massaging their surroundings.

It had been barely a minute like this when Ricart swung the door of the office open. "Councilor Dryden," he called.

She opened her eyes too quickly, and the light blinded her. All she saw were blinking circles. As she returned to a sitting position, she pushed a few papers off her desk with her legs.

"Ricart," she chided. She could only see his shape without her glasses on. "For God's sake, haven't I told you to knock first? What now?"

"It's the headmaster, Councilor. He wants to talk with you."

"What does the old man want with me now?" she asked, scrambling to find her glasses.

"I asked, but he didn't say. He demanded you go to his office right away."

"Does he understand I don't work for him anymore? He can't boss me around like this."

"Shall I . . . shall I tell him you won't go?"

"What?" Alex's tone was a pitch higher than she wanted. "No, I'm going right now. It might be something important, you know, if it's this urgent."

A few minutes later, she knocked at the headmaster's door.

"Come on in, please," a voice said from inside the room.

As she opened the door, she found the room illuminated by the faint light of candles. There were many of them on a candelabra on the headmaster's desk, others on the cabinets that ran along one side of the room, and more on the chandelier that dangled from the ceiling. She could not grasp what was the root of the headmaster's aversion against modernity, but the room was still like the first time she had entered it.

Even the smell was the usual mix of wax, wood burning, and old books, so many of them stored in the same cabinets that hosted the candles. The very first memory she had of the School was in this room. Just like him, she hadn't aged much since then, but at least she had let the simplifications of modern life have the best of her. In a way, it still made sense for someone as old as Headmaster Tylanus Spencer to be nostalgic.

The man sat in an armchair behind his desk and looked straight at her as she walked a couple of steps inside. He smirked, and she found it ironic the man could still be so full of himself when dealing with her. The high and mighty Spencer, who had turned himself into an immortal capable of doing magick, hailed as a hero of the School. He was a legend.

Yet, she knew the truth now, that it had all been by accident, and no one, including him, had been able to repeat this feat. All the others since then had been created from his blood, and then from the blood of the ones he turned, and so on. Alex was among the first the council had turned, or so she was told.

The council had wiped any memory of the events from her

mind, a habit they had kept when turning wizards from outside their VIP club. But she was in the club now, so she knew their secrets, and as much as she hated it, she had to keep them such.

"Ricart said you had asked for me. What can I do for you, sir?" She stood, hands folded behind her back.

"Alexandra, my dear, you used to wish me a good evening when you were little," said the man with a smile. "Look at you now, always ready for business. Take a seat, please."

The headmaster was a plump man. His cheeks full, eyes too tiny for his face, a broad nose, and a large bush of curly hair on his head. As he spoke, he gestured for her to sit in one chair in front of the desk.

She sat, saying nothing.

"Alexandra Dryden," the man said, clasping his hands. "Look at you, all sitting straight. It seems yesterday you used to sit on my knees."

"That was half a millennium ago. People would talk if I did that now, sir."

"Always a smart answer," said the man with a bitter grin on his face. "If only your old man could see you. First in class, accomplished witch, and even appointed to the high council."

Alex gripped the flesh of her own thigh. "Not thanks to you, sir. You voted against me at the council. Would my old man be glad of that too?" She looked out of the window beside the headmaster.

"I tried to protect you from yourself. I've held my position in the council for many centuries. I understand it isn't just about talent or skills, and you are not what one would call a people person. Had I been gifted with a talent as bright as yours, I would have spent less time studying and more time learning how to be liked by my fellows." His voice turned from sweet to low and serious in an instant. "Speaking of which, I heard what happened to that kid today."

"He did it to himself. He should have listened," she replied. "And how did you hear about it already?"

"That's just a perk of the headmaster's job," he said, leaning back in his chair. "That, and he is a Blake. His family will make my ears hurt, you know that."

"Did you call me here just to talk about this, sir?"

The headmaster leaned forward, both hands under his chin. "You and I both know that one day or another you'll annoy enough of them. You need to be more careful now that you are a council member."

"Yeah, the prestige of the council is important to you."

"You paint a worse image of me than you should," said the man in a condescending tone. "I care about your safety."

"Sure, you care about the safety of the order, sir."

The man laughed and smirked. "Anyhow, that is not why I called you here." He took an envelope from a drawer and slid it over to Alex.

"What is that?" she asked.

"An invitation to a party for you to attend."

"You send me to parties now?"

"Well, it's from an important friend of the order in Paris."

"Paris?" she asked, dragging her chair back. She was about to stand up, but restrained herself. "The courses have just started. I can't go on a trip now. I have to monitor the state of the programs."

"The School will be fine. As a councilor, your time is better invested away from teaching, and the place has survived for a while without your monitoring, anyway."

"That is what I'm trying to fix, sir."

"Read that letter, Alexandra," he said, leaning back again and looking at the ceiling.

Her hands shook as she reached for the letter. She almost tore it apart while opening it. How could he dare give her, a member of the high council, such a direct order?

She pulled the letter out with some trouble and skimmed it up and down. Then her eyes stopped on the signature at the bottom.

"Is this some kind of joke?" she asked. "The man has been dead for what? A few centuries?"

"We never said he was dead. He retired from the spotlight."

"And what would Mr. Demeure want from me, anyhow? I have never met him or been at his parties."

"Beats me if I know," the headmaster sighed. "He is an eccentric man and comes from a time when he could do anything he wanted. I think he has sent this invite to me under the false assumption I still hold any authority over you."

Alex tapped her fingers on the desk. "Are you saying I can refuse?" she asked, grinning. She knew the answer already.

"No, I'm not. The order requires you to go," said the headmaster. "That man was an important ally for us in our early days. From what it says there, you are not to bring any servants with you, so make sure you can arrange your security somehow."

No servants. It sure sounded suspicious, but as much as they disliked her, the other councilors would not do this to her. Not this soon. She still had enough support.

"You know what the man was famous for, right?" asked the headmaster, interrupting her thoughts.

"All of those stories about fulfilling wishes?"

"Exactly those. I have seen him with my own eyes. I have been to those parties. Those are not stories."

"I'll take them for what they are then," Alex said, standing up. "Now, if you'll excuse me, sir, I have to prepare myself for this trip if I have to leave so soon. I also have to arrange things so everything here keeps running as it should in my absence." She half-bowed and headed to the door without looking back. "Have a good night, sir."

"Alex . . ." said the man behind her. Something new was in his voice. Concern.

"What now, sir?" she asked, one hand still on the knob.

"Nothing," said the headmaster. "Just have a good night and safe travels, Alexandra."

Evidence L-0472 to the investigation I-7242
Letter, Arnaud Demeure to Tylanus Spencer (Councilor of the School
of Winchester)
24 February 1532

I have received the stone. The inscription is authentic, so I will pay my side of the bargain. And yet, I know you don't fully trust me, despite what you have seen with your own eyes. I couldn't fathom I would live to see the day when a wizard would not trust the infinite ways of magick. But you were there when I, an immortal, did the impossible and performed the art.

Let me tell you, there is hope in your quest for knowledge. With eternity in front of you, you will have the time to discover every secret this world offers.

Go east, in the land of the Strigoi. If you want what I have, you must make an enemy of them. One Strigoi lord has a jewel, a weapon of my making that hides in the guise of a child. Find it, and in the blood of that child, you will find the secret I carry.

Once you find the child and discover the secret of how immortals can do magick, you will keep the child with you and use it for the glory of your dear school. But remember, the child is mine and mine alone. One day, when I will come asking for it, you will return it to me.

Arnaud Demeure

3

THE OLD PRINCE'S PARTY

The fireplace was lit and ready to consume his life, or, at least, the memories of what it had been. Roman had waited for this day for so many centuries, and now?

That piece of paper, that invitation, didn't want to leave his hands and, instead, kept moving in them. The letters, piled on the table beside the armchair, stood there too, looking at him, scared of the fire but not bothered by how hard this was to him. The invitation was proof his time had come at last.

This was how his end started. If so, he wanted to go unhindered, and burning all the letters to his dead sibling seemed the best way to get rid of any burden. Those letters were the only thing he still cared about. He had to burn them.

Roman picked up the first one. His memories didn't weigh as much as he thought. His eyes followed the paper as it flew into the fire. It talked of his betrayal. Just like Cain, murderer and betrayer of his own brother, only one thing he feared for almost half of a millennium: dying. He chuckled at the irony.

With the letter, pain, guilt, and neglect went up into smoke. All those emotions, caught in paper, twirled in a gray cloud over the fire that called him by his name. All those stories gone and, with them, that infant left in front of a church, the drunkard father, and his lonely death—stabbed, suffocated in his own filth —such a relief.

One letter gone, many others still to burn. A long process he savored. The pain of taking out that tooth had left him with the pleasant feeling that his suffering, his real suffering, was behind him. A second letter flew into the fire, and again, Roman felt the same pain.

If a new world, even a better one, had to come, it must do so through screams and pain. No birth arrived without pain and blood, and the memory of the sea of blood in the prince's eyes was Roman's last memory of him.

The first time Roman met the prince, it was amid a crowded party in Paris. The old man, the prince, could go through it unnoticed. His gray hair, small body, and face, one out of many, were built to be forgotten. Roman met him as the prince came down the stairs of his palace. "Old friend" the prince had called him, and to this day, Roman still didn't know why he had received such a salute.

He had lost himself searching in those icy eyes, as he had seen something behind them. The eyes of someone else who had died alone many times. Someone old who had escaped the world many years before. Those eyes called him *old friend*, but whose eyes were they? Those of the man who stood in front of him or those of a monster who stared at him without a shred of light?

He would die because of that man. He had seen the sea of blood in which the monster was swimming. Roman would spend years swimming in there himself.

Now that invitation.

The wolf quivered within his guts—everywhere within him —chained for so long that it yearned for the day it would be free to drown in its fury. Nothing mattered anymore. And yet, fear took hold of him. Dread that the prince might be a monster far worse than he was himself.

Roman closed his eyes and reached for the flame where his letters were burning, and the fire, driven by a higher intelligence, tried to reach him. And perhaps, who knew, the best end would have been to burn by the fire. The wolf winced. For the beast, no time would ever be a good time to die.

He threw another letter into the fire.

His centuries whispered into his ears, talking of nasty and mysterious things, of caverns and wars, worlds above and below, philosophy and magic. A rant of fire and smoke of which, after so many years, he could barely hear the words but not understand the meaning. They talked of arcane knowledge, worlds beyond this world, keys and doors, rituals, sacrifices, and monsters from before his own long story.

"Enough," he said, gripping the armrest.

The fireplace stood in front of him, silent now, just barely crackling. No words or whispers.

The pile of letters almost gone, he threw the final paper into the fire and stood to look at the last words on it burning. A name, one he had chosen, Azurine. And with it vanished, he was finally ready.

The fire had gone out, but Roman stood there watching its cinders. He took the phone and called the only number saved in it. "I'm ready, sir. It is all done."

"We are in luck," said a hoarse voice. "We spotted the target in Paris."

Roman's fists clenched so much his knuckles whitened. Despite the centuries he had spent in the order, Roman had never met the high priest in person and knew only his hoarse voice, his face always hidden behind the shade of a confessional or the handset of a phone. Even so, the high priest had been a father to him, much more than his real one had ever been. It was the high priest who had given him a mission, a target, and with it, purpose.

"Listen," the voice kept going, "help with the search. I want you to catch the target before the party starts. The others will take over from where you leave off, but we can't let that man have it."

"I will make sure it won't happen," Roman said, his teeth grinding against each other.

"Then, all the best, brother Roman. Stay under God's wings."

"Always under God's wings."

Evidence J-0006 to the investigation I-7242
Extract from Arnaud Demeure's journal
13 July 1258

Hurt, scared, and hungry, this is no place for me. If only Father were here, in this cold, ugly house, he would teach them how to treat a noble of France. But he is not here, and the day will come when I won't need a father to give them a lesson.

The old cassette's noise had filled the room. Finding one of those old players had been harder than Hermann thought, but at the end, he was there, in an old motel with carpets the same color as rats that smelled a bit of rat too. The warm tobacco flavor that lingered in the air was a sweet distraction from that reek.

Valentine, his sire, had demanded a swift job, but the tapes meant more to Hermann than they did to her. It had never been easy to understand her intentions, and this cleaning job, as she had called it, was even stranger than usual. Valentine had been stranger than usual herself since the moment she had received that letter from Paris. She hadn't let him read it, but her face when she saw it was that of someone uncertain about which direction to take. A face Hermann had never seen on her.

As he spent his time sticking newspaper to the windows, an old man's voice and that of a young boy took turns speaking out of the cassette.

"Nice to meet you, Hermann," said the old man's voice. "Your mom and I talked about you at length. She is proud of you. She said you are a bright student. How is life at school? Are you making lots of friends?"

"No more, no less than the others, I guess," said a youthful voice. "Most of my friends are on my softball team. All good, anyway."

"Softball, that sounds interesting! And you have a team, you say?"

"Yeah, I'm the captain," said the young boy with pride in his voice. "First in the league but going up and down from second. We might win this time."

Both voices disappeared, replaced by the striding noise of the tape moving in fast-forward.

Hermann pushed play.

"Dr. R.J. Millard, 27 August 1978," said the same old voice as before. "This was my first visit with Hermann Walker. These are the notes at the end of my session. Hermann is a polite kid, studies hard, and his mother describes him as having a normal ability to interact with others and make friends. Hermann has been through therapy before, one or two sessions after his father's death.

"According to his mother, he is one of the best students in his class. She says he is a well-mannered and methodical kid. After having met him today, I can't say I disagree. There is something that bothers me, though. I'm not sure if it is the way he speaks, the way he moves as he talks, but there is something, for lack of a better term, unnatural, about this kid. The whole time I sensed he was hiding something.

"His own mother sent him to me for this very reason. I wasn't sure of what to think of a mother that brings a fourteen-year-old boy to me without a clear motivation, but now, I admit, the whole thing is fascinating. But I'm an old man who is too easy a prey to his curiosity."

"Same dream again?" Millard asked.

"Yeah . . ."

A creaking noise came out of the tape. Doctor Millard leaned on his armchair every time Hermann talked about his dreams. "Would you mind telling me about it again? Anything new you noticed?"

"Nothing too different from the other times, Doctor. I'm bouncing up and down in slow motion. Beneath me is a man. I have no idea who he is. And behind him is a woman. I know her, or at least myself in the dream knows her. She floats behind him, naked and surrounded by light. She brushes her hair as it falls on her back. She turns and smiles at me. Then nothing; it's dark and something shrieks. I always wake up at this point."

"And what do you feel when you wake up?"

"Nothing too special. Nostalgia, I guess."

The time was passing fast as Hermann listened to the tapes. He found some entertainment in listening to them. His entire story danced in the motel's putrid air, while outside of his window a man was puking his stomach out and another shouted at the traffic.

"You are quiet, boy," said Doctor Millard from the tape. "Did you miss some sleep?"

"Yeah. I keep having the same dream and that stupid nightmare."

"What kind of nightmare?"

"I don't know, people shouting. Light shines behind a glass, a window. I don't know, a fairy or something? A sphere of light traveling at a crazy speed and nothing after. It bumps against the glass, and there is a crash. After, it's just yelling and a lot of red all over. I guess they are shouting a name. I'm not sure who they are calling. All around is a white light that wraps me, and I shine all over."

"And?"

"Nothing, Doctor. Nothing. I wake up after that."

"I see," Millard said, his scribbling so furious it came through the cassette. "What name are those people calling? Your father's name?"

Hermann stood on his feet that day, he remembered. Not that he didn't want to talk about his father, but Millard just could not stop with it. "What does my father have to do with all this?"

"Hermann, your father died in a car accident. Do you still hold a grudge?"

"I think he should have stuck around just a little more, but no, I wouldn't say so. I've managed."

The tape shrieked again as he pushed fast-forward.

"Is it already time? Are you sure about it?"

"Yes, Hermann," said Doctor Millard. "We spent at least one hour today trying to carve out something from you, but despite the time, I don't think you want to trust me. It's been ten years, and you still can't open up to me."

"I don't get the point, Doctor."

"Okay, let's try again. Can you explain to me why you need to spend your days with your nose in books? Why do you need to win every game you play? Why at all costs?"

"What's wrong with it? I mean, that's what she . . . I mean, what my mother always wanted. Is there anything wrong with it?"

"Hermann, we are done for the day. I'm tired. You are frustrated. Let's move this discussion to another time, okay?"

"Doctor R.J. Millard, 27 August 1989. Last session with Hermann Walker. This day, eleven years ago, a fourteen-year-boy entered my office for the first time. Today, a twenty-five-year-old man came out instead. A man who has spent the last eleven years in therapy. He is like a son to me, and the biggest mystery of my career. I can't stop being obsessed with his way of speaking and the way he moves. There is something in the way he sees things, and perceives the world around him, such a level of depth and speed that I can't follow.

"He has built a character and a plan for his life I can't understand, or maybe he just doesn't want me to understand. As if something or someone bigger than him talks from the shadows, and he puts effort into hiding it as much as he can. But he can't hide the thirst and hunger he has for the world. Such hunger that he might swallow it whole. His mother's death has worsened this further, and as she disappeared from his life, another woman entered it. He talks of her as one would talk of an old friend who came back from a lifelong travel.

"In a short time, she has gained more and more of a grip on him. I am not sure if this is a healthy relationship for someone like Hermann. From him, no real attachment toward a partner. She is more like a mother figure; an attraction toward opportunities he can't describe. On her side as well, from the way he talks of her, the pushes are toxic. He might not understand it, but she has a plan for him, I am sure of it. Maybe the surprise of receiving his call tonight and his desire to cancel every other appointment biases me. He is following her to New Orleans. This burns like a failure.

"There is something broken, but I can't put my finger on it. Any colleague would laugh at me for keeping him in therapy for so many years without a diagnosis. But an aura permeates from him. I sense it, I can't get it out, and now, my pity, I might not be the one to fix it."

It had been weird for Hermann to listen to the whole summary of his own therapy. Even more to discover the notes and comments of the doctor that had followed him. How little he had understood. But Valentine had asked him to close his ties. She never said to listen to the cassettes, and he suspected she would not like it, but so it was. He was certain she would discover it somehow. She had always been able to.

It was night again, though, and as he threw everything he had collected in a garbage bag in his trunk, some dull misery took hold of his heart.

The drive from Houma to New Orleans had been fast. Faster than he had thought. He sighed. It might have been worth enjoying the breeze of the night, refreshing, for once, in a place always so muggy. There was music in the air that night, for sure. Something important was coming.

Why did she send him on this mission?

It could even be something Doctor Millard knew or the recordings in the garbage bag. He wouldn't ask. Valentine would never give him a straight answer, anyhow.

She had bossed him around for the good part of two decades. Scared of a danger that never arrived. New Orleans, the old city, was safer than Houma. Safer from what, he didn't know. Hermann sighed. One day, if this kept going as it was, they would have to move somewhere else.

When he arrived in New Orleans, he took the bag from his trunk and threw it on the side of the street. He then took a tank of gasoline from the trunk and poured half of the liquid on the bag, and with the rest, he created a path running from the bag to a point a few meters away and went back to leave the tank, still one-third full, near the bag.

Hermann took out his lighter. It was a good lighter, one of those that keep the flame when left open. He sighed again and threw it on the gasoline path. Everything was done according to the instructions he had received.

Now, he could drive to her without interruptions, hoping Valentine had something less burdensome for him to do this time.

Hermann had been away just for a few days, but now, the periodic flashes of the streetlamps as he drove into town played the rhythm of his welcome song. He was home.

The excitement had been enough to awaken the wolf and his sharpened senses. His foot pushed on the accelerator more than he would have wanted.

He was hungry.

It hadn't taken Hermann too much time to accept that the wolf that lived within him needed an offer from time to time. In fact, it wasn't much of a price to pay for his immortality and the benefits that derived from it. At first, by the way Valentine kept referring to it, he thought she had turned him into some sort of werewolf, but then he realized how much less literal this whole wolf thing was.

At the same time, the wolf was him and was something else. It was like carrying a silent passenger within him. A bundle of instincts that communicated in growls and winces. An exaggerated caricature of himself, furious when he was angry, frightened when he was scared, voracious when he was hungry. It was no more humiliating than eating or defecating.

Mortals had become disgusting to his eyes in most ways, and he could not stop the thought of their nasty habits from crossing his mind. His stomach twitched as he pictured their hands grabbing food and bringing it to their mouths, hands dirtied by the grease of the food they ingurgitated every day while humors drooled out of their lips.

Their flat teeth crunched and melted everything, reducing it to what they themselves, disgusted, would have called vomit had it moved in the opposite direction. Their guts contorted in the desperate attempt to compress, squeeze, and extract something good out of that mire. The idea of how all of that would end horrified him: the vilest act, when naked, vulnerable, and bent on themselves, they would expel the result of their intestines' work between sighs and grunts.

It was nauseating.

His sight clouded at the idea, and he slowed down just to speed up again a moment later. He had to stop for dinner as soon as he arrived in town. This was the deal. He would feed blood and meat to the wolf, and this would give him enough time to reach his wildest dreams. He had signed the contract long before.

It was an easy protocol. He just needed to find some cheap drinks and someone stupid enough that his car could mesmerize them. At that point, he would take out enough blood to keep going for one night, perhaps avoiding killing his victim, shower them in whatever bad alcohol he had at the back of his trunk, and drop them near a dumpster. Wolf fed and mission accomplished.

Yes, once again, mission accomplished.

———

Hermann entertained the idea of not going to Valentine right away, but he had to talk with her about his little adventure out of town, and either he would go to her, or Valentine would find him, anyhow.

She had made the little theater in Vieux Carré her own, perhaps because the buildings with their old European style and the French café at the corner fed the longing for her old life in Paris. Walking through the Creole areas of town to land in the French district, Herman tried to imagine Valentine's life in Paris.

He smiled, thinking the red walls of Vieux Carré and its red brick roads were hints that the woman had left for him. Her Old-World origins gave her the freedom to take on an entire district without turning up anyone's nose. Vieux Carré was Valentine Duchamp's domain, and every nightcrawler in New Orleans acknowledged it.

She lived there, straight in his brain, as he walked around those old streets, and the thoughts of Valentine walked with him until he reached the theater.

It was late at night and the streets around the theater were deserted. The building was closed at that hour, but Valentine loved spending time there in activities that reminded him she might be a bit mad. The theater would have been empty and the stage silent if it were not for the dirge that kept repeating itself. It would have been hard for a mortal to move around in that darkness, but Hermann's eyes allowed him to walk around using only the faint light filtering through the windows.

Someone dear to him sang the dirge, a failed lullaby, in honor of a teddy bear left on the ground. Since the first time he saw Valentine, she had struck him, not much for her beauty because, to be clear, she had never been beautiful, but because her innocent blue eyes trapped between voluminous scarves and blonde locks made her somehow attractive.

Those eyes looked at the world in awe, unaware of what to expect from the future and trusting everybody. Those eyes were her biggest lie, her most dangerous hoax as they hid her true nature.

Hermann came close to the woman, and running a hand through his hair, he reached into the inner pocket of his coat to take out a cigarette. He looked at her for a while, but as soon as he was about to raise his hand to greet her, Valentine stopped singing and stared at him with motionless eyes, her head tilted, and a curious smile on her face.

"Hermann, my dear, welcome home. You have mail," she said without standing from the ground where she sat. She then took an envelope from under her bulky sweater and threw it at him. "Read!"

No sender and not opened yet. On the envelope, only the recipient's name: Valentine Duchamp. "For me, all right," he said.

"You need to leave tonight," she said, her eyes still fixed on him.

He glanced at the letter again. And her name wasn't on the envelope anymore. Instead, it read Hermann Walker.

The man took another puff of his cigarette, the best thing to calm his nerves. "I imagined I'd spend some time in New Orleans."

She glanced again at the teddy bear and grasped it to rock it like a child. "I need you in Paris."

"You do? Stop acting like a child then!" he said and bit his lip.

He expected anger, but Valentine smiled. "You chose to see me like this. Of all the ways you can choose to see me, you keep picking this one. It's kind of inappropriate if you ask me, but what kind of comfort are you seeking, my dear?" she asked, tilting her head to catch his eyes.

"I . . . How much time before I go?" Hermann asked. It would be useless to debate her if she had decided already.

"Mr. Walker," said the voice of one of her servants from behind the stage. The man emerged from the shadows. "I've organized everything according to the instructions. Nobody will annoy you during your trip, sir."

Hermann didn't want to listen to him. Did she have to send him over like this? On a whim? Hermann took another whiff, flipping the envelope around with his fingers while he followed the servant. But before he could turn to say goodbye, Valentine wrapped him in a hug behind his back. She was warm, and her hair tickled his neck.

"Be careful, please," she whispered.

When he turned, the theater was empty. Nobody was there beyond him, the servant, and a teddy bear on the floor. An old radio sat on the stage playing a lullaby. Hermann could not resist a smile. He needed to be in Paris.

———

Evidence J-0074 to the investigation I-7242
Extract from Arnaud Demeure's journal
5 August 1259

"Who is she?" I asked the others who, like me, watched the schoolmistresses chasing a blonde girl away from the courtyard of the orphanage. She was one or two years older than me.

"A gypsy," one said. "She comes along now and then to sell

her junk, but really, she comes to kidnap the little ones. She lives with a witch out of town, and I bet they eat babies for breakfast."

The others laughed.

"Does she not already look a bit like a witch herself?" another asked.

I didn't know about them, but she was, to me, the most beautiful thing I had ever seen.

4

DON'T GO

"My friend, you need a woman in your life." A guy stood in front of Daniel. He was sure he knew him, but he didn't remember his name. The guy looked tall. He must have been standing while Daniel studied him from the bottom up. So many people all around, and way too strong a stench of beer and smoke. "You must find another one to forget the previous. It's like, you know, what you do when your cat dies or something," the guy said. He must have been drunk, this self-proclaimed love professor.

Whatever he said didn't matter. Daniel still felt her arms around his neck, her smell in his house.

"Daniel? Are you asleep?" Sophia asked. He was in bed. Not in a pub, not with that annoying guy who kept drinking and talking, but in bed with Sophia. Was she back?

He faked being asleep so she would sleep too. Maybe she would not leave.

Sophia sobbed. "Daniel, what will we do the day they come to tear us apart? What will you say when they come and ask about our love?"

How many times had she asked that question? Was it a serious question or just a lover's one?

She sighed. "Maybe one day," she said, "I will tell it to your face and not to your back."

"Ouch!" Daniel said. She had pinched him on the neck. He turned to face her, but she looked scared, startled. The warm touch of her lips still lingered on his neck. Did she kiss him? Bite him?

"Shh . . ." she said and pushed him down on the pillow. "Sleep."

His eyes opened and closed, an empty glass shaking in his hands.

"I have told you already, and I'm going to repeat it," said the annoying guy sitting beside him. "You need a refill."

"I don't," Daniel said. His voice sounded like someone else's, older than the self he had just met in bed and way drunker. The old pub, the place where he had met most of his friends, was empty and silent. At the table, only him, the annoying guy, and their booze. It must have been late.

"She won't come back."

"And I told you," Daniel said, pushing him on one shoulder, "I can't forget her like that." The words were delivered in shouts.

"Okay, okay. I give you that she hasn't escaped from the toilet's window. But you have to admit, a girl like that, with whatever we can call you?" The man talked right into his ears, wrapping him with one arm. There was too much noise and people pushing from all sides to reach the bar and get a drink.

"She hasn't," a voice said behind their backs. Sophia. She shouted close to their cheeks. She smelled good. Not like flowers, but like grass after a light rain, like the peace of a lazy afternoon. Was this the first time he had met her? It must have been. "There is too much noise over here," she said. "Shall we get a table?"

It was just him and her at the table. She pushed herself close so he could hear her. "You have a dark past, you say," she laughed. "What kind of dark past can a major in philosophy have?"

Before he could answer, he found himself transported to the middle of a clay field. He recognized the place. They had left stones on the ground to act as goalposts. A kid, a middle-schooler, lay on the ground. Blood came off his head. Next to him stood another one, shaking, with the face of someone about to puke and a stone in his right hand.

"Run!" Daniel bellowed. His voice was the one he had as a young boy.

After, it was all footsteps and panting, the other kids gone. He stood in front of his own house, the place where he grew up. The white walls he remembered, the red door, and a garden where no one ever grew any grass. He glanced at the only tree in the garden, and there he hung, a man, both feet up, tied to a branch with a rope. His head pointed to the ground and dripped blood. Daniel looked away. He was too young. He should have been strong enough to burn this sorry place down.

On the ground, in front of the door, an envelope. He grabbed and opened it. Just money inside—he ran through the bills with one finger—the usual amount.

His head was spinning, and he just wanted to sleep. He pushed the door open, and the reek of blood filled his nostrils. His feet squelched as he moved one step into the house. Blood covered the entire floor. There were no windows, and the room was empty except for two chairs and a cot.

A man sat on the ground, legs crossed, between the chairs and the cot. His eyes empty and pointed at the ceiling. Asleep or in a trance, his face contorted into a morbid smile. He knew that stupid face: Marcel.

Another man, a larger one, held Marcel by the shoulders with his face stuck to his neck. Blood leaked out of Marcel's neck, and the other sucked it in gulps.

"Stop," Daniel yelled. "You are killing him!"

The large man ignored him. And so Daniel leaped and pushed him away. The man slipped on the blood and fell on a wooden chair, crashing it into pieces. Daniel moved before he had time to stand back up, grabbed one foot off the chair, and smashed it on his head. His eyes bloodshot, the large man was still alive, and so Daniel hit him again, and again, and again.

The man's red eyes still stared at him as he turned back to check on Marcel, who lay faceup, smiling, while blood streamed out of his neck. Daniel sat beside him and lay in his arms, so tired he closed his eyes.

"No secrets," Daniel said to Sophia, who was still waiting for an answer. Back at the pub, the woman he loved sat in front of him. The annoying guy was half asleep between them as Sophia busied herself with turning his hair in a mess of braids. "I thought it sounded cool. You know, western-hero-like cool."

"One can't be too excited," Sophia said, still busy with the man's hair. "I'm not sure he will enjoy it when he finds out tomorrow," she said with a guilty smile on her face.

"I'm pretty sure he won't," Daniel said.

"So, we should stop messing with him and get another drink. Let me fetch you something."

He blinked, and she came back to the table, upset, her eyes moving between his face and the door.

Daniel tried to dissimulate the smile that kept appearing on his face. "I never thought I would see you again . . ."

"I'm with you now, but you need a drink."

"Do I?"

"Drink, my love, please, drink!" She forced herself on him, pushing the glass against his mouth. "Stay with me, okay? Stay with me!"

The fiery liquid dripped from his mouth down his throat, and again, the empty room appeared around him. He crouched over Marcel, his wrist slit and blood pouring into the man's mouth. "Stay with me, okay? Stay with me!" Daniel kept repeating.

Everything became dark.

"'He who makes a beast of himself gets rid of the pain of being a man,'" said an old, hoarse voice coming from the darkness. Descartes liked his riddles.

"You quote Dr. Johnson now?" Daniel said.

Descartes chuckled. "You'll excuse the hubris, my friend. Perhaps I'm too old and full of myself, but it seems written for just you and me."

Daniel shook his head, finally awake from the haze of the drug. He had drooled on the pillow. His lips and tongue were numb, and his mouth was as dry as if he had crunched on sand. The syringe rested on the bedside table. Whatever came in those things wasn't making him sleep, but that wasn't the point.

The Shadow said to lie in bed before taking his doses, and luckily, he had been following their advice. At least the mixture made her reappear in his dreams. For every time he had to listen to Marcel complaining about the long-term effects of whatever that liquid was, this still sounded like a good deal.

"Don't go full junkie on me while I'm gone, okay?" Marcel had said. "You can source your blood reserve from everywhere, but I have just you to use for transfusions." Since then, only one message to tell him he was on the right track, and nothing else. It was time to worry. But since his last shot, he didn't really know what time it was.

Even in the darkness of his room, his head still spun. He pushed himself against the bedside table, and the syringe he had left there rolled onto the ground. He didn't care. A small card stuck to his palm, the invitation.

Arnaud Demeure, the so-called old prince of Paris, some

important guy, invited him to a party. The Horror Vacui, as people called these recurring gatherings when they used to happen centuries before, were so packed it was hard to move. Demeure hadn't held one for ages, but out of the people that man could reach, why would he invite him, someone he had never met before?

The prince will grant any wish, if true, said the invite. That fit the legends any brother in town talked about. Without thinking, Daniel reached for the card and raised it in front of him. Not that he could see it in the darkness, but he preferred this temporary blindness to the torture of the light when he dosed himself. Something told him that piece of paper was hiding a secret, but nothing he could see.

He dropped the card on the mattress, fell back against the pillow, and rolled himself under the blanket. As he moved in them, the bedsheets, soaked in sweat, stuck to his skin. Until the first time he used whatever the Shadows had been selling him, he never dreamed, and one of the many regrets he had about his turning was the loss of this pleasure.

His bed had become a mere shelter where he hid during the day. Closing his eyes didn't differ from turning off a television. Nothing had remained of the slumber of mortals or their pleasure in sleeping. No sore muscles or clouded eyes, no yawning or drowsiness, only the darkness of two closed eyes and nothing else.

He grew bored with his own thoughts, jumped out of bed, put on an old gown, and traveled to the kitchen, crossing the living room without bothering about turning on any light on his way there. It was dusk outside the windows. Like every other day, he prepared tea and a few toasts. It was like having breakfast late in the day, and it sounded transgressive enough to make this habit survive even the fact he would have to puke up everything he ate a few minutes after having consumed it.

Daniel had just finished eating when he checked his watch.

He would be late to the party if he didn't get ready. Still wrapped in his gown, he walked back to his bedroom to take up some clothes. But as soon as he turned on the light in his room, his legs began shaking. On the wall in front of his bed, someone had left a message written in thick red paint: *Don't go*. Under the message was a drawing resembling a little rolled-up cat. Was it painted in blood? Quite possibly, considering how the wolf inside him shook.

What if the author was still in the house?

Daniel jumped to reach the drawer of the bedside table where he kept a knife. With it in his hands, he checked in a hurry under the bed. Nothing. His hair was still brushing the ground when he realized he was showing his back to the wardrobe. He jumped up and turned to open one door. Again, nothing.

He had to check the rest of the house.

Daniel pushed himself against the wall near the door of the room, keeping the knife in his hand. He slid into the corridor, still keeping himself flat against the wall. Bathroom or living room?

He chose the bathroom and jumped to snap open the door and turn on the light without going in. He found nobody inside. But the curtain of the tub was closed. What if someone was hiding behind it? Daniel swallowed hard as he gathered the nerves to slide the curtain, and with a deep breath, he opened it. Nobody was behind it, but footprints impressed with blood covered the bottom of the tub.

Before he could decide what to do, the thump of his front door echoed as it slammed open. Daniel ran back to the living room but found no one. The door was still open, and it was closing itself after having hit the wall. Someone had left near-invisible footprints stamped in blood all over the floor. Nobody was outside.

Daniel locked it and scoured the house to check for any

intruder. He found no one but his reflection in the bathroom's mirror. His eyes gray and his hair of a blond so light it was almost white. Despite the youthful body he inhabited, he looked old.

Daniel went back to his room and studied the drawing. The blood, still fresh, was drying out. But one thing that bogged his brain was he recognized that drawing.

He might have needed drugs to keep precise memories of the woman in mind, but two things he still remembered even after so many years: the piercing green of her eyes and the tattoos on her shoulders—a weird circle on the left, and a rolled-up cat on the right.

Daniel walked back to his laptop and searched between the old recordings of Marcel, and there it was, from one of the man's travels to the Americas. Like the others, he had heard it tens if not hundreds of times, but pressed play to listen to Marcel's voice.

"Hey, Chief. I might have some good news. To be fair, it's not much, but I had lost any hope, so I take what Heaven sends me, right? At least I didn't have to do too much hopping around this time. I paid a fortune in drinks, but between one alcoholic and the other, I met one local who recognized the symbol and remembered where he might have seen it.

"I bought him more rounds, paid him a few bucks, and the guy brought me to an old woman. You won't believe it. The moment I showed this thing to the lady, she went crazy. She dragged me inside her house, offered me food, and called me names. She showed me a little altar, one of those within cabinets. The damn symbol was all over the place, carved in the wood, painted on it, and even in the fucking blankets she used as decor for the altar. The only thing beside it was a tiny doll; an evil idol if it was any scarier. Then she told me a story as my new bestie translated it for me.

"It talked about a young girl from before the Europeans landed here, a messiah of sorts. Miracles included, you know, healing people, exorcising, nothing new. She told me that when the invaders came, they kidnapped the girl. The locals still wait for her to come back.

"Now, everything matches what we have seen in Egypt with Isis and Bastet. Once again, a young girl with green eyes. Even in this case, some ghostly cat follows her everywhere, some sort of messenger or guardian. The same story that the Shadows told us in Paris. The Scarlet Woman, or whatever they called her.

"But this time is different, and that's big news. She battered me with her legends for hours, but she also told me this child had chosen a European name for herself. You guessed it. She chose Sophia. You might have made love to a goddess, my man!

"Now, listen. I gotta go, but I have everything recorded on video. Once I'm back, we can hit the Shadows again. In the meantime, I hope I can collect a bit more info before my flight back. Call you soon."

Could it be that, after so many years, Sophia had paid him a visit? All of that to tell him not to go to a party. But if it involved her, he had to go. There was no way he would let her run away again without seeing her.

Evidence J-0085 to the investigation I-7242
Extract from Arnaud Demeure's journal
14 November 1259

I followed her away from the orphanage and into the woods. I tried so hard to prevent her from noticing me, I didn't realize I was being followed myself.

By the time I arrived at the hut where she lived, I had already lost sight of her. It was then my pursuers revealed themselves. As usual, I was far from popular among the kids of the orphanage, and they had planned to blow some steam off by using me since we were so far away from any schoolmistress.

I lay on the ground, ready to take my daily beating when someone saved me. I don't know how. All I could see when I opened my eyes was the girl running behind them with a long stick spinning at her side. By the time she grew tired of chasing them, they had escaped.

"What are you doing following me here?" she asked, her chest still going up and down.

I didn't have a reply. I could not say I wanted to spy on her.

"Bring him in," said the gruff old voice of a woman from inside the hut.

"But it's a boy," the girl shouted back. "You said never to let a boy in."

"Do as I say," the woman said without showing herself. "That one is special. So much greed for power I have never seen. Hurry, before I change my mind and leave you both to the wolves."

5

HIS BLADE

The light ring of a bell announced the elevator, and the valet showed Violette the door. His tight red jacket contrasted with the gray of the parking lot, and he beamed at her. That was the smile on every man's face the first time they met her.

The bell rang again, and a light blinked on top of the door as it opened. The air moved behind her as if someone had been standing next to her neck. She turned, but no one was there, only a faint scent of moss.

As the doors fully opened, the smile never left the valet's face, even as his legs bent like paper, and he flew wide-armed as if he had jumped to hug her. The man's knees slammed against the floor with a loud crack, then his chest and head reached the ground a few inches from her feet.

A young man stood where the valet had been a moment before. His brown hair moved, still falling back on his shoulders. He looked at her with puppy eyes as his lips, surrounded by a light beard, curled in a pleading smile. The second smile that someone had offered her that night, besides that of the valet, who lay on the ground, leaking blood from his mouth, his neck livid, broken.

The elevator's doors closed again with no one going up as the man stood in front of her in his gray pinstripe suit. He had been way too fast. Not even nightcrawlers moved that fast.

The wolf within her winced and all her muscles jolted. She showed him her teeth and hissed.

The man showed his palms in response. "Quiet, quiet, quiet. No need to get violent. I wanted to talk to you with no one listening."

His black eyes pierced hers. So, Violette used her gift. She threw her own mind in his eyes so she could read his soul to find out if that man had ill intentions, sure, at least, he was hiding something. Yet, she found nothing in them but a deep and somewhat soothing icy darkness.

"What made you think killing that poor bastard was the best way to chat with me? These aren't the dark ages. You can't kill people in a parking lot and go unnoticed. This town has so many immortals already it's hard not to get noticed even without killing people at random!"

The man looked embarrassed, rubbed his own neck, and grinned. "I might have gone too far, you are right. We will have to hide him, don't you think?"

"What do you want from me?" she hissed.

"Company," said the man, blushing, but it sounded more like a question. "For a party."

Violette looked at him in disbelief. A dandy, wrapped in his gray suit so deadly and as beautiful as no one else had ever been for her, now looked somewhat awkward, almost childish. So much that she laughed in his face. She had many customers, immortal or not, and this allowed her to live like a princess in the capital.

"Do you think you can afford my company?" she asked, still giggling.

The man pondered it for a moment. He took something out of his pockets and handed it to her. It was a small, flat wooden box. It looked ancient and had something engraved on top that she could not read. She turned the box up and down, still looking at the man inviting her to open it with his eyes.

Violette opened it, and inside was a piece of paper, a blank check already signed. This man for sure knew how to attract her attention. "Leto Sieberg, eh? It sounds like a name I've heard."

He shrugged. "I must be more famous than I thought. You are popular too. They tell me you accompany old gentlemen whenever they go to parties. I have one to go to, if you care to accompany me. You set the price, of course."

Just a day before, Leto was in his apartment in London and sat in his armchair, reading. He didn't care too much about sitting and reading, but that was how a gentleman should spend his time. When the phone rang, he could have answered immediately, but his master had taught him never to answer on the first ring. It meant one had nothing better to do, as he would have said. His master was all he had, and had taught him everything he knew. The way he dressed, the way he lived, fought, or spoke, everything came from his master.

The phone rang again. He could answer at last.

"Leto, it has started. We need you in Paris," said a hoarse voice on the other end of the phone. "You know who to search for you to get your part of the work done. As a side note, we might have lost the package again, and it's always a pain to get it back when it happens. I might need you to do some extra work this time."

Leto stayed silent. As his master always said, he should not ask questions on the phone whenever they were talking business. Impossible to say if anyone was listening. "You'll give me details when I arrive in Paris. I'll see you tomorrow," Leto said, ending the call.

There wasn't much he hadn't already arranged. He had already packed shirts and suits in a suitcase, prepared for the day his master would require his service. He searched for his checkbook, signed one, and put it in his pocket, ready to go. A small wooden box caught his eye.

It sat on a table in the hall, and it had been there since the day his master had gifted it to him. Engraved on it, in Latin, a passage from the gospel. *Man shall not live on bread alone, but on every word that comes from the mouth of God.* It was right, as his master wasn't a mere man. Not at all.

Violette Renoir, the name his master gave him to follow, would act as the ignition they needed. No one else would work, his master said. It had to be this precise woman. Leto didn't know why, but it wasn't his place to ask.

He had followed her the entire night. Many would have said she was stunning as she moved, shaking her hips, wrapped in her latex dress while walking through the streets of the capital at night. Her brown hair swayed in the wind, and thanks to his ability to stay hidden in the shadows, Leto savored the tangerine scent of her skin.

Nobody, in all the years he had been alive, had realized he was spying on them, even when he stood a few inches from their shoulders. This Violette wasn't any different. So, he followed her from one club to the other. She was beautiful, indeed, perhaps a bit tawdry with her blood-red lipstick and fake eyelashes.

Destiny wanted that in order to visit the club she had to pass through an underground parking lot, and that was a peaceful place to chat with her alone. Perhaps he hadn't managed the whole situation in the best possible way, because she was shaking. Maybe angry, maybe scared. He didn't really know. Then he remembered the lessons his master always gave him.

"You might not grasp it," he used to say. "You are an attractive man. If you can play your cards right, you won't lose a beat, my son." All he needed was his neat suit and a rich puppy act. She would fall for it.

***

"If you need to think about it, it's fine," Leto said, maintaining his trembling voice while the woman handed over the box to him but not the check.

"Do you have a pen?" Violette asked with an impish smile.

She took a pen from him, wrote something on the check, a high number he supposed, and stashed it in her bag. "You say you are having this party, where?" And she offered him her right arm.

***

The complete act had worked, just the way his master had always taught him. Not surprising. As always, his master's teachings were the only thing that kept him moving. The man had treated him like a son since the day he had found him hugging the dead body of his mother. He remembered little from his life before. He must have been five or six. His master told him someone had killed his mother and sister. Since that day, his master had been a father to him.

"Many," he used to say, "would consider what happened to you some form of misfortune. But it isn't. Can you hear what's at the bottom of your heart? Or rather, do you understand what's missing? Some people would call yours a condition of apathy, but I'd rather call it ataraxy, complete freedom from any human emotion. You are free, Leto. Do you understand? Out of all of us, the only one who is free. Free from all the burdens of being human without the need to be dead."

His master's blood had been his own blood for a long time before he himself had become immortal. And now he was his blade. Deprived of pain and joy. He could smile while remembering his mother now, if he needed to.

"The elders' palace," Leto said. "On the old prince's invite."

Violette's entire body shook at his side.

"We better hurry, then. We don't want such an important man to wait," she said in a trembling voice.

The two left the place arm in arm. The bright streets of Paris were in front of them when a scream came from the parking lot behind them.

"Someone found him," Leto said, and Violette chuckled.

Evidence J-0272 to the investigation I-7242
Extract from Arnaud Demeure's journal
7 September 1265

I was crying by the river when my sister came. My parents's carillon, on the ground next to me, played a music only I could hear in my head. I had put effort into hiding so nobody could find me while I drew and listened to my music. To that end, I had gone far away from the trail that led from the town to the hag's place. I went down by the riverbank where the grass gave place to mossy stones, and hid behind a bush, lying on the ground.

A cool breeze soothed the drowsiness of the sunlight, and I hoped the splashes from the river would mask my tears.

But my sister had always been better at finding me than I had been at hiding. And I enjoyed that of her, but for the first time, I didn't want to see her or, at least, I didn't want her to see me like that.

"Are you sad, little one?" She closed the broken carillon, and the shrieks of metal, music only to my ears, stopped. Only the gurgle of the river remained. She glanced at me and tossed me an apple she carried.

"Those are for the old hag," I said.

She shrugged and snatched the papers from my hands. "What are you writing?" She snorted. "Nasty child. You should not be drawing me like this. I'm your sister," she said and winked.

"First, we are not children anymore. Second, you can't read. And third, she is not you," I said, and my cheeks flamed hot. "She is a princess I came up with. I'm writing stories."

"Sure she is," she said, still grinning. "You know, any time you want to draw straight from the subject, I can let you peek, just like when we were kids."

She dropped the diary on my lap and looked away as red in her face as I was.

My heart ran fast, but I looked down at my papers, unable to write for real.

"What were you crying about? She turned you last night, didn't she? You waited for years. Is it not all you wanted?"

"I asked to be turned for power, and all I got is meek illusions. I can do some sleights of hand if you want me to," I said, and laughed at myself. "But you got an even shorter straw, didn't you? I have never seen you using any gift."

"You see it every day. I told you many times."

"Yeah, yeah," I mocked her, waving one hand. "Everyone sees you how they want to see you. That sounds boring, and you kept telling this story from when we were kids. She hadn't yet turned you back then."

"I would explain it better if it wasn't a secret the hag doesn't want me to tell anyone."

"Okay," I said, still laughing. "I will tell you a big secret about the hag if you tell me this one."

She thought about it, then she reached out an arm in my direction. "Deal."

"Deal," I said and shook her hand.

"The hag never turned me," she said. "I have always been like this. She told me my father was a knight. He was hunting in the woods when he saw a beautiful woman, and they fell in love, so he brought her to his palace. That night they, you know . . ."

I nodded.

"Turns out my mother was a fae, a sylph, the hag says, and so the morning after I was already born. The knight got scared, kicked my mother out, and dropped me by the witch's hut."

I looked at her with my mouth hanging. "But you grew up," I said. "You aged until you stopped!"

She shrugged. "The hag made me eat. She said people like me turn the first time they eat human flesh. We are just humans with odd powers until then."

I think I believed her. It was a better story than the ones I heard about her when we were kids.

Her eyes widened as she looked straight into mine. "Your turn now."

"Me? Oh, yeah, I found a book in the hag's hut. It talks about a place nearby, an underground labyrinth. From what it says, it's a place where one can find power beyond understanding. Perhaps that is our way out? What do you say?"

"I say you didn't give me much in exchange for my secret." She puffed her cheeks and spun, kicking a stone into the water.

She stayed silent and offered me only her shoulders as she

focused on a few leaves that floated on the water carried by the river.

"It's true, and it might be the real deal!" I insisted, but she turned and looked at me, unfazed, with her arms crossed. "Okay, you know what? I will teach you to read so you can see it for yourself."

"You would? The hag will kill you if she finds out."

"I don't care," I said, and I knew I was in for a lot of trouble.

She jumped and hugged me so tight she didn't need to say thank you.

I laughed. "So, you love me, don't you?"

She peeled herself off me, stepped back, and stared into my eyes with a serious expression on her blushing face. "Never," she said, rushing back on the trail toward the hut.

6

THE HOUSE OF CHOICES

Evidence N-0113 to the investigation I-7242
Arnaud Demeure's handwritten note
Extract from The Chymical Wedding of Christian Rosenkreutz—
copy found in Arnaud Demeure's palace

This day, this day, this, this
The Royal Wedding is.
Art thou thereto by Birth inclin'd,
And unto joy of God design'd,
Then may'st thou to the Mountain tend,
Whereon three stately Temples stand,
And there see all from end to end.
Keep watch, and ward,
Thy self-regard;
Unless with diligence thou bathe,
The Wedding can't thee harmless save:
He'll damage have that here delays;
Let him beware, too light that weighs.

She didn't know her own name, nor the reason she was there, but she was lucky the tired sun of the winter had gone to sleep early that night, and this had given her more time to complete her task. What task? All she could remember was herself rushing out of his house, warning him before it was too late.

Him, Daniel, she remembered, but more like in a dream than in a memory. Had he seen her? Recognized her? She hoped he would just stay hidden, far from the dangers and the darkness that followed her.

The Parisian night, cold on its own, was even more freezing to her bare feet as they touched the ground. If anyone could have seen her, they would have been surprised by the naked woman running in the middle of the city. But it didn't matter. The lights of the city were like needles in her tired eyes. People talking, the cars rushing on the streets, and the loud music of the shops were an untenable agony.

What was her name? If only she could remember. But she didn't have the faintest idea. The last jump had cost her too much.

Where was she going? Was she trying to catch up with someone? Was she running away? Had she really achieved anything?

She tried to focus. All she needed was a reason for such despair, and in the end, she remembered. It was Daniel. What if he had gone, anyway? He was in danger, and she would not let him go. She decided to travel where she had just told him not to go.

She stopped short, naked as she was, between a few passersby who could not notice her, so many were the shadows wrapped around her body. She studied both her legs and arms. Bloodstains covered her entire body in stark contrast to her amber skin. Had she lifted a hand against him?

Her stomach writhed and a whistle, loud as a train, filled her head. Her legs shook and almost gave up under her weight until something came up into her mouth. She puked a few gulps of blood as her stomach squeezed itself. She had no idea when she had eaten last.

Her green eyes glanced in search of a solution, a place to hide. The hiss was stronger every second, while lines and multi-colored sparkles blocked her sight. She needed to move, but she might faint any moment.

She shook her head, trying to regain sight. She just needed a few minutes. One last glance between the colored lines barring her eyes showed her a corner of the street well-hidden between two trash cans.

The woman ran with all the energy she had, as keeping herself unseen among so many people tired her beyond belief. Blood rushed to her eardrums, and everything around her moved twice as fast. Lights, people, and cars were nothing more than colorful stains. The icy hands of the night ran over her body and the chill burned her skin.

She reached the alley at last. Again, she tried to remember her name and the reason for all that fear, but she failed. The only thing she remembered was that she had to save him. She had to jump once again. This time, and she was sure of it, she could not stand it. Her mind was far too compromised; another offer would lead her to insanity. But it didn't matter. Only he mattered.

The woman brought her fangs to her wrists, and with the blood spilled, she drew a circle on the ground. She didn't need memory to remember the permutation. She drew the letters of creation around the mandala, and at its center, she drew Dalet, the door, the symbol of nullification.

Roman had followed the smell of her fear, but he didn't sense it anymore—she had disappeared.

On the ground, and he was sure the woman had drawn it, was a circle of which Roman recognized the type but not the meaning. He huffed. He had lost his trail. And he was sure the high priest would not like it.

He took his phone out of a pocket in his leather jacket, typed a number, and explained what had happened.

A white scar ran on his dark skin, crossing his face from the cheek just below his right eye till it reached the lips where it branched in two before disappearing. The scar shone, following the movements of his face as he spoke. For as thick as it was, his beard could not hide it.

"Sir, I lost her. I think she might have used the same trick as last time." His face turned sterner as he listened to the phone.

"Anyhow," he continued with the face of someone who has just received a punch in the stomach, "your track was the right one. She visited the young immortal."

His black curls fell back on the phone as he nodded in response to the new directions.

He shot a photo of the symbol before he left. He had another mission for that night and needed to get ready for a party.

———

Daniel scratched his eyes and brushed the tears off his face. If all the waiting wasn't annoying enough, his eyes hadn't stopped itching for a second. He scanned the place for a washroom, but the room had only two doors. The one he had arrived from and another one, a few meters tall, he supposed would lead to the courtyard outside and to the party.

Despite all the years spent in Paris, he had never visited this side of the elders' palace. But the surprise of visiting these unused rooms had already left space to boredom. The room had no texture, no personality to it, as if someone had tried to make it purposely unremarkable. The floor was made of old, rigged hardwood, the walls empty.

There was no furniture, if not for some chandeliers hanging low from the ceiling and a few chairs placed along the white, undecorated walls. On one of these, Daniel remained seated, thoughtful, bent over himself, elbows on his knees, chin on his palms, and a frowning face. His right leg could not stop moving up and down.

Why was he in this room? Why would someone send him a message? Was Sophia back? Too bad his companions tonight were a group of people he had never met before and out of whom, he could swear, almost none lived in town.

In fact, among the other six guests in the room, Daniel recognized only one, Ioniță, another Parisian resident. Despite the excessive number of immortals in town, most of them still knew each other. This Ioniță, or Ioan as he called himself, had always seemed a good one. A man with ancient mannerisms and a scholarly demeanor, always discreet about asking and giving away any information.

As much as he liked the guy, many were wary of him. His heavy accent didn't help him hide his eastern European origins, and as people whispered, he might be much older than he wanted others to think. But right now, if he had to choose the one thing suspicious about him, it was that the man—blind—moved with no aid or discomfort.

Ioan, as if to confirm his suspicions, leaned on his walking stick and waved at him from the other side of the room. Daniel was sure the man had arrived after him. How did he know he was there?

Daniel smiled as the old man beamed at him. He was lively despite his almost transparent skin, his gray hair, and his black-on-black attire that would have fitted him much better when he was younger.

"I hoped there would be someone I knew here," said the

man, displaying all of his accent, "as I believe it will be long before the party starts for real."

"Hi, Ioan. So, you received one of those weird invites too?"

"Weird?" said the man. "More cryptic, I'd say. But nothing I wouldn't expect from someone like Demeure. He has always been peculiar, that man. At least I have a friend here," he said, sounding happy.

Who knew where Daniel's best friend was now instead? He hadn't heard from Marcel for far too long now. "That's right," Daniel said, smiling and taking out the invitation from one pocket. "I got little out of mine too."

"Neither did I, but at least there is a monad behind yours too, so it's not on mine only."

"A what?" Daniel asked. "There is nothing on this invite besides the address and the weird thing about wishes."

Ioan looked perplexed. "Uh? Did you look at the invite," he said, lowering his voice, "for real? I can feel that you have the sight. Didn't you think of using it on the invite?"

The man called it sight, but Daniel knew what he was talking about. "Oh, sure . . ." he said. "I didn't think about it."

Daniel tried to focus on the piece of paper the man held in his hands. He still remembered how to do it. After a few seconds of concentration, a splitting headache took hold of his head, and an image appeared on the card. It was shining like gold and looked like a little man with short arms, bent knees, a single eye, and a half-moon attached to his forehead that looked like the horns of a little devil.

His headache was killing him as the old man tapped him on one shoulder with his stick.

"You don't use your gifts too often, do you?" Ioan asked.

"Not if I can avoid it, no," he said, wiping his sweaty forehead. The beast inside him growled. "What's that thing anyhow?"

"All I can guess is that this is going to be a wedding, one of the magical sort."

"A magical wedding?"

Instead of answering, the old man recited a short poem in verses. Something talking of a royal wedding.

Daniel frowned with half a smile on his face as he finished. "What was that?"

"Just an old man and the memories of when he was young," he said, smiling and still looking at the ceiling. Then his face turned serious. "To your question, the symbol and the rhymes come from an old alchemy book, *The Chymical Wedding of Christian Rosenkreutz*, that talks about a magical wedding. My best guess is that this party is a wedding or something similar for a supernatural purpose. But if he is doing something odd here, why would he leave us clues?"

Daniel ignored Ioan, distracted as he was by the lights and colors that floated all around the room and wrapped around everyone. Dense reverberating water filled the room and thousands, if not millions, of translucent threads floated in it. The wolf growled again within him and brought him to reality.

"I see you are enjoying it," Ioan said close to him, snickering. "You should control the wolf, not suppress it unless you want it to run away with your body. And that gift is special, very rare. I am, in fact, surprised there are another two in these rooms doing the same thing you are."

Daniel looked around the room, fixing his eyes on each of the other six guests and trying to see if his newfound sight could reveal anything about them. The young-looking nun sitting on a chair straight in front of him showed him nothing. Neither did the giant man, Roman, the announcement had said, who stood, arms crossed, against the wall on his left. He was by far the largest man Daniel had ever seen and must have had a nasty accident in his previous life, given the deep scars that covered his face.

He switched his attention to a man and a red-haired woman who stood chatting in the center of the room. The man, who had been announced as Hermann Walker, must have been so annoyed at the idea of being there he could not resist the urge of tip-tapping with his feet the whole time. He hadn't stopped smoking since his arrival.

He had a young, muscular build, and if not for the scarred giant, he would have been the tallest in the room. Aside from this, he had a flavorless beauty, but his jock mannerisms and his loud complaints attracted everybody's glances. As Daniel was about to focus his sight on them, intermittent sparks of light, invisible until then, moved his attention toward another guest, a bespectacled, dark-haired teenage girl with a broken nose.

She had turned immortal at such a young age, and with her goth vibe, she didn't fit the profile he expected for a guest of a boring party. He didn't remember her name, although she had arrived a minute after him. She stood alone, staring at Ioan, wrapped in a long sweater and tight jeans. Around her wrists, she wore two silver bracelets, each with its own pendant attached. On the right a cross, on the left a little sphere. At her neck, she had a similar chain with an amulet attached, a tiny hook.

Unlike everyone else, the light strands connected all over her body so much she appeared wrapped in flames. Sparks of every color moved away from her body in every direction, some falling toward the ground, others disappearing, and others following small paths that connected back to her. Any color he could imagine was there around that young girl, and it was so bright it overwhelmed him.

"A witch!" Ioan shouted way too close to his ear, and this stopped his vision. "We have a problem." Without waiting for an answer, the old man continued, "You don't see well enough, my friend," and smacked Daniel's forehead with one palm so strongly Daniel lost his sight for a second.

In an instant, the room turned dark, and a light mist rose from the floor. Trembling golden lights drew shapes on the wall, floor, and ceiling. Symbols and patterns he didn't recognize. Tears wetted his cheeks once again as the mist cleared.

Evidence J-0304 to the investigation I-7242
Extract from Arnaud Demeure's journal
27 June 1266

"Is the hag . . . dead?" my sister asked, turning toward me. In so many years, this was the first time I saw her scared.

"I don't know. I just desired for her to suffer, pictured her in Hell, and she fell down," I said. "Do you think it was me? It can't be right."

"Your gift creates illusions, and she always said it's strong. Maybe she is living whatever you imagined."

"Oh God. I'm so sorry. I didn't mean to. But for years, all those men in and out of this house . . . the things she made you do. I just couldn't watch her again, shouting at you and beating you so much. I couldn't stand it," I said.

But she shushed me and squeezed me in her arms. "It's fine," she said. "We will be fine. I promise."

7

SISTER TO THE WOLF

Evidence N-0114 to the investigation I-7242
Arnaud Demeure's handwritten note
Found written on an ancient text—the title translates as "A weapon
that pierced the heavens"

A brother must kill his sister twice for the door to open and the
weapon to be forged.

"I can't show up like this at the prince's," Violette said, her voice
way too loud. "I look like a slut," she added in a whisper.

Leto, at her side, smiled and kept walking, so she unwrapped
her arm from his, sped up, and placed herself standing in front
of him, arms crossed, and legs spread as much as that damn
tight dress allowed her to.

"One thing is dressing yourself to hook dinner at a club, a
different thing is to visit the old prince. You understand this
thing is plastic, right?"

The man smiled again, scanning her from head to feet, but

didn't seem to get her point. He was instead, again, looking dumbfounded and rubbing his neck.

"So?" she asked, trying to put all the effort to sound mischievous. The exaggerated heels of her red shoes seemed short compared to the miles of her legs. The latex suit barely covered a body that, paired with her dark gift, could wake up anyone's desires, alive or not.

Her arms, folded below her chest, showed, even more, the line of her perfect breasts, ready to escape the grip of the dress she would have liked to get rid of. Violette put on a falsely sulky face. That, with the scent of her hair, and her lips frowning, should have made him want to kiss her, but nothing.

The man disturbed her. He was cunning one second and behaved like a child the one after, unaware of how handsome he was. But he was way too handsome not to realize it. She had already witnessed him killing someone and pulling such a stunt she had never seen before. And now, he appeared insensible not only to her body but also to her charming gift.

"We can fix that. With the right dress, you'll be a princess. Shall I buy you something?"

Violette had to resist a smile but reached again his side and took his arm. "No need. I have the right dress already."

"*Ask her something,*" his master would have said.

Perhaps Violette expected the same. Leto had caught her two or three times, glancing at him in silence as she walked at his side. She sure was trying to play her own game as well. She must have tried to use her charms on him, but those never worked. On the contrary, his dark gift was quite effective on her.

"Did you grow up around here?" he finally asked.

"Kind of," she said.

"Kind of?"

"For a few years with my mother when I was very young. I remember little aside from the day I left."

"It must have been a glorious day."

"In a way," she said, shrugging and looking at the sky. Her eyes were wet. "At least I could breathe some fresh air. I couldn't suffer the horrid smell this place used to have." She smiled. "This air," she continued, waving one finger and mimicking a voice lower than hers. " 'This air is not good for the girl. She will get sick!' " She chuckled, but her eyes were still wet.

"What was that?" he asked.

"Nothing. Just fooling around." She squeezed his arm and looked at the shop's windows. Then, a few steps later, she stopped in front of a window and murmured something, looking serious again. Two white ballet dresses stared at them from behind the glass, and shoes and accessories spied from the sides.

Leto had no idea of what might go on in her mind, and so he decided to wait and see.

Before he could think of anything to say, the woman sighed and turned to face him again, smiling. "Shall we go?" she asked, and offered him her arm again.

It took Violette a while to extract the scarf from the pochette, using only one hand stiff with the cold of Paris's streets. But she managed. She left Leto's arm to cover her head and shoulders in the wool, and as she did, a thick fog was lifted off her brain.

What was she doing bringing this man to her apartment? She had seen him kill the valet, and for sure, he would have no problems in killing her if he wanted to.

Violette turned to face him, ready to tell him to go on his own. She would reach him at the place of the party. She knew where it was, anyhow. But she stood there, looking into his eyes without speaking.

"Are you okay?" asked Leto.

"Yes," Violette said, smiled, and grabbed his arm again, "we are almost there."

They arrived at her apartment not long after. The stairs of the building rose in a spiral. Dark wooden handrails, supported by fruit and flower decorations, flew up, following the rhythm of an unknown music. The columns, the red carpet along the steps, the candelabra on the ceiling, and the adornments on plaster and marble, typical of the area, gave her the idea of being a dancer accompanied by her patron, ready to enter the scene in a theater.

They didn't speak while climbing the steps. She watched him as he stared ahead with the same innocent smile he had reserved for her at the start of the night. So clumsy, yet so confident at the same time. She was so lucky he was by her side, a knight bringing his dame to the prince's ball.

The light of the streets filtered through the window and made the crystals of the chandelier sprinkle light across the short corridor and the kitchen at its end. The ceiling was a night sky covered in stars. In the kitchen, a small round table was ready for a breakfast that would never come.

"Do you want to wait here?" Violette asked, showing him the sofa near the entrance. "I'll turn on the lights."

Leto took his seat on the sofa, moving a pillow to his side, while she wondered why she had bought pillows in the first place, as if anyone ever needed a pillow on a sofa.

"Lots of mirrors," he said, pointing at the walls as she turned the lights on.

"Yeah, I'd rather have those than boring portraits. The place is kind of small also," she said, twitching her hair with one finger, "but I managed to fit the sofa through the entrance."

The man didn't answer. He sat with his arms relaxed at his side and a frown, like a child worried he would have to wait.

"You are a lucky one, you know? You are going to be the most envied man at the party."

Leto grinned. "I can already imagine."

"Good. I'm going to get changed then, and remember, beautiful things need some patience, so no peeking!"

Leto was likely still waiting, seated on the sofa on the other side of the door. At that moment, Violette didn't care. That dress had waited a long time to attend such an event, so it deserved its celebrations. Across the centuries, she had it adjusted many times to match it to the period, always waiting. Out of the original, only fabric remained, but it didn't matter.

Once again, the fabric caressed her skin, and she admired herself in front of a mirror. This time it wasn't the small mirror of a common dormitory, but one the size of a wall in her bedroom. Violette saw herself wrapped in the sky-colored veil that enveloped her, following her shape along her hips and her thighs, and falling toward the floor to cover her feet. White embroidery covered her bust and back. The decor thickened, moving upward, and stopped on the chest to leave the shoulders naked.

Violette almost dropped it as she remembered that very dress covered in her own blood, the stench of a nasty tavern, the eyes of an old man, and a hand slitting her throat from the shadows. She sat at the foot of her bed, her breathing coming harder and harder until she clenched her arms. There was no need to think about that. She had survived.

She crawled her way up to the mirror and smiled. She looked pretty. She had just removed all the heavy makeup that covered her face, and the mirror already betrayed her, revealing the young age at which her body had stopped aging. She admired herself in the mirror, turning around and bowing as she used to in the old times when she was a young girl.

The check abandoned on the bed screamed she hadn't been a girl for a while. It was getting enough on her nerves that she locked it up in a drawer. She sighed with the relief of having slammed the door on an enemy's face. So, she surprised herself when she opened the same drawer to take it out again, a mere instant later.

"Sieberg? Where have I heard this name?" For sure she had heard about him. For the old prince to invite him, he must have been famous.

As Violette headed to the other room, she could only imagine the dances she would have that evening with her knight. She was already looking forward to when she would come back right to this room with him to take off this dress she had wanted to wear so much.

Violette found Leto where she had left him, absorbed in his thoughts, and for the first time, she could observe him unnoticed. She would have expected to find out something about him from his expression. Was he bored? Dreaming? Eager to see her appear? She read nothing. Leto sat there, motionless, eyes closed, and arms relaxed at the side of his body. It seemed as if someone had built a mannequin with his appearance and had abandoned it right there on the sofa. It didn't last long, though.

The man must have noticed the door had opened and, perhaps, also that she was watching him. His muscles twitched for a second, and as if someone had pulled the mannequin's threads, his innocent smile reappeared on his face. Leto got to his feet and observed her while massaging his neck. His gaze stuck on her in such an innocent way it embarrassed her.

Leto approached her, held out one hand, and wrapped her hip with the other. "Will you give me the honor?"

She smiled back, moved away from him for a second, bowed, then returned to his arms. She could hear her own laughter during the only round of dance they did. As she left his arms, she kept spinning, giggling till she reached the front door. At first, she was about to reach for the doorknob, but, turning around, she saw a hint of disappointment in his gaze. And she didn't want to disappoint him. He deserved what he expected.

Violette let her hand slide along the door, abandoning the doorknob, and turned toward him with such eyes and a smile he must have been stupid not to understand. With her back still leaning against the door, she let herself slide onto the ground.

The disappointment had vanished from Leto's face. The man approached. When he reached her, he dropped to his knees and looked into her eyes, reaching out as if to give her knight's first kiss. But the wolf inside her jumped. The beast that had been silent all evening screamed to run away.

There it was, like the first time, the absolute, disarming certainty she was going to die. The man's claws slashed through the flesh of her neck, scratching the door behind her. This time, the last one, she didn't have time to ask herself why, but a tear had time to furrow her face, perhaps at the thought of her beautiful dress soaking again in her own blood.

And Violette was there again, in the dark old tavern that smelled like piss, with its wet carpets, creaking floors, and pictures of sea and ships filling the walls. She remembered the woman at the entrance. She must have been beautiful at some point in her life, but her beauty, perhaps bored with her, had departed, leaving behind only the shadow of what she was.

Her nails bitten, her bones protruding, and way too much skin on her arms and chin. That woman had crossed a name from her registry as Violette and the old man with icy eyes had arrived at the tavern that night, and the name she had crossed was Sieberg.

Leto had to move fast. He dipped both his hands in Violette's blood, and with it, he traced a circle on the floor. At the center of it, he drew three symbols—Beit, the house, the free choice, the world to come; Shin, the change; and Samekh, the end nested in the beginning. He then drew the twenty-two letters of the permutation around the circle, following his master's instructions to the letter. He didn't need to know their meaning to remember how to do it.

As he touched the center of the circle, he looked up. Sitting with its back against the door was the corpse of the woman he had just killed with her beautiful dress, her cheeks wet with tears. One moment after, he disappeared.

It had started. The house of choices had received the last one of its guests.

Evidence J-1552-a to the investigation I-7242
Extract from Arnaud Demeure's journal
25 January 1268

"A year and a half we have spent in the labyrinth, and we have no treasure or power to claim," I said. All at once, the air was thin, and my head light. "They will never believe I'm some marquis, even less I found anything in those tunnels!"

"Look," my sister said, staring straight into my eyes, "if I say that you can do it, you can. If it makes it any easier, stop trying to believe in yourself and just believe in what I say."

I didn't answer. She was holding my shoulders so tight that it almost hurt.

"I understand you dislike your powers, but they are going to be useful. You killed the hag using just your mind. Believe it or not, she was a powerful one. She must have been around since the times of the Lord's son. Is that being weak?"

"But maybe—" I tried to say.

"No, no, I said. Look at me." She raised my face up to meet hers. "Just look at me. You are the man for the job. The son of a noble, you have the looks now thanks to the labyrinth, and if you use your illusions, they will believe anything you say."

Whether she was right or not, it was too late to run away.

I took a deep breath, straightened my back, held my right arm out so she could take it, and knocked on the door. A door that separated my past life from my future one. Only God knows how much I wanted that door not to open. But it did.

8

THE ALCHEMICAL CHAPEL

Evidence L-0481 to the investigation I-7242
Letter, Conrad Ashdown to the most illustrious Tylanus Spencer
(Councilor of the School of Winchester)
16 April 1538

I'm no one to discuss your wisdom, only a soldier honored to serve the cause of the School. But my duty binds me to the companions I have lost in this war.

We fight and die by the dozens at the hand of these animals. They call themselves Strigoi lords, but are just wolves hiding in the guise of men.

This land is cold and crude. It can't grow crops or sustain life, its magick is vicious, its populace sad and weak. But the lords of this land defend it fiercely. I saw it with my own eyes. One of them can kill ten of us. Magick or not, they move faster, hit stronger, and don't tire. They are not men. They are monsters. I have seen them eating from the corpses of their kills and murdering their own people if it helps them in battle.

Every day we spend here is a day closer to a brutal defeat,

one so burning the other schools might come after our heads. No amount of sacrifice can save us.

Sir, in your infinite wisdom, end this war. Do it in the name of all the soldiers who have perished and the others who are about to.

In faith,
Conrad Ashdown

Daniel saw the room where he had been an instant before as an out-of-focus image that overlapped the place where he was now. The others still moved around, speaking to one another, ignoring he had departed that place. Their voices grew fainter and fainter.

The windows, closed with bricks until a moment before, in this unknown world, had decorated glass in them. On each, a drawing filtered a ghostly light while leaving the room immersed in shadows. There were no walls to keep the windows that floated in the air and no ceiling above them. The whole place was submerged in an infinite blackness into which floated a myriad of symbols. Where the floor should have been was a huge emblem. A circle, surrounded by many other signs he didn't recognize.

His eyes burned and leaked tears even more than before, while both his legs and arms suffered enough spasms that his entire body kept shaking.

"You'll get used to it," Ioan said. He stood at his side. He wasn't an afterimage like the others. Instead, there were two copies of him in the same place. One blurry, on the other side with the others, one with him. Ioan had tears on his face too, but seemed accustomed to the space. "Just relax, breathe, and try to move as little as possible. It's like controlling two bodies, one over there and one over here. It takes practice, so don't strain yourself."

"What is this place?"

"Well, it's complicated. Let's say it's the same place, but in a different plane of existence."

"What?" Daniel tried to move closer to Ioan, but both his legs didn't respond, and he almost fell to the ground.

"Move carefully. It's going to get easier. I hoped someone taught you, you know, since you have the sight."

"Well, I'm sorry I haven't read the manual. What's with this place?"

"Okay, the best way to put it is that there are many worlds. Humans, mortals or not, live in the lowest one, Asiyah, the world of action, which is split in two: the physical Asiyah, where you are used to staying, and the spiritual Asiyah, where the dead live, and we can't go. This is a space, a dimension, between the two. We haven't really changed place. We just shifted ourselves away from the physical plane, into a shadow of the spiritual one."

"Madness! How did I do this?" he asked, glancing around.

"Well, I brought you here."

"You did?"

"Yes, and I'm sure another two will reach us here."

That somehow didn't sound important now. "So, is this the same as using the sight?"

"Oh, no, no, no, it's all different. That's just you using your sight to see behind the veil. That way you can see the divine water and the floating strings—"

"Would you stop teaching nonsense to that poor kid?" said the voice of a woman. It was the young girl with the pendants who had just detached from her own image on the other side. "And you, blondie," she said, "don't listen to the geezer. There is no such thing as divine waters. It's just your mind trying to understand something it can't perceive with its senses. Think of it like gravity. Also, stop scratching your eyes. You'll harm yourself."

"Your eyes cry, for they are facing the divine," muttered Ioan.

The woman chuckled. "That or just a physical reaction to the pressure of the field in this place. Pick the one that sounds less dumb."

"I thought that even within your lines one could find some faith in the old creed," Ioan said. There was a new bitterness in his voice Daniel hadn't heard before. "But the School of Winchester never ceases to surprise me with how low it can fall."

"Well, I guess we can afford to fall, since we are not becoming extinct," she said, grinning.

Ioan clenched his fists and opened his mouth without replying.

"Yes," said another voice. Another woman with a clear tone of mockery. She gave Daniel a nasty feeling. The way she moved and the grin on her face made her look like a snake ready to bite. She was a short, milky-white, red-haired, thin woman. Her eyes, of such a pale gray they seemed white, moved quickly in all directions behind the small round lenses of the glasses on her nose and gave her the looks of a professor.

As she moved in their direction, her shadow kept conversing as if nothing had happened. "That must have burned. But, please, ignore me or the young Italian. We wouldn't dare interrupt such an interesting debate. It's not an everyday thing to have a Strigoi and a witch from the School of Winchester in the same room. We'll stay put here and enjoy the spectacle of you two reenacting the past few hundred years of war your kinds have been fighting. Waste as much time as you need. We don't have any pressing issue at hand."

"Who do we have the pleasure to speak with?" Ioan asked.

"Van Vloed," said the woman, offering her hand. "Aylin. But you can call me by my surname."

Ioan took a breath and shook Van Vloed's hand. "I'm Ioniţă Sturdza, and this with me is Daniel Cortese."

"Fresh blood," Van Vloed said. She licked her lips, and her eyes darted from Ioan to Daniel and back, which increased Daniel's overall sense of uneasiness. She glanced at Daniel again and smiled. "Good. Very good."

Then she glanced at the witch, and both Ioan and Daniel followed her eyes.

The witch shrugged. "Alex Dryden," she said without looking at them, scanning the symbols that floated in the air.

"Why did she call her a witch?" Daniel whispered in Ioan's ear.

But Alex heard him too. "She calls me a witch because my people and I do magick."

"Yeah, like the real deal, not just the dark gifts we immortals have. Well-rounded, reality-bending kind of magic," Van Vloed said, then whispered in Daniel's ear. "You don't want to see her nasty side."

The witch eyed her, shook her head, and rolled her eyes.

"What do we have here?" Van Vloed asked, walking and looking around. "Glyphs that resemble Hebrew letters, numbers, a few planetary symbols, and metals."

"And what would you make of it?" Alex asked, keeping her eyes on the symbols.

"Alchemy, I guess," Van Vloed said.

"Nice," Alex snorted. "More hogwash . . ."

"Excuse me?" Van Vloed said, her voice high-pitched. "I'm an alchemist myself. I must know what I'm talking about."

"Oh God . . . you're right," the witch said without even looking at Van Vloed. "It's not hogwash. You guys get something right from time to time. I have seen little right done since Paracelsus, but yeah, something."

Even Ioan smirked.

Daniel realized he was the only one in the dark. "Can someone explain what's going on so I can understand?"

"Some kind of ritual, I guess. If I didn't know that it was impossible, I'd say it is . . ." Alex said, half-minded. She moved her index finger, pointing at one symbol at a time as if she was counting.

"An alchemical chapel," Ioan said, completing her sentence. "He is preparing the ground for a chemical wedding."

Alex kept counting while spinning on her heels. "There is no such thing. It has something to do with the number seven. I mean, it's a typical number in our line of business, but these symbols are not random. Look there," she said, pointing at a stylized glyph shaped like a bird and moving through others in unrelated places. "These animals are the seven deadly sins: the peacock is pride, the snake is envy, the lion wrath, the toad greed and over there"—she turned to point at something toward Daniel's back—"the snail is sloth, the boar is gluttony, and the goat is lust."

The first thought that came to Daniel's mind was that the witch was making it all up. She was seeing what she wanted to see. But before he could go further in his thoughts, Alex continued.

"As Van Vloed said, planets, but only seven of them, the classic ones: the moon, the sun, Jupiter, Venus, Saturn, Mercury, and Mars. And then there are seven metals, four elements, and three principles, which is seven again." At this point, the witch was spinning and pointing so fast it was hard to follow her. "And the virtues, look, the sphere is faith, the hook is hope, the cross is charity, the wheel is temperance, the shield is fortitude, the book is prudence, and the sword is justice."

"All nice and good," Van Vloed said with a grin on her face. Her eyes moved all the time, pausing on each one of them. "But what about the twenty-two glyphs similar to letters of the Hebrew alphabet all around?"

Alex stopped counting and sighed. "What about them? If you look up at the windows, there are twenty-two major arcana over there."

Daniel looked up at the windows again. She was right. Those weren't saints after all, but images from the tarot. Even he could recognize a couple of them.

"At the beginning, I thought it made zero sense too. But then I noticed that." As the witch spoke, she pointed at the floor.

Where there should have been the floor under their feet was the circle painted in light he had noticed at his arrival in this place. Two lines split it into four equal quadrants, and all around were twenty-two symbols that now even Daniel identified as the letters Van Vloed had pointed at. He still couldn't get her point. Both Van Vloed and Ioan looked as confused as he did.

"Don't you get it?" Alex said.

The others glanced at one another. Daniel shrugged.

The witch stared at them without speaking and gave an exasperated sigh. "It's a circle with twenty-two letters and two diameters crossing it. Not that hard. A circle with a diameter of seven has a circumference of twenty-two."

Van Vloed snorted. "I'm surprised to say the old man's theory sounds more sensible than yours."

Alex didn't reply at first. Whatever conclusion she had jumped to was far-fetched, but to her credit, her brain moved way faster than all of theirs combined. "If this is a ritual, we are all in danger," she said. "You don't invite people to rituals. You use them as sacrifices. I told you, there is no such thing as a chemical wedding, that's nonsense, and even if it wasn't, by the book, it would require nine people, not seven."

Alex talking of danger and sacrifices made Daniel think of the weird message he had found written on the wall of his bedroom. Witches, alchemists, and powerful immortals. Was this really the world he had to live in? A new place he didn't understand, and that he didn't want to understand. One that now, apparently, was trying to kill him. There was no hope of going back to a world where sacrifices were a thing out of a story.

Vomit rose from his stomach pit, and he pushed it down, but his head spun. Ioan, maybe believing he was dizzy because of his powers, held him in place, gripping him by one arm.

"You are both wrong," Van Vloed said, breaking into his thoughts. "Because there are eight of us."

There couldn't be eight. Daniel was sure he had counted only seven guests, himself included, just a few minutes before. He glanced around, his head still spinning. Besides the three talking with him, only the same people he had seen before: the nun still sitting in her chair, alone; the ancient giant leaning in silence against the wall; Hermann Walker, somehow still talking with Van Vloed's shadow; and that overly dressed man, Leto Sieberg.

Daniel didn't remember looking at Leto, but he knew for a fact he had been there since the beginning. Van Vloed was right. Including himself, there were eight guests. Had he miscounted before? But as Daniel glanced at Alex, he found her staring at Leto with a frown on her face he couldn't interpret.

"What if we are both right?" murmured Ioan, but the others, aside from Daniel, didn't hear him.

"Okay, I'm done waiting!" someone roared. It was Hermann, who marched toward the big door.

"Crap," Alex said. "It wouldn't have killed him to wait a while." As she said so, she vanished and reunited with her shadow. Van Vloed did the same as both her figures laughed. Not likable, for sure, but someone who could be useful.

Ioan clapped his hands, and Daniel felt as if he was being

sucked by the drain of a bathtub, and an instant later, he was back in his body, staring at Hermann, who was walking and mumbling something he didn't understand.

Hermann reached the door and yanked it open, but then stood still, looking abashed. Alex, who had followed him, had a similar reaction, and as she reached the door, she moved a couple of steps back. The others rushed toward them.

Daniel, instead, still strained by his experience in the spiritual Asiyah, had his head spinning and his eyes burning. Everything was out of focus, so he stood where he was, rubbing his eyes.

It took little for the voices of the others to attract his attention, and so he teetered his way toward the door. On the other side was not another room of the palace, but an outdoor space, a large square Daniel didn't recognize. Nobody, not a single soul, was around.

At his side, Ioan sniffed the freezing air. "This doesn't smell like Paris at all."

Evidence J-1552-b to the investigation I-7242
Extract from Arnaud Demeure's journal
25 January 1268

"You took your time to introduce me to your sister, and a woman of such beauty to add to the offense." The duke patted me on the back as he spoke. He sure still had the strength of the knight he used to be. "Arnaud Demeure, accompanied by such beauty, you must be the luckiest man on Earth. Allow me to say, the difference in age is striking. Your father must have been a lively old man."

The duke expected us to say something, but none of us spoke. All we could do was stare at each other and smile. He was right. Our time in the labyrinth had turned me into an old man and had done nothing to her, but we could not tell him. The duke looked at us, puzzled. I thought he would not buy it, but to my surprise, he burst into a roaring laugh and clapped me on the back even harder than before.

"An interesting old man, indeed," he said with a raucous voice as he broke out of his laugh. "Let me arrange with my men. I'll keep company to my granddaughter while you arrange with yours." And he moved away.

"I thought I was your wife," my sister whispered.

"Yeah . . ." I said, scratching my back that was still burning. "I guess I screwed it up, didn't I?"

"If that was the only thing! How did you do that?" she said under her breath. She wrapped her arm in mine so tightly she hurt me. Her eyes stared far away.

"Did what?"

She moved her eyes to point at someone behind us. "The girl."

I turned. The duke, who had offered for us to stay at his place, stood by his cart a few steps behind me. Close to him was a girl in her early twenties. She was restless and hopped from one leg to the other. Catching my eyes, she smiled from ear to ear and waved.

Her skin was so white it almost shone under the light of the fires, and every feature in her was gentle. Her eyes were wide and dark. They were as alive as my sister's, but something made them youthful and full of hope. Her hair was so black it shone more than her skin did. She beamed at me with such intensity that I blushed and looked away. I had the faint impression of having seen her before, but didn't know where.

"That girl? What did I do to her?"

"Stop joking now. Did you make her believe she can walk? How safe is that? How long is it going to last?" She shot the questions at me, keeping her head close to my shoulder.

"I don't know what you are talking about," I said, restraining myself from gesturing. "The whole evening is kind of blurry to me. I guess I'm just not used to the wine."

"You are joking, right? That girl strolling behind us—the Duchess Renée d'Albert—she came to the party carried in the arms of a servant. She could not walk."

"Are you saying I fixed her legs?"

"Well, you did something. The duke came over, and just a second after he introduced himself, you muttered something like, 'Your wish is granted.' Even for you, that was weird, but then the duchess screamed she could walk."

"It sure sounds a bit preposterous to think I made her walk."

"That's what I thought, but the duke didn't," she said. "The rest I can explain with your dark gift, but this one?"

I didn't know what the rest she referred to was. "I'm dead serious. I don't recall any of it. All I can remember is coming to the party, greeting some folks, and drinking."

She gave me a puzzled look and sighed. "We will sort this out, I think. I just hope, whatever it is, it doesn't wear out. The man is obsessed with his granddaughter. I remember the night he came over to see the old hag and have her turned to fix her legs, but even the witch said it. Turning someone can't always solve all their problems. You can, though."

Before I could answer, the duke called for me. In his words, the ladies should enjoy each other's company while we talked business.

9

THE SCHWARZSCHILD BOX

Daniel, like the others around him, stood petrified in the freezing December air, but it didn't take long before they looked at one another in search of an explanation.

"What the hell . . ." Hermann said, the first to wake up from the trance everyone had plummeted into. "If there is no party, why did they keep us in that room?" These few words were enough to shake the others awake.

"This isn't Paris," Daniel said. "I don't remember a place like this near the center. We must be somewhere else."

He walked down the stairs that faced the door. Alex followed while the others did not move.

Daniel and Alex both turned to face the building. It was a small church. The walls were rugged, some plaster had fallen, and the wood of the door on the outside was rotten and cracked. White bricks, newer than the rest, walled up the windows, and weeds had grown out from some cracks in the walls.

Alex, a few meters from Daniel, looked around, turning her head left and right, again and again. Daniel had seen her doing this before, and he was sure she was looking at something he could not see.

"This is not an illusion," Ioan said as he came out of the door and reached the two.

Alex rolled her eyes. "I can see that. Thanks a lot."

Ioan clenched his jaw but didn't reply.

Daniel stared at both of them. It sure wasn't the best time for bickering. He pulled out his phone and checked the GPS. "No reception," he said. This was bad, really bad. He was still waiting for news from Marcel.

"We have bigger issues," Alex said. "We didn't arrive here through magick. The network is all tangled, but I don't sense any dissonance."

"I'm not sure I got any word you said besides magick," Daniel said.

Alex's eyes darted at him. "Every time you do magick, you reshape the telluric network to get the results you want. But when you do that, you cause dissonance in the network. If you know how to search for it, you can find the dissonance, but here, there is none."

Daniel hoped Alex didn't expect anyone to understand what she said.

"No worries, pal," Van Vloed said, chuckling behind him. "She is saying if someone had done witchcraft around here, she would know it. What about a dark gift then? Those are for free, no?"

Alex shook her head. "They are, but I've never seen anyone with a gift this impressive. I mean, whoever did this just moved us and the room to another place."

Van Vloed shrugged. "The prince used to do miracles. If someone can—"

"Anything new?" Hermann yelled from the top of the stairs.

None of them answered.

In response, he lit a cigarette, walked down the stairs, and took the street that skirted the church.

The young nun who stood beside Hermann when he shouted didn't follow suit, but stared at him with so much interest that even Daniel noticed. She breathed slowly, inhaling from her nose and exhaling from her mouth in a regular rhythm. Her dark skin contrasted with the white collar of her dress, and Daniel couldn't stop staring at her hands as they squeezed a rosary.

The giant with the scars on his face had absorbed the initial surprise, and the moment Hermann shouted, he went back inside without a word.

"Did you find anything interesting?" Leto asked, coming closer to the four.

"No," Daniel said, his heart pounding. As the man appeared out of nowhere, the wolf within him winced, as if standing too close to a tiger. "Everything is normal, but I'm not the expert here."

"Interesting stuff. Anyhow, I almost forgot my introduction. I'm Leto Sieberg. It is a pleasure," he said to all of them, but offered his hand only to Alex.

The witch glanced at his hand, didn't take it, then studied his face.

"That's Alex Dryden, but we call her Winchester," Van Vloed said. "I'm Van Vloed. This one is Ioan, and the other is Daniel."

"We don't call me Winchester, and I never said everything is normal. I just said no one did magick, but we are far from normal here. If what I think is true, we have a problem."

"Oh boy, another theory," Van Vloed said.

"Well, you are free not to trust me, but you've got the eye yourself. Check the strands in the area. You'll see they all lead straight there"—Alex pointed at the church—"and more strands are gathering."

"It's true," Ioan said, his face stern.

"What does this mean, Miss Dryden?" Leto asked.

"Well, if I'm right, and I am, this . . ." Alex said, looping an index in the air, "is a Schwarzschild box."

"A what box?" Daniel said.

"A Schwarzschild box, a singularity in the quintessential field." Alex must have read in their eyes they were not following. "Okay, I'll make it simple, but I have to give you some basics. I told you we do magick by changing the shape of the quintessential field, the water you see whenever you use your sight, right?"

Daniel nodded. The others were interested too, so he suspected that while knowing more than he did, they might not know as much as their confidence suggested.

"Good. The quintessence manages the interactions between shards in this world."

"Shards?" Leto said, interrupting her.

"Me, you, everything else, every atom composing anything. All connected in a mesh, a network, that links everything with everything else, sometimes directly and sometimes through many hoops."

"What for?" Daniel asked.

"It makes energy flow through the mesh. We call it telluric energy, and you can see the strands of tellur floating in the quintessential field. Those strands form a network, a mesh, used to exchange information between the shards so they can establish and enforce the rules of the world. Everything you know about reality, from gravity to time, to the smell of this place, all is an agreement reached through the network. All magick does is send a message through the mesh strong enough it can go up to where the entire network joins in a single point."

"The Kia," Ioan said.

"Right you are, old man. If the magician can impose their will on the Kia, the message comes back through the network, and the rules of the agreement change, at least for a while."

"For a while?" Daniel said.

"Told you. Trillions of parts decide in agreement how everything works. As strong as your will can be, the network will always enforce the original agreement, and the backlash, the dissonance, will be opposite to the ask of the enchanter. The bigger the change, the bigger the backlash, and the price to pay."

"What does this have to do with that box you were talking about?" Daniel asked.

Alex nodded. "Oh, yeah, the Schwarzschild box. It is the name for a place where many strands connect, a crowded knot in the mesh. Many suspect they exist to preserve and replicate information within the network, but we don't know enough yet about the structure of the network to understand them. All we know is that the pressure of the quintessential field is so high in the boxes the rules of magick go awry."

"So, the big problem we have," Van Vloed said, pointing at the witch, "is you can't do magick without it blowing up in your face?"

"That's not the problem at all," Alex said. "I can manage myself well within here. Penrose, the house I grew up in, is a Schwarzschild box just like this one. The actual issue is—"

"This is insane!" cried someone from behind them. It was Hermann, and he came from the opposite direction he had gone a few moments before. "You five," he said, now pointing at them, "I bet one of you knows what is going on."

"It's not like we have any idea of what you're talking about in the first place," Van Vloed said.

"I went down the street and saw the sign at the corner. It says, '*Rue de la*' something, and under it says, '*Provins*,' so I figured I would search it on the map, and here it is. We are one hour outside of Paris."

"Wait, your GPS is working?" Daniel asked.

"Not at all. I just downloaded the map on the phone before coming. But the GPS is not the issue. Something is weird about this place. It's not like I want to deal with whatever this madness is, so I searched for a cab to go back to Paris, but every time I turn a corner or two, I find myself back here."

Alex snorted. "This is the problem I was talking about. It's what a Schwarzschild box does. You can't just leave a box once you are in it. This place will tamper with reality, create rooms, streets, even people, and push you deeper inside every time you try to escape."

"You said you grew up in one. You must know a way out, right?"

"Well, I bet I can find one, but it took me about five years to learn how to get in and out of the other one on my own."

"Five years?" Hermann and Daniel said at the same time.

"That's good, actually. Most people take over twenty years, so I was pretty fast, and I was seven years old when I started trying. Maybe I can crack this one in three to six months."

Daniel could not believe his ears. "Three to six . . . But wait, isn't Provins the place where the old prince moved after leaving town?"

"Straight into the belly of the beast," Van Vloed said with a grim smile.

This all made sense. Where else if not Provins would he bring them? But why did he need them in his house? He wasn't sure if any of them had ever met the man, but it felt like Demeure didn't want them to leave.

"And the prince controls this place?" Van Vloed asked.

"No, nobody can control a place like this. In theory, with some unbelievable amount of energy, it should be possible to create one. Nobody ever reported a box just outside of Paris, so I have to believe he has created one and must have done so only recently. At least there is no way he can control it. Once it starts, it sucks tellur in until it stabilizes, and once it has enough tellur, it behaves more like a living creature than a place, so powerful it acts of its own accord."

"Okay, I'll cut through all this," Hermann said and marched back toward the church.

Alex and Leto were the first to react and followed him, and the rest were a few steps behind. Celeste, the nun, still stood at the entrance, looking at Hermann with her mouth half-open.

As Daniel entered the room again, music came from the other side of the second door. But that was the door he had come through on his way in, and behind it was only a long dark corridor he had crossed with one of Demeure's servants. Yet, considering they had teleported to another town, music coming from there wasn't the weirdest thing.

Hermann had already hammered the door with his fist and shouted for someone to open it many times, but nothing came from the other side besides music—the glorious music of a grand ball.

"Okay. Everybody, step aside," Alex said, her face stern. Veins ran through her neck and her eyes were bloodred till they started shining a shimmering blue and sparks of electricity enveloped her hands.

"What are you doing, Witch?" Ioan asked in a tone so severe Daniel would not have expected it to come from him.

"Well, we are being kept prisoner here, so whoever this guy is, I'm going to make my way into his house and have him free us."

As the witch was about to raise her arm, Van Vloed leaped to block her. She had almost touched the witch but retreated, screaming as the sparks reached her hand.

"What are you doing, you idiot?" Alex asked. All the sparks disappeared from her body.

"Listen," Van Vloed answered, still clenching her hand, scarred by heavy burns.

The noise of keys unlocking the door from the other side filled the silence that had fallen in the room as Van Vloed had spoken.

Then the door opened.

A man appeared from the other side. He frowned, perhaps surprised to find all of them standing in front of the door. He glanced at them all, his face relaxed while a smile appeared on it, and he spread his arms, welcoming them.

As soon as the man appeared, Roman, who had stayed seated the whole time, stood. So did Van Vloed, who was crouched and taking care of her wounds. She had fully healed already, reminding Daniel that none of them, he included, were human anymore.

Alex moved a couple of steps back. Ioan grasped Daniel's shoulder with one hand. Around him, most of his companions were distraught. Some looked scared, or perhaps excited. All of them had eyes only for the man who had just come out of the door.

At a first glance, there was nothing particularly striking about him. Not too tall, like Hermann, not too short. Well-fit, but not as bulky as Roman. His pointed chin, the shape of his face, and the light in his eyes made him look somehow smart, but he didn't have the look of a scholar Van Vloed had. His age, gray hair, and spacious forehead gave him an elegant look, somewhat reassuring, but not as fatherly as Ioan's. Not as noteworthy as Alex was, nor as timid or melancholic as Celeste. He wasn't ugly by any means, but neither was he a beauty like Leto. There was nothing in this man one could use to remember him. He was built to be irrelevant, forgotten.

One thing struck Daniel like an arrow, the smile the man reserved only for one of them: not him, but Hermann. Envy rose within Daniel, and for a moment, he wanted all the others to disappear. He looked at the man in the eyes. Those eyes of such an icy blue they seemed unreal. In them, he found all the understanding that the world had negated him.

The invitation didn't matter right then, the party, the ritual, and the box too, he'd rather stay there, forever looking in those eyes. He knew who this man was. Despite all the effort that nature had put in designing him to be forgettable, Daniel would always remember his eyes.

"Descartes," Daniel said, and before he realized it, the man wrapped him in his arms.

Descartes, as usual, held him for much longer than was comfortable, but at last, the man released him.

Daniel sighed, smiled, and hugged Descartes again. He had missed him without realizing it.

"I welcome all of you to my house," said Descartes once freed from Daniel's embrace. "There is a lot to celebrate, and I won't hold you here any longer."

"Your house?" Daniel asked. "Mr. Demeure, the old prince, invited us here."

"That's a name I use, my friend," the man said as the group looked at both him and Daniel in awe.

None of them moved until Demeure stepped aside and showed a vast hall hiding behind the door. "Please, come on in. The others are waiting for you," he said. "You and I, my friend, have a lot to talk about," he said to Daniel as he took his arm and drove him inside.

The group looked at each other, then, with Alex at the helm, they marched into the party.

But there was something else Daniel had seen in Descartes's eyes for the first time. A faint light somewhere within them, as if someone was hiding at the back of a dark room. Something wrong that startled his wolf, but very different from what he had felt when he had seen Leto. If Leto was a tiger, and it was natural to fear a tiger, in this case, it was something unnatural, primordial, and revolting. Then it was nothing, just his old friend. So, he walked arm in arm with the man as sweat ran down his forehead.

Evidence J-1558 to the investigation I-7242
Extract from Arnaud Demeure's journal
31 January 1268

"You did what?" my sister asked, her cheeks red and her eyes flaming in rage. I had misspoken, and she had interpreted my words in the worst possible way. All she must have been thinking was how she wanted to slap me in the face, and how she could explain to the others in the room if she did.

"Not for real. I only made her believe I did," I said.

She looked at me, baffled.

"I had to use my gift. You should have seen her. She jumped on me."

Her cheeks and eyes twitched, then she exploded in a roaring laugh.

At a table on the other side of the room sat the duke with two guests. They all turned toward us. The guests' disgusted faces showed how disgraceful they thought my sister's behavior was. The duke, instead, smiled, amused. I don't think there would be anything we could do to upset him. Except for perhaps one thing.

She must have thought along the same lines because she stopped laughing and looked at me with the eyes of someone who had realized they had missed something big. "What if she tells her grandfather?" she whispered. Her head was tucked in to be closer to me.

"That would be bad, I guess. But he is the last one she would ever tell, right?"

"Sure, until the day the fun ends, and she claims you forced her into it. Or worse, until she gets married and the husband discovers it!"

"Well, I mean . . . I didn't touch her. So, everything should be in its place."

"With that attitude, who knows?" she said, her voice bitter.

And because I enjoyed it, she punched me on one shoulder. "Stop smiling, you fool!"

"I have a plan," I said. "I thought of it last night, and so I told her not to tell him and to come by my room again before dawn."

"Are you mad?"

"Listen, she might be our age, older even, but she knows nothing of the world. She is a child. She had the time of her life. I told her we can be together . . ."

Her eyes widened even more. "You're mad."

"Let me finish. When her dream ended, she turned to me, guilty for what she believed we had done. She feared she would never find a husband, and that got me thinking. What if?"

"No, you are not suggesting!"

"I told her I will talk to her grandfather, but we need to let everything simmer for a while or the old man will get what we are up to. To him, we are rich, and I can use my illusions to glue the story together. In the meantime, we can be guests here, then we will be part of a noble family."

She stayed silent for a moment. "Let us suppose this works . . ."

As she said so, I knew she was on board with it.

10

A PARTY OF GHOSTS

Evidence L-1141 to the investigation I-7242
Part of a letter, Roman de Polony to Azurine de Polony (never sent)
Not Dated

Had you walked with us on the roads of Paris in the old days, you would have heard many stories. And yet the nightcrawlers cared only about those talking of a man: Arnaud Demeure. The one with the gift to fulfill any wish. Only one rule—it had to be your one true wish.

If while walking in the shadows of a dark alley at midnight, you met one of ours and asked him, "What news do you bring, brother?" They would respond, "Have you heard of Arnaud Demeure?" And if by the witching hour, while hunting for prey, you talked with those of us who spy and report, they would tell you, "Arnaud Demeure . . ." So, when dark gave in to the light, on your way home to escape the sun, you thought, *What's my true wish, Arnaud Demeure?*

Consider what you'd do if that fine little man invited you to his castle. Imagine, any wish you have he'd grant it, if it is true. They say the hardest thing for those like us is dying. Others say it is to stay human as time carries us around. But we are like you. We want something; we don't know what it is and never get it. For you, it's years, for us, centuries. Now you understand why that night many years ago, when I received his invite, against any logic, I accepted.

———————

The room was larger than Daniel had expected. Many crystal chandeliers descended from the ceiling and spread the yellow light of their candles, scattering it in thousands of floating sparks. A fresco, painted straight on the ceiling and enclosed in an embossed oval, peeked through the chandeliers. It told the story of the clash between two groups of angels.

A multitude of angels wrapped in a white light flew spiraling in the sky near the sun. On the ground, a group of men shielded themselves behind an angel with golden wings and dressed like a Roman soldier brandishing a flaming sword. Some men leaned against his back as they took cover. One of them was whispering into the angel's ears while he pointed toward the other group.

Where he pointed stood two angels in front of a crowd. One painted as a man wearing a robe and a crown and the other as a woman in armor wielding a sword. The man blocked the woman with one hand as he leaned forward, ready to fight, his other hand pointed at the sky.

The fresco gave Daniel an uneasy feeling he could not explain, and the more he studied it, the more sadness mounted in his heart.

Sparkling decorations filled the room. Along all the walls and a few meters high ran a small balcony crowded with people. On the walls at the top of the balcony, windows alternated with large paintings that covered entire sections up to the ceiling. Each of these paintings depicted biblical scenes. Daniel recognized the Genesis, God creating humankind, and Lucifer's fall. Red drapes blocked the view of the windows.

At the lower floor, where they were now walking behind the prince, again windows and paintings gave space to each other, separated only by small columns. Against the columns were statues of muscular men that emerged from the wall, each looking different from the others, and each supporting the weight of the balcony on his shoulders.

Dozens of people populated the room. Some chatted in groups, and others on their own were tasting the food on display on the tables running near the walls. Food provided little to immortal bodies, but it was something that most night-crawlers stuck to, perhaps with the vain hope of remembering what it meant to be human. But Demeure had also provided food more suitable for immortals. Some guests used ladles to pour blood out of enormous glass bowls or ate slices of uncooked meat, likely human, as they chatted. Daniel's wolf howled inside him, but his stomach twitched.

None of the eight following the prince cared about the food.

"I can't believe all of you came. You are giving me a great honor, and I'll repay you for it. For now, enjoy the party and this magnificent palace. It took a long time to get it back to its old glory, but I have had the place for ages, and time is not that big of a deal for people like us."

Again, none of them spoke, and Daniel limited himself to a nod.

"This palace is the most interesting place. It was a dormitory for young orphans. Nobody knows how it came to be, and underneath this ground are catacombs, a labyrinth that reaches every part of the town. Can you believe it? No one has mapped it yet, or not all the tunnels at least. Oh, where are my manners," he then said, halting. "I was taken by my story, and I didn't ask. How were your travels?"

"Travels?" Alex asked in a high-pitched voice. "We don't even know how we came to be here."

"Well, Miss Dryden, I hope you trust me when I say it was the safest way to bring you here. I might have retired, but I have quite a flock of enemies still."

"Trust, you say. It would be easier to trust you if we didn't already know there is no way out of this place."

The prince smiled. "This is the issue? I guarantee you it is all so we can deal with our business here without being disturbed. The reason people called me *prince* in the old days is they treated me like one. Those nights, kings and princes were the first ones to die with a knife in their backs. I'd rather keep us off the grid from mortals or anyone else with ill intentions."

"Or you'd rather keep inside those of us who want to leave instead," Alex murmured, but loud enough the man heard her.

"Miss Dryden, I see that Spencer's pupil is still a bit hot-headed. Youth, I guess, but please, just enjoy the party. Now, now," he said, turning toward Ioan, "what can my favorite prophet say about my future?"

Ioan shrugged. "Nothing. I lost the gift as soon as I left my land."

"That is sad," said the prince, but his voice betrayed a tone of mockery. "Ignore me. It is just the fretting of a groom curious about his future married life."

"You already had my prediction many years ago, and it remains valid," Ioan said, and his face contorted as if he was about to spit.

For a second, Demeure's eyes changed from those of a polite old man to something alien. But it lasted only an instant, and Daniel thought he had imagined it.

Before the prince could answer, Van Vloed spoke. "Are you getting married?"

"I am," said the prince, his chest out.

"Excellent! When will we have the pleasure of meeting the future spouse?"

"There will be many opportunities. All of you will be my guests till the wedding day. For now, my future wife is"—he paused, perhaps in search of a word—"unavailable. Women can get emotional before their wedding."

"Till the wedding day? For how long—" Alex tried to say.

But the prince cut her short. "Miss Dryden. Your headmaster has already been informed, and it will be only for one or two nights. In the meantime, I'll provide you with anything you might desire."

Demeure gestured in the air, and in response, someone arrived from the back of the room. It was a stocky man so much that he looked fat despite his monstrous height that made him as tall as Roman. He came bouncing from one foot to the other, his walk reminiscent of a gorilla. His head was a ball, smooth and shiny, and judging from the little skin that came out of his clothes, the rest of his body must have been hairless too. His hands, feet, and nose seemed too big for his body, while his eyes, mouth, and ears were awfully tiny. The man came close to the group and stopped in front of Demeure. He bent his knee and dropped to the floor, letting gravity do its job with a thump so loud Daniel worried for his bones. In this position, he bent his head, leaving his arms dangling.

Demeure caressed his bald scalp in the same way someone would do with a dog, while the man, still kneeling, didn't seem to care for this display of affection.

"This is Guillaume. Wherever you are in this palace, you can call his name. Ask him to do anything for you, and he will do it."

"It's a pleasure to meet you, Mr. Guillaume," Daniel said, but the bald man didn't react.

"I'm so sorry, my friend, Guillaume can't understand your kindness and can't reply. He's been mute since birth. Treat him as you would treat a servant. He will do as you wish. Now, I must go," Demeure said, stepping away from them, but then he turned back. "Daniel, don't think you can run away. I want to have a chat once done. We have a lot of stories to tell each other, I bet."

After the prince gave them a quick bow, Daniel observed him moving to a chair decorated in Louis XV style placed next to another identical empty one on a low stage. A pipe rested on a small table in front of his chair. The prince took it and started smoking it while watching the group.

Guillaume kneeled in front of Daniel and Ioan without moving a muscle. Leto and Roman had disappeared somewhere already, and the others instead came closer to him and Ioan, while the young nun stood alone a few steps away.

"An interesting guy, right?" Hermann asked, while coming closer to the two. As he spoke, he placed a hand on Guillaume's head and rubbed it in the same way Demeure had done.

"Guillaume?" Daniel asked.

"No, poor one, I mean Demeure. You both seem to know him."

"My question too," Alex said. She also had come closer accompanied by Van Vloed.

"He was there when I woke up the first time like this," Daniel said, waving his hands. "I didn't know he and the prince were the same person until a minute ago. I have always called him Descartes."

Alex's eyes narrowed. "We can't trust anyone."

"I think you are getting this all wrong," Daniel said. "He knows you too, and the way he beams at Hermann. I mean, he invited us to his party. Isn't it obvious he'd be familiar with who we are?"

"Hey, don't drag me into this," Hermann said. "I'm not even

sure why I'm here. That guy invited my sire, and I got the short straw, that's all."

Van Vloed's laugh interrupted their bickering. "Look at you, all fighting like a happy family. At least we know the Strigoi was right. It is a wedding, after all. Congratulations, one for Ioan and zero for Miss Winchester here."

"It's both," Alex said, and Ioan nodded. "We have two mysteries to solve."

"What mysteries?" Hermann asked.

"Well, there is one guest missing for a wedding and one too many for a ritual."

Daniel shook his head. "I don't know how to tell you guys. You have gotten it all wrong. He is my friend. I would have been dead if not for him. I think you are reading too much into the whole thing."

"And there are plenty of people around anyway," Hermann said. "He can pick anyone he wants."

Alex didn't reply, glanced around, and walked away muttering as she headed toward the tables.

"A piece of work, that one," Hermann said, nodding in Alex's direction. "Not to change subject, but what should we do with the big boy here?"

As he tried to move his hand off Guillaume's head, the bald man slid on his knee to get closer to Hermann.

"Maybe he doesn't enjoy being touched?" Hermann said.

Van Vloed chuckled. "It seems quite the opposite to me."

Hermann pulled his hand away as if he had been touching a stove and watched Guillaume for a long moment. Before Hermann could speak or move, Guillaume stood up and walked away. Daniel followed him with his eyes and saw Demeure, a grin on his face, gesturing with one arm in the air. Guillaume walked to his right and dropped to his knees as the prince caressed his head once again.

Hermann chuckled and opened his mouth, about to speak,

but then something distracted him. "I have to go," he said and rushed away, leaving Daniel puzzled.

Daniel stared at Hermann from far away as he gestured to an empty table. Was he mad, too? Alex wasn't too far away from him either and was, once again, looking left and right. Daniel sighed, about to invite Ioan to take a seat so they could talk more about how they had met the prince, but before he could do it, the young nun came closer.

"So, you both know him?" she asked.

The young woman was on her own. Her black dress was worn out, and her face tired, but in her eyes was a smart light.

"Yes," Daniel said. "From a long time ago. Anyway, I'm Daniel and these two are Ioan and Van Vloed."

"My name is Celeste. Celeste Moreau."

"In search of some business with Mr. Walker?" Ioan asked.

Daniel glared at Ioan, then he glanced at Celeste. It was true, Celeste's eyes kept darting at Hermann even as she spoke to them, and Ioan didn't need sight to notice it.

"Business? No, not business. He looks familiar, nothing else."

Ioan sighed. "Just reminiscing, then."

Van Vloed, who had been scanning the room in silence until then, giggled. "Reminiscing, uh? That other one is bigger if you are searching for someone to have fun with." As she spoke, she pointed at Roman who was, once again, standing with his eyes closed and his back against a statue.

Celeste, red in the face, glared at Van Vloed and walked away without answering.

"What is wrong with you?" Daniel asked.

Van Vloed shrugged and walked away.

The moment Hermann had seen her, he couldn't believe his eyes. She could not be at the party, but there she was: Valentine.

That woman had the absurd ability to swoop out of nowhere, and now she sat at a table just a few meters from him. With one hand, she held a teacup, and with the other, she supported her own face. She was blowing hard on whatever she was about to drink, but she kept blowing and drank nothing with a pout on her face.

Someone else might have thought Valentine was sad, but he knew she was mad about something. She might have been a force of nature, maybe too smart for him to keep up with, but she wasn't able to express her emotions in any way he could call normal.

The dress she wore wasn't her usual style. She had arranged herself like a doll, as she always did, and her puffy dress hid both her legs and the chair she sat on. Something was wrong with her. For the first time since he had met her, she didn't wear her scarf. Instead, she had tied it to a purse hanging on her chair. He had never seen her with a handbag. She had put way too much makeup on. Her lipstick was smudged, and her eyes were trapped in a cage of mascara that leaked down her cheeks.

Hermann smiled, but remembered he should have been upset.

As Hermann came closer, Valentine mumbled something he could not understand. Then she paused and stared at his puzzled face, and realizing his confusion, she repeated it aloud. "I said, what a bastard!"

"Who are you talking about? And what are you doing here in the first place?"

Valentine didn't reply or move her head, but she used the hand under her chin to point at the old prince, then went back to blowing on her drink.

"That's the vibe he gives, for sure. But what's spoiling your party?"

She blew hard once again on her cup, but then struck it

against the table so hard Hermann marveled it didn't break. Luckily, none of the surrounding guests appeared to care.

She pulled herself up, pushing on the table. "I have been trying so hard and for so long to stop him from doing stupid stuff like this, and now, not only hasn't he stopped, he is even getting married."

"Are you jealous?"

Again, she didn't answer. Instead, she took her purse, about to leave, but he grabbed her by one arm. She turned on her heels and dropped the handbag on the table. "Madness!" she said under her breath.

"Valentine?"

"What?" she asked, with spirited eyes.

"Can you explain what's going on?"

"Explain you—" Valentine mumbled, and she sat again, breathing hard. Then she wrapped her neck with the scarf and crossed her legs, regaining composure. "Hermann," she said. "Are you enjoying the party?"

"For real? Stop playing games with me, Valentine!"

"You shouldn't be so angry."

"And why do you think I am angry? Perhaps because an old bastard teleported me to a place I can't escape? Or maybe because you pop out of nowhere and don't explain anything to me?"

Valentine's mouth trembled, resisting a smile.

Hermann looked at her in disbelief, letting his arms fall by his side. "Can you at least tell me what is going on?"

A hand touched Hermann's shoulder before Valentine could answer. "Mr. Walker?"

Hermann spun and found the young nun standing in front of him. Celeste stood there without speaking, ready to say something that for some reason she wasn't spitting out.

Hermann didn't care.

He turned back to face Valentine again, but she wasn't there anymore. The table was empty. He glanced in every direction to spot her, but there was no trace of her. "You," he said without looking Celeste in the face. "What do you want?"

As Hermann faced her, the young nun trembled.

"Next time don't interrupt people if you have nothing to say."

As he spoke, Roman arrived behind Celeste and placed both hands on her shoulders. "Leave that guy alone, not worth your time."

Celeste glanced at Roman, then back at Hermann with watering eyes.

"I'm not sure what's going on, but I'm not interested," Hermann said, leaving to get something to eat.

"Hey!" Alex's voice said, one inch from Daniel's left ear.

Daniel turned to see if she was there, but found no one.

Alex cackled. "I'm not there. I'm just thinking in your ears."

"What?" Daniel said. He was so loud that some people turned to stare at him.

Alex, still close to the tables, was shaking her head with a pained expression on her face. "Oh man, don't shout, please. I was joking. I'm transferring the vibrations that my voice produces to your inner ear, and I'm doing the same with yours. Give me one second to connect the others."

"Nice trick, Winchester," Van Vloed's voice said. "I guess you'd do anything to keep talking."

"Instead, I'm wondering why I added you to this conversation. We should hurry. We don't have the entire night for this," Alex said.

"And Demeure has likely realized what you are doing," Ioan said.

Alex sighed. It was as if a gust of wind had filled Daniel's ears. "He has, but he can't hear what we say, so we are safe on that front. Listen now. All these people you see around aren't real. They are just illusions."

"Oh, come on, Winchester," Van Vloed said. "I used the sight to search around, and they all seem regular to me."

"I hate to say it, but I have to agree with Van Vloed on this," Ioan added.

"Well, I hate to say it, but you are both wrong. I thought as you did. I looked around and didn't notice anything weird. I even talked with some of these folks, and nothing looks fake about them. They could even keep up with conversation. So, I thought it wasn't an illusion after all."

"And what made you change your mind?" Daniel asked.

Alex hummed and spoke again. "I hadn't decided on the idea of being wrong in the first place, so I ran a little experiment on a couple of them, and they failed at it."

"An experiment?" Ioan asked.

"Yeah, it took me a while to do something small and controlled enough to prevent anyone from noticing it. I raised the temperature of a sphere of air, around one of these people's heads to about one hundred degrees. He should have died but nothing, not even a minor discomfort."

"What?" Daniel said, once again raising his voice. "You could have killed a man just to prove a point."

"Well, I didn't, did I? And, please, don't shout. You are going to give us all a headache if you keep going. Also, not to displease you, but I tried it on two of them. I redirected the dissonance into his companion' head. Even taking the temperature of the room into consideration, to counterbalance my one hundred, the other should have been at least at eighty below zero but, once again, nothing."

"So, you think they are all fake?" Van Vloed said.

"I'm pretty sure of it," Alex said. "They really are convincing, though. I have seen plenty of immortals with dark gifts that produce illusions, but never at this level. I bet that even the food is fake, but I tasted it, and it was very good. And these people, they are so real it's almost as if he is creating life."

"But why didn't you tell the others?" Daniel said.

"Told you, we can't trust anyone blindly here. I'm pretty sure that one of us is working with the old prince. To be honest, I wouldn't have told you either, but you already know enough it would be more useful than—" Alex broke mid-sentence and let out a wild scream.

Daniel's ears rang, and his sight blurred. He had avoided glancing in Alex's direction during the entire conversation, but now turned to stare at the woman.

She kneeled on the floor, both hands on her ears, blood dripping from between her fingers.

Without knowing why, Daniel glanced in Demeure's direction, and he found him standing in front of his chair, his icy eyes fixed on Alex and every muscle in his face tense. Daniel felt his own wolf's desire to flee.

Demeure came down from his stage, Guillaume following at his heels. He then walked in Alex's direction until he was a few steps from her. "Miss Dryden, it isn't the politest thing to use magick within the walls of someone else's home. The flows of tellur in this place are unpredictable, and you don't know what you are doing."

Alex raised her head. Blood still dripped down her neck. She breathed hard and looked at the man with an accusatory expression.

The prince turned his back to her. "We are done here. The party is over. Guillaume will show you to your rooms." He then walked away, waving one hand in the air, and left the room.

As he did so, the curtain went down on his play. The golden lights of the chandeliers left the place to the dim ones of candles. There was no longer any trace of the guests or of the tables and the food. The room would have been empty if not for the eight people who had entered it together and Guillaume.

The eyes of the angels in the painting above them looked at Daniel as sternly as Demeure had done with Alex before leaving. Could Alex and the others be right about his friend?

Evidence J-1722 to the investigation I-7242
Extract from Arnaud Demeure's journal
3 March 1269

"You can read?" I asked.

Renée bowed her head, but raised her eyes to look at me. "Yes, I could not walk and stayed home all the time, so my grandfather took a scholar in to teach me. It is unusual to teach women, but books kept me company. I also read stories to the maidens from time to time."

She looked embarrassed, but there was pride in her words. At that moment, she was less of a child than usual, but kept her eyes staring into mine. I didn't know what to say.

"This is impressive. My wife can read! You must read a story to me and Sister from time to time."

She giggled.

"But you can read on your own, and Sister can too."

"Well, she wasn't great at the start, but I taught her. She can manage herself now."

Renée looked briefly dispirited, then smiled again. "She is smart and brave and strong. I would like to be more like Sister."

"You know what," I said. "I was talking with one of my guests from our last party and he said that I was the luckiest man on earth. I have a beautiful sister, but my wife is even prettier and full of grace."

Her eyes widened, and a smile opened on her face. She jumped with both arms around my neck and squeezed me.

I might not have shared the thought of my guests, but I saw their point. Over the years, my sister had grown into an indomitable force. She could ride horses, and she would not have had any problem at wrestling down most of my men. She had the fierce beauty of a wild animal. Renée, on the contrary, was a princess, a doll, almost. The perfect companion at my parties, loved by all my guests.

My sister's hair might have been a rare jewel, but she didn't bother combing it and arranged it in a long braid. Renée's black hair instead was the talk of other women, so thick and long, but soft and heavy. I often caught the wives of my guests putting their hands under it and laughing in wonder.

Where my sister's eyes would look at you in a curious and challenging way, Renée looked at people with hope, as if everybody who she talked with had some life-changing truth to share with her.

While I daydreamed, a servant rushed into the room. "Sir, your sister, Miss Valentine, demands an audience."

"Can you please tell your lackey I don't need announcements in my house?" Valentine said, appearing behind the man and pushing him aside. "Am I intruding on the lovebirds?" As always, she wore a pair of my trousers and a light white shirt. She had a stick in one hand, and she tapped it against one shoulder.

"Sister!" Renée greeted her and ran in her direction to hug her.

Valentine, caught by surprise, almost stumbled.

"My husband said that I am the prettiest!" Renée said.

"Of course he said it," Valentine replied, stroking Renée's head. "He is dense, but he would be mad to say otherwise."

Renée pulled away from her hug and looked Valentine straight in the eyes. "I saw you in the courtyard with the men. I worried for you but then bam and bam." She gestured with her arms, as if wielding a sword. "Where did you learn all that?"

"Well, I always liked to pick a good fight, I guess."

That wasn't true. She had always handled herself when we were kids, but for sure, she had enjoyed all this much more since we had left the labyrinth.

"Will you teach me?" Renée asked.

Valentine glanced at me, her eyes puzzled, and took her time to answer. "Sure, why not?"

"And will you let me brush your hair today?"

Valentine's eyes swiveled from Renée to me. I shrugged.

"Fine," she said, defeated. Renée clasped her hands and pushed Valentine out of the door. "See you in the evening, dear. The women have work to do."

"Yes, please," I said, chuckling. "Make her look like a woman before the party tonight."

To this, Valentine turned her head toward me and stuck out her tongue.

"Your wish is granted," she said, imitating my voice and waving one hand in the air.

11

THE GUIDING LIGHT

Daniel had spent five minutes in his room and was already out in the dark corridor in front of his door. He had way too much to think about. The message in his bedroom in Paris, the radio silence from Marcel, and now also Descartes, or Demeure, as the others called him.

He was a friend, not an evil man. But the witch was convinced Demeure was planning something bad, and he had to admit it, she had a point, especially after the scene at the party.

Now, he walked without a destination, absorbed in his thoughts, and he couldn't stop wondering how much he really knew Descartes. After all, many years had passed since the last time he had seen him. He didn't even know that the old man who had taken him in when he had just turned was, in fact, the prince of Paris everybody talked about.

Without realizing it, Daniel found himself in a large room full of books, a library. He recognized it as the first room he had passed through following Guillaume once they left the failed party. The entire room would have been pitch black if it weren't for a fireplace. The light coming from the fire created shadows that danced on the surrounding walls.

Because of the darkness, he couldn't read the names of the books stored along the walls, but bookcase after bookcase filled the entire perimeter of the room from the floor to the ceiling. A series of statues or busts ran along one wall, but he couldn't glimpse their features.

In front of the fire sat two armchairs and in one of them, maybe asleep, was Demeure—one arm dangled from the armrest, the other rested on his lap.

He wasn't his Descartes, nor the prince. He was an old, tired man, small and frail, taking comfort in the fireplace's warmth.

Daniel was about to leave and go back to his room when the old prince spoke. "So, you didn't forget that you promised me a chat? Do you want to talk, like in the old times?"

Without answering, Daniel took a seat in the armchair in front of him. The fire crackling and the warmth coming from the fireplace made him notice how cold the rest of the palace was.

The two sat in silence. The old man didn't speak and kept looking in the fire with tired eyes. Many times, he glanced in Daniel's direction, about to speak perhaps, but every time he didn't.

"Is everything all right?" Daniel said.

The other sighed. "The best I can afford, I guess. Since I saw you tonight, I started doubting something I had decided many years ago. Can I ask you something as a friend?"

"For sure," Daniel said.

"Did you ever love anyone?" Demeure asked.

Daniel tried to resist laughing and felt relieved. Whatever the old man was worrying about couldn't be too bad if this was the topic. "You have love issues? I thought you were getting married," he said, still laughing.

Demeure went on, ignoring him. "I remember in your first nights you kept talking about a woman. Someone who left you. You wanted to find her at all costs and never succeeded. She was life to you, and you lost her. Despite this, you survived. How? Why did you keep living? Why didn't you take your own life?"

What he said, and how he said it, made Daniel stop smiling. "Is that the question you want to ask me after so many years? Why haven't I killed myself?"

Demeure leaned toward him and nodded without speaking.

"Because she is still out there, and one day I'll meet her again and she will explain why she did this to me. I didn't have any other reason. And yeah, I think I might have loved that woman if that's what you want to ask."

The prince kept looking into the fire as if there was something there only he could see. "If that's so, what would you do to find her, and what if she were in danger, and you were the only one who could save her?" Demeure kept going, gesturing with both his hands and staring into his eyes.

"I'd do anything," Daniel said.

"Even if that means sacrificing others you love? Even if that means giving up every value, everything that makes you who you are?"

Daniel studied him. He had never seen Descartes like this in the old days. He had never seen such doubt or restlessness in the man before. His quiet and determined demeanor was gone, replaced by someone who was lost. "Old friend, is there any way I can help you with whatever this is? You know I—"

"I asked you. Would you?"

"Well, if I knew that she was in danger, I'd do everything I could. Nothing else would matter."

At these words, Demeure fell back into the armchair, exhausted, frailer than before for an instant, but a new fire surged within him. His face contorted, and his body became rigid as he came closer to Daniel again, his eyes full of malice. "And what would you know about love? About anything! Like dogs, you bark, failing to imitate your masters' speaking, that's what you do!"

Daniel's skin tingled at his words. He tried to reply, but his lips moved without any sound coming out. The demon within him was alert, as if ready to run for his life.

The spark of fire from within Demeure dissipated as fast as it had appeared, and he fell again in the armchair, lifeless and paler than before. "I'm sorry, my friend. I'm just tired. Would you mind leaving me alone for a bit?"

Daniel didn't reply at first, but stood up. "Have a good rest then," he said, having resolved to give him some space. So many questions he wanted to ask, from his wedding to his illusions at the party to the odd conversation they just had, but it didn't seem the right place or time. Daniel glanced at the man while leaving the room. He sat there as pale and motionless as a corpse.

"Hey, Daniel?" Demeure called to him as he was walking back through the dark room. "Your wish is granted, my friend."

Evidence J-1891 to the investigation I-7242
Extract from Arnaud Demeure's journal
3 July 1288

"How come you always say, 'Your wish is granted,' to our guests, but they never tell you their wish to begin with?" Renée whispered in my ear and squeezed herself to my right arm so none of the guests could hear her.

"It is not in the nature of men to know their own desires. Even if they asked, they would wish for the wrong thing."

Everything started with a *bang*. The walls trembled as if a tree had fallen, smashing against the door of the castle.

"Stay here," said a man close to the child. She loved him. He was a good man. But she didn't listen to him. First, she checked in her pockets. There were trinkets inside—one, two, three, she counted. It was all of them. She then followed the man and hid behind a door that led straight to the entrance hall.

Another bang came and the big door came off its hinges. An enormous animal stood where the door had been a moment before. It must have been two times as tall as the good man. The beast panted. She imagined its bad breath. Fangs came out of its mouth, pointing both upward and downward. Fur covered its entire body; its shape had something of both wolves and lions. Its feral eyes glanced around, ignoring the good man as if searching for something.

Many soldiers followed the beast with blades in hand. They, too, searched for something.

The good man rushed in one of the soldier's direction, but he didn't go far. The beast grasped him by the shoulders.

Those arms could have snapped the good man in two, she was sure of it, and its claws and fangs were ready to rip him apart.

The child's heart jumped, and she was about to storm into the room to save the good man, but he didn't need help.

His body dissolved between the beast's fingers as if made of dust. The smoke that had been the good man's body spread in the room as a dense mist like that of a smothered fire. The beast turned its head left and right, confused.

With the beast still standing at the center of the room, the smoke moved around from one soldier to the other, filling their mouths and nostrils. One after the other, they collapsed to the floor. Some coughed, some shrieked, others sounded like cats crying.

The child didn't like the noises they made.

After just a few moments, none of the soldiers stood alive and the beast was alone in the middle of the room, stupidly trying to catch the smoke that surrounded it with its enormous claws.

It was then that the cloaked man entered the room, his face hidden by the hood.

The cloaked man raised one hand to the ceiling, and as he did so, the smoke that had spread around the room converged back to a single place on the ground.

Out of the smoke, the good man reappeared. He struggled to get back up again but kept falling, and so he stayed on all fours, unable to stand.

The beast ran in his direction and kicked him in the stomach with all its might, making him roll along the ground and smash against a wall. As the good man lost consciousness, the monster roared and rushed in his direction with such speed that it hit a table in its way, making it fly.

In the meantime, another group of soldiers, four or five of them, entered the palace. The cloaked man gestured their orders. At this signal, the soldiers dispersed around the castle. Two of them marched up the stairs that led to the living quarters. Another one went to the kitchens. Only one of them moved in her direction.

The child was about to close the door to run and hide, but she glanced once again at the good man.

The beast had straddled him and was punching him savagely on the chest. His ribs cracked and a splash of blood painted red on the beast's fur and on the wall. She could not keep herself still anymore.

A faint light surrounded her entire body as she rushed into the room to save the good man. One soldier tried to stop her, but as he came close enough, her light enveloped him, and he fell numb to the floor.

The child rushed through the entrance hall and reached the

monster. In doing so, she passed straight in front of the cloaked man who gestured something, but she didn't care.

The child's light was quick to wrap itself around the beast as she jumped on its shoulders. The beast's fur was rough and wet with rain. The monster struggled, trying to get rid of her, and shrieked so loud it shook the room. So much it tried that at the end the beast grasped her by one ankle and smashed her to the floor.

Her right arm and shoulder moved on their own with a loud *crack* as they touched the ground. Pain like that of a thousand needles pierced her skin, spreading from the shoulders all down her arm.

She lay on her broken shoulder, her arm pressed against her body and a cheek resting on the floor. Straight in front of her was the lifeless body of the good man lying in a pool of blood.

The beast was coming for her.

Seeing the good man in such a state made her heart beat faster and faster. Her body moved on its own. The bones strode against each other as the arm came back into its socket. The pain and the warmth were gone. Her feet left the floor as she rose up, hovering inches from the ground.

The beast in front of her screamed. Smoke came out of its enormous mouth and its eyes leaked a thick black liquid.

Then nothing. The child's sight blurred. The bones of her face had been crushed and a throbbing pain spread across her cheeks and mouth. A soldier, appeared out of nowhere, had just punched her straight on the nose.

The beast came closer and took her once again by one ankle, dragging her outside. Her cheek scraped the ground, but she glanced at the good man, and he was breathing. He was alive, but she had just lost consciousness.

Alex woke up to a loud whistle ringing in her head. She touched her neck. It had swollen, but the blood on the pillow was dry, proof something had improved. Yet she was having that weird old nightmare again. She tried to bring back images from her dream, but the faces were blurry, and she couldn't remember past when the young girl lost consciousness.

She raised herself from the bed, then fell, sitting on it once again, her head spinning. There she waited until the room stopped whirling around her, took a deep breath, and stood. She stumbled a bit, but reached the bathroom. As she turned on the light, Alex saw her reflection in the water-speckled mirror above the sink. Her eyes were hollow and she had encrusted blood on her earlobes and neck. She washed it away, splashing herself with cold water, which relieved the ringing in her ears, even if for just a minute.

As Alex came out of the bathroom, she turned back to look at the door, but there wasn't any—no bathroom. She smiled. At least the box, the house, was taking care of her.

The prince might have created it, but nobody could control so much magick.

Still smiling, Alex walked to the window. It was still night outside while it should have been morning already, but that wasn't surprising. Like in Penrose, time must be unreliable in here too. She shrugged and decided she would wait for the ringing to fade before reassessing the situation.

Suddenly, a door downstairs creaked, opening and closing. As she glanced down the street, Daniel came out of the palace in a rush.

Daniel reached his room, still thinking about the private chat with his old friend. He wanted to believe that everything was fine and that nothing was wrong with Descartes. But that outburst?

He checked his phone, but there was no reception and so no way for messages to either leave or reach the device. The clock on it ticked five in the morning, but the one in the room, just above the bed, said one thirty. What was going on?

He paced the room many times, wondering whether he had sent Marcel to his death this time.

A movement outside the window startled him.

It was a cat. Its fur was black and shiny under the pale moonlight and the lampposts. Its eyes must have been green, but its pupils were so dilated that only a thin circle remained of the green. The cat stared at him from behind the glass with the stillness only felines are capable of.

"What are you doing here?" Daniel said, tapping on the window.

The cat trilled and drew a quick circle in the air with its head. Daniel took it as a greeting, and that made him smile. He tapped on the glass again, waved at the cat, and closed the curtains.

Daniel lay in bed staring at the ceiling without moving a muscle. The clock above his head was ticking and his finger tapping on the bed had synchronized with it. As the two drifted apart, his eyes clouded and everything went dark, then again something hit the glass of the window. Daniel struggled to open his eyes, but the noise kept coming, so he got up and peeked behind the curtain.

Again, he found the black cat there, staring at him. The little animal was hitting the glass as it had done a few moments before, but now that it had seen Daniel, it meowed again and again without rest.

Daniel opened the window. The air came against his face like a blade and he had to brush off some snowflakes. The cat, in the meantime, walked back and forth on the windowsill, purring and rubbing his face and tail against Daniel's arms. He peered down. They were three floors from the ground, so how had the little beast arrived there unless it could fly?

The cat hopped on his arm and bit his hand. There was no actual strength in the bite, but Daniel withdrew his hand, anyway. In response, the cat jumped away from the window onto the nearby desk, and with another jump, it reached the bed. Once there, the cat sat and stared at him, meowing and stretching one paw in his direction once more. Daniel came closer to it, but before he touched it, the cat bounced down from the bed and back on the windowsill.

Daniel chuckled and walked back to the window, expecting that the cat would repeat his jumps around the room. The cat instead stretched its neck to push its head against Daniel's hand, but then turned to face the street and jumped down.

"Fuck," Daniel said and looked straight down, expecting to see the little cat's body smashed on the sidewalk. But the cat just sat on the snow and stared at him from below.

Once again, it meowed and stretched one paw in his direction. Did it want Daniel to follow it?

Daniel shook his head and closed the window. In response, the cat cried again. It was so loud Daniel heard it through the glass. Maybe he was going insane, but he had seen more magic in a few hours than he had in all of his immortal life, and in this case following the cat might as well have just been the sanest thing to do.

So Daniel found himself once again running through the dark corridors of the prince's palace. He passed through the library, but this time there was no Demeure, nor a fire lit to wait for him, so at least he didn't have to explain himself.

Once outside, Daniel didn't know if he could reach the same place he had seen the cat land. He had gone through so many twists and turns within the building that it was impossible to say where to go, and even if he could find that street again, this whole idea was already sounding stupid. In the absolute silence of the place, the lampposts stretched the shadows of the cars and created ghosts that walked with him.

He sniffed the air. Nothing. But he shivered, patted himself on both shoulders, and rubbed his hands and legs. As he stood still, looking at the door, something brushed against his ankles. Without a noise, the cat had appeared at his feet.

Daniel bent to reach the cat's face and brushed some snow off his fur. The cat thanked him with a headbutt and a meow. The little animal turned toward the street and, tail in the air, started walking. Daniel sighed and followed.

He had to walk faster than he was comfortable with to keep up with the cat's pace, especially with the snow pushing against his feet, and now, many turns into this trip, he had no idea where he was. Suddenly, a noise came from behind him, as if someone was about to turn the corner he had just crossed.

He stopped but no one was behind him and nobody came from the corner, or at least no one he could see through the falling snow and the reverberating light spreading in the air. When he turned back to follow the cat once again, the animal had disappeared.

Daniel searched in all directions to spot his guide, but nothing. He reached for his phone, but the display showed nothing. The snow squeaked behind him again. He glanced, but nobody was there. The snow hammered against his face, and despite the fact he couldn't see anyone, he was sure that someone was out there with him. But if he could not see them, they could not see him either, so he ducked and hid behind a car and waited.

A shadow appeared in the middle of the road, straight in

front of the car he was hiding behind. "Where is that dumbass?" asked the shadow—it was Alex.

Daniel came out of hiding, hands in the air, as Alex stared at him, shaking her head. "What were you doing down there?"

"Nothing, I wanted to make sure it wasn't someone dangerous."

"Dangerous? You eat people as food!"

He did, but he didn't need her to remind him. "What were you doing out here anyhow?"

"I was following you," Alex said, looking away. "A box can be a dangerous place."

Daniel eyed her and shook his head. "You thought that I was planning something nasty."

Alex shrugged. "Well, blame me all you want, but it was the only logical conclusion. You are, after all, on friendly terms with the prince."

"I told you, he is not an evil man. He must have his reasons—"

"And what are you doing out here anyway?" she interrupted him.

Daniel looked around before speaking. "I was following a cat."

Alex stared at him wide-eyed with her mouth open, but didn't say a word.

"It wasn't a normal cat. I'm sure it wanted me to follow it."

"At least you had a smart one to follow," Alex said.

Daniel tried to think of something smart to rebuke her with, but she was better than him at that game and he needed her help. "I think it's related to this entire story."

Alex huffed, moved a couple of steps away, and glanced around. "How so?"

"I found a message in my house before coming to the party and it said not to come. The symbol of a cat was underneath the message."

Alex clenched her jaw. "You tell me that now? Okay, let's find your cat, but you must explain to me everything as we walk, and if anything happens, you do as I say and don't ask questions. Do we understand each other?"

Daniel nodded.

With an air of satisfaction, Alex lifted the left sleeve of her sweater and raised her arm in front of her with the hand parallel to the ground. A sphere-shaped jewel dangled in front of her face.

"What's that?" Daniel asked.

Alex eyed him. "Just an old heirloom, it's been with me since I can remember. I customized it a bit. Now, be quiet while I concentrate."

At first, nothing happened, but the pendant lit up with a pale blue light, and fireflies or sparks, tied to the woman's wrist, began floating in the air. Looking straight at the light gave Daniel a sense of serenity he hadn't felt since this entire trip had started.

The light spread by drawing a line in the air in front of them, causing an infinity of glitters that spread between the snowflakes suspended in the air. It was almost as if someone had blown diamond dust and created a path that now stood in front of them. Daniel looked away from the origin of the light, but then immediately returned to it. The light pulsated. It talked to him. Nothing could go wrong, provided that he kept looking into the light.

"You should not be staring straight at the amulet," Alex said.

He had kept his eyes focused on the shining jewel for so long he didn't notice that the body attached to it had moved closer. Daniel ignored Alex, but she elbowed him in the ribs hard enough he lifted his eyes from the pendant.

"It will suck the will away from you, so stop staring at it."

Daniel tried to shift his focus to Alex as much as he could, and that absolute peace faded away from his mind. "Are you looking for the cat?"

"Couldn't care less about the cat. I'm searching for the place where we are meant to be. Follow me."

Daniel rolled his eyes behind the woman and didn't reply. She would not have been his first choice for that stroll, but at least she was helping him.

"So, who do you think has left you the message and sent the cat?" she asked, breaking the silence.

"I think it was the woman who made me the way I am."

"She must be a powerful one," Alex said, glancing back at him. "Few immortals know how to sire, and fewer can do it."

"I don't know about that. It's been many years since I saw her. I was still human. I'm not even sure she is the one who made me."

"You moron!" she said, turning back to face him. The blue mist thinned as she moved her arm away. "You fixated on some chick and are wasting my time in the hope of meeting her again. Do you know how much pain I have to go through to enchant one of these pendants?"

"No, wait, this is not like you think it is. I mean, I searched for her for years without success. The last time I met her was the night I turned and I met Descartes, I mean Demeure. Now, I received his invite, and she came back to leave me a message."

"You can't even be sure that she left it."

"I'm sure," he said. He had to come clean if he wanted her help. "She signed it with a symbol she has on her shoulder, a curled-up cat. I followed her trail everywhere, and I found a lot of stories. All about the Scarlet Woman."

A weird light gleamed in Alex's eyes. "The Scarlet Woman, you said?"

"Yes, why?"

"Okay," she said, turning her back to him. "I'm going to

follow this trail. You stay here, I'll be back soon, and it should be safe enough if you don't go roaming around."

"What? I'm not just going to sit here!"

"You are going to be in my way," Alex said, as the light formed once again in front of her. "Now, be a good sport, and don't make me force you to stay here, okay?"

"Wait," he said, as she had already started walking. He was about to jump and fetch her by one arm but he knew already that he was no match. "She has sent the cat to fetch me, not you," he said under his breath.

Alex quickened her pace as Daniel stood looking at her as she was walking away.

"I know that immortals like you can't understand. You don't even remember what it's like, do you? Did you ever love anyone? Did you ever have any purpose? Something you wanted to find?"

But Alex didn't show any intention of wanting to stop.

"Why do I even ask you? You are just monsters. You could never understand."

Alex stopped and turned to face him. Daniel attempted a smile that disappeared from his face as he saw her eyes and her clenched fists.

"You child, you have no idea what makes people like us go on. You think you are special with your love and purpose, you moron! But you're just like us, doing what we all do. Obsessions are all we have. How do you think we can go on for hundreds of years with a hungry monster inside without going mad, huh?" She turned her back to him once more and kept walking.

Daniel had lost any hope that she would allow him to follow her.

"Are you going to walk or not?" she said without facing him.

He ran to reach her. He would have hugged her, but she would not have let him survive it. "What made you change your mind about following the trail?"

"I said it already. No questions, and just do as I tell you." As she spoke, her voice hissed between her teeth. "And if you go wagging your finger at me ever again, I'll kill you."

They walked in silence for what seemed like hours. Daniel stared at his own feet and at the houses around to avoid the light of the pendant, and so he struggled to follow Alex's pace as she walked on the trail of light.

They were crossing a few streets barely wide enough to fit a single car. From both sides, the houses of the old town looked down on them. They had pitched roofs and sat enclosed within walled gardens. From above their walls, branches and flowers, covered in snow, poured out on the street as if trying to escape. The plants were so dense that, to avoid dealing with them, Daniel and Alex had to walk in the center of the street.

Daniel checked his watch once again and not even a minute had passed. No news from Marcel yet, so he tried to send him a message without taking the phone out of his pockets. He wrote, as best as he could, *"Everything okay? Found anything?"*

In the meantime, Alex didn't take her eyes off the trail as she sighed. "I told you already that phones and watches don't work here, right? And who is that for anyhow?"

"A friend . . . he might be in danger because of me."

Alex rolled her eyes and moved one hand in the air as if to say, *"Whatever."* Daniel took the phone from his pocket to check that he had lost no messages. As she had said, there was no reception.

"Say," Daniel, his phone still in his hands, said, "you don't like old Ioan much, do you?"

Alex hummed and eyed him. "What makes you think that?"

"Just a hunch," Daniel said with half a smile. "Also, Van Vloed said your people were at war."

Alex sighed. "She talks too much, that one. There is no war going on in the shadows. You don't have to worry. The School won that war many centuries ago and the Strigoi tribes have been crippled ever since."

"That sounds"—Daniel tried to search for a word that would not upset her—"harsh."

"They deserved everything that came to them. Let me tell you, Strigoi are dangerous, they are an old species, and way scarier than any other immortal. They have so many dark gifts up their sleeves that if it weren't for my magick, I would fear them myself. Those animals have killed hundreds of ours. All we wanted was to visit their lands in search of the secrets of immortality. We've been lucky to create immortal wizards soon enough to wipe most of them out."

All her ranting was one-sided, but Daniel knew better than to tell her. He shrugged. "I'm not even sure which species of immortal I am. For all I know, I could be one of them."

Alex laughed, but kept walking without turning back to him. "You'd know if you were one of them. But it's not that unusual not to know exactly what you are. Most immortals are unclassified, anyway. It's a rare condition and it doesn't come with a manual. The School estimates there is one immortal to every one hundred thousand people, many of them clustered in a few hot spots. Most mortals won't even know immortality is a thing, and that's good, otherwise who knows what would happen. But this is also why it's so hard to study immortals. Each one seems to have little in common with the others and so only a few species have been classified."

"Alone, with no one else like you, and nothing in common with anyone else. It sounds pretty much as lonely as it is."

Alex stopped and looked at him, grinning. The bluish light still floated in the air. "You really enjoy your self-pity, don't you? Well, if it makes you feel better, you are not as unique as you think. There are a few things all immortals have in common.

For a starter, they all lack strands connecting them to the network, and for all we know, this seems to be the very reason they are immortal in the first place. Which also means that, excluding those like me, immortals—"

"Can't do magick," interrupted Daniel.

Something brightened in the witch's eyes and a large smile appeared on her face. At first, Daniel feared she would smack him for talking over her. Instead, she simply nodded and snorted. "Not a lost cause, after all. A few hours spent in my company and you can already make smart deductions."

Daniel stopped himself from answering in kind. The witch didn't seem pissed for the first time since he had met her, and he'd rather keep her in a good mood. "Well, you said that to do magick you use the network, so I figured," he said. "But it's not like I get much beyond that. I don't even understand how what you do differs from normal dark gifts."

"Simple," Alex said. "Immortals operate on the agreement from the outside and with a focused purpose, which means their impact on the agreement is immune from dissonance but has limited versatility."

Daniel looked at her, puzzled, his mouth half-open, unsure if he should say that no one, absolutely no one, could ever understand what she just said.

Alex sighed and hummed, and Daniel knew he was in for a long explanation. She stopped and looked pensive for a minute. As much as Daniel was curious to know what she was about to explain, he glanced at the floating light and resented himself for having asked any question because it would keep him from his destination.

"Come on," she said, resuming her walk and gesturing until he followed her. "I'll explain as we walk."

Daniel hurried to reach her, excited that, for once, he could have his cake and eat it too.

His surprise must have shown as Alex glanced at him. "Who

am I not to entertain genuine curiosity? But I have to warn you, my view is scientific, and as you've seen with the Strigoi, for some people it isn't a matter of science. They've turned these concepts into a religion. So, be careful when you deal with people like those. Even in Winchester we have many zealots." As she spoke, a few dots of light broke away from the pendant and floated in the air, like fireflies, a step or two ahead of them. After a few more appeared, she spoke again. "Do you see this one?" She pointed at a large, bright one in the center. All the others were randomly distributed around it.

Daniel nodded.

"This is a core soul. Just like the others"—she pointed at each dot surrounding the large one in turn—"it is just a universal entity or, as the old folks call it, a shard. Remember when I told you that trillions and trillions of parts agree on how our reality works? This core soul is one such part, and it isn't too different from the others surrounding it, if not because it's bigger and it concentrates a higher amount of tellur. Because of this, it distorts the quintessential field and forces other shards nearby to orbit around it, just like planets do around a star. Now," she said, and bright bridges, like sparks, connected the small lights to the big one. "When these shards spin at the same frequency, they entangle and connect. This is pretty much how every living being looks to someone with the sight: a core soul with a high concentration of tellur surrounded by minor shards of telluric energy connected to it via very robust strands. Are you following me?"

Daniel nodded, eager for her to continue.

A few other constellations like the first appeared in the air, then more sparks connected the core soul of the first with some other dots around it, at times through large branches and at times through thinner ones. "When the core soul is large enough, you have sentient beings, more and more human. They also loosely connect to each other. The larger the core soul, the more connections it has, and the more it can influence the network. As I said before, the way we do magick is by sending a message, our will or desire, through the network."

"You said you have to reach a single point where everything joins."

"Correct. That point, we call it Kia. We don't really understand the precise mechanism yet, but we know it controls and mediates the agreement achieved through the network. While it doesn't directly express any will on the agreement, it functions as an arbiter of what the agreement, and hence reality, looks like at every given moment in time."

"Then, if it's a matter of changing the agreement, how can immortals even have a dark gift in the first place?"

Alex smiled. "Well, for you to understand that, first I have to show you what an immortal looks like." Again, as she spoke, the lights in front of them flickered and changed. This time, some of the sparks that connected the lights disappeared until one constellation found itself separated from the others. "So, as you already know, immortals are not connected to the network. In fact, this is what an immortal looks like: a region of the telluric network completely disconnected from the rest."

"As you said, this is why it isn't possible for immortals to do magick. Right?"

"Correct. No strands connecting you to the network means you can't do magick. And I'll spare you the theorem showing that the exchange of telluric energy is always negative for any single shard, but it also means that you can't die."

Daniel was about to open his mouth to speak, but the witch raised a hand to shush him. She was on a roll.

"Now, when a cluster of shards is cut off from the others, it can express itself without the network mediating it. That's what a dark gift is: the shape assumed by the will of an isolated region of the network that influences, from the outside, an agreement it isn't part of anymore. It isn't versatile because it is a perfect expression of the immortal it originates from. Also, there is no dissonance, because there is no connection to the system that enforces such an agreement.

"It is likely for the same reason that we immortals have those animalistic instincts, those wolves, within us. While this ventures a bit too much into philosophy for my taste, we can't exclude that immortality and its wolf are just the shape men would assume in a world where they wouldn't have to share their reality with others. Their true face, so to say."

Daniel found this thought depressing but she was talking so feverishly that, once again, he thought better of disappointing her. "Well, I'm kind of proud I followed your explanation this time, but I feel you made it simpler for me. So, thank you," he said, smiling at the witch.

Alex smiled, but became serious again. The lights she had used for her explanation faded away. "It is good for you to know these things if you want to be of any help. Now let's hurry."

They walked straight on the same street for a while until, at last, they reached a corner where the bluish light turned. But before taking the new road, the witch stopped. "Daniel?" Alex said, friendly for the first time.

"Yes?"

"This box might still be dangerous, so, just try not to screw up."

They turned the corner and continued in silence for a few meters. The wind howled, and they both had to shake the snow off their clothes once or twice. The light went through a small alley, one so small that cars wouldn't be able to go through. Alex walked in with no uncertainty. Daniel looked around and followed. Nobody seemed to be there, but the streetlights were all off, so it would have been hard to be sure about it.

The alley was one of those places where houses are built on top of one another. One of those places that cities forget about. A small lamppost attached to one house lit the end of the alley, but it made the darkness even bleaker where they were. Despite this, grass and moss were trying to take possession of that corner of the town.

The magical light passed through the whole alley and turned the corner. Daniel and Alex followed it in silence. He didn't know if she was feeling as he was, but out of respect, he avoided asking any questions. As they turned the corner, they found a flight of stairs attached to the wall of a house, its railing reddened with rust. At the top, a group of three waited. The light of the pendant made their faces visible even in that dark place: Ioan, Van Vloed, and Roman.

Evidence J-3451-a to the investigation I-7242
Extract from Arnaud Demeure's journal
23 May 1371

"Give it back," I asked, attempting to hide my anger.

At this, my wife, Renée, gave a soft giggle and looked at Valentine, who smiled back. "I just want to know what all this studying and notes are about, my dear."

"Renée, don't make me ask you one more time. Give that book back to me."

"Be patient with this silly wife of yours, my love," she said, winking at Valentine. "I'm a woman after all and so I'm bound to be curious."

She spun, jumped, and landed near the fire on Valentine's knees. Both laughed at each other as my patience faded.

"Hear, dear sister, your brother is a gloomy man." She read from the book, lowering her voice to sound pretentious. "'It took the work of six hundred thousand men to build the tower, and many of the same to build his bow and arrows. Some of his men shot arrows to the sky, and these came down tinged with blood. At this, the men cried. They were killing them, everyone in the higher sky. To this, the old father sent his elders, and they confused the men, so they could not understand each other and separated from one another, so that the memory of the tower would be forgotten and with it the science behind Nimrod's bow and arrows.'"

Valentine's smile left her face as she frowned at me.

Renée didn't seem to notice it, turned the page, and was about to read another piece aloud.

"Enough!" I shouted, hitting the table with my fist. "I said to give it back!"

Guillaume, who sat on the ground near the fire, startled. As I saw the look on Valentine's face, I regretted what I had done.

Renée jumped to her feet. Her eyes full of tears, she was trying to keep herself from crying. She looked at me, half scared, the book still clinging to her hands.

Valentine stood up, put a hand on her shoulder, and kissed her head without speaking. She then took the book from her and moved toward me. "Don't you worry about your husband, dear, he likes to be boring." As she said this, she dropped the book on my table without ever looking me in the eyes. "Let us go to the library and leave this one to his work," she said, taking Renée, who was still looking at me full of tears, arm in arm. "I will read you a story."

Evidence J-3451-b to the investigation I-7242
Extract from Arnaud Demeure's journal
23 May 1371

Like many other mornings, I made sure that Renée was sleeping before reaching Valentine in her room. I found her silent in bed and she didn't greet me as she had every other day. She gave me her back, and I could not see her face. I assumed she had been sleeping already, but she broke her silence. "You don't have to treat her like that, you know?"

"She is just a child. It doesn't matter. She will have forgotten everything tomorrow already."

"She is a friend to me. A sister even. You are way too busy with your parties, your miracles, your studies, and God knows what else. For the little we both see of you these days, she might as well be the only friend I have."

"And yet you lay in bed with her husband," I said and chuckled.

She turned to face me. There was a fire in her eyes I had never seen before.

"Out!" she shouted, pushing me off the bed with both arms.

I tumbled out of bed and looked at her in shock.

"I said, out!" Her eyes were so full of contempt that I left in silence, not knowing what to say.

THE SCARLET WOMAN

"What are you all doing here?" Alex asked the three of them as they appeared in sight.

"The same as you," Van Vloed said.

A grin formed on Ioan's face. "They met me while I was leaving the palace and followed me, but we just arrived ourselves. Someone sent a guide."

The three stood at the top of the stairs in front of a battered door, but the space on top wasn't enough for all of them now that there were five of them, so the other two stood on the stairs. Aside from attempting the door, there wasn't much else they could do at this point.

The pendant's light disappeared, its metal, once silver, charred. The sudden vanishing of the light caught everyone's attention.

"Depleted, I guess," Ioan said, pointing at the jewel.

Daniel was still amazed at how Ioan, supposedly blind, seemed to notice just about everything around him. But Alex ignored the old man. "So?" she asked, struggling from her position to point at the door.

The other four stared at each other until Ioan broke the

silence, sighing. The old man turned toward the door, grasped his stick with one hand, and used the other to push the handle.

Daniel's mouth was dry, and Alex's must have been as well, because although he couldn't see her face, he was sure that she had taken a deep breath as soon as the old man had put his hand on the handle, and she hadn't breathed till he pushed it down.

The door didn't open at first. Ioan struggled to push it while the others didn't bother helping him, but just watched. The noise of wood scraping against the floor was loud and was even louder when compared to the veil of silence that had enveloped the whole place. After getting stuck many times, the door squeaked open at last.

The wind didn't want to miss the opportunity to visit the old house and rushed in through the door they had just opened, bringing flurries of snow with it. In the meantime, the five tried to glance beyond the darkness inside, but it was so deep that even their immortal eyes could make nothing out of it.

Ioan hesitated, which gave Daniel the opportunity to take the lead. After an entire night made of rituals, spells, and other supernatural madness, fighting a normal danger felt like a cakewalk. The others didn't seem to think the same, and this gave him a hint of satisfaction.

Daniel walked up the stairs and went in, using his phone as a torch. The others followed behind without saying a word.

The creaking of the wood under their feet accompanied every step. As they all walked in, the floor complained so much that Daniel worried it might break under their weight. Holes and cracks covered the boards on the floor and cold air found its way through them to roam freely in the house. The whole place smelled like rotten wood. Some pieces of furniture were still there, covered with thin white drapes, as if whoever had vacated the place planned to pick them up one day that never came.

Perhaps the same person had taken care to cover the

windows by nailing boards to compensate for their smashed glass. The little light that filtered through the wood boards only made the whole place appear ghostly. The house had no other doors besides the entrance, and this was somewhat reassuring, as they could see through the entire floor.

There was a small room to their right and on the left some stairs. The space they were in was larger, perhaps a living room. A table, almost as long as the room, sat at its center, with a few chairs scattered at its side, all covered by white drapes. A couple of armchairs filled a corner of the room. The wind made all the drapes move, and the light of Daniel's phone made it look like ghosts surrounded them.

Daniel explored the floor before moving upstairs. At least he could avoid finding himself trapped upstairs for having missed someone hidden around there. The other four walked around in silence while Daniel explored the only other room on the floor. A few pipes and some bare wires came out of the walls. A kitchen, perhaps, but lacking anything that would make the place warm. At least there was nothing, or better, no one, inside.

Daniel came out of the room to find Van Vloed with a foot on the first step of the stairs. The wood made such a noise that the woman pulled her foot back. Another noise followed, something like a sob that came from the floor above. At first, Daniel thought he had imagined it, but a glance around at the others' faces showed they must have heard it too.

Whereas Daniel had accepted the idea that the noise was real, he decided it was only another of the many the old house produced while fighting with the wind that wanted to tear it down. But the noise repeated itself, and this time he was sure it was a woman crying.

Once again, he glanced at the others. Alex nodded, so he moved up the stairs. They were immortals after all, and some of them had spent hundreds of years feasting on mortals. If someone had to be scared, it wasn't them.

The flight of stairs complained about their weight, but it survived. As they ambled up the stairs, more and more sobs came from above them. It looked enough like a trap that Daniel took a glance behind his shoulders at every step, somehow unable to shake off the thought that, despite having checked the entire floor below, someone might have still been following them.

A few steps later, they were already up the stairs. At the top was a small hallway with no doors separating it from the rooms it led to. As they reached the place, an icy breeze bit them in the face. Straight in front of them was a tiny window with its glass broken. It wasn't good enough to bring light to the place, but it carried frost and snow inside.

The small space gave access to two rooms, both filled with darkness. One was on their right and the other was behind them on the side opposite to the window—the cries came from the latter and it was now clear that whoever was crying was a woman. Daniel paced in the noise's direction as the others trailed behind him.

As he was about to reach the room with the noise, a hiss came from behind him. Alex stood still in front of the room they had ignored, shaking and staring at the darkness.

The witch hissed. "There is someone in there."

Roman pushed through the others to come closer to Alex while the sobs from the second room became louder. "Mr. Cortese," said the giant, looking at him straight in the eyes and pointing to the room from where the noise was coming. "You watch that room." His voice was so resolute that Daniel didn't struggle to obey.

"Mr. Sturdza, you stay behind Mr. Cortese," Roman said. "Miss Van Vloed, you go to Miss Dryden's left. I'll keep her right."

Something in the way he spoke had been convincing, as even

Van Vloed executed his orders without mocking or debating him.

"So?" Roman asked. "What did you see?"

Alex kept her eyes on the room. "Someone's inside there. I saw a shadow the moment Daniel's phone illuminated the entrance as he passed by."

Daniel turned to look at them. The three acted as a wall, shielding the room where Alex had glimpsed someone. No one could have gotten out of it without passing through them.

Another sob came from the darkness Daniel was supposed to be watching.

"Eyes on that room, Mr. Cortese, please!" Roman ordered again and glanced at him. His eyes had turned gold and bright in the darkness, like those of a cat.

Daniel turned back as fast as a boy caught disobeying his mother.

"There are at least five of them in there," Roman said. The floor complained under him.

Alex exhaled. "They are not connected to the telluric network and are not moving. I don't know what is going on here." Her voice was flat, relaxed almost.

"Five?" Daniel asked, struggling not to turn and watch.

"You stop worrying about this and keep your eyes on that room," Roman said.

"Daniel?" someone asked. It was the voice of a woman coming from the shadows.

Daniel shivered. While on one side were five enemies ready to attack them, on the other was this woman speaking from the shadows. Daniel knew who that voice belonged to, and without thinking he moved one step toward the darkness in front of him.

"Boy, listen, this could be a trap. Stay where you are." Roman's voice shook as well, but it was enough to stop Daniel on his spot.

A sound of steps came out of the darkness that Daniel was surveilling, accompanied by the noise of the wood bending under the footsteps. "My love, that's his name. The name of an angel . . ." said the woman from the shadows, her steps coming closer and closer to Daniel.

Daniel wanted to raise his phone up to shine a light on her, but couldn't. What if it was all an illusion, and she would disappear as soon as he pointed his light at her?

"Will you remember our love forever?" the mysterious woman asked. "What did you tell them when they asked you about our love?"

Daniel tried as much as he could to stay still, to avoid thinking or doing anything stupid. He squinted his eyes so hard he made them water, or perhaps he closed them because of his tears. He even shut his mouth and fists to keep his body from moving, but he failed. Despite Ioan reaching toward his shoulder to stop him, his feet moved of their own volition and his legs followed. Before he could stop himself, he was already halfway there.

"I told you not to move!" Roman yelled.

"Daniel, please, do as he says," Alex added, her voice sounding worried.

But he could not stop himself from moving.

Someone came out of the shadows in front of Daniel. It was a woman. Daniel's phone was shining some light on her feet and legs. Her wet skin shone, reflecting the white and bluish light of the phone's flashlight—mud and dried blood covered her entire body. "The song of the angels, they don't sing it for me. They want my music," she said, coming closer to Daniel. "But I can give my music only to the man I love, to the man who loves me."

Daniel's face was wet with tears as he moved to hug her.

"Okay, that's enough. I'd rather make my move first," Alex said.

A flash of light illuminated the whole room accompanied by

a high-pitched hiss. An instant later, a *bang* resounded in the air and the noise of something cracking followed.

Roman, his hands clawed and covered in fur, had rushed over and was almost on Daniel and the woman who had come out of the shadows. Before Daniel could understand what was going on, Ioan had jumped in front of him and had tapped Roman on one knee with his stick, making him tumble to the ground.

"Mannequins!" Alex said. "Who would fill a room with mannequins? This box is a pain!"

Someone else was shouting too. It was Van Vloed and she was loud enough that the woman ran back, hiding in the dark room she had come out from.

"What is your problem?" Alex asked. "Why are you always in the middle every time I shoot at something?"

Daniel turned, about to yell at them to stop bickering, but he restrained himself. Van Vloed was losing blood from one hand and a sizable chunk of it, including a couple of fingers, was missing.

"Go out and put that hand in the snow. It will slow down the bleeding until it heals," Alex lectured her.

As strange as it was, Van Vloed obeyed without a word and went down the stairs in silence.

Alex turned in Daniel's direction. "She'll survive, I'm afraid. But who was that? Is she the woman you were looking for?"

He nodded. The light had guided them to something important, at least to him.

"Sophia?" Daniel said, but the woman didn't reply.

Daniel got a grip of his phone again and walked into the room, using it as a torch. Alex followed on his heels.

Sophia sat on the ground. She was naked, and her body

shone in the light. Her bright green eyes stared blankly into space and a faint but vibrating light gleamed within them.

Daniel reached her, kneeled close to her, and covered her body with his jacket. "Sophia, it's me, Daniel. You're safe now."

The woman glanced at him, then stared at the ceiling. "Are you my love? Am I yours?"

"Yes, yes," Daniel said. "I'm here." And he hugged her tight. He was crying again, and his tears mixed with the mud and the blood covering her body.

Sophia put a hand on his head and finally looked him in the eyes. "One day they'll come, and they will ask you if I have ever loved you and if you have ever loved me. That day you must not speak. So, my dear, what will you tell them when they will ask you about our love?"

"I don't understand," Daniel said, sobbing. "I'm here. Can't you see? I'm here."

"She doesn't," Ioan said, placing one hand on Daniel's shoulders. "I don't think she is capable of understanding. Something must have happened to her."

Daniel loosened the grip of his hug, and Sophia stared at the old man and smiled. Daniel followed her eyes. She glanced at Alex, who stood beside Daniel with her phone in hand, and at last, she spotted Roman, who stood by the door. As she saw the giant, she punched and kicked to free herself from Daniel's hug. She squirmed enough to get on her feet and tried to flee toward a corner of the room. But a few steps away, she slipped and tumbled on her knees, hitting her head against the floor.

She didn't seem to care. As possessed by fear or rage, she hit the ground with both fists, screaming. "I don't even want it! Take it. Take it if you want it, it's yours!"

Daniel stood back up. He was about to reach her again but hesitated and, instead, stood in place with his arm stretched out in her direction. Once again, he felt Ioan's grip on one shoulder. The old man smiled and nodded.

As if Ioan's smile had pushed him, Daniel reached for the woman and stroked her hair. She quieted a bit, and he put her back on her feet. But as she glanced again at Roman, she started crying and ran to hide in the shadows.

Daniel glanced at the darkness where she was hiding, but then turned to face Roman. "Why is she scared of you?"

Roman averted his eyes and didn't answer.

"She knows you, and she's frightened. Why?" Daniel insisted. His angry eyes met Roman's, and the giant clenched his jaw and once again looked away.

"I'm a hunter, and she is my prey," Roman said.

Daniel rushed, both fists closed, in Roman's direction.

"No!" Ioan shouted before Daniel could hit the giant.

Daniel's legs stopped where he stood, and as much as he wanted to, he could not move anymore.

"Let him explain, then I'll let you do anything you want," Ioan said.

The young man glared at Ioan with the same anger he had reserved for Roman until a moment before. "Explain then."

Roman ground his teeth and took a gulp of air without replying.

"Listen, big man," Alex said. "I don't have the entire night, and I can't say I'm enjoying the company. So, please, speak already."

The giant's eyes moved to Alex for an instant, then he glanced at the other two. He clicked his tongue and sighed. "It is for the order. We must keep her away from that monster."

"Demeure?" Ioan asked.

Roman bit his lip and spoke. "Yes, we don't have the exact details of what he is trying to do, but we know that he needs her to complete it."

"Wait a minute, wait a minute," interrupted Alex. "What is this order you are talking about?"

The giant sighed again. "I'll start from the beginning." As he spoke, he opened the first couple of buttons on his shirt. On the right of his chest, he had the tattoo of a cross with a rose vine wrapping around it. "I'm a Knight Kadosh of the Rose," he said, buttoning his shirt back again. "I have followed Demeure for centuries."

"Descartes? But why?" Daniel asked.

"He had made himself a name in the time between the two holy wars," Roman said. "You must have heard the stories too. Mortals believed he was a new noble just arrived in Paris, but the Shadows told different stories, that he had found an ancient power in the labyrinth under Provins."

Daniel glanced at the others, then back at the giant. "An ancient power?"

Roman nodded. "Biblical is the word that most of them used. The legend said that there was a secret room in the labyrinth, but no one ever found it. We don't even know if that's true, but given how close he seems to be to this place, the order ended up believing the stories."

"But those are just stories, right?" Daniel asked, glancing at Alex and Ioan. Both were staring at Roman.

The giant shook his head. "Not at all. Nobody can negate that he did miracles at his parties. Things extreme enough that he was the talk of everyone who moved in the shadows. Everyone was interested in the man—the four schools, the Strigoi tribes, pretty much everyone."

"What does this have to do with Sophia?" Daniel asked.

Roman bit his lip and took his time to reply. "This entire story is older than me, and I don't know every detail, but during the first crusade, the knights of the temple found a treasure, a set of tablets that described a ritual. A bow and an arrow to pierce the heavens, that's how they described it. The School of Winchester had bought them, but the fact is that the tablets disappeared as soon as the knights reached Europe. We believe that Demeure somehow took possession of them."

"The School . . . a bow and an arrow . . ." Alex murmured.

"All this still doesn't explain why he would need this woman," Ioan said.

"It does," Roman said. "The tablets didn't contain only the ritual but also a story of a previous imperfect attempt to perform it by the hands of a wizard king called Nimrod."

"Nimrod," Alex repeated. "A bow and an arrow. You are talking about the Tower of Babel."

Roman nodded. "The tablets counted over four hundred thousand deaths so that the arrow could fly. And it must have done some damage, as blood fell from the sky and the Lords broke the languages of men, so they could not understand the ritual. Both the knights and the wizards tried to decipher the tablets, but could only collect scraps of their meaning. All they could understand, and all we know, is that the ritual works somewhat like a cannon."

"But why would Descartes build a cannon? To what target? And what would he be shooting, anyway?" Daniel asked as questions flew from his mind to his mouth.

"We don't know his reasons," Roman said. "As to what he would shoot at," he continued, pointing at the ceiling. "As I said, it pierces the sky, quite literally making a hole in our world to let the other worlds, the higher planes, leak into this one."

"This is how all these people died when Nimrod tried it?" Daniel asked.

"No," Roman said. "The order believes that was only collateral damage from the blast. Nimrod never managed a successful shot, but the consequences of the worlds merging would be a disaster. If not for the damage from the merger itself, for what's on the other side."

"The Great Ones," Ioan said. "The Lords. Creatures so powerful not even the immortals or the wizards could challenge one of them."

"Roman," Alex said. "You didn't answer one of his questions. What does this cannon shoot?"

"The word '*soul*' was all the order could translate from that part of the ritual. A human one, immortal or not, would not work. It would not hold enough tellur. We don't know where he has taken one that is large enough to have such an effect, but that man is no fool and we suspect it might have to do with whatever he has found in the labyrinth."

Alex frowned, pressing her lips against each other.

Roman continued, "To work, the ritual needs an ignition mechanism, an action, a trigger that kick starts the process. All we know of this part of the process is a single sentence that translates as '*a brother must kill his sister twice for the door to open and the weapon to be forged.*' We never understood what it meant, but the order is sure that Demeure has completed this part, otherwise he would not have invited us here. If he has indeed completed the ignition, the next thing he needs is gunpowder: the sacrifice of seven people. We don't know the exact conditions he needs to fulfill to select or kill these people, but they must be complex if we are still alive."

Alex shook her head. "It can't just be that. Rituals are a mundane form of magick. They follow a predictable and repeatable logic. So, tablets or not, anyone with time and knowledge of alchemy could have deduced a process like this if it made sense. He must be trying to change the rules using magick somehow to make it work."

Roman nodded again. "There is more, in fact. For as much as the order doesn't have details on the ignition process or on the conditions of the sacrifices, my superiors were convinced from the start that it couldn't work. So, they studied Demeure's moves. There was a pattern to his parties and in his activities outside of those, and it all leads to this final one to which he has invited us. Since those old nights, he has been searching for something. The fruit of knowledge, a power that would allow him to perform the ritual in its perfected form. The old knights founded my order with the sole purpose to stop that man from getting it."

"And you think that woman has such a power? Is she the one he wants to marry?" Ioan asked.

"We didn't know it at the beginning," Roman said, "and I don't think he did either. It took him centuries to get her at first, and we snatched her from him immediately, but she ran away from us too and went into hiding. He must have taken her only recently, and that is why he believed he had everything to execute his plan. But he has lost her again, it seems."

"The fruit of knowledge," Alex said. "The Scarlet Woman, born from the creators. Just like the Kia, it's a single node through which most of the network has to pass." She stumbled into Daniel and almost fell. She must have walked a couple of steps backward. "She is a monster. I don't understand how she could be immortal and yet be connected to the telluric network. But even if we forget that, she has so many strands connecting to her that not only could Demeure use her to perform magick, but he could really change the rules enough to make his cannon work."

"What?" Daniel asked. His hands trembled. This couldn't be true. For all the Shadows and these people could say, they knew nothing. She was just Sophia; his Sophia. His secret, his mystery to solve, not theirs, and not Descartes's.

Daniel looked at Sophia. He could barely see her amid the shadows she had used as a refuge. She sat on the ground and moved her lips as if mumbling something.

"I glanced at her," Alex said. "So many strands go through her. It's like looking at a living Schwarzschild box."

"So, you are a believer, after all," Ioan said.

Alex sighed. "That's not the point. You know the old stories about the Scarlet Woman, the Kia, and the Idea of God, being the three spawns of the Demiurge and the Great

Mother. Those are stories from old folks, but their intuition led them to real facts. We have studied the quintessential field for decades now, and we know that the cosmic microwave background is the result of its own self-organizing mechanisms. The old farts might call it Lord of Shards all they want, but we understand it. What we later found is that there are three additional frequencies that split from the background, independent and interfering. One is the Kia. Every wizard uses it to perform magick when they send a message through the telluric network. A second one is faint and distant; we've never been able to find where exactly in the network it is. The third, we pinpointed it close, local to our world, maybe not the origin of the frequency itself, but a catalyst, like a pin, through which a vast portion of the network connects."

Daniel grinned in disbelief and glanced at the others, but he only met serious faces. "Oh, come on, you are just making stories up. Descartes can't have planned all this, and Sophia, I mean, there is nothing powerful about her."

"Yet here she is," Ioan said. "And this entire party is a wedding, Demeure said. It is a chemical wedding. The entire purpose of them is for one spouse to access the powers of the other. Didn't you find it suspicious that his bride wasn't available the night of her wedding?"

Alex nodded. "We will have to talk with her."

Alex looked down at Sophia, who was pushing her back against the wall. She had tried to carve out something from her, but failed every attempt. "I don't think we are going to get much out of this one. But if we have to give it a shot, big man," she said, pointing at Roman, "you must leave the room. Wait in the hall outside and keep watch while you are at it."

Roman walked out of the room, his lips tight, and groaned as he reached his post.

In response, Sophia stopped pushing with her feet against the floor and didn't pant as much as she had been doing until then, but she was still wary of the man who stood at the door.

"Out of sight, please," Alex said in his direction.

The man grunted and moved to the side, where Sophia could not see him anymore.

"Good," Alex said, turning back toward Sophia. "Now some light would help." And she raised one finger, pointing at the ceiling.

"Light . . ." Sophia repeated before the witch could do anything and scribbled something on the floor using the dirt on her hands.

Both Daniel and Alex bent to look at what she was drawing. It was a circle surrounded by tiny glyphs and another larger emblem straight at its center. While the two still watched, Sophia tapped the circle with one finger.

A burst of white light came out of the circle, and a fluctuating orb the size of an orange emerged out of the radiance. The sphere itself was shining, illuminating the entire room.

"There is no dissonance," Alex said, looking straight at the sphere. "This is impossible."

Sophia beamed at the sphere and giggled.

Alex took a deep breath and glanced at the circle. "Tet," she said.

"What?" Daniel asked.

"The hidden light. It's the name of a Hebrew letter," Ioan said.

Alex ignored them. "The other letters are not in order. It's a permutation." She looked at Sophia, who was still simpering. "How did you do that?"

Sophia smiled at her in silence.

"Listen to me. How did you do that?" Alex said, grabbing

Sophia by both shoulders.

"Alex," Daniel said, going close to the women. "She doesn't understand what you are asking."

Alex didn't look at him. "Just stay out of this." Her voice trembled in a way Daniel hadn't heard before. Again, she talked to Sophia, pointing at the glowing light that hovered near the ceiling. "Tell me how you did it."

Sophia's eyes filled with tears, and she tried to free herself from the witch's grip by shaking her shoulders.

"Leave her alone!" Daniel shouted, grabbing Alex by one wrist.

Alex glared at him. The veins on each of her temples throbbed. "I'd suggest you listen to me when I boss you around."

Daniel flew in the air as if someone invisible had punched him straight in the face. He fell on his back against the ground. His arms moved behind him as the invisible force twisted them. His legs did the same, moving up until his feet reached his hands. The more he tried to free himself, the more his arms and legs pulled in the opposite direction.

Sophia lurked over Alex's shoulder to see what was going on. As her eyes and Daniel's met, she kicked with both legs to break free from Alex's grip. The witch, in response, pushed her on the ground with all her weight and straddled her, pinning both her arms to the floor. Sophia grew even more agitated and kept shaking her head left and right, while Alex came close to her face.

"Would you calm down?" Alex said, grabbing Sophia's face in her hands, her gesture too deliberately gentle. "I don't want to harm you."

Sophia stopped, still breathing hard.

"I think you are smart enough to realize that it must seem quite the opposite to her," Ioan said.

"And I think you are smart enough to see that what she did is the same as the spell we saw at Demeure's palace."

"Oh! You are just scared because you don't understand her magick. You're not that different from the rest of your school's riffraff."

"Stop, both of you!" Daniel shouted, his face still pushed against the floor. "She can't even understand what you are saying, and you're beating her up. How do you think she is ever going to answer your questions? If you are that good, why don't you bring her mind back to normal?"

Alex bit her lip. "I can't do it without being prepared."

"What does that even mean?" Daniel said, as he slid his face so that the floor would not push against his nose.

"It means that she can't do it without someone to suffer the damage," Ioan said. "That's how they are, these wizards. Happy to change the rules but not willing to pay the price for it."

"Right you are, old man. And sorry if I don't want to die when I can spare myself the annoyance."

"Is that true?" Daniel said.

"Yeah," she said. "I told you there is dissonance produced every time I do magick. If the magick is simple enough or if I can understand its consequences well, I can bend it to make sure it doesn't rebound on me, or I can even use it to my advantage. But if I don't understand the mechanisms I'm changing, I can't do it. This is why I don't do magick on human biology or minds as is the case here. It is impossible to predict the consequences and control the backlash. And that's when wizards use effigies. We can mark someone before the enchantment, and they will pay the price to rebalance the agreement in our place."

"But wait, what if I do it?" Daniel said. "I don't care what happens to me."

Daniel's arms and legs fell to the floor, free from whatever was bending them. The witch didn't need much to accept the idea of using him as an effigy. And so she had freed him by lifting one hand in the air.

Alex dismounted from her seat on top of Sophia and moved in the man's direction. "Are you sure about this?" she asked.

"I'm sure."

"All right," Alex said, sighing. "If you say so. Let me set your expectations, though. Whatever I can do is likely going to be just temporary. She has somehow broken and burned a sizeable chunk of her core soul—the sole thing that prevents her from becoming one with the network. Her soul is what gives her conscience. I don't know how she broke it, but without it, she would be just like an inanimate object. Having their soul in such a condition would be bad for anyone, but for someone like her, with that monstrous number of connections . . . I'm not even sure how she can still have an individual identity. She should be dominated by the network."

Daniel was about to speak, but the woman raised one index finger to shush him.

"Given what she is, I'm not even sure that killing you would be enough to bring her back to normal. We would need tens, if not hundreds of effigies. But I can stabilize her for a limited amount of time, and even in this case, I have no idea of the consequences it would have on you. You might die, for all I know."

"It's fine," Daniel said. "You can stop trying to convince me otherwise."

The witch puffed her cheeks and blew out some air. "I couldn't care less about what happens to you. Now sit down on the floor near her, and let's get this over with."

Daniel obeyed and sat, legs crossed.

Alex searched in her pockets and took out a Swiss Army knife she used to cut a deep wound in her right palm. She then kneeled and used the wounded hand to paint Daniel's entire face red. By the time she finished, her wound had already healed.

"Blood magic?" Ioan said.

"Yes, we took a page out of your book," Alex said, glancing at Ioan. "And, Daniel, please stop touching your face." She moved closer to Sophia, who lay faceup on the ground, glaring at her wild-eyed. Alex tapped Sophia's forehead with her index and middle fingers. "Done," she said unceremoniously.

"What?" Daniel asked. "But nothing happened."

"Did you expect fireworks? I told you it's done, just trust me."

But as she spoke, a warmth traveled under his skin, starting from his face and moving across his whole body. The beast inside him howled as he had never heard it doing before. Both his hands shivered, and he was lucky he had been sitting, otherwise his legs would not have kept him standing.

"Daniel?" Sophia called to him, and he forgot about his own body as she spoke. She sat beside him with his and Alex's coats covering her otherwise naked body. "Daniel!" she repeated with a leap, and hugged him tight against her chest. She then pushed him away, holding him by the shoulders and studying his face. "Your eyes . . . they are so old," she said, tears coming down her cheeks. "What have I done? Oh my God, I'm so sorry."

"What are you talking about?" Daniel said, wiping away her tears. Whatever it was, he didn't care.

"Gosh, can you be denser?" Alex said. "She is regretting having made you immortal, and I agree with her, by the way. Now, can we please talk business? We don't even know how much time we have."

Sophia glanced at her without taking her hands off Daniel's shoulders, smiled, and extended one hand in Alex's direction. "You must be the witch."

"I guess so . . ." Alex said, looking at the hand as if tempted, but she didn't take it.

Sophia chuckled. "You have a kind heart," she said, and Alex's weirded-out expression in response made Daniel smile too. "And you are from the Strigoi tribes," she said, smiling in Ioan's direction. "You give away a warm energy. My messenger did a good job." Then she looked at the door, no trace of a smile left on her face. "Why did you bring that hunter with you?" she asked, pointing at the wall beside the door.

The giant must have been eavesdropping as he rushed inside the moment she spoke. "I was only trying to stop the prince."

"That's right," Alex said. "Do you know what he is planning?"

"I don't," Sophia said. She looked again toward the door as if she could see through Roman. "All I know is that he wants access to this energy that flows through me, and to do it, he wants to marry me. He also needs a circle of sacrifices, people that have to die for him to start his spell."

"So, it's all true," Daniel said, clenching his fists. "He took you and now he is planning to kill all of us?"

Sophia nodded, staring at her own lap. "I'm so sorry. That's why I ran away many years ago. That's why I asked you to never talk about our love. I'm so sorry that I made you like this, but I hoped that one day, I could meet you again. Instead, you are in this circle because of me."

"I knew it," Alex said, punching the air. "But wait, a circle like the ones you use? We have seen some of those in the palace too. How can they do magick without dissonance?" the witch asked, bringing her face a few inches from Sophia's.

"I'm not sure about this dissonance thing. I'm not a trained witch myself, but I learned two or three circles by watching Demeure, and it's not too hard once you get the gist of it. Each circle is like a formula. If you know the circle you need, you draw it, then you just have to focus on your soul and imagine a piece of it burning. That will make it work."

"This is how you mutilated your soul?" Ioan asked, putting one hand on Daniel's shoulders.

"Yes," she said, lowering her eyes. "There were no other ways to escape."

"And after that, when you realized Daniel was here, there was no other way to come back and save him," Ioan said, and the grip of his hand on Daniel's shoulders tightened. "Ah, youth, so much energy!"

"Burning souls," Alex muttered and raised her voice again. "If that's as you say, how come Demeure is not in the same state as you?"

"You haven't gotten that yet?" Sophia said, looking at all of them. "He is not like us. I don't know what he is, but he is not just immortal, he is something more, something different."

"Something different?" Alex asked.

"I'm not sure of what he is, but yes, he differs from everyone else. Maybe you two, with your knowledge, can discover more. There is a door within the palace. It is in the library. The house will lead you there if it knows that you need to go. I'm not sure of why, but it seems like the house desires people to find that place. The door leads to the tunnels below the town, and through those, one can reach the room that was my prison. It is a tomb but works like a catalog of these circles, and I'm sure that in there you can find a way out."

"But didn't you say that you have escaped from this place twice?" Alex said.

"I did, but it took me many attempts to imitate what the old prince was doing, and every time someone travels through the portal that brings you out, the permutation of letters changes."

"That must be the box not liking someone going in and out without having solved it," Alex said. "You have tried way too many combinations, haven't you? That's how you have depleted so much of your soul."

Sophia didn't reply but looked down once again. "It was faster the second time. I told you that, once you get the gist of it, it isn't too hard."

"If by getting the gist of it you mean getting used to the pain of ripping off pieces of your soul," Alex said.

"But why did you come back after all that? Why, if you knew he needed you?" Daniel asked, taking Sophia's hands in his.

"Oh man," Alex said, shaking her head again. "I can't believe how slow you can be. Isn't it clear that she is doing all this for you? I bet she has also figured out the new permutation and wants to use it to bring you out of here."

"Yes, I have," Sophia said, hesitating. "And I have to use it now so that Daniel can leave."

"What? I'm not letting you do it," Daniel said.

But Sophia didn't listen and took to scribbling on the ground. "In time, you'll understand. You will forget about me and at least I will have fixed the wrong I have done to you."

"Stop it!" Daniel said, grabbing her hands. "I said that I won't let you do this. You can't keep burning pieces of your soul."

"He is right," Alex said. "The cure was temporary. In a few minutes, you'll lose reason even if you do nothing, so I'm not sure what will happen to you if you do a thing so complicated as opening a portal out of a Schwarzschild box."

"I know, and I have made peace with it. It's my soul, my life, let me give it the meaning I want."

"No, you can't. I've spent so many years searching for you, and now this? I won't let you do it," Daniel said, and turned toward Alex. "Please, stop her. I know you can."

But the witch looked at both of them, expressionless.

"Fine," Sophia said. "I'll do it my way if I have to." And as she said so, she closed her eyes. A moment later, her body fell back against the floor, despite Daniel still gripping her hands. At the same time, a faint circle of light appeared on the floor at the center of the room.

The light of the circle rose like a wall, forming a column that reached the ceiling. Once the column had disappeared, in its place, now floating in the air, appeared something resembling a mirror or the surface of water that faded on the edges as if it was boiling away. Through the surface of the mirror was another place. It was an alley illuminated only by the light of the sunrise. No one was around.

Alex let out a sharp scream. "She did it."

Even Roman, who had kept his composure until then, gasped.

Daniel's phone rang—a message, but he ignored it. "How? I've stopped her from drawing, but she is dying!" Daniel screamed in the witch's direction. "Help her."

Alex shrugged. "Not much I can do. She's not dying, she is just unconscious. I think she overdid it, but what she achieved is remarkable. She must have used the image of the circle in her mind to do the spell. She might not be a trained witch, but she is far better than most of my students."

"What do we have here?" Van Vloed asked. She had appeared at the door. Her hand, now healed, showed no trace of her previous wounds.

"You took your time to heal," Alex said. "I hope that teaches you not to get in my way. Anyhow, that's a portal that Daniel's sire opened, to Paris, I suppose."

"Excellent," Van Vloed said. "Time to leave this place, so we can live to die another night?"

Alex scoffed at her. "I wouldn't recommend it. For starters, that thing is so unstable it can barely carry one person. It might evaporate as soon as someone passes through. But, please, go through, I'd like to see you get stuck in between."

"You can make it stable, can't you?" Ioan asked.

"What if I can?" Alex said. "I have no intention of traveling back to Paris and dropping the opportunity to discover more about these circles."

"I wasn't talking about you traveling. We should have this young man go as she wanted."

Daniel stared at Ioan. "Why would I ever do that?"

"That's right," Van Vloed said. "Why this child out of all of us?"

"Because it is the right thing to do," Ioan said, tapping his stick on the floor.

Daniel stroked Sophia's hair and stood up, trying to hide the tears in his eyes by wiping them with one hand. "You don't need to fight about this. I won't travel back leaving her here."

"We should move her instead," Roman said. "It would stop the prince from completing his spell, and he will have to give up on killing us too."

"She is naked, weak, and not in her own mind. He is going to find her in no time if we drop her on the other side like this," Alex said, waving one hand in the air. "I won't suffer a rebound for a plan this bad."

"My order can pick her up and keep her safe and away from the prince," Roman said, stepping forward in the room. He had responded to Alex, but he kept his eyes on Daniel.

"No way!" Daniel said. "I've seen how scared she was of you. For all I know, your people might kill her so that the prince doesn't take her."

Roman, red in his face, came a few inches from Daniel's nose. His arms were shaking. "The order would never harm her. We are a religious order, not thugs."

Van Vloed chortled, and her voice covered the others. "Religious fanatics, much, much better people than thugs. Now, I don't know what you are talking about, but I'd rather have her out of here."

Alex sniffed and shook her head in response, then flicked one hand in the air. The surface of the mirror bubbled and a circle of white light started running around its border with a loud fizzing sound.

"What are you doing?" Daniel's heart pounded as he imagined the answer already.

"I'm stabilizing this thing and getting her out of here. I hate to admit it, but Van Vloed and Roman have a point. Leaving Sophia in those people's hands might save us all." Her voice was cold and emotionless. Daniel had just met her, but he knew what this meant: she had already made up her mind.

"And who are you to decide that? She is my sire!"

"You want to keep her here? She'll die. She'll die such a brutal death in front of your eyes that you'll lose yourself. Then we'll all die. Is that what you want? Perhaps these people will kill her too. Fine. But at least you have some hope that she'll survive. If you want to leave her here, it's fine by me, but I'll do the most humane thing I can do, and I will just kill her right now rather than letting that maniac get his hands on her." She eyed Daniel, and he could do nothing but lower his eyes in silence. "Good boy. Now you, big guy," she said, glancing at Roman, "do you know where this place is?"

"Yes, I'm pretty sure that it is the same street where I lost sight of Sophia as I was following her before the party."

"Well then, I heard one phone ringing, so I assume yours works too. Please call those friends of yours and tell them where to get her. All of you," she said, moving her eyes in sequence over each of them, "this is going to cost me a decent rebound, so you owe me big time."

Roman took his phone out of his pocket, moved away from the group, dialed the number, and brought the phone to his ear.

"Speakerphone, please!" Alex said.

Roman glanced at her with the phone still against his ear. He then looked at the others, and understanding that everybody agreed with her, he took the phone away from his face and turned on the speakerphone.

The phone rang only once, then a man with a hoarse voice answered. "Roman?"

The giant remained silent. He looked at the others, keeping his body stiff and his face deprived of any expression except for his lower lip that trembled on its own.

"Roman?" pressed the voice on the other end.

Alex uttered a syllable, but Roman silenced her with one hand.

"Roman!" the old man repeated, further raising his voice.

"Yes, yes, high priest, sir," Roman said.

"Oh, good Lord, at last. I didn't expect to hear from you for at least another day. How is the Demeure situation going?"

"Not much to report on that account, sir, but I have news on the other assignment."

"The target?" the man asked. "At the party of any other place! Don't tell me that the prince already has it."

Daniel's heart pounded hard in his throat and he could not stop his fists from clenching. *The target,* that was what the man on the phone had just called her.

"No, sir, quite the opposite. I have her here."

Only silence came from the other end of the phone for a few seconds, then the old man broke it. "Why isn't she here with the order then?" he asked, and a metallic noise accompanied his voice, something like the sound of two metal scraps grating each other.

"It is a long story, sir. Another of his tricks. She . . . I mean, it isn't in the best condition. It might fall prey to that man's intentions, and I can't leave this place. I need support. One, or better, two men to get it off my hands."

The man on the other side of the phone took his time to answer. As he did, the metallic noise tortured their ears. "Fine. Tell me where you are, and I'll send you people."

"First, tell me what you are going to do with her," Daniel said, loud enough so that his voice could reach the phone from the opposite side of the room.

Roman's eyes widened and every muscle in his face stretched.

"Who is that?" the voice on the phone asked. "Who is there with you?"

Roman's eyes swiveled across all the others to land on Daniel.

"Roman!" the man insisted, loud enough that his voice, dry and stern, echoed in the empty room.

"Sir, he is another of the guests at the party. As it appears, the target sired him. He was instrumental in the recovery."

The metallic noise kept going in their ears while the man stayed silent. Daniel knew he wasn't the only one waiting for him to speak again, but whoever he was, he must have been as much an expert at managing silence as he was at choosing his words. "Young man," he said, breaking the silence, "we have no intention of harming your sire, and I promise you we won't keep her one minute more than needed."

Daniel's and Roman's eyes met once again as the former hesitated in giving an answer. Roman's face had relaxed and he nodded in encouragement.

"So," asked the man, "what do you say? Will you let us protect her?"

Daniel thought about the question. As much as this world was unknown to him, his problem now was a practical one. Contrary to what the others might have thought of him, he was used to handling these situations in a calm, analytical way, and in this case, he had little choice, anyhow.

If Demeure had wanted to take Sophia or harm her, he would not have been able to defend her. Hiding within the box wasn't an option either, and there was no way for both of them to leave, but these people might have the means to hide and defend her. As much as something didn't sound right, as much as he didn't trust any of them, he had no other choice.

"Yes," he said, disturbed by the tone of defeat in his own voice.

"That is the right choice," the man said. "We are done here. Roman, send the coordinates for the pickup." Without waiting for an answer, the man hung up the phone.

Daniel stared at Roman, who was using his phone to send a message with the location for his order to pick Sophia up. The woman was still lying on the ground, dead-looking. Her bare skin showing off the jacket he had left on her shoulders made her appear weaker than he would have wanted to see her. Was this the right thing to do? He should have tried to ask for something, a condition that would guarantee Sophia's safety, but whatever he could have asked for, what difference would it have made?

It didn't take long for two men to appear on the other side of the mirror. Both of them were overdressed for the job, with the shabby and unfit suits only a police officer would wear. Somehow, they were both built in such a way that he was sure he would forget their faces as soon as they turned their backs on him. As they arrived, Daniel looked at Roman, who nodded in confirmation. These were the people they were waiting for.

"Make her hand touch the surface of the portal," Alex said, one hand in the air rotating a finger at the same rhythm as the light surrounding the mirror. She was breathless, and a sheen of sweat covered her forehead. "Just make sure you don't touch it unless you want to vanish into nothingness."

Both Daniel and Roman grabbed Sophia from the ground and got her seated. Daniel raised her right arm with his and pushed her hand against the floating mirror. In the same instant that her fingers touched the portal, she disappeared to reappear seated specularly on the other side, and given Daniel's absence, she fell on her back. One of the two men took her on his shoulder, and Daniel was about to reach the mirror before it vanished in front of him.

Before Daniel could accept what he had done, a muffled growl came from the witch behind him. Alex was on the ground, knees and palms against the floor. Her skin, wherever visible, was moving as if something were sucking away the muscles and flesh from underneath it.

Her arms dried out so much that the bones were protruding from her wrists and fingers. The turtleneck she wore now was like an empty bag, and the jeans gave the same impression. Alex's white skin turned thin and yellowish, showing the green of the veins that ran underneath. The same was happening to her face where the only dark parts were the circles around her eyes.

Despite burying themselves more and more in their sockets as if to disappear, her eyes were still lively. Her glasses had grown larger in contrast. Alex let go another muffled scream as her skin grew wrinkled and her hair went gray. The spasms in her body continued for a few seconds more.

Ioan, who stood beside Daniel, lowered his head as if, despite being blind, he couldn't watch such a mess. Van Vloed, by contrast, appeared intrigued by the phenomenon.

It took a few moments before the woman's convulsions faded and she breathed regularly as if she were regaining her strength. Once again, she grunted and pushed on her bony fingers as if she wanted to take a piece of the floor with her.

A single long contraction of all the muscles crossed her body that covered itself in sparks. Her hair, starting from the root up to the tips, went back again to her usual jet black. The witch's muscles regained volume underneath the skin, which reclaimed its color and lost its wrinkles.

Finally, Alex's look returned to that of a teenager, except for her left arm and hand. There, the sleeve of the sweater still looked loose compared to its contents. The hand was still withered and white. Before Daniel could stare too long at it, Alex got to her feet and hid her hand with the sweater's sleeve.

"Let me help you up," Daniel said, and moved closer to help her stand. "You still seem dizzy."

But the woman raised one hand and groaned, finding her feet. "The day I need someone's help to walk has yet to come. Now, please, let's leave this damn place before the prince finds out about our trip."

———

The wind pumped so much air in Alex's nostrils she had to stop and breathe. At least the chilling air was soothing on her headache, and somebody might have believed her tears came from the wind rather than the pain.

So, despite the wind, Alex tailed the group and pushed through the snow, unwilling to raise her feet up and down, a thing that would have spared her the effort of fighting the snow but that would have required energy she didn't have. At her side walked the Strigoi. If she didn't know better, she would have thought that the old man was keeping her company.

The group took what they believed was the fastest route back to Demeure's palace, hoping that box hadn't deviated too much from the layout of the real Provins. In this part of town, the streets were larger than the ones Alex had walked through with Daniel before. The houses faced the street without any walls or gardens isolating them. Some of them had signs above the arches that encased their wooden doors—restaurants and cafes. Alex wondered whether they really existed somewhere outside the box.

She tried to move her wounded hand while keeping it hidden within the sleeve. With some effort, she moved a couple of fingers, but they clicked and cracked, and the pain that followed was like shots of electricity running up her arm.

"How are you holding up?" Ioan asked while struggling to walk through the snow. Here and there, from under his feet, the red and gray bricks of the sidewalk emerged out of the snow. "You don't really seem good."

"It's not a big deal," Alex lied. "I will be back in shape in a few hours." That wasn't true, either. Maybe in a few years, but most likely never. "And aren't you supposed to be blind?"

The man chuckled. "I just feel that we have lost much tonight. You must have noticed the young man."

Alex sighed. Daniel, after all, was the one who had asked to pay the price for Sophia's temporary cure. "Yeah, he doesn't look good. I'm not sure he accepts his condition. The ones like him are always the first ones to turn fully, and now his wolf is leaking out. I hope he doesn't turn on us."

"Well, maybe there is something that can . . ." Ioan said, leaving the words hanging, and stopped to turn facing back, sniffing the air.

Alex stopped, too, and looked around. There was something different in the air, but she couldn't put a finger on what exactly.

"Are you two going to up the pace?" Van Vloed said. She, like the others, was walking a few meters ahead.

"Miss Dryden," Ioan said, ignoring Van Vloed and pointing at her right with his stick.

Alex didn't wait for him to say it twice and with her right hand covered in sparks threw a backhander in the direction he was pointing.

A man, invisible until a moment before, flew to the ground, holding his jaw—it was Hermann.

Evidence J-4282 to the investigation I-7242
Extract from Arnaud Demeure's journal
11 October 1534

"Why don't you go to bed?" I asked Renée as she struggled to stay awake even while sitting on the ground in front of the fire.

A golden griffin shone on the otherwise crimson carpet under her body. Guillaume sat on the carpet too and, silent, stared straight into the flames.

Renée's head sat on Valentine's lap as she stroked her hair, guiding her to sleep. Valentine looked at her with sweet eyes, but there was a glimmer of worry in them. Renée's eyes were closed, and she breathed deeply.

"I don't want to, my love. I want to stay here with you and my dear sister."

Her voice was so soft that I could barely hear her.

"Just let me stay . . ." she said, fading into a dream.

Valentine kept stroking her hair, looking more and more worried. "I think we are losing her," she blurted out.

"You are being too dramatic," I said, going back to my book.

"She is dying, Arnaud."

"She can't die," I said, nonplussed. "She is immortal."

I didn't know how this could be possible. People like us don't die.

"Every night she is weaker. Every night she wakes up later and has to go to sleep earlier. She is barely with us at this point."

I raised my head for a second to glance at Valentine. Her eyes were full of tears, but I didn't know what to say.

"Do you even care?"

"Of course, I do, but why do you think I know more than you do?"

"Well, you would spend some time away from precious research to understand it if you cared! Maybe you could skip one or two of your parties. Where is all that 'your wish is granted' of yours when we need it?"

"That is not how it works. I can't just grant wishes; it needs to come from them."

She fell silent for a minute as the light of the fire illuminated her muted eyes. I thought we were done arguing at last.

"I think it's you . . ." she said, and she almost raised herself from the chair. She would have done so if Renée's head hadn't been resting on her lap.

"Excuse me?" I asked.

"Yes, that is it. Your dreams, your illusions, it must be it."

"My illusions have never . . ."

"Killed anyone? You know that is not true!"

She must have caught my expression at these words, and she looked away from me for a second and bit her lip. I believed that the remorse for what she had said would close the argument at once.

"They killed no one I didn't want to," I said. She should not have brought the old hag up. We were over that.

"I told you. You are killing her," she insisted, her voice broken. The argument wasn't over at all. "Every time you are not around, she looks weak and sick. She can't live outside your dreams anymore. This is it, is it not?"

"Listen, you're talking nonsense. You don't even know if what you are saying is true."

"Stop fighting, please," muttered Renée, rolling her head without opening her eyes.

We both fell silent.

"My love," she said, still half asleep. "Would you kiss me good night, please? I have the worst nightmares if you don't."

My legs shook as I walked from my seat to the one where the two women rested. I dragged myself there and kissed Renée on the forehead, as I had done every night since our first one. I gave her a pleasant dream.

While coming back to my seat, I tried to avoid Valentine's eyes. They were likely piercing my back, so I sat down again and set the book in front of my face.

"If you were a decent man, you would at least see what you can do," she snapped. "Or . . . or you would put her out of her misery."

13

MY HERO, MY KING, MY BROTHER, AND MY LOVE

Supplement S-0021 to the investigation I-7242
Provins underground tunnels

We found the map among the documents in Mr. Demeure's possession. It represents an unknown area of the catacombs under the grounds of Provins. We have compared it with all the documentation we could find on the tunnels, and we have several entry points (see: PUT-1A for notes on the locations). Previous explorations have not documented the passages in the map, so we expect some drilling might be necessary.

The overall surface represented in the map covers an estimated area of a few kilometers in radius, larger than the town above, which indicates the known catacombs might be a small, peripheral part of a larger unexplored structure.

Unfortunately, the map is incomplete as it does not report the tunnels in the most central area. A Leviathan cross fills the center of the map accompanied by a note that says, *"Visita interiora terrae rectificando invenies occultum lapidem."* We suspect it might refer to a location within the tunnels. The motto, which translates to *"Visit the interior of the Earth, and through purifica-*

tion, you will find the hidden stone," suggests that a ritual must be performed once at the location on the map.

We have not determined the age of the map yet (our lab in Penrose is performing chronological dating at the time of writing), so we doubt its reliability. We will use caution and wait for the reconnaissance teams to reach us in Provins before starting a full exploration.

The others, who were walking scattered a few meters ahead, all rushed back toward Alex and Ioan. In the meantime, Hermann was on the ground with both hands on his face, muttering something Alex could not hear.

"Why were you following us?" Alex asked.

Hermann ignored her and drew nonsensical shapes in the snow. He took his time to sit, legs crossed. Heavy burns covered half his face beneath his left eye, and his lips twitched with spasms. The man took some snow from the ground and, with more focus than needed, formed a ball with both hands.

For an instant, Alex suspected he might throw it in her direction. Instead, Hermann smashed it against his own cheek, massaging the wound she had left on his face. "You sure are nasty, aren't you?"

"Yes, she's a peach," Van Vloed said, chuckling.

Alex glanced at her, then glared back at Hermann. She wondered if the best course of action would be to hit him again, and she sure would have done it if Ioan hadn't spoken.

"She chose not to kill you. The least you can do is to answer her questions," he said.

Hermann stared at Ioan for a long moment and shrugged. "I guess I wanted to take a walk to get some fresh air."

"Oh man," Alex said. "Please keep saying this kind of crap so I can kill you."

Van Vloed kneeled to face Hermann, adjusted her glasses, and licked her lips before nodding toward Alex. "Perhaps you haven't noticed it, but she can be very violent."

"Okay, okay . . ." Hermann said, raising both hands. "I saw you two leaving the castle and followed you." He glanced at Alex and Daniel. "I was curious."

Roman came closer. "What did you see?"

Hermann yawned, looking at the sky and scratching his head. "Everything."

Roman shook and growled at his answer.

Alex huffed and glanced at the others. "What shall we do with this one now? I guess we have our best candidate yet to be our extra for the ritual. He might be spying on us for Demeure."

"Me? Spying for Demeure?" Hermann asked, about to laugh. "No way! Listen." He turned serious and stared into her eyes. "I'm in this mess because my sire forced me into it."

It wasn't all that different for Alex either. She was there because the council had asked it from her. The problem was that this man, who despite what he was saying might well still be working for the prince, had seen everything they had done with Sophia.

Alex looked at the snow on the ground along the path they had followed. As invisible as he might have been, the snow must have been squeaking and crunching under his steps. She glanced at his feet, and they had sunk in the snow as much as hers.

Hermann had somehow worked out what she was thinking. "I don't become invisible, and I don't fly either. It's simpler, if I don't want people to see me, they don't."

Van Vloed came closer to the man and peered at him from head to toe. "Interesting."

Alex agreed with her. It was interesting. Even Ioan smiled with an unusually wicked smile. They both had the same idea.

Van Vloed took off her glasses and licked her lips again. "Can you use this trick any time you want?"

Hermann didn't answer, but glanced at Roman. The giant was staring at him, too, with the eyes of a beast.

"Hey, big man," Alex said, waving one hand in their line of sight. "Get a grip, okay? He's discovered your secret club, so what? Breathe some fresh air and calm down. And you," she said, glancing at Hermann. "Stop staring at him, and please, Daniel, you too. What's wrong with you? Can you please stop looking so shocked? He won't bite you, I promise."

Roman hid his face with one arm and gave his back to the others, moving a couple of steps away.

"We are lucky, though," Van Vloed said with one hand covering her mouth. "At least he hasn't peed on our shoes yet."

"Back to you," Alex said, once again, targeting Hermann. "For once, Van Vloed here asked the right question. Can you do your trick every time you want, even on the same person?"

Hermann scratched his head and cleaned the snow off his legs and shoulders. "Yeah, I never had an issue with that."

"I think you might be quite useful," Ioan said.

Hermann studied him. "Useful, uh? Not interested."

Ioan tapped the ground with his stick. "You said you have seen everything. If you have also heard everything, you understand we all are in the same boat."

Hermann took some time without answering. He studied each one of them in silence, stroking his chin. "What about you?" he asked in Daniel's direction. "Do you trust them?"

Daniel glanced at Alex. "Me?"

"Yes, you. I can't bring myself to trust the old guard, but you seem naïve enough I can trust you."

"Well, I . . ." Daniel said, biting his lip. "I would at least listen to what they have to say."

"Okay, but just because you say so and because the lady here"

—he nodded at Alex—"reminds me of someone. So, how can we help each other?"

Alex wasn't sure she trusted him yet or that having anything to do with him was a good idea. He sure didn't appear as nasty as Van Vloed did, but he didn't ooze stability either. If there was ever hope to find some information on the ritual, this man with his ability was it. "We need to do three things," Alex said. "The first is to learn more about this whole ritual, the second is to find a way out of here, and the third, if everything goes south, is to manage the old prince. You are going to help us with the first of the three."

The six took to walking once again toward the palace and had just taken the last turn to reach the street where the entrance was located. Alex walked backward, explaining her plan to the others while Ioan nodded from time to time as if she was repeating something he had thought first.

"It is quite simple," Alex said. "We have two places we want to go. One is the secret room in the labyrinth that Sophia talked about. She learned those circles in there, and Demeure's secret powers come from there too. Perhaps there is something in that place I can use to bring us all back home. The other place I want to check is the prince's room. If he is trying to complete such a large ritual, he must have notes somewhere and his room is the best place to search."

"You want me to visit Demeure's room without being noticed?" Hermann asked. "It sounds like I'm the only one doing all the work."

They all were in the same boat, she thought as her heels reached the first step of the palace's entrance. "You are also the only one among us who can do it," Alex said, talking to the others from the steps with her back to the door. "Once we investigate everything, it will be up to me to build counter-measures."

Of course, those thankless people thought her work was

work, and that she could do it while staying in a safe place. It was up to Hermann to risk his life big time.

Hermann must have been thinking along the same lines as he seemed ready to rebuff her, but his mouth didn't move. Instead, he stood in awe. The others were doing the same.

Alex frowned. "What is it?"

Hermann didn't answer, but raised a finger, pointing at something behind her.

As she turned, her heart jumped. Guillaume's inhuman face was peering at them from behind the ajar door. He had somehow opened it with enough discretion that she had missed the noise. She moved one step back to face him.

"Hey, man," Hermann said, stepping forward. "You scared the hell out of us, you know?"

The servant didn't reply. He continued to stare at them with his expressionless face. Making no noise, he threw the door open, standing by it with a camping lamp hanging from one hand.

Alex and Hermann looked at each other and at the rest of the group. The man shrugged and moved up the stairs. Alex and the others followed.

The moment they crossed the entrance, the man shut the door behind them. He walked through the room where they had waited the first time they arrived at the palace. The torchlight showed a very different place from the one they all remembered. Benches covered most of the ground. A small altar sat on the short side of the room, close to the door that led to the ballroom; an enormous cross watched it.

They traversed both rooms without speaking a word and reached the old library. Two armchairs sat close to the fireplace, turned toward the center of the room, and in front of them was a coffee table and another four armchairs. Someone, perhaps the servant, or the house itself, had prepared the room for their arrival.

Guillaume left the lamp, still lit, on the table, walked away without a parting gesture, and disappeared in the darkness.

Hermann walked to the table, lifted the lamp, and put it back. "What do you think is going on?"

"Beats me if I know," Alex said, still looking at where the servant had disappeared. She pointed at the lamp. "I hope this isn't the only light we have in this place."

"I'm pretty sure it isn't," Van Vloed said, flipping a switch on the wall.

The new light showed them every detail of the room. Bookcases ran along the walls, from the floor to the ceiling, storing tomes amassed on top of each other. Along those on the shelves lay hundreds of tiny objects, ornaments, and knick-knacks. Alex feared she might crash into something if she moved too much.

Columns sat in front of the bookcases, separating the space between one and the next. They were tall enough that the bust statues sitting on them could look at the guests straight in the eyes. At a first glance, given the armor, Alex thought they must have been soldiers, but in a way, their features were way too gentle. Each bust had a name carved underneath.

"Armoniel," Ioan said, touching the engraving on a column with one hand.

Daniel read another one. "This one says Shamshiel."

"The watchers," Roman said. "Protectors of humanity. They failed at their task because they wanted to possess the sons and daughters of men. God punished them because they whispered the secrets of the heavens to their loved ones."

"Fascinating," Hermann said. "But what does it mean?"

"No idea," Alex said, and none of the others answered, either. "I bet we will learn more if we investigate it."

"Don't you think it would be too risky now that Guillaume has seen us?" Daniel asked.

"Yes, it's dangerous, but what do we have to lose? If we do nothing, we are dead. The best we can do is fight back. And before any of you mentions it, yes, I realize he knows what we are planning to do, and he is mocking us by having his servant deliver us a torch. I say screw him and let's go." It also meant something else, but Alex would rather not think about it, least of all mention it in front of Daniel.

Van Vloed shook her head. "All you care for is learning more about some weird type of magick."

"That doesn't make her wrong," Roman said, coming closer to Van Vloed. "Miss Dryden, Mr. Cortese, I owe you the success of my mission. I will follow you anywhere if you ask me to."

Alex glanced at Daniel, who was looking back at her. She didn't know what to answer to something like that. "Sure," was the best she could mutter.

"Good then, I will prepare myself for anything awaiting us," Roman said. "I'll be ready for your orders in the church." And he left in direction of the chapel.

"What is going on with him?" Hermann asked.

Van Vloed waved one hand in the air. "He is just a dog. Who knows what goes in that animal brain he has?"

"A dog?" Daniel asked, his gray eyes narrowing.

"Ignore Van Vloed. That is just a slur people in the old days used for those who let themselves commune with the wolf. Roman is a soldier from the old times," Ioan said. "Honor and loyalty must be the most important values to him. And he is not a dog. He must be ashamed of having fallen to the wolf while we were on our way here, but turning into beasts is the destiny of people like us, so it's hard to keep control for the oldest of us. It must be harder for him, I guess."

Daniel frowned. "Why would it be harder for Roman?"

"He is a Wurdulac," Alex said before Ioan could. "An immortal who is in closer communion with his inner wolf. They are rare, and they die early, often going crazy under the influence of the wolf. It's a horrible way of living, especially when other people, like Van Vloed here"—Alex glanced at the

Dutch woman—"spit on you and call you names. If making an immortal is hard enough, siring a Wurdulac is much harder. Whoever did this to him must have hated him a lot."

"How do you know all this?" Daniel asked.

"You must have seen it," Ioan said. "In the house, when he turned part of his body into the wolf. That's the sign of a Wurdulac. He must be old and with no more to lose if he shows it around."

Alex grabbed her own left arm. "The thing has its advantages. If we need a fighter, we have the best we can get. So, now back to the plan."

"What plan?" Hermann asked. "Someone can get into the labyrinth if we find out how to enter, but how am I supposed to sneak into the prince's room if we don't know if he is in there right now? And even if we knew, we still don't know where his room is, right?"

It was all true. Alex hadn't planned for that as she hoped they would get an opportunity if they waited long enough, but how long they could wait, she didn't know. There must have been a way to exclude potential room candidates based on the positions of their own rooms.

"I could stay here forever watching Winchester's brain spinning and going nowhere," Van Vloed said, grinning. "But I think I can help." As she said so, and as if it was nothing, Van Vloed stuck three fingers in her own left eye's socket—index and middle finger above the eyeball and thumb below. She extracted the eyeball fast enough that none of them had the time to look away.

A second later, blood fell down her fingers, dripping on the floor, and the eyeball looked at them from her hand. Despite all this, her usual smile hadn't left her face and the other eye still moved, glancing at each of the others in turn.

"What are those faces?" Van Vloed asked. "Is this the first time you've seen blood?" But before any of them could answer, she raised one hand. "Let me show you how I'm going to help."

With the attitude of someone executing a religious ritual, Van Vloed walked close to a wall, clenching between her fingers what used to be her eye. A new, half-formed one had appeared on her face, and this gave her an overall asymmetric look that made her appear possessed by a demon.

As she glanced at them and smiled once again, she pressed the eyeball against the wall as if trying to smash it.

Alex prepared herself to see the eyeball breaking and releasing humors all over the wall, but the eyeball penetrated the plaster as if it were fusing with it.

"Do you like the trick?" Van Vloed asked. Her face was back to normal again, and her eyes jumped from one of her companions to the other, waiting for an answer. The eye on the wall followed the same movements as the ones on her face.

Alex studied the eyeball stuck to the plaster. She had to get up on her toes to face it and tried to jerk her head left and right to study it from every direction. "How will this help us?" she asked. A nasty smile opened on her face, and as if it were nothing, she poked the eye on the wall with one finger.

"Ouch!" Van Vloed yelled, her face twisting in pain. "Can you just look without touching?"

The eye merged itself with the plaster, disappearing within the wall. On the plaster, there were no signs anything out of the ordinary had ever been stuck to it.

Van Vloed regained her composure, and with a satisfied expression on her face and a slow gesture, she pointed at a corner of the room close to the ceiling. The eyeball was there, peeking on them.

Alex stared at it. "This is interesting."

A large, pleased grin appeared on Van Vloed's face as her eyes glanced at every other person in the room. Most of them, Alex included, seemed surprised by the trick she had just pulled off, and this somehow made her complacent. Only Ioan was unfazed.

"I still don't get it," said the witch. "It's all nice and fun, but even if you were to search each room, you wouldn't know which one is Demeure's unless he is in it, and he might notice if he is in there."

The grin on Van Vloed's face grew even larger. "It isn't too hard, given I've already found it." She raised one hand, circling in the air with one index finger.

Nothing happened for a few seconds while all of them stayed in silence and the pleased expression didn't leave Van Vloed's face. Just as Alex was about to open her mouth in protest against Van Vloed's antics, a low buzz reached her ears.

It sounded like a swarm of roaches was about to crawl out of the walls. The guests turned around following the noise, then, all at once, they appeared. In the same way the first eyeball had done, tens of eyes popped out of the walls and the ceiling. The eyes moved in all directions as if they were searching for something, until they all pointed at the guests in the room.

Hermann muttered "What the . . ." under his breath, Daniel's mouth hung open, and everybody stepped away from the walls.

"So, this is what you have done," Ioan said. "Since before I left the palace in the morning, I had the weird feeling of being observed. I see you've taken the liberty to spy on me while I was in my room."

Alex glanced at Van Vloed. Judging from her face, Ioan had guessed right, and she was sure the Dutch woman must have spied on her too. She had underestimated these people. Roman was a Wurdulac, the game with the eyeballs must not have been all there was to Van Vloed's dark gift, but most of all, the Strigoi had noticed Van Vloed was watching him while she, a pupil of the School of Winchester, hadn't.

"Good job, old one," Van Vloed said, clapping her hands. "You don't miss a beat. But I'm sad to say you didn't show me anything interesting. Winchester here, however," she added, moving all the eyes to the witch, "was much different, much more, how to say . . . vulnerable."

Alex's face grew red. At first, she herself thought it was shame, fury perhaps, but for sure not fear. Nobody, especially someone like Van Vloed, could push that button. "So? Did you find Demeure's room or not?"

Van Vloed nodded without taking her eyes off her and yawned with one hand in front of her mouth. "Yes, yes, last floor on top. He has spent most of his time in the third room on the left, coming up the stairs. I saw him leaving the palace just a few minutes ago while we were speaking. I had to follow him around for a bit. This place has a lot of entrances." As she spoke, she gestured with one hand in the air and the eyes disappeared, going back within the walls.

"You didn't say a word before. Why?" Alex asked.

Van Vloed bent in her direction to get Alex's face in front of hers and smiled once again. "I wouldn't have missed watching your brain spinning round and round while trying to find a solution for anything in the world."

Alex rolled her eyes, ignored Van Vloed, and walked past her to reach Hermann. "I guess you have everything you need. Van Vloed will give you support to make sure the prince doesn't catch you there."

Hermann nodded. "Works for me, but wouldn't she be more useful to you if you are going down into the tunnels?"

"I don't think we are going to find anyone trying to stop us. The prince must be sure that whatever we find there won't be a game-changer. If he wanted to stop us, he would have done so already."

"We don't even know how to get there," Daniel said, looking around.

"Sophia said that the door will be in this room. Right now, there are only two doors here. One leads to the church, so the other," Alex said, pointing toward a door that stood opposite to the fireplace, "must lead us to the tunnels."

"That leads you to the kitchens," Van Vloed said. "I looked everywhere in the palace; I would have noticed if there was access to underground tunnels. You know, I have pretty good eyes."

Alex ignored her once again and walked to the door and opened it. Behind it was a kitchen, like one in a restaurant.

Van Vloed giggled.

Alex shook her head and closed the door to reopen it immediately. A dark passage lay behind it, excavated in crude stone. The light that filtered from the library illuminated a couple of meters, showing the centuries-old stone bricks.

"You might have good eyes," Alex said, "but I grew up in a house like this."

It had been easy enough for Hermann to reach the room that Van Vloed had pointed him to. Visible or not, it would not have made any difference, as he had met no one on his way there. Van Vloed's dark gift, on the contrary, had been instrumental. With all those corridors looking the same and the entire building filled with vast halls and tiny bedrooms, it would have been way too easy to get lost.

Hermann wondered if the house had gone overboard knowing it would receive guests, or if this was because, as Demeure said, the place had been an orphanage in the past, and he was visiting its living quarters. He'd rather it be the latter.

The actual issue was, though, that if he had to run out of the place fast, he might not make it without losing track of the path, and he wasn't sure he could trust Van Vloed with guiding him out either. With one hand on the handle, Hermann looked up at the ceiling and there he found it, one of Van Vloed's disgusting eyes. That woman was a creep.

Hermann kept his hand on the handle long enough that it didn't feel cold against his skin anymore. Still in doubt, he peered around to make sure no one was coming down the corridor and pushed it down. Not enjoying the loud creaks that followed, he hurried to go inside and close the door, hoping that no one, not even a servant if there were any in the palace, had heard the noise. And so, once inside, he stayed with his forehead against the wood, inhaling and exhaling to calm himself down.

As he turned, though, a face and two large blue eyes just inches from his nose startled him. His heart leaped in his throat, and he jumped back, slamming his back against the door. The long hair, the wide blue eyes, and the ever-present sweater and scarf confirmed to him he stood in front of his sire—Valentine.

Still panting with fright, he turned to the woman, who giggled, shielding her mouth with one hand. "What the hell are you doing here?"

She stared at him, puzzled, with those huge blinking blue eyes.

He knew that, as usual, he would not receive a straight answer.

Valentine lifted her scarf in front of her mouth up above her nose. "I could ask you the same," she said, and she turned away from him as if she didn't want to be seen. She walked up to the bed behind her she took a seat, facing him once again. She then yawned, raised her feet on the bed, and lay staring at the ceiling.

"I'm trying to get out of the mess you've thrown me in. Your turn!" Hermann said, coming close to the bed so he could tower over her.

Valentine didn't reply.

The woman shrugged and rolled on one side, showing him her shoulders. "They will hear you if you shout like that."

"You are such a child," he said, getting away from the bed.

"I told you already. This is how you want to see me. Now, be a lamb and don't complain about it."

Hermann sighed and looked around the room. There wasn't much to look at, and it was like his own room. A window on the wall opposite to the door showed the world outside, hiding it behind a layer of condensed water. No light came from the window itself, as the box had given them a never-ending night. The little light in the room came from the lamp on the ceiling where two of the three bulbs had given up on living. A single bed sat at the center of the room with its head against the wall, no bedding on it.

Valentine, who now lay on her side on the naked mattress, faced an old wardrobe. The prince had left it open, and it showed a full set of suits, each a copy of the others with pairs of identical shoes underneath each of them. The only other piece of furniture beside these two, if he ignored a tiny chair, was a writing desk placed at the foot of the bed. It didn't look like the room of a prince at all.

"It is his room," murmured Valentine under her breath.

Hermann glanced at her out of the corner of his eyes. "Well, I'll do what I need to do. You rest there or help if you want."

The desk was only big enough for one person to work at. Cracks, scratches, and stains covered its top, its feet, and the drawer that popped half-open out of the front. On it sat a lamp that, having lost its glass covering, showed its lightbulb attached straight to the base. Beside the lamp were a pen, a book, and a wooden box.

Hermann studied the box. Its lacquered wood had scars all over as much as the desk it sat on. A circle as wide as the box itself was engraved on the top, with a hole in the center. As he took the box in his hands, the bed behind him creaked. He didn't look at Valentine, but was sure she was peeking at what he was doing. He found nothing inside besides a lever attached at the bottom of the lid.

As he moved it from its position, the box produced a shrieking metallic noise. Hermann turned it back to stop the noise. It sounded familiar, but he wasn't sure where he had heard it. He turned the box up and down, but there wasn't anything interesting about it. He put it back. A broken carillon or something of the sort? Old people didn't give up on their trash so easily, and immortals weren't any different.

The book was the second thing that piqued his interest. A cover made of black leather wrapped it, and the pages were sewn together with a thick thread. As Hermann opened it, a few pieces, not secured to the rest, fell to the ground. He cursed under his breath while collecting the pieces one by one and putting them back on the desk.

"Crap! He will know for sure now."

Valentine turned on the bed behind him. "Him not knowing was never an option to begin with."

Hermann glanced at her. She hadn't moved at all. He shook his head and threw the remaining pieces of wood on the desk. Someone had drawn on them a forest of signs. The writing matched that in the book, but he didn't recognize the letters, so he had no hope of understanding what it all meant. All he could see was that each page was made of a different paper. The prince had taken notes on scraps he had bound afterward in a book. That thing would have looked good in a museum. Hermann took a few photos of the pages. Maybe the witch or the Strigoi would know what to do with it, or, at least, understand what the symbols meant.

"No hope," Valentine said.

He kept taking photos with his phone. "I'm pretty sure they would want to try."

"I'm pretty sure of that, too, but it won't work. There is a magic lock on the book, and unless one with the key opens it or the author dies, that is going to be just unreadable gibberish."

"How do you know this stuff?" he asked, dropping the book on the desk and going close to the bed once again.

Valentine didn't answer.

"Whatever," Hermann said, going back to the desk and now opening the drawer. It was full of letters. These were covered with the same dense handwriting, but in a language he could understand. He didn't bother reading them. At this point, he just wanted to get out as fast as possible so he took them out one by one, placed them on the desk, and took photos of them in groups. "I'm not even sure you are here or just in my head as usual," he said while doing his work. "But just so you know, I'm risking my life in this place."

"You are not. He would never harm you."

Before Hermann could answer, a stack of pictures wrapped in an elastic band surfaced from under a pile of old letters. The first was a charcoal drawing. It was a sketch of two women dressed in ancient fashion. One of the two looked at him from the picture with eyes so full of hope that he struggled to take his own off hers. Her hair was long and full and fell over her shoulders on both sides as she sat back straight, smiling at whoever had drawn the picture.

The second woman had hair collected in a long braid that fell over her left shoulder. She sat next to the first and smiled too, but her eyes were lively and fiery. She was identical to Valentine, but there was no childishness in her. Instead, she gave off a vibrant, overwhelming feeling of confidence.

Hermann glanced at Valentine, still lying in bed as he took off the elastic band. She was looking at him, but she moved her face away. How was she involved in all of this? He was about to ask her that, but once again, the pictures in his hands distracted him from doing so. The pictures, photographs in this case, had no one else on them but Hermann himself.

At first, he tried to understand what those meant. Maybe the prince had taken photographs of each of his guests, but no, he was the only subject. He kept going from one image to the other. Some were old, some more recent. The prince must have followed him for years, as some images portrayed him as a teenager. There were even newspaper clippings referring to the road accident that killed his father.

"You wouldn't understand," said Valentine, still unmoving before he could ask.

"Well, you really have to try me." He dropped the pictures back in the drawer and came closer to the bed. "It's me in there, you and me, but mostly me."

"Don't get too flustered." She sat up and tapped her hand on the mattress. "It's me he follows, not you. And I have already told you, he will never do you any harm."

Hermann sat down where she had tapped. "But he won't be this nice to the others, will he?"

"You never struck me as someone who would worry for others."

"I couldn't care less about those people, but I want to understand what is going on. As of now, I'm not so sure I can trust you. Tell me more about this man and who he is to you."

Valentine sighed and massaged her eyes with both hands. "He has been many things. When I say that you wouldn't understand it is because I can't myself."

"I guess you could start from the beginning." Hermann's voice was so quiet that he surprised himself.

She looked at her lap and smiled. "Yeah, that's always a good point to start a story." She stayed silent for so long that Hermann thought she would never tell him, but then she did.

———

"At first, he was my hero.

"We lived in a place far from the reach of any other people, with our brothers and our father. The light shone so brightly in our land that nobody would call the place any other name that wasn't Heaven. You ask me who he is for me, but a better question is who he has been. I didn't know him in my first days. I remember the colors of our father's palace lost in the infinite light and the long, winding debates of my elders. There were so many of us, I have no memory of him in those halls.

"My very first memory of him is the memory of a war. One we had never seen before and have yet to see another. When our elders fought, we both took the side of our father. Not a day would pass when I didn't have to kill one of my brothers or one of them tried to kill me. In those days, I found him fighting by my side. In all the horror, every time one of us stumbled, he was there, his arm stretched to get them back up. He gave us hope.

"No one, aside from our father and the eldest, had shone so brightly before. You could watch him and think he was all there was. If he was with us, we could not lose. He wasn't like the eldest. He wasn't born to be mighty, but he had made himself one of them. Because of him, we won the war.

"And so, he became my king.

"Father gave him a crown to wear as a sign of his kingship. We built our country outside of the lands of our father and there lived younger, more innocent people. We saw them growing, raised them, changed their shape so they could resemble us. Before we realized it, we had built a kingdom so vast and rich it rivaled the beauty of our father's land. And we loved every single one of those people.

"We loved them so much that we whispered the secrets of our land in their ears so they could use them to grow stronger. But that was too much for our father and the eldest among our brothers, and when they came to take us, the ones we loved betrayed us. Once again, many of my brothers had to die, and this time we had to disappear with them. For thousands of years, they tortured him in the darkness as I watched him suffer, scream, and die.

"But when two children of men walked the halls of a labyrinth, everything changed. We woke up, the darkness disappeared, and suddenly he was my brother. My little one to protect.

"He looked up to me, and I loved him for it. I think he still believes he loved me first. We lived not too far from here, he and I. He read me stories and wrote tales about me, and in his adventures, I was a princess, and he a king. Out of this dream, we came to the tomb to discover its secrets.

"When we came out of it, he was everything: my brother, my lover, and my family. We conquered Paris together. We were happy, until he traveled back through the darkness, and I could not pull him back. All of it for me . . . so, I left his side, not once but—"

Valentine stopped speaking mid-sentence and glanced at the door.

Hermann followed her eyes.

One instant after, a voice came from the other side. "Mr. Walker, are you in there?" It was that annoying little nun.

How could she know he was there?

As he turned back, Valentine had vanished.

"Mr. Walker," insisted the nun from the other side of the door. "It is dangerous to stay there." And she pushed down the handle.

Before she could walk in, Hermann had already taken the handle and slammed the door open. "Woman, you know how to pick the worst times. What are you doing here?"

The nun moved one step back and looked around. "I came to warn you. He is back in the house."

Hermann and Celeste rushed down the stairs connecting the third and second floors. He ran so fast that the woman struggled to keep up.

Hermann kept going without looking back at her. "How did you know I was in there?"

The other panted, trying to get closer. "Miss Van Vloed told me. I found her looking at the ceiling in the library, and she started shouting that you were in danger, and I should come and warn you about the prince being back."

"Why didn't she come herself. The witch will kill her . . . Fuck!"

Out of the blue, a familiar figure appeared as soon as they reached the second floor: Demeure.

Hermann stopped still so abruptly that Celeste went stumbling against his back. Demeure looked him in the eyes and Hermann did the same while both stood still. No one spoke. The moment went on for long enough that Hermann thought he might have had to give some explanation about what he was doing up on the third floor, but the prince didn't seem interested. Instead, he had a creepy smile on his face as he passed around them and walked up the stairs.

Was this really the same man that Valentine was talking about?

Evidence J-4355 to the investigation I-7242
Extract from Arnaud Demeure's journal
6 January 1535

Renée lay in bed on her side; the room was dark. Not a muscle moved in her body, but she was awake. Her eyes, wide open, were following me in the room wherever I moved. Something told me she knew what I was there to do, but I could not see any sign of fear.

She always looked at me like this, and she did the same to Valentine. I was her savior, a hero. Valentine, her wise older sister. She looked up at us, and at least for me, this filled the cup of my pride. This time, for a moment, I thought I could not keep up with what I was doing as her eyes looked at me like this. It was then that the door opened.

"I thought you didn't want to be here." I tasted spite in my own words.

Valentine ignored me and walked straight to the bed. She lay behind Renée and hugged her just under her arms, wrapping her chest. Her face disappeared behind Renée's hair. She whispered something I could not understand. Renée didn't speak. She had not done so for days now. Her eyes following us every moment, screaming that she trusted we would save her, that we would be a family again.

Now, the same eyes were giving away some tears, and I knew what she was thinking. I had been in her head and knew that for sure. She would have screamed at us, if she could have, to stop fighting. "I don't know what has gotten into you two." She kept admonishing us until she lost her voice.

I kneeled at the foot of the bed while Valentine kept whispering in her ear, repeating the same thing, over and over. Still, I could not understand it.

I took Renée's hand in mine, stroked her hair, and kissed her on the forehead. "Don't be afraid now, my dear Renée, it's time to sleep. Your wish . . . your wish is granted."

She exhaled in response and closed her eyes.

I stroked her hair again. "I will give you the most beautiful dream, a dream of love. And I will be in the dream and your sister too and even Guillaume will be there sitting on the ground as he always does. And Valentine will read you stories and your head will rest on her lap, and I will kiss your forehead. Don't be afraid . . ."

As I was done talking, her body relaxed. Valentine fell silent but didn't loosen her grip.

My face was wet as I tried to reach for Valentine, but she didn't give any sign of wanting to move. All she did was sob into Renée's hair. That was no place for me.

I left the room and closed the door behind me. Valentine screamed and cried, but she would not welcome any consolation from me, so I sat there and cried my last tears in my own hands. Alone.

14

THE TOMB OF GIANTS

Supplement S-0032 to the investigation I-7242
Results from laboratory investigation.
School of Winchester—Department of Magical Encoding and
Cryptography

The pictures were taken in an unknown location and found on Daniel Cortese's phone. They contain poems and short stories in verses. A spell renders the text readable in the native language of the reader. The symbols in the text don't match any known alphabet.

Any reproduction of the pictures in their entirety retains the same effect. Partial copies lose this property.

fMRI analysis suggests the spell works by altering the electrical connections in the language center of the subjects observing the image.

Given that neither the phone nor any copy of the pictures show signs of alteration in their connections to the telluric network, we can't exclude the hypothesis that the spell has been implanted directly in the neural structure of every human brain.

As Alex walked, the others behind her scratched and wiped tears off their faces. The place was so quiet she could hear them. Only the Strigoi was handling the telluric pressure with decency. "Roman, Daniel, you both will end up gouging your own eyes out. Stop that." Her words broke the absolute silence that had fallen on them since they had entered the tunnels.

"Do you think it has been a good idea?" Daniel asked in response to her remark.

She didn't know what to make of the question.

"Uh . . ." Alex muttered in response as she struggled to keep her focus. She glanced around. Bricks and naked stone merged all over the walls, as if the place was trying to resist being conquered by the house. The tunnel was small enough that Roman, so tall and broad, had to walk hunched over as he trailed the group.

Daniel, who held the light, and Ioan walked side by side, the old man leaning even more than usual on his walking stick. Alex led the pack in silence, looking at every detail in the structure of the tunnels, and thanks to a spell on her eyes she hadn't bothered sharing with the others, she didn't need any light to see in the darkness.

The witch sniffed the air. She would have expected to smell death and mold, but there was nothing like that. On the contrary, the air was dry, and a faint wind pushed against her face. Keeping the spell on her eyes and studying the network's currents were enough of a burden to her without having to deal with people's questions. She glanced at the walls and sniffed the air again.

"Van Vloed," Daniel insisted. "Do you trust her up there watching Hermann's back?"

A fork opened in the path in front of her. "I don't trust her at all, but I don't trust most people, anyway. I just don't think she would do anything weird this time." She glanced left and right twice and took the left path. The others followed.

Alex was more worried about Van Vloed than she dared admit in front of the others, especially after what Hermann had told her just before they entered the cave. The man had seen Van Vloed out of the house where they had found Sophia, likely when Van Vloed had left the group because of her wounds. The curious thing was Hermann saying she was staring into the void, which Alex feared meant she might have been spying on her and the others.

As she was immersed in her thoughts, Daniel kept pestering her with questions. "How do you know where to go?"

"The flow of tellur. She is going to its central knot," Ioan said.

Alex glanced at the old man and pointed forward again. If anything happened, he would be the most useful, but likely the most dangerous too, if he turned out to be on Demeure's side. This felt unlikely somehow.

"And you can do it too?" Daniel said.

The old man was also more tolerant than she was to questions. "To a certain extent, but not in here like she does. The telluric pressure is so high that the strands are all wrapped and tangled. Following their movements when they are so dense must require a talent that I don't have."

Alex sniffed the air again and tried to make sense of the path ahead. "I'm flattered, Strigoi."

"Telluric pressure?" Daniel asked.

Alex released the spell on her eyes and gestured to Daniel to give her the lamp. It would have been too dangerous to do any magick farther down the path. With such tremendous pressure, she wouldn't be able to follow the flow and handle the dissonance. "The density of the strands," she said. "As we approach the singularity, the quintessential field is so compressed that the strands are too close to say where one starts and the other ends. Just like two lights shining too close to each other."

Daniel stared at her with his mouth half-open and did not react to her gesturing.

Alex chuckled. "The lamp, please. I'm at the point where not even I can see anything or do any magick, so let's hope that there aren't too many forks ahead."

But Roman stepped forward and took the lamp off Daniel's hands. "No, I'll lead the way. You are way more useful, Miss Dryden, so it isn't worth risking you." He pushed through. "I also owe you my mission, so please walk behind me."

Alex's and Daniel's eyes crossed each other, and both shrugged. The giant was serious about all this knight code stuff, and he was better than any of them in any situation that required tactics and likely fighting. It was for the best he led the pack now that they were blind.

As Roman moved through the group, lamp in hand, something gleamed on the wall that Alex, so focused on the telluric currents, had missed while passing by. "Wait," she said and nosed her way back to the stone. It was an inscription. "It says, *'Behold, the man has become like one of us, and now, he might stretch out his hand and take also from the tree of life.'*"

"From the Bible," Ioan said. "Genesis, three, twenty-two."

"I think it might be older . . ."

Roman cut her off and turned himself so quickly that he almost smashed the torch on Daniel's chest. "Miss Dryden, another one here: *'Your right hand, oh Lord, is majestic in power. Your right hand, oh Lord, shatters the enemy.'*"

"Exodus, fifteen, six," Ioan said. "Do you think there are others around?"

"These weren't here a moment ago," Alex said. "I think the house wants us to read them. Keep your eyes open while we push through."

The way forward went smoother than Alex expected. Sure, it

was for longer than she would have wanted, and the place was dark even for their immortal eyes, but at least they didn't meet many other crossings. Perhaps this was what Demeure wanted, or was the box helping them? Places like these always cared for her. Even the Penrose house had always picked her as a favorite.

"Stop." The giant blocked their path with one arm.

"What is it?" Daniel asked.

"Something is coming," Roman said, and as soon as he spoke, a pair of red eyes shone from the darkness, illuminated by the faint light of the lamp.

Roman raised the lamp to show what had just come out of the darkness. The black form of a massive beast, a dog, emerged from the shadows. The animal looked at them warily, but it didn't move or bark in their direction.

"A dog?" Daniel said, pushing his head to peek at the beast. "What is a dog doing down here?"

"It's not a dog," Ioan said as Roman crossed himself. "It's a grim, a guardian of holy places. They say that when you see one, God must be close."

"So, what do we do?" Daniel asked, looking at each of the others.

Alex studied the dog as it studied her from afar. Something gleamed close to its paws. "He doesn't seem aggressive, and look at his feet, another message." She walked to where the dog was.

The beast bared its teeth and growled.

Alex halted and studied the dog that still growled at her. She glanced at both her hands. One disfigured by the spell on the portal, the other fresh and young. Her hands were majestic in power. She kept walking.

The dog growled louder but didn't attack, and as she drew close, it whined and sat.

She braced herself for a bite, stretched her undamaged hand, and placed it on the dog's head. The beast didn't stir or rebel, wagging its tail instead.

The witch sighed. At the dog's feet, as she had seen from afar, was an inscription. *Stretch your hand and grasp it so it can become the staff symbol of your power. For it ought to be not the strength of your arm, but the power of God imparted through your open hand.*

As she was about to read the inscription aloud, the dog patted its paws on the ground and jumped up, pointing toward the dark passage ahead. "Hurry, it wants us to follow it. And that makes it the second time I have to follow a pet tonight."

They followed the dog without knowing where it was leading them, but since they wouldn't have known where to go, tailing the animal was their best option.

———

"What do you think is beyond this point?" Daniel asked.

The dog had led them to a corridor that ended in an arched passage. A larger room must lie behind the passage, as the space beyond was so dark that the light showed nothing from the outside. As they hesitated before entering, the dog disappeared within.

"Wait," Alex said as Daniel almost walked in. "See that?" And she pointed at the top of the passage where a stone, as wide as the corridor, with an engraving on it, looked at them from above.

"*Guard thyself from crossing me because I guard the greatest sin. Only darkness I can let in and only light I can let leave. If thou wish to cross me now, I will be the one to weight thy worth.*"

"What does it mean?" Daniel asked.

"There must have been a door here sometime in the past," she said. "It sounds like a warning."

"And they wrote it in Italian?" Daniel asked.

"Not Italian," Roman said. "It's Latin."

Alex took the lamp out of Roman's hands and raised it to the inscription. "It is neither. I read it in English. Try to look at it without reading it, you'll see that the characters are gibberish. It's fascinating."

"Shall we proceed?" Ioan walked close to the passage and touched the floor on the other side with his walking stick. As soon as the stick crossed the shadow it disappeared in the darkness as if it were going through a thick, dark drape. It then reappeared as soon as Ioan pulled it back.

Alex studied the process. Some ancient form of magick played here, and this made it even more interesting. "Sure," she said, about to cross the threshold.

But Daniel called her back, pointing at the engraving. "Wait, didn't you say it's a warning?"

"Whatever was in there is long gone since the day the door was open, and I bet you two things. One is that the singularity is in there and with it the library that Sophia promised me. Two is that the person who opened this place first was Demeure."

"Let me be the first, then," Roman said. "If something happens, at least it will be to me."

Once again, the man was knightlier than she would have expected. "Thanks, but I don't need a bodyguard."

"I know but please, let me do it," he said, grabbing the torch from her hands and disappearing into the darkness as if a pool of tar absorbed him.

For a moment, there was only silence. Then Roman shouted an all-clear from the other side and the three followed him in, one after the other, with Alex at the helm.

The room was circular and spacious enough to host a ball. Columns, Alex counted nine of them, ran around forming an inner circle and creating an external corridor shaped like a disc. The place had no windows, but flaming torches attached to each column filled the room with so much light that she could see everything as if it were day. Roman stood a few steps ahead of her and the others, studying the place. Of the dog, there was no trace.

Alex moved around to inspect the walls and the columns. The place smelled like burned wood and the air was warm in a comfortable way. The only things she assumed to be man-made were the columns, sculpted with wrinkles and furrows, and two altars at the center of the room. Naked rock composed the walls, the ceiling, and the floor of the place. As she came close to a wall, she touched it. It was smooth and, contrary to what she expected, warm to the touch.

"What is this place?" Roman asked, spinning to glance in every direction.

Alex gestured toward the object at the center of the room and moved back to study one of the columns. "Judging by these and the altar down there, it must be some kind of church or a tomb, as Sophia said." As she spoke, she went around the column, running one hand against its surface, and despite the wrinkles, it was warm and smooth as silk.

Daniel approached the same column and brought a hand to the fire. "How can the torches be lit down here?"

Alex sighed. They all asked so many questions that they were becoming annoying.

Sophia had said this was a tomb and a library, but it had no books. Alex walked around the column, studying it. There was a symbol under the torch stuck to the stone. It was a circle made of glyphs, like the ones Sophia had drawn, with one larger sign at the center and many others surrounding it. Someone had engraved it on the stone. Alex moved one finger around the profile of the circle.

The others' chatter disappeared in the background as she walked from one column to another to find symbol after symbol carved on them. Each time a different one, and as she finished one round, the symbols changed, never the same even on the columns she had already visited.

She must have been going around for a while when she stopped again in front of one column and took to studying it from the bottom up. At its base, the column split as if roots sprouted out of its trunk to secure it to the earth. A trunk, she thought, and roots. She glanced at the other columns, and all of them had trunks and roots. They weren't columns, but trees, petrified trees.

As the idea crossed her mind, the symbol on the column changed right in front of her eyes. Instead of the complicated pattern, only a circle with another nine, one inside the other.

Nine circles, she thought, a tree, her hand. Should she stretch out her hand and take what was hers, as the engraving said?

She placed the palm of her only working hand against it.

The symbol burned under her skin, and it was as if she were merging with the stone, which creaked, more like wood than rock, until her hand, and only her hand, was inside.

A forest of twigs must have been on the other side. She pushed her hand through the twigs, feeling her way around until something slithered, touching her skin.

At first, she was about to pull her hand out, but forced herself to stay and search for whatever it was. Stretch out your hand and grasp it, the inscription had said, and so she did until she found it again. It was smooth, like a snake or a worm. It wriggled away once again through her fingers. But before it could go too far, she grasped its tail. The snake jerked on the other end. The burning pain of its teeth pierced her skin.

Once again, she was about to take her hand out, but thinking of the inscription, she tightened her grip. The snake again jolted and opened its mouth.

The snake stiffened and straightened within her fist. Not a serpent anymore, but a stick or a staff.

"These aren't altars," said someone from far away. "I think

they are tombs. Look, there is something written here. Alex, you want to see this."

"Witch," called another voice closer to her ears.

She ignored it. The staff had vanished. Her hand was on the stone. The warmth of the symbol burned so hot that it was scarring the skin of her hand. Her burning skin smelled like wood, fresh grass, and flowers.

"Witch," said the voice again.

The circle shone with a bright light and disappeared. "What?"

Ioan stood a few inches from her. "What are you doing? The strands around you . . . you were doing magick."

"Me?" she said, looking at the palm she had kept pressed against the column until a minute before. There was no trace of it being burned, but the circle on the column had disappeared. Two white dots, scars, shone on the back of her hand. And she didn't need to use her sight to know that she was connected to the network as if ready to perform an enchantment. She tried to disconnect, but failed. "I think I did something."

"Witch, what did you do?" Ioan asked.

"I think I absorbed it, learned it. I understand it now."

Before the old man could speak again, she ran toward one of the nearby columns. Here, again, she found one circle, but it was already disappearing by the time she arrived. "I know what this means. I can read it, whatever it is. These are not Hebrew letters, similar but older. Maybe Phoenician or Amorite, I'm not sure."

"You learned the circles? How?"

"I don't know, I used it, like a key. I touched it, and I think it downloaded the circles into me from the network." Her hands, no, her entire body shook. "I think it's in my brain somehow."

"It might be a good thing," Ioan said, but didn't sound convinced. "You can use this magick?"

Alex closed her eyes. All she could see were sequences and

sequences of circles. "I'm not sure I can use the magick these circles do yet, but I've learned them. It's like knowing the words, billions of them. It will take a while to make sense of them all and also learn how to use them . . ." She was speaking faster than she wanted to.

"Look," Ioan said, coming closer to her. "Roman and Daniel have found an inscription on the tombs over there. If you understand this language now, maybe you can read what it says then?"

"I guess," she said.

Alex followed Ioan. So much blood pumped into her brain that she kept seeing stars, as if someone had blinded her with a flashlight. Circles kept floating and flashing in front of her eyes.

"Everything okay with her?" Daniel asked as she pushed two fingers against her eyes.

"Yes," she said before Ioan could. "It's nothing. What did you want me to read?"

Daniel and Roman glanced at each other and shrugged. The giant pointed at one altar's side. "Here. There is writing there. It looks like old Aramaic but different."

Alex studied the engraving. It wasn't in a language she had ever read before, but it was the same as the circles still flashing at the back of her eyes. Most of all, she could understand it. "Just an epitaph. It's for the angel Semeyaza. Something about misunderstanding love." Semeyaza, this didn't sound good. Despite the flashes still going in her brain, she hurried to the other altar. "This one is the same, but for Azazel."

Alex stared at the others. Roman's and Ioan's faces gave away that they understood. Daniel, clearly, had no clue.

Roman preceded her in explaining. "The commanders of the watchers. Same as in the library above; they betrayed the sky when they took humans for spouses."

"Yes, that," Alex said, leaning against one altar, her head still spinning. "And according to the Thrice Great, they were killed for teaching men all the secrets of the sky. Agriculture, hunting, primordial science, and even magick. I guess you can say they were eliminated for smuggling secret weapons. Still, I don't understand—what are these tombs doing here?"

"Sophia talked about a tomb," Daniel said. "The stories say Demeure found something down here, right? Perhaps this is it."

"The stories say he found power, not a couple of old coffins," Alex said. "I would have thought that it might have been this magick based on circles, but it can't be. You have seen what it has done to Sophia in such a short time. It would never have worked with him for so long."

Roman's face became sterner than usual. "Sophia said it. He is not a normal immortal. He is something else. What if the coffins were not empty when he found them?"

"That would mean we have those Grigori to deal with, and it would be a nightmare." A drum was still beating in Alex's head, so loud she worried it would crack open any time. If she could disconnect from the network, she would heal whatever damage the circle had done to her. But her strands were not responding, and she couldn't detach them. This might become a bigger issue if any problem were to arise, considering that doing magick in there would be hard because of the telluric pressure. "I don't even want to think about it."

"We have a more pressing problem," Ioan said, pointing with his walking stick toward the door.

There stood Guillaume, looking at them with his usual empty stare. Without taking his eyes off them, Guillaume stomped one foot.

"Miss Dryden, watch out!" Roman shouted next to Alex's ear and jumped toward her, pushing her away.

Alex landed, sitting on the ground, one or two meters from where she had been standing. There, in her place, had grown a column of what seemed like solidified mud or clay that shot from the ground to the ceiling. At first, she thought of using her lightning. Perhaps with it, she would have a chance to defend and attack, but she couldn't, not unless she severed her connection to the network. This was an issue.

She glanced again toward the door. But Guillaume had vanished. As she turned to check where Roman had landed, there was Guillaume; he stood tall between her and the giant who lay on the ground too.

"No!" Roman said, leaping up from the ground in Guillaume's direction. His voice was cavernous this time, and as he jumped, both his arms went straight through Guillaume's chest.

Guillaume should have died on the spot. Instead, he was unfazed. A thick black fur covered both Roman's arms as they came out of Guillaume's chest—his hands mere inches from Alex's face. The witch would have expected a flash of blood, but none of that came out. Instead, pieces of wet clay fell from the holes in his chest.

Roman didn't care about this oddity as much as she did and opened his arms, cutting through Guillaume along the line of his chest.

The head fell down, shoulders and arms attached, sliding against the rest of the torso that was still standing. As they touched the ground, they melted in a splash of gooey mud.

Roman sighed and his tired face hinted a smile toward Alex, who still lay on the ground not too far from him.

Before he could raise a hand to help Alex up, the mud at the top of Guillaume's decapitated torso started boiling and suddenly two arms shot out in Roman's direction from where Guillaume's shoulder blades should have been.

Both arms hit Roman straight in the chest, bumping him a few meters away. The giant rolled on the ground, hit a column, and stopped moving, blood dripping down his forehead.

Alex tried once again to disconnect from the network, but again, nothing. This time, she might end up killed if she didn't get it together.

In the meantime, the long arms retracted and shortened against the remaining clay body, and soon enough a new head had appeared over Guillaume's shoulders. The man glared at the witch with his tiny eyes and stomped once more.

Again, columns of clay sprouted from the floor nearby Alex.

"Get a grip!" Daniel yelled. He rushed to her, took her by one hand, and dragged her on the floor out of the place where the pillars were forming. "Do something. He is made of clay. Can you use fire?"

"Fire?" Alex repeated. "I—"

A tentacle of clay flew over her head, hitting Daniel and smashing him against the ground a few meters away.

The young man jumped back on his feet and ran against Guillaume, who was once again pointing at Alex, ready to stomp. Daniel moved faster. He leaped on Guillaume's back, kicking him on the hips with his heels and punching him on the head.

It wasn't elegant by any means, but it was somehow effective. Guillaume struggled to get him off his back. "Witch! Come up with something," Daniel cried.

If that was how it had to go, so be it. Using magick within so much telluric pressure would kill her with a loud recoil, but for whatever reason, that animal had decided to murder her. "Okay," she said. "Daniel, get out of the way."

The young man jumped off Guillaume's back and sprinted away from him.

The witch was ready to weave the flow of tellur and cast her spell, but as she closed her eyes, her body moved on its own. Instead of concentrating on the strands, she kept seeing circles flashing in front of her eyes. So many at first, until only one remained in focus. As if it was the most natural thing for her, she bit one index finger, scribbled something fast on the ground with the blood, and slammed one hand over the circle she had just drawn.

A dull pain filled her chest with sadness, as if someone had dropped a stone against her heart. It was cold and lonely, any hope, desire, or love gone from her. Was this the feeling of burning away a piece of one's own soul?

The circle expanded on the floor so broad it enveloped her together with both Guillaume and Daniel.

"Run farther," she yelled at Daniel, but the man didn't have the time to move.

A blast of flames shot up from the ground, and she was at its center. This was her end, a blaze of glory in every sense. But before the flames could burn her, a cloud of thick smoke and dust cocooned her body. It was as if the smoke was eating her away, but it wasn't painful, and so she let herself disappear within it. She didn't know what it was, but it was better than being burned alive. And in an instant, she wasn't within the symbol and surrounded by flames anymore but looking from the outside at the flames still bursting from the floor and shooting up at the ceiling.

Alex scanned her surroundings. Ioan stood close to her. Daniel was on the ground, coughing. The smoke spiraled around the old man's body that was still fully forming out of the dust.

"I guess I should thank you for pulling me away from the fire," she said, getting back on her feet. "I wouldn't have guessed you'd risk your own life to save an enemy of your people. Why did you do it?"

The old man smiled and leaned on his walking stick, tightening the grip on its handle. "I didn't risk my life," he said, but the burns on his hands and face betrayed him. "And I wasn't being generous. Roman said it best: you give us the most chances of getting out of here alive."

"And we all like each other at this point, right?" Daniel said, now standing up.

Alex rolled her eyes and shook her head. She didn't like any of it, but couldn't stop herself from leaking a smile.

She looked at the towering flames. It was like staring straight at the sun for how bright they were burning. Such was the power those circles released by burning someone's soul.

"That's a big one for someone who couldn't do magick," Daniel said. He hadn't figured out what she had done. The young man ran to check on Roman, who still lay on the ground. "At least the big guy is still breathing."

Alex sighed in relief, but not for Roman. His being alive was no actual news—the man was immortal. Far better news was that the circles had stopped flashing at the back of her eyes, and her head wasn't exploding anymore. She finally disconnected from the network. The painful icy feeling of getting herself unwired from the strands was nothing compared to the dull ache that still lingered in her chest.

"You used one of those circles," Ioan said. "Can you control them now?"

"Not even close." There were way too many of those combinations in her head. So many it would take her years, centuries, before she could understand them all. Was it even possible? Enough of these spells, and her whole soul would burn away. This wasn't magick designed for humans, mortals or not.

It took a minute or two for the tower of fire to consume itself. The four, Roman having regained consciousness, watched the fire while resting from the fight. Alex and Roman both sat on the ground near Ioan while Daniel toured around the room, shooting photos of any inscriptions he could find, as he said, just in case.

"There is stuff written everywhere," he said. "Someone has been stitching pieces of the Bible together to make poetry."

It must have been quite the opposite, Alex suspected, as the flames vanished. Guillaume's body still stood where they had left it when the flames had erupted. Alex walked close to observe him. He seemed even more of a statue now, naked and featureless. His skin, darkened and sturdy, had turned him into a terracotta sculpture that sat at the center of a circle of burned stone.

Roman came closer to study the statue. "Dead, you think?"

Alex shrugged. "I do hope so, this bastard."

"He focused on trying to kill you," Daniel said. Both he and Ioan had reached Roman and Alex.

Roman pointed at the columns of mud Guillaume had built. "Not killing. Look at those columns he was building from the ground."

At a first glance, they looked like nothing special, but Roman was right. It wasn't about the columns themselves, but the way Guillaume had placed them. It was as if he was trying to build a cage out of them.

"He was trying to capture me," Alex said.

"I think so," Roman said. "That's why he didn't stop us from coming down here."

Daniel frowned. "It makes no sense. He could have captured Alex so many other times. I mean, she slept in a room in the palace, right?"

"I think something hasn't worked the way he expected. He must have believed we would spend our time going around the tunnels, but he didn't consider the house would guide us here. The affection of the house makes me a liability."

"Why would the house help us? Didn't you say that he created the box?" Daniel asked.

"I told you already. He might have created it, but magick is collapsing at a single point. A box is not just a place, it has a brain of its own, and I told you, for whatever reason, places like this one seem to like me a lot. This is what he might be worried about."

A creaking noise came from behind her. It was like ice on the surface of a lake cracking under someone's weight. But there was no ice, nor water. It was trouble, and judging by Roman's face, he was thinking the same.

She was about to turn and check on Guillaume when a gust of wind traversed the room, and something carried her away. A blink later, she was a few steps away from the others. A few pillars of stone had formed in front of them, and they hadn't had the time to realize that she had moved. Two arms were carrying her as if she were a newlywed bride.

Alex raised her eyes to see Leto's face looking down at her with a smile. Every feature of his face was so perfect, a beauty. He smelled of fresh moss, and for a moment, she liked it. She shook her head. "What are you . . . Put me down!"

Leto chuckled. "I just saved your life."

"Hey, you!" Roman called in his direction. "Put her down."

"Bigger fish to fry," Leto said, pointing at Guillaume.

The statue had cracks all over the place. Out of those bubbled and leaked a substance that resembled mud or wet sand. The ugly liquid was dripping on the ground at the statue's feet and had already formed a little pool.

"What the hell?" Daniel said as the shape of an arm grew out of the pool.

"Allow me," Leto said, putting Alex back on her feet and raising one hand in Roman's direction. The giant's expression suggested he was ready to pick a fight.

At the same time, Guillaume's head and torso had pulled themselves out of the mud.

Leto disappeared with another flurry of wind to reappear with a bang and the sounds of rock cracking and mud spattering near Guillaume's newly formed body. Alex hadn't seen what he had done, but the man was now standing where the statue was before, smiling at her with Guillaume's bald head held in the grip of his right hand.

Leto's pinstripe suit hadn't met any sprinkle of mud. His hair waved, so, while he had moved fast, at least he hadn't teleported. This reassured Alex. Still, if this guy wasn't a friend, he could be another nuisance—a big one.

"Is he?" Daniel asked, staring at Guillaume's head.

The expressionless face of Demeure's servant had changed little after Leto had severed his head. Mud was still fizzing and boiling from the neck.

"No, he is not," Alex said, reaching the others who had already gathered around Leto. "Give me that," she said, pointing at Guillaume's head.

Leto stared at her for a long moment, then shifted his eyes to her hand. At last, without a word, he handed Guillaume's head over.

"The hell with this. Strigoi," Alex said. "That smoke trick. Can you carry me and the sandman here to a place in this maze where I can do magick without worrying about the pressure?"

Ioan's lips curled. "Yes, no problem at all."

"Great, let's go then," Alex said, coming closer to Ioan.

"Wait, no, that sounds dangerous," Daniel said, jumping between the two. "Wouldn't it be better to move together?"

"I know what I'm doing. Let's go. And you, whatever you are," she said, glancing at Leto. "You are not off the hook; we need to have a chat after I deal with this thing."

A cloud of dense gray smoke wrapped Alex, Ioan, and Guillaume's head, and flew away from the room.

Daniel rushed through the corridor with Roman and Leto at his side.

The giant frowned. The dandy instead smiled, as if he was

enjoying himself. He was no more dangerous than the others at first sight, but in Leto's presence, Daniel's inner wolf winced and howled, forcing him to keep the dandy always in his line of sight.

Even without the witch, going back on their footsteps was easier than he would have thought. Perhaps now that Alex wasn't with them, the house wanted them out of there.

As they arrived, Alex stood in a pool of what must have been her own blood. She had deep cuts all over her already rotten arm. She had rolled up her sleeve and now it wasn't just her hand anymore, but her entire arm that had dried out to a point it wouldn't have looked bad attached to a corpse. Ioan stood close to her, and they both were watching a restored Guillaume strolling away along the tunnel toward the palace.

"Hey," Daniel called from the distance. "What happened?"

As Alex heard him, she startled and rolled down her sleeve.

"Nothing," she said. The contorted expression on her face betrayed her. She was in pain. "All done."

Daniel glanced at Ioan to search for confirmation, and the old man, having noticed it somehow despite his eyes, nodded. Blood dripped from his hand, down the walking stick, and to the floor.

"All done?" Leto said, tilting his head. "You let him go on his own legs?"

"Yes," she said. "I made him forget his mission. A friendly message to his master not to bother me."

Daniel glanced at Roman. The man was frowning. Why not kill him, though?

"You instead," Alex said to Leto. "How did you find us here?"

"I was walking around the palace and found myself in the tunnels just before Guillaume attacked you. I saw you in danger and stepped in," Leto said, reaching to take her hand in his. "As you said, this house must have taken a liking to you."

She pulled her hand away before he could touch her, so fast

that she almost jumped back. "Are you trying to hit . . . no chance!"

Daniel snorted.

Leto tilted his head again and opened his mouth without speaking. "I guess I should just go," he said, following Guillaume on his way out.

"I don't like that guy," Alex said through gritted teeth.

Evidence J-4689 to the investigation I-7242
Extract from Arnaud Demeure's journal
12 March 1535

One of Leto's screams woke me up again. I was surprised to have found myself in my reading room when I raised my head. Books surrounded me and my desk from three sides; many on the shelves, many more forming piles on the ground. The sun was still up in the sky, and nobody had bothered closing the drapes. My stomach wanted to come out of my mouth and a headache was splitting my brain. I guessed that, as usual, the light of day was weakening me. Not having slept properly all night and day must have taken its toll on me, and with Leto screaming, I tried to cover my ears and massage my temples at the same time.

It was then that the door slammed open.

"What is with the kid?" Valentine asked, entering the room. She was having a tantrum. The sun never had so much of an effect on her as it had on me. She didn't seem about to puke, but she didn't look her best, either.

"Did you just arrive?" I asked, trying to keep the image of her in focus. She still wore the same dress from the night before.

"I asked you a question. What is going on with the kid?"

"Would you just sit so we can talk?" I said. Since Renée, it had been hard to have a civil conversation with her. "You have blood on your hands. What have you done?"

"Not my own. Now answer me!"

One of my men arrived panting in the room, and another followed a few steps behind.

"Sir, we tried to stop her," said the first in the room, still taking deep breaths between one sentence and another. "But she would not listen."

"Answer me!" she demanded again.

"Sit," I said, signaling to the chair.

"No!" she shouted back. Metal, like that of two swords crossing each other in battle, resounded at the back of her voice. The glass on the windows wavered as if they were about to crack. She grabbed a vase from the top of a cabinet and threw it in my direction, missing me by one inch and hitting the books behind me.

"Miss, you cannot—" the man close to her said, but she grabbed his forearm. The man screamed. Valentine's hand squeezed his arm as if it were made of butter, his blood bursting from between her fingers. The sound of his bones cracking to dust filled the air.

"These are not our servants. Who are these people? Why are they dressed like this?"

Valentine fell to her knees, still keeping her grip on his arm. She was crying now. From rage, from sadness, I still don't know. I used to understand why she cried when she did, but I could not this time and it made me almost shed a tear too.

"Valentine, would you just sit?" I asked her again. "I will explain, I promise."

The second man tried to reach her, perhaps to pull her out or save his comrade.

"Don't you dare touch her!" I bellowed. My voice had the sound of a storm. Wind blew in every direction, and it was strong enough that it pushed the man back a few inches. The papers on the table flew across the room and Valentine's dress and hair flapped in the air, but she didn't move. "Take him and leave," I said, pointing to the man at Valentine's feet with the thunder still resounding in my voice.

The man moved a few steps forward, watchful of Valentine and me. After catching the other under his arms and freeing him from Valentine's grip, he left as fast as he could and closed the door behind himself without looking back.

"Tell me the truth for once," Valentine said, still sobbing.

"What is there to say? I'm doing what I have to."

She raised her head from her hands and glared at me with her eyes full of rage again.

"All this for a dream? You don't know if anything that happened in the labyrinth is true. You can't even tell if Mother was real or not."

"She was, and you know it as much as I do."

"Even if it's true, is it worth it? Renée, that kid, us?"

I moved across the desk to reach her. "Listen to me," I said, grabbing her by the shoulders.

"I won't," she said and pushed me away. "I don't understand what this is. In my head, in yours. I . . . You were my little one, remember? A hero. And now this? Is this what you are? What has happened to you?"

"You are just confused. I'm still trying to do what is best for us. We have to go back home. We have to. This plan will fix it."

"We are home. Together, like a family."

"A family . . . I thought you were not seeing it, but I believed you had opened your eyes to the truth now."

"Opened my eyes to what? To this damn plan of yours? You are not even sure that what you are doing will work." The air around her, moving like blades, cut the rugs under her feet. Many covered the floor, lying on one another, in memory of Renée's passion for collecting them.

"It will, I say. Do you remember the Englishman? The

wizard? He sent this to me." I searched around the room for my notes. "Look." I pointed with my finger at the paper. My hand was shaking. If she read it, I thought, she would understand.

She glanced at me first, then at the paper.

"It is a ritual." I smiled and pushed the paper toward her. "As Mother said in the labyrinth, a bow and arrow to pierce the heavens. The wizard's school recovered this from a crusader. The soldier didn't translate it all before escaping the Holy Land, but this is a start. It took them ages to translate a little piece, and I'm way ahead of them in just a few days. This, see?" I said, pointing at the part of the ritual that talked about the ignition. "A brother and a sister . . . this is why we need the kid! The rest is easier. All I need are sacrifices. People willing to put something above their lives, and I have the power that Father had bestowed on me. I fulfill wishes, don't you see? Mother had thought this through from the very beginning."

Once again, Valentine glanced at me and at the letter, but her eyes widened, her tears dry. Had she finally understood that all of it would work?

But she hadn't. All I could see in her eyes was disgust, anger, and fear. She backed away from me.

"What did you do to the kid?" she asked.

"Not much. He is young. It was easy to alter his memories with my illusions."

"Alter his memories?" she asked. She was being careful in picking her questions.

"Yes," I said. Not much to hide. It was the most practical thing to do. The only thing to do. "We need him. You read it yourself. He doesn't know he has a sister. I'm just changing him into a person who could reasonably kill her."

"Kill her . . ." she repeated, then she backed away from me and stood up. "It was our duty to love them, to protect them. You were their king. Father didn't bring us here to slaughter them or make them kill each other."

"I'm not doing more than they have done to us. Do you remember how they betrayed us on their first occasion? And even the ones that didn't, how many of them defended us? You can't have forgotten their joy in torturing us!"

"Vengeance?" she shouted back. "All this for vengeance?"

"What if it is? Have you forgotten? For eons, we watched each other's backs in a war that we didn't understand. We followed orders, and this is what they gave us. In a snap, all my brothers, our brothers! I still pray to their signs in the sky. And the torture! We were ripped apart, deprived even of our own suffering, what they did to us—"

"These are not our memories. They come from those things in the tombs; from whatever creeped inside us. And even in that dream, nobody tortured me . . . the other me!" she bellowed, hiding her face in her hands. "They didn't. Nobody ever laid a hand on me. All I could do was watch you being torn apart for thousands of years."

As she sobbed, my legs trembled. I could say nothing, nor could I ask her the question that had jumped to my mind. Had she stayed with me out of pity? Out of guilt? Even that first night?

It didn't matter, her reasons, my reasons, nothing did. I had to save her.

"You know it isn't just revenge," I said. "You are smart enough to have realized it as much as I did by now."

She stood still, breathing hard and studying me, but she didn't speak.

"We are going to disappear," I said, and in that instant, I knew it was what she had expected me to say. "It has been happening to us since the moment we were reborn in the labyrinth. We can't exist in this world if the door to the sky is closed. We won't even die. This world will forget us. We won't have the honor of death, not a sign in the sky in our names. We will fade, disappear, vanish into nothingness, as if we never existed. It took me a while to understand it, but I managed soon enough. I bet you knew it even before I did, didn't you?"

She averted her eyes.

"And despite knowing all this, you would not try to stop it?" I asked. "I don't care if you stayed with me out of pity, but we are not so meaningless that I will let us disappear. You are not so meaningless. I won't let that happen to you."

"It could be in a century, a millennium even. Would it not have been better to be happy in the meantime?"

"But we can, and we will do it forever. I showed you! We need not for that to happen anymore."

Valentine clenched her fists and went for the door. "This is madness. I won't stay here to watch it. Whatever you are planning, do it without me."

"No!" I yelled, and thunder again resounded in my voice. The door slammed shut in front of her.

"You are mad," she shouted back, and opened the door to leave.

"Can I be mad if I still love you so much?" I heard myself asking her. There was something different in my voice. All the anger that had boiled for thousands of years vanished. I sounded weak.

She stopped on her feet, trembling, her hand still on the doorknob.

"Little one?" she asked and turned to face me again, her eyes full of tears. But she must have seen something that disgusted her. A monster. And I knew all at once it had been me.

"I'm going," she said. There was something definitive in her voice. She had decided something that I would not be able to change. "Please, don't search for me."

15

MIHAELA

When Alex and the others emerged from the tunnels, they found Hermann walking up and down the library.

"What is she doing here?" Alex asked, pointing at Celeste while she tried to hide behind Hermann's back.

Hermann moved aside, revealing Celeste again to the room. The others gave him and the nun a suspicious stare.

"Listen, all, I don't find her useful either, but we are where we are, okay? Also, it's Van Vloed's fault."

"Of course it is," Alex said. "Who else?"

Van Vloed, who until that point had been fiddling with the position of the marble busts, shrugged and sat on an armchair. The fireplace in front of them was still lit. "Well, Celeste, or better, I saved his ass."

Alex shook her head and rolled her eyes. "What did you find?" she asked Hermann.

"Some old garbage, an unreadable book, and a lot of photos and documents, like notes and letters. I took pictures of everything," Hermann said, tossing his phone toward the witch, who caught it. "You can keep that for a while; I won't receive any calls, anyway. But so you know," he continued, sitting on an armchair beside Van Vloed, "he has been stalking us for a while. He has addresses and timelines in there—creepy business."

Alex sighed and frowned as she pocketed the phone. She should have been angry at the situation but couldn't summon any strength to be. Instead, she was worried.

"What about you?" Hermann asked. "Did you find anything useful in those tunnels?"

Alex tapped the floor with one foot and adjusted the sleeve of her sweater to hide her left arm. "We found both Guillaume and Leto, which wasn't fun. There must be other entrances in the house. The rest is all about what Demeure has found in the tomb, or what he might have awakened. We reached the tomb of two Grigori angels—as Roman says, kings before the men had kings, if you believe in this kind of stuff."

"Shit," Hermann said, melting into the armchair and checking his own pockets for a cigarette. "It can't be true, can it?" He put the cigarette in his mouth, lit it, jumped to his feet, and started pacing in the library.

"What now?" Alex asked.

Hermann rubbed his eyes and temples. "My sire was in Demeure's room."

"Now you say," Alex said.

"I don't know if she was in his room for real or not. She might have been in my head. She does that. But what you said, it doesn't even matter where she is, it must be true."

"And he goes nuts at the end," Van Vloed said with the side of her mouth, glancing at all the others.

Alex glanced back at her, shaking her head.

"It would make sense if she was there. He needs nine for the wedding . . ." Ioan said.

Hermann pushed himself up from the armchair. "Quit that. It doesn't matter. It's what the witch said. I mean, what my sire said too. She talked about the two of them, Demeure and her, being kings of young people and before that of a war in the name of their father.

"I thought she was raving, but by the way she talked, she sounded as if she had lived two lives and was mixing them up together. They didn't just find something in the labyrinth. Whatever they awoke there is in them now. I mean, she practically said it to me, they did something down there, and since then they've never been alone once—"

"I had the same feeling," Daniel said, interrupting him. "While talking with the prince, it was as if two people lived within the same body."

"If that's how it is, we know which soul he intends to use in his cannon," Roman said. "It must be his own."

"We should just kill him before he does us then," said Hermann.

Van Vloed, Roman, and even a more reluctant Daniel nodded, but they looked at Alex in search of an approval.

Alex took a deep breath and walked around the room. She glanced at the books in the cabinets and the titles on their spines blended together, while far too many thoughts filled her mind. Still silent, she looked up at the ceiling, where a flowery decoration emerged from the plaster.

"It's out of the question," she said. She grabbed her bony hand with the other and kept it from shaking.

"What? It's eight of us against one, perhaps two if you count Guillaume," Hermann said, coming close to her face. He towered over her. "There is no way he would survive!"

"I said it is out of the question," Alex repeated, challenging his stare. "End of story. We wait and play along until we have a plan to escape this place."

Van Vloed rose from her seat and circled around Alex. "Am I hearing fear in the witch's voice? Is the bad witch scared?"

She was right. As much as Alex hated to admit it, Van Vloed was right. But it didn't mean that Alex could accept it. The witch clenched her fists, ignoring the pain on her bony arm. "I am, and you should be too. You haven't felt his power on you as I did."

The others gave her a puzzled look.

"When you did your magick at the party," Ioan said.

As usual, the Strigoi was the fastest.

She nodded. "It wasn't like anything I had ever seen. The tellur hit me with such strength it was like trying to stop an ocean. But it isn't just that. Even ignoring that, we have other problems. We have no idea of who is an ally and who is an enemy, and we are in his house; if he has invited us in, he must be convinced he can deal with us."

"May I?" Celeste said with a feeble voice, raising one hand. The others stared at her.

Alex studied her. She had seen her during the party, but now she was looking at her for real. Her wide brown eyes, timid at first, were bright and curious. The nun must have been hiding more wit than she wanted the world to know.

Celeste continued, "Miss Van Vloed and Mr. Walker haven't told me much about what you think the prince's plan is. But if he really means to kill us all, why hasn't he done it already?"

She was right. It could only mean one thing.

"Rituals have conditions," Alex said. "Whatever ingredient you use, be it a plant, an animal, or a human, they need to be prepared so that the conditions are met. He must still be missing something."

"And if that is the case," Celeste said. "Wouldn't it be wiser for him to keep us prisoners in our rooms until we are ready, instead of leaving us free to roam around his palace?"

"That must mean that our free will is part of his ritual, too," Alex said, without thinking too much about it, but then stopped and stared at Celeste.

The nun's face was unperturbed, but her eyes betrayed her. They smiled, as if inviting Alex to go on.

It was then that Guillaume appeared at the door behind her.

The servant walked to her as Alex glared at him with such eyes the servant might have burst into flames. But all Guillaume did was hand her an envelope and walk away in silence.

The woman studied the letter and glanced at the others. She tore open the envelope and took out the letter inside. "'My dear guests, it is with infinite delight that I invite you all to the church for the wedding. The ceremony will take place in thirty minutes.'"

"But that can't be right, can it?" Daniel said, stepping closer to Alex.

The woman stared at him and squeezed her eyes shut, biting her lip. "'Miss Moreau,'" she kept reading. "'It will be a great joy for the spouses to have you officiate the wedding. Please reach the groom in his room to receive instructions.'"

The young nun was taken aback and stood still, looking at each of them.

"You should go," said the witch. "Do whatever the prince tells you to do. It is our best bet, for now."

Celeste hesitated for another second, nodded, and rushed down the corridor where Guillaume had disappeared a moment before.

"No, for real," Daniel said with a nervous smile on his face. "He doesn't have Sophia, right? Who is he marrying?"

The witch avoided his eyes and peered down at her feet.

"I get it," Daniel said, half laughing. "He is bluffing, isn't he?"

Only when the Strigoi put one hand on his shoulders, Daniel stopped talking. Instead, he stared at Ioan with an odd smile on his face. The old man nodded, and Daniel melted, as if someone had stabbed him.

"Where are you going?" Alex asked Hermann.

All the others were already in the church. She had caught Hermann instead, walking toward the palace.

"I need to understand this story better," he said without stopping. "My sire will talk to me."

"Listen, I don't think that's a good idea, now that Demeure is making a move. We should play it all together."

Hermann stopped and chuckled. "You talk about team play? Your concept of team play is barking orders at us and expecting we comply!" He laughed, but his laugh came off as fake. He pushed one armchair away and moved one step to leave the room. "This is none of your business."

"I said that's a stupid idea." She raised an arm and whirled one finger in the air that she pointed at Hermann.

Hermann halted. He tried to keep walking, but couldn't move. He looked at her, clenching his jaw. "Whatever you are doing, stop it."

"This won't let you move away from me. I don't intend to let you leave until we talk this through, and you tell me more about this woman. It must be important."

Hermann moved one step in her direction. Given how simple such an enchantment was, she had let the dissonance balance itself. But it hadn't been her brightest idea. As he couldn't move away from her, she couldn't move away from him, either. Somehow, Hermann had understood.

"Well, if that's the case," Hermann said, moving another step in her direction. "I said it already: stop it."

"Don't you dare touch me!" Alex yelled, panting, and used her rotten hand as a shield. Sparks of electricity ran through her hands.

Hermann ignored the warning, moved closer, and grabbed her hand to cast it aside.

He squeezed his eyes shut. Her coating of electricity must have caused him some pain. Alex didn't want to hurt him or kill him, but she wanted to push him aside, so she tried to send a stronger shock.

Hermann yelled, but it somehow backfired.

All of Alex's muscles tried to contract at the same time. For an instant, the pain was unbearable, but then it slid away. Everything turned pitch black and a dense fog surrounded her. No Hermann around.

Alex thought she must have been hallucinating somehow. It must have been the effect of the shock.

In the absolute silence, a voice reached her. It was the voice of a young woman she didn't recognize. "Are you sure about this?"

"Yes, how many times do I have to repeat it? There is no other way. We have to go back," said a man's voice. He sounded older.

Alex couldn't see them, and their voices were somehow muffled. She moved a few steps toward the voices, and the shape of a little girl formed from the fog in front of her.

The child crouched in front of a door opened by a sliver. Alex was less than a step behind the girl, but the girl didn't see her.

"I'm asking you to reconsider. She is only a little girl," said the woman.

"There is no other way. If you want no part in it, you can leave."

"You know I won't," the woman said. Her voice was tired.

"Then, please, don't look at me as if I'm going to do her any harm."

"But—"

"Valentine, please, would you understand? I have told you

many times now. We are a long way from home, way too far. We are nothing if we don't go back."

Alex could see them now. It was as though she were seeing through two pairs of eyes. With her own, she saw the little girl looking at a chink of the door; through the girl's eyes, Alex saw what she was seeing. The woman, Valentine, as the man had called her, sat on the side of a bed. The man had interrupted her and kneeled in front of her with his hands in hers. Both their faces appeared as blurry as their voices.

"It just . . . it just looks like you are getting used to it," Valentine said. "I fear you might even enjoy it sometimes. I understand this is your way to fix things but—"

The man dropped her hands into her lap again and stood up.

"Watch your words!" he shouted. His fury came through, despite the muffled voices. "Sacrificing myself is all I do. You came back on your own. Why did you do it if you think so low of me?"

"I guess I can't let you slip away, can I?" Valentine said. Her voice was broken as she tried to smile while looking at her feet.

The man huffed. "Then listen, would you? Get yourself ready for the work ahead. I'm going to have a word with the lord of the castle."

Valentine didn't answer.

The little girl outside of the door frowned at seeing the old man moving toward her.

Alarmed, she tried to hide as he opened it to come out. She failed because she was the first thing he noticed once in the corridor. He startled and the little girl was about to run away. Then the man kneeled, and smiling at her, he patted one hand on her head. His icy eyes followed his mouth in the grin. There was something dishonest in his smile, but the girl was as hypnotized by his eyes as Alex was.

As the fog faded away from his face, Alex studied his features. He was the old prince of Paris: Arnaud Demeure.

"I think it might be too late to be around for a little lady."

The girl muttered something; an excuse Alex couldn't hear at all, despite being in her head.

"I will make sure you get safely to your room, but I will give you better company than that of a ragged old man. Valentine, would you come out, dear?"

The woman appeared at the door with a look of surprise.

"Valentine, would you accompany the little Mihaela to her room while I reach mine?" he asked his companion, and grabbed the girl's hand in his, gifting it to the woman. "It will be better if the servants don't find the young lady in the company of an old man at such a late hour."

Valentine glanced at him and at the child. There was something in her eyes that Alex could not describe.

"All set then," Demeure said. "I bid good night to both of you."

This said, he disappeared amid the fog.

The little girl, Mihaela, as Demeure called her, was now alone with Valentine. The two walked down a dark corridor. A deep fog hid most of it, and Alex could see only a fraction of the rooms while the two passed through them.

Valentine's concerned expression never left her face. Every time the little girl looked at her and she noticed, she smiled back.

"Is he your husband?" Mihaela asked, staring into the woman's eyes.

Valentine moved her lips but exhaled, making no sound. She gasped for some air and answered the girl who, in the meantime, hadn't stopped staring at her. "You could say something like that."

"That is not a straight answer," said Mihaela. "Father tells me to always give straight answers, and I'm old enough to hear them."

"Well, I guess your father is right. Then, no, we are not

married by any law, but for us, it is as if we were."

The girl thought for a bit about what Valentine's answer meant and stopped talking until they reached what was likely the door of Mihaela's room.

"There we are," Valentine said. "Now you go cuddle under your blankets. It is a frosty night."

The woman kneeled in front of the little lady and took the girl's head in her hands. She was about to kiss her forehead when Mihaela asked, "Do you love him then? Like in the stories?"

Her expression was inquisitive, as if she were asking a question while feeding an answer. Not a positive one. Valentine was taken aback and giggled. "You are a peculiar girl."

But Mihaela didn't budge and kept staring straight into her eyes.

Valentine herself assumed a more serious expression.

"Well, let me think about it. Arnaud is the person I respect the most. He gave me more than I deserve. You know, he saved my life countless times and did the same for my brothers. He still fights for the two of us so I owe him a lot."

Mihaela exhaled and turned on her heels to face her door.

"Good night," she said, opening it.

Valentine called her back. "Would you wait for one moment? I want to give you something."

Mihaela turned back again, her eyes on the woman.

Valentine reached her own neck to take her necklace off. Three pendants were attached to it—a hook, a sphere, and a cross. Alex recognized them at first sight.

She detached the pendants from the necklace, took Mihaela's hands in hers, and left the three charms to her.

"I saw you staring at them during dinner tonight, so I thought you might like to have them."

Mihaela's eyes swiveled from her hands to Valentine's face. She looked as if she was about to give them back, but Valentine, noticing it, pushed her little fingers to close her hand around the jewels.

"Keep them. They will bring you good luck."

The little girl stared at Valentine with a curious look, and without saying a word, she brought back her hands to her chest and studied the pendants. She looked back at Valentine, as if worried she would change her mind. Finally, she nodded. "Thanks."

"Nothing to thank me for. We are your guests, so consider this as me repaying you for your hospitality. And now, straight to bed!"

Mihaela stepped again within the darkness of her room, then she hesitated and glanced back at Valentine. Again, she had a stern look on her face. "You didn't say you love him," she said and went back into her room, closing the door behind her.

In an instant, Alex found herself right where her journey had started. Darkness and fog were gone. Next to her, as if someone had just hit him hard on the head with a bat, was Hermann. Her own head was spinning, and as if drunk, she was having trouble standing still. Hermann gave the same impression.

She wasn't sure what the vision meant. The only thing she had a strong feeling about was that those memories were both hers and his. How could that be? Neither of them was in that vision, but what about the jewels? Those were the same she had since she could remember. Was this Mihaela a blood relative? Were the memories of the little girl flowing somehow through her? Or perhaps it was through the jewels themselves?

Alex wondered if it was possible and if the same was happening to Hermann.

Alex suddenly realized she stood less than a palm from him. She fell on her back to the ground and slid away from him.

Hermann took a few seconds more to recover and didn't seem to care too much about what she was doing. He let his legs go and sat on the ground, looking in her direction. "What the hell did you do, Witch?"

Alex stared at him, shrugged, and regained composure as she paused to think. "Me? I have no idea but, maybe . . ."

"Maybe what?"

"Maybe those were memories. Not ours . . . theirs. I mean, you have a strong connection to this sire of yours. You saw her up there in the room, didn't you? And I bet it was her, this Valentine from the vision, am I right?"

"Even if we say so, how will that help us?"

"Well, didn't you hear what they said? They were planning something and needed the girl somehow. There are stories about a wandering couple from the time of the war between the Strigoi and the School. Wizards who helped my side. Every time those two showed up at a castle, the School would attack it and gain traction. I think they did something to that kid, Hermann."

Hermann waved his head left and right, as if he didn't want to listen. "If this is true, and I don't believe it is, I would know about it. Valentine would have told me. I mean, this isn't a thing she would have been hiding."

"What are you two doing still here?" Demeure asked. He had arrived in the library without them noticing and stood beyond the door, smiling at them. He gestured for them to hurry. "Come on, you don't want to get to the church after the bride and groom, right?"

Alex stared at him for a long moment, then glanced at Hermann, who was glaring into the prince's eyes.

Demeure once again gestured with both his hands and head.

"We should go," Alex said, and pulled Hermann by one

sleeve.

The man resisted her, somehow enthralled by Demeure, but in the end, he let himself follow Alex.

Evidence J-4697 to the investigation I-7242
Extract from Arnaud Demeure's journal
26 March 1535

"Sir," the guard said as he came into my rooms, "your sister is back."

My legs made me stand up before I could force myself to keep composure. "My sister?" Perhaps the madness was over. She had forgiven me.

"Yes, sir, but she seemed in distress. She ran to her rooms and is not letting any maiden in."

"I must go visit her at once," I said, and I was about to rush past him.

As I walked, the guard stopped me. "Sir, before you go, there have been rumors in town. A man, some drunkard, telling the story he had intercourse with a woman and that the morning after she had already delivered a baby. Some plebs are hunting for what they think is a witch, and their description of the woman matches your sister."

I stopped and tried to hide my anger. "What about the baby?"

"Nobody knows. The man says he gave it to his son to kill. Nobody has seen the baby ever since."

"What is the name of this man?" Whoever he was, he had made the worst possible mistake.

"Jacques De Polony, sir, and his son's name is Roman. Say the word, and we will take care of it."

"I will take care of it myself." I could barely stand still. "Now go, I just want to visit my sister."

16

THE LABYRINTH

Note to the evidence J-0376 to J-1541 to the investigation I-7242—the "Labyrinth section"

Important: the following set of documents, from here on referred to as the "Labyrinth section," are verbatim entries from Mr. Demeure's journal covering a period, between 27 June 1266 (supposed date of Mr. Demeure's sire killing) and 25 January 1268 (date of Mr. Demeure's debut in Paris), that Mr. Demeure and his associate Valentine Duchamp have spent in the underground labyrinth of Provins.

Given their value to the investigation, we have collected them into this folder. A copy should be delivered to each member of the scouting team assigned to the exploration of the labyrinth.

The veracity of the content is still disputed.

Evidence J-0376-a to the investigation I-7242—Labyrinth section
Extract from Arnaud Demeure's journal
15 July 1266

"Look," Valentine said, pointing at the top of the wall.

There was a single block of yellow stone shaped like a half-circle. On the stone, an inscription, "*Guard thyself from crossing me because I guard the greatest sin. Only darkness I can let in and only light I can let leave. If thou wish to cross me now, I will be the one to weight thy worth.*"

I ran the words in my head over and over while Valentine watched me. I had the feeling she already had an answer, but was letting me have the spotlight. Despite the thinking, I could not come up with anything better than sticking my hand in the hole. A moment in, something like a long thick needle pierced it, and warmth filled my entire arm, as if I had immersed it in a dense fluid.

I forced myself not to pull the hand out and a voice whispered in my head. "You can pass, son of the darkness, but I warn you, only death lies behind this door. Leave now, and I will make you live like a king."

"Who are you?" I asked, and a glance at Valentine told me she was hearing the same I was.

"Some call me the Holy Ghost. Others have given me more entertaining names. I was the Morrigan in the North, but in the East I had two names. I am Wakan Tanka across the waters and Advaita I am in the land beyond the winter. The wise ones call me Kia, the wisest don't call me by any name," the voice said with a rhythm that was more like chanting than talking.

"So, you, son of the darkness," the voice continued, "do you accept my offer?"

I hadn't come this far to back away.

The voice spoke, "So be it."

One instant later, the entire universe moved around me as I stood still, waiting for the voice to speak.

Valentine shook me by one arm. "Look! We are somewhere else."

With my hand still in the hole, I turned to see that an immense circular room had somehow been summoned behind me. The place was somewhat bare, lit by torches stuck on a set of columns that formed a smaller circle within a larger one.

We moved around without speaking, inspecting the columns. On each was carved a unique symbol, a set of small signs placed around larger ones—nothing I had ever seen before.

Right in the center of the room sat what, at first, I thought was a single, broad altar. Coming closer, I saw that they were two sarcophagi placed side by side. On each of them was the carving of a hand with a spike in its center, like a knife stuck in their lid with the blade pointing up. I glanced at the side of one.

There was an inscription written in a language I should not have been able to understand. I read it aloud, "'Here lies Semeyaza, greatest among the great ones who came to watch the sons of men when they were young. The one who read the stars and mastered the power that molds the world. The one who whispered our father's secrets to the young ones. The one who lies here having misunderstood the meaning of love.'"

Valentine, who stood on the other side, stared at me as I spoke, and read something herself. "'Here lies Azazel, greatest among the great ones who came to watch the sons of men when they were young. The one who wielded fire, molded iron, and could guide legions. The one who whispered our father's secrets to the young ones. The one who lies here having misunderstood the meaning of love.'"

I didn't know what all this was about, but it didn't take a genius to understand what the carved hands and the spikes were suggesting. I took a deep breath and Valentine did the same. We stared at each other, each with one hand in the air. A moment later, we both had slammed them against the blades.

My eyes clenched, and Valentine's and my own screams filled the place. My heart beat harder and harder as the pain in my hand faded. Once I opened my eyes, I found myself in a dark and featureless place. In front of me, still visible despite the darkness, was Semeyaza's sarcophagus.

The voice spoke again. "Son of the darkness, this is the place where the ones such as you were born. Shells, husks. When She bent His power, the impetus of His creation, She had to shape it within the vases that make up the tree of life. But He was not perfect, and neither was She. And they left dust in the jars. And that dust, son of darkness, is you. Covered in the light of the creators, but never filled with it. This is the place where you must die so you can be born again."

I didn't really understand what the voice meant, but for as much as it talked of my own death, its echoing lulled me.

"Lift the stone in front of you and seek rest within this tomb. This is where your travel begins."

I studied the coffin, trying to find the determination to open it and enter. Valentine had disappeared, but I was sure she was facing the same choice. The thought of her made me swallow my fear and move on with my task.

With nothing to look at, nor the voice talking to me, I just closed my eyes.

Evidence J-0376-b to the investigation I-7242—Labyrinth section
Extract from Arnaud Demeure's journal
Not dated—supposed date between 15 July 1266 and 19 January 1268

"Open your eyes, son of the darkness, as we enter the first of your travels," the voice said.

As I did, I wasn't in the coffin anymore, but I stood in what now I know must have been hell.

It was the middle of a temple, around it was a broad meadow all enclosed by trees as if in the middle of a deep forest. I stood on the white marble surrounded by columns. Above my head was no ceiling, but a sky of such a blue I had never seen in Paris. The sun shone so brightly that I could not lift my head, and my skin burned all over as if too close to flames.

Something flew in the sky, like golden rings, winged and covered in many eyes, twisting and turning as they flew between the clouds. A nightmare surrounded me.

The entire floor was stained, or worse, flooded with blood— so much blood—and thousands of feathers floated on it as if someone had slaughtered a flock of birds.

Ten or twenty people were in the temple with me, all of them wounded. Two men lay on the ground, facedown, dressed in white drapes and light silvery armor. Their blood and innards I had just stepped on.

The blood, the smell, the splashing noise under my feet, all of it was so much that my mind could not see where I ended and where the misery surrounding me started. All I could do was stay in awe of what I was witnessing. And so, my heart fell victim to an uncanny peace. I wondered if I was meant to be a spectator or a character of this story. Maybe, for someone watching, I was as horrifying as the scene in front of me—not a bystander, but a part of it.

Women cried around me. Some leaned against the columns, others lay on the ground. Every one of them was pregnant.

One of them, who held a knife, cried louder than the others. "No, God of the skies, no! Don't let it be born, please. I don't want it to be born!" In the meantime, whatever was growing inside her tried to carve its way out. She lifted the blade to the sky and stabbed herself in the abdomen. One, two, three times while screaming horrible screams. Only the shrieks coming from her stomach were louder than her voice.

I turned away in horror, but on my other side were two other women with knives in their hands. With their eyes shut and hands on their mouths, they mumbled something. "Please, God of the skies, I slay it in your name, and with it, I die. Take me to your kingdom."

Another shouted. A mix of terror and pain. It was so fast when she slit her own throat that all fell silent. She collapsed to the floor. A loud shriek, like that of a pig, came from her, and something emerged from under her vest. A half-formed baby, covered in blood, too big for a stillborn child. It crawled on his arms down the steps on the temple.

Many other newborns were crawling their way down the temple toward the forest. Men in armor ran around the meadow, piercing the children with their swords.

The worst I saw last. A pile of corpses had been stashed near an altar on one end of the temple. The bodies had been cut into pieces and flies roamed around them. Not much was human about those remains. Overgrown legs, heads without eyes or with too many, all mixed with parts that must have come from birds, lions, goats, and animals I didn't recognize.

A naked man, a creature with skin dark as coal and ragged with cracks, stood in front of the pile. Through the cracks in his skin glowed the muted red and yellow light of a suppressed fire. He looked down at another creature sitting on the ground. This one had nothing of a man. Bark covered its body and its limbs were oblong, with no hands that I could see. Its chest grew thick and split into thin branches it used to hold a baby, still alive. The creature had no face, but a wide crack near the top of its trunk breathed and growled, so I assumed it was its mouth. Other branches hid the trunk at the top. They had no leaves, but black feathers, like those of a raven.

The monster grabbed one of the baby's legs and ripped it off.

The baby shrieked and cried, but the creature had already dropped the stolen limb into its mouth. As it did so, a thick gray fur grew out of the bark on its branches.

Suddenly, thunder broke the sky, so close that I thought lightning must have struck a few inches from me. At the same time, the loud sound of metal hitting metal blasted the air. Both were so loud they made me jump. When I opened my eyes, two young kids had appeared in front of the monster. They were barefoot, dressed only in white sleeveless shirts and white trousers. Both were built to be equal and opposite—one blond and fair-skinned, the other brown-haired and tanned dark. The blond one carried a sword secured to the hip, the brown a crown on the head.

"So, this is the respect you show to our father's creation?" the dark one asked—the voice was a faraway storm of thunders resounding in the air.

"Walahraban," said the scorched man as he bowed, and his voice was like fire crackling under the ashes. "Look, the monarch of this land visits us. We must bow in front of the king." Then he turned back to the kids. "I am so sorry for my companion. You must have met its kind. Such a fool it cannot talk, the poor soul!"

"Cut it, swarthy one, you have no business in this place," said the crowned kid.

"Is this the way you greet an old friend, Semeyaza?"

"You are no friend," hissed the blond kid with a voice that was that of a vibrating sword. "You are killing our people. If Father was not watching us, you would feel my sword in your guts."

"I would hold my tongue if I were you, Azazel," said the charred man with a voice so greasy it made me shiver. "We never lay our hands on them. They are doing this to themselves."

"Would they if it was not for Walahraban's illusions?" Azazel shouted.

"I will say it once, scorched one," Semeyaza bellowed. The thunder rumbled so loud and close that the others stepped away. "You can't be here. This is land for men and the Grigori that watch them. Out of here, before I remember which side you took during the war and show you the power that Father granted me. And I am less mellow than the Eldest Lords."

"Are you?" said a voice coming from above us. It echoed until those two words came at me from every direction. At first, only a hiss, it compounded so many times it exploded in my ears like a loud chorus, like music. It was sweet as the sweetest song, but resolute at the same time. The sound of a thousand wings followed and a gust of wind ran through the temple, so hard that the air blinded me and its pressure stormed over my entire body.

Something stood beside me, a shadow that I saw from the corner of my eyes. As I turned, nobody was there, but again it appeared on the other side. So, I turned at once, but nobody was there, and all I could catch was a glimpse of white and black feathers, the shape of a man. And so, I stopped trying to catch it in plain sight, as every time I turned, it disappeared. Instead, I glanced at it from the side of my eyes, unable to see it straight. At times, I glimpsed youth; at times, the wrinkles of age or the maggots of death.

"Lord Uriel," said the scorched one, lowering his head and kneeling.

The others followed. Even Walahraban dropped the baby corpse on the ground and grossly imitated the others.

"Poor creature," said Uriel. Again, I did not see it. Yet I sensed it had walked toward the corpse of the woman who had stabbed herself to death. "She died to spare the others of her womb's pain." A light wind rushed through the temple. The woman's body throbbed, took a gasp, and opened her eyes. Then she fell asleep, breathing soundly.

"So, Azazel, tell me of your desire to pass your siblings to the sword," Uriel said.

Azazel's mouth opened, ready to speak, but closed as an enormous shadow cast itself on the temple.

As I looked up, nothing was there but the sky and the sun, but I was sure I had caught the glimpse of a hand and thousands and thousands of eyes.

"This is your doing," said Uriel's many voices. "Whatever power Father has bestowed upon you, whatever right to lead the Lord of Shards, whatever honor in war, you threw it away the moment you whispered our secrets and took advantage of them."

"Advantage?" Semeyaza said. "We came to this land and found them naked, starved, killed by the cold of rain and the heat of the sun. We raised them from the ground where Father had left them. We taught them how to light the fire that guards their night, how to hunt and feed themselves, and gave them the magick of the sky. How can you think that we took advantage of them?"

Uriel broke into a laugh, so loud it resounded in my ears for long after it had stopped. "You know what I find tragic, Semeyaza? They prayed for us to come. Jealous of your glory, they asked Father to rid them of you Grigori and your sons because you had become their monarchs. This much they loved you back."

Once again, a shadow with a thousand eyes appeared behind me, but before I could turn, both Azazel and Semeyaza had fallen to their knees. "Of all the ones who deserve our punishment, one has escaped," said Uriel. "So, tell me, both of you, where have you sent Esterah, your favorite child. Why can't we find her anywhere in this world?"

Semeyaza struggled to speak, strangled by an invisible hand.

"You think Father made me king for nothing. My sons had dreamed of their own end, and we saw the signs of our brothers in the sky as you finished them. The Spirit told me you would close this world to the others, so, before you arrived, I gave Esterah the key our Father had passed down to me. A key not even I, nor you, can use.

"I taught Esterah the Ineffable Name, and she is now above the stars, there, where the Spirit, the Kia, our Father's sister, lives. My magick will bring my vengeance. Esterah will come three times again until one day the sky will crack open under your feet, Eldest Lords."

Those words weren't a mere prophecy, but a promise or a curse.

Even in the chorus that made Uriel's voice was some sign of agitation. "Well," he said, and I caught the glimpse of a smile. "You must attend to your punishment."

And everything became dark.

Evidence J-0376-c to the investigation I-7242—Labyrinth section
Extract from Arnaud Demeure's journal
Not dated—supposed date between 15 July 1266 and 19 January 1268

Within the deepest darkness of Uriel's spell, my eyes burned in pain, as if someone had just pierced them with needles. I screamed and Semeyaza screamed with me, our cries tangled.

Many voices rang in my ears and hands ran over my body. One voice was louder than the rest, one made of thousands of others: my older brother, Uriel. "Do you hear them? These are the creatures you raised from the mud. They still sound like animals to you, do they not?"

Uriel was right. My people were ready to torture and execute me.

Someone lifted me and dragged me for a long time. Their feet marched around me, and they laughed as the wet ground scorched my heels. At once, something hit me in the head first, then in my rib cage. Tens of blows all over. A last one straight at my face, and a ringing noise filled the darkness.

A bucket of cold water woke me up. Someone was pushing my head down in it long enough that I could not breathe. As soon as I hoped that it was my time to die, they took my head out and dropped me seated on a bench. Still blind, I could not see what was happening, but a door slammed. All around was silence. My torturers had left. But in that perfect silence, I somehow knew I wasn't alone. Uriel was watching me, looking for any sign of surrender. But while he had the power to kill me, I would not give him the pleasure to crush me.

The door broke the silence again as my torturers came back, and I was sure they were bringing fresh pain with them. Some of them came close enough that their rotten breath filled up my nostrils. They laughed and pressed something against my face. Perhaps a glass or a jar, so hot that it burned me at once. As they took it away, it brought my skin with it enough that I screamed. They cracked up louder than before.

Still laughing, they pulled me down by my hair and dragged me to the floor. From their giggles and the heat in the air close to my face, they must have been planning something terrible. One of them slapped me and shouted something I didn't understand. Another spat in my face.

Once again, they pulled me up by the hair, leaned my head on one side, and poured a liquid in my left ear. It was like molten metal entering and finding a straightforward way across my skull. My ear, nose, and mouth were about to burst into flames while the quavering liquid bubbled down my throat. Without waiting for my head to stop spinning, they turned me on the other side and gave me the same service on the other ear.

I screamed, but I couldn't hear my voice. Blood filled my mouth, and I could not breathe.

They dropped me on the bench, but without the strength of my own legs, I fell forward so hard that the ground cracked my skull.

Someone lifted me and dropped me faceup on a table. Nothing happened for a while and all I could think about besides my pain were Azazel and Valentine. Were they suffering the same fate? Had they seen their end at the hands of Uriel as all my other brothers before them?

Suddenly, someone grabbed my head and opened my mouth wide. I worried they would do the same as they had done to my ears. But they didn't. It was fast this time. Two fingers grabbed my tongue, took it out of my mouth, and passed it through the blade.

A thousand worms crawled under my skin as the hot knife moved on top of it. They stabbed, cut, pulled, and peeled my skin away.

I could not die by their hand, so they were giving me to the oblivion.

While my body burned in pain, a familiar voice came, one I hadn't heard since the start of this dream and since my sons had told me of theirs. "Tell me now," it said. "Do you want this to end? Do you want to reach your brothers?"

"Uriel won't defeat me," Semeyaza and I said with one voice.

"Ah, beautiful creature, you have nothing left but your hope. But the Lord of Death will take that away. Once it is done with its punishment, I will ask you again."

Silence fell again, almost peaceful. The pain carried me along as I floated in a sea of darkness. But Uriel's hand came from the darkness and wrapped, not my body, but my heart. A hand so cold and rotten it took away all the pain, and with the pain, it sucked everything that kept me alive.

I had nothing but despair. Not even the sound of my own

cries. I wanted it to end, and even if that meant defeat, I wanted to die. I could not hear myself doing it, but I was crying. Then the voice came again.

"It is time for your choice. The Lord of Death will make you live this over and over, but I can spare you. Do you wish to leave this place? Do you wish to come with me to a world of peace where none of this pain can reach you?"

Yes, was the only answer I could give. It would make me free. Free from living and reliving this darkness, this numbness. Free to be weak for once.

Then someone's fingers wrapped around mine, and the frigid grip of Uriel's touch weakened. Valentine. Even in this place of darkness, she had found me. How could I leave her alone? I might have wanted to die. Still, I had to live for her. I might have lost every reason to keep going, but I could not bear the thought of her waking up and finding me dead.

"No," Semeyaza and I said once again.

"So be it," said the voice. "I will wait for you to be born again as my son."

This was how my prison was built. Senseless in the darkness, and reached by Uriel's hand. Tortured again and again for hundreds, maybe thousands of years, then again abandoned in the darkest oblivion.

I don't remember my thoughts during my time in this prison, and perhaps I didn't think in the same way I was used to thinking. There were not dreams in there either. Joy never reached me and hope never came back. But Valentine's hand was in mine to remind me I had to survive. If not for me, at least for her, because her smile was all that mattered.

Evidence J-0376-d to the investigation I-7242—Labyrinth section
Extract from Arnaud Demeure's journal
Not dated—Supposed date between 15 July 1266 and 19 January 1268

The infinite darkness ended as it had started, in blood and faraway screams. Then I opened my eyes to a faint light and the voice of the tomb spoke again. "My children, wake up," it said, and it wasn't in my head but close to me.

Waking up wasn't easy. I could not see what was beyond the deep fog in my eyes, and the more I pushed myself up, the more I stumbled back down. The room was chilly and the air running on my body told me I was naked, on the ground, and covered in something wet and sticky.

Someone else crawled near me. It must have been Valentine. Before I called my sister, a hand caressed my head. "My son and daughter," the voice said. "They are so beautiful."

I squeezed my eyes until I saw her. A woman was looking upon us, so tall that her head pressed against the ceiling and the corner of the walls locked her shoulders—no arms came out of them. She had long, red hair falling to her waist, covering her otherwise naked breast. Her face was gentle, and her lips curved in the loveliest smile. Above this, she had nine eyes, each of a different color. Under the waist, she had the egg-shaped black body of a spider, covered in fur. Out of it sprawled eight thin human arms, six of which she used to push herself up. The other two were caressing our faces.

From these words, she might seem like a monster, but she was the sweetest thing my eyes could see, and all I felt for her was the love of a child to his mother.

Her face was tired and her clenching eyes betrayed her. I looked at her abdomen to find a pool of blood and yellow mucus just underneath her.

Valentine had noticed it too. "What has happened to you,

Mother?" she asked and paused on the last word as if it had come out unintentionally.

That word gave me an odd feeling, and Valentine must have felt the same. She never had an actual mother, and the old hag could not live up to the title.

"Dear daughter, you should not be worrying about me. I could not be happier to have brought you back to this world. I have to die now, but I am only an avatar. A splinter of the First-born who lives in the highest sky."

My heart sank. I had just met her and didn't want to lose her so soon. "Why do you have to die?"

"You have seen it yourself. The Eldest Lords fear the people in this world for what they can become. To stop them, they closed the sky and made me prisoner, alone in my own world. They thought I was senseless, energy to consume whenever they wanted to bend the rules. But I would not stand by looking at them defacing the world that took my father's and mother's life to create. So, I gave Semeyaza's sons their dreams, and he offered me his favorite child to be reborn three times and teach my magick to the young people of this world."

"I saw them," I said. "Why did Uriel not kill Semeyaza and Azazel?"

"You will discover the magick of old in you, my son, and you will know that it isn't as easy. They changed the rules when they closed the skies, and that needed a price. It had to be imperfect, reversible. That is why you, my son and daughter, could be born. Don't worry about all this just now. The stronger you will get, the clearer it will become."

"We don't want you to go," Valentine said. For the first time in my life, I saw her crying.

"There is no time to waste crying on me," she said and lifted both hands from our heads. She coughed hard again and again until a small piece of parchment came out of her mouth. She handed it over to me. Then, with the nail of one finger, she pierced my right index finger and did the same to Valentine. "Write your names on this," she said.

All I could do was look at her—she was dying in front of me.

"Hurry," she said, and it was an order. "We have no time. You came here seeking power, didn't you? You have found it, but now you need to survive."

But there was no new power in me. I was numb, confused, and tired. I followed her order and wrote my name on the parchment. Valentine did the same.

Our newfound mother took the parchment from Valentine's hands, rolled it, and dropped it in the hole in which I had put my hand to hear her voice at the beginning of my journey.

Both Valentine and I stared in silence while nothing happened for a few moments. Then a cracking noise came out of the wall surrounding the hole and a small rift spread from it, till a larger door-like opening appeared on the wall. Something sat on the opening, though, and the more pieces and debris fell, the more a human skeleton emerged from the rock. It sat on the ground, legs crossed, with the parchment in its mouth.

As if animated by a magical force, the dust and debris moved toward the skeleton. As they touched it, they turned into flesh that wrapped around its bones. A man grew around the skeleton, round, muscular, and lacking any genitalia. He didn't have any skin to cover his muscles so I could see and hear the blood pumping within his vessels.

Whatever he was, he was alive and convulsing and rolling on the ground as if in a great deal of pain. He opened his mouth wide to scream, but no voice ever came out. He gasped for air in large gulps. The more he rolled, the more his flesh covered with the remaining dust on the ground and the debris became his skin, giving him a more human appearance.

He took one last gulp of air and stopped rolling. His chest still going up and down, he took a stance in the middle of the opening he had come out from and blocked the corridor behind.

As I looked at him standing there a bit more, he didn't seem human at all. His entire body was featureless, no hair on his chest or arms or between his legs, no nipples or belly button. His posture was all shifted forward, with his head and shoulder pushed down by the weight of his arms.

Despite being one of the tallest men I had ever seen, he still was somewhat round, his body shaped like an egg. For sure, he was muscular but maybe his build, his short legs, or his rather enormous feet and hands gave him a fat appearance. Even his head looked somewhat artificial. It was round, with two tiny slits where he had his eyes, a broad nose, and a thin-lipped mouth. This, paired with his boldness and tiny ears, gave the impression that his entire face had been squeezed so it would use the least space possible out of that available on his head. Overall, he looked made rather than born.

Despite his odd looks, I found in myself some attachment to him, like one has when they see an old friend after a long time. But before I could think of anything to say or do, a loud thud reached me from behind.

It was our mother. Her abdomen, no longer supported by her arms, lay on the ground. Her limbs sat motionless, and her human bust leaned on one side.

"Mother!" Valentine shouted and stood up for the first time. She moved one step and stumbled, her legs unable to support her weight.

Mother smiled. "There is no reason to be sad. I die for what I love and to die for what you love is the greatest joy of all." And as she said this, she stroked our hair one last time.

The moment she closed her eyes, thousands of tiny strands of light came from every direction and passed through the walls and ceiling. They reached her body and enveloped it in a shining light. Her lifeless body shrank and became so small that it disappeared into nothingness.

Valentine wept herself asleep, and I could not stop myself from crying either. I hoped that she hadn't felt like this when I killed the hag. I would not have forgiven myself otherwise.

Tired of the silence, I fell asleep too.

I woke up to Valentine hugging me from behind. As her bare skin pressed against mine, her hair tingled my neck. I could not give her warmth, but my heart pounded for her. I didn't open my eyes and acted as if I were asleep so she could do this unseen —I owed her this much, at least.

Evidence J-0377 to the investigation I-7242—Labyrinth section
Extract from Arnaud Demeure's journal
Not dated—supposed date between 15 July 1266 and 19 January 1268

I don't know how long we slept like this, but when I woke up again, Valentine's arms were not wrapped around me anymore. I was lying on one side when something hit the back of my neck. I scratched, but a few seconds later, it happened again. Awake and waiting, when the third one arrived, I spun on the other side.

Valentine sat, her legs crossed, and she hurriedly hid a hand behind her back. A small pile of stones, each the size of a pearl, sat on her lap. The impish smile on her face told me she was in the middle of one of her antics.

It made me happy, but I knew I had to act grumpy. "Grow up!"

She raised her chin. "I did nothing. And, by the way, never oversleep a lady in bed, especially after a night of passion."

"A night of what?" I yawned.

She faked loud sobs. "You filthy pig! How could you forget about it? After everything you made me do last night?"

Her skin was pale and she was thinner than usual, her eye sockets deeper. Nonetheless, seeing her joking around made me happy enough. It hadn't happened since the hag had died, and I preferred this to the long silences.

"Ah . . ." I said, waving one hand, "nothing special."

Her cheeks turned red, and I sensed danger. "Nothing special?" she asked, and her eyes turned into two slits. "You. Filthy. Pig," she said, and at every word, she threw a stone in my direction. "The day you will have a piece of this," she added, pointing at herself, "you won't forget it." She crossed her arms and puffed her cheeks.

I studied her. She wore different clothes from those she had when we arrived at the tomb. She was dressed like a man, with a pair of beige trousers, a simple white shirt, and no shoes on her feet. Everything was way too bulky. Her hair was shiny but much shorter than it used to be.

"Where did you get those?"

"You mean the clothes?" she asked, now out of character, pinching her shirt. "Guillaume brought them. He carried a bathtub as well," she said, pointing at a rather sizable bucket. "More like a trough, but we can't complain, can we?"

She stared at me as I sat in front of her, naked and speechless. "You have yours right there." She gestured toward a sack on the ground near me. "But take a bath first, you stink!"

"Who is Guillaume?"

She shrugged. "The man that came out of the wall. I called him that. I guess you wouldn't know."

"You guess right." I searched around for the man. He was nowhere. I had forgotten about him, and in many ways, I thought it had been all a bad dream.

Yet I noticed that, while we were still in the same circular room where we had fallen asleep, a few things had changed. The coffins' lids were opened, all the decorations on the columns had vanished, and a large hole connected the room to the corridor outside.

"You know," Valentine said, "he doesn't talk much. To be fair, he doesn't talk at all, but he can be an excellent servant."

Once again, I searched around for the man. "Right . . . and where is Guillaume now?"

"Not sure. He comes and goes. He does what I ask, otherwise, he just tries to help, I guess. Last time he stopped by, he brought fresh water for your bath."

"And you just play along?"

"Well, why not? It is not like I can do much on my own." Her blue eyes focused on me while I failed at giving her a rebuttal. "Now, please, relax, and wash yourself. Then, we can have dinner together. Guillaume brought food." As she spoke, she lifted a heavy blanket that lay behind her. The face of a man looked back at me from underneath. "I'm sorry," she said. "I took a quick bite while you slept."

For a second, something within me, something new, winced out of disgust at the sight of the dead man and the large wound on his neck. That went away soon, as a more usual hunger kicked in.

"No matter how hungry you are, I won't let you touch it if you don't take a bath first, little one!"

I startled. My inner wolf stood silent as an unfamiliar voice rose within me. "Little one? Who did you just call little one?"

She grinned. "Why so upset? You are my little one, aren't you?" And she waved one hand as if to stroke my hair from afar as I paused, puzzled by my spike of anger.

"Just take a bath. It will cheer you up," she said.

To reach the bathtub I had to crawl. My legs had no strength in them. Raising my arms to wash myself was a similar labor of pain. Whatever had happened during my dream had reduced my body to bare bones, with little flesh on them.

As I was done, Valentine tore the meat off the dead man—it was a tough job without a blade. As she went on, she glanced at me, but every time I caught her eyes, she turned away. At times, she seemed on the verge of asking me something, but she said nothing. Before I could ask her, she finally spoke, "What did you see?"

"What?"

"When you entered the coffin, what did you see?"

I wasn't sure I wanted to recall everything I had seen. "Odd stuff. A temple, baby-eating monsters, and two kids coming over to save the day. An old, winged shadow captured them." I frowned and tried as hard as I could not to pronounce Uriel's name.

"What after that?" she asked and worked on the bones without looking at me.

"What about you instead?" I asked. I would rather bicker.

"The same," she blurted. "What after that?"

A shiver ran through my back. "The after was confusing and dark. I think they tortured me." I shrugged. "But it was just a dream, right?"

"Right." She glanced away.

"What was it like for you?" I felt guilty for asking. "The torture, I mean."

"The same," she answered, so fast that I didn't believe it, but I didn't want to inquire any further.

"Why do you think I look like an old man?" I asked as she handed over some meat.

She shrugged. "Stop thinking about it. I'm sure it's temporary. Just enjoy being the big brother till it lasts. I will let you call the shots now and then."

The time was lazy after dinner. Valentine crashed and polished the stones she had piled and used to wake me up. She was trying, for no apparent reason, to make them flat and round like coins. I instead mixed the dead man's blood with some dirt to make ink and built parchment out of the scraps we had.

Just as tiredness turned into slumber, Guillaume came back. He carried something in one hand, half wrapped in a piece of cloth. He was dressed this time, and what he was wearing was like what we had. For all I knew, he might have murdered an entire family just to get some clothes.

For sure, he looked less charming than Valentine in them. The trousers barely covered his legs to the knees. They stayed up by the sheer tension against his thighs as the button on top was open and bulging. The shirt was half-open, as he had misaligned the laces that would close it on his chest.

Valentine chuckled at the sight, and I shook my head at her reaction.

Guillaume stopped in front of her and stared at the top of her head until she glanced back at him with a dignified expression on her face. But as he dropped the package at her feet, she joyfully clapped her hands, hugged one of his legs, and said *"thank you"* at least three times before letting him go. "Ahem . . ." she said, regaining composure. "You can go now."

I gave her my best sarcastic smile while her hands unwrapped the piece of cloth. A pile of trinkets fell on the ground. There were cards, pick-up sticks, dice, and a wooden chessboard.

"What is with all that stuff?" I asked.

"I sent him to get games," she said, glowing in her smile even more than she had for the food. "This way we can spend our time playing."

"You are telling me you sent a bald giant into town to buy games?" I asked. It was upsetting how immature and dangerous that sounded. "You aren't even good at them! You know he killed someone, and he doesn't have the looks of an innocent man. It is not like he has any money. What do you think he did to get these? Did he slaughter some poor kid? A bunch of them?"

She just shrugged and took to sorting the cards aside from the rest.

"Valentine, we need to be cautious with what we do here. What if someone follows him to this place?"

"Listen," she said. She was now more severe than I had ever seen her before and stared at me straight in the eyes. "You and I are weak. You think I didn't see you in the bath before. You could not even lift your arms. It was hard enough for you to crawl a few steps from here to there and back. I can't move that much either, and I'm much better than you. We will spend weeks here, maybe months, before we recover.

"I get it. If they follow him, we are dead. I'm fine with that. But if we don't have him fetch food and comforts for us, we will either starve or go crazy and eat each other's faces, and I'm usually hungrier than you. So, now, be good and help me sort this stuff."

I wanted to open my mouth and reply, but I couldn't.

She smiled at me again. "Look, I have selected these flat ones so we can play checkers. And these others"—she showed me a selection of stones sorted into categories based on their shape—"we have enough of them to play chess."

"How did you know he would not bring the pieces?"

She looked down and saw her short hair again. That is when I realized what she must have done.

"You gave him some of your hair to trade for this stuff?" A hole opened in my stomach.

She offered me a weak smile. "You should not feel guilty, you know?" she said in a soft, serious voice, still not looking at me. "The hag deserved to die. I would have done it myself one day."

"I haven't done one thing right by you. I dragged you here, and once again you have to care for the both of us."

"You could not drag me anywhere, even if you wanted to. I

came here on my own. Now, do you want to play chess or checkers because I'm feeling lucky?"

I smiled. "So, you do love me, sister!"

"Never." She sighed and crossed her arms.

We played five or six times that night, and Valentine lost every single time. Every time she got upset with herself and acted annoyed at me for my mocking of her. Then she laughed, blackmailed me into another game, and lost again in a more spectacular way.

We talked and talked. I'm not sure how we fell asleep; I just remember a conversation that we had while we were half-awake and half-dreaming.

"Valentine, are you awake?"

"Yes," she said, sleepy and annoyed.

"Will you promise me something?"

"Anything that would make you sleep, little one."

"Well, promise me you will never let me wake up alone again. Promise me you will never wake up before I do."

She stayed silent. I didn't know why I cared so much about something this little. It was stupid, and she was likely thinking the same.

"I promise," she said. From the decisiveness in her voice, she had been awake. "Until you see me in the sky, or I see you, or we both earn our signs to live up there, I promise."

I didn't understand what she meant. I turned to face her, but when I looked, she was asleep.

17

THE CHYMICAL WEDDING OF ARNAUD DEMEURE

Evidence J-1541-a to the investigation I-7242—Labyrinth section
Extract from Arnaud Demeure's journal
A date (19 January 1268) appears to have been added at a later time

Guillaume was back when we woke up. This would be our last sleep in the cave, and that made it the most restful one I had since we had started our life there. Guillaume had been away for much longer than usual and he brought us nothing for the first time. I guess whatever Valentine ordered him to do had busied him enough the poor creature didn't hunt.

Seeing the empty room was saddening. As Mother said, we were reborn in there, and I'm not sure I wanted to leave the place. The only thing we left there was the trough we used as a bathtub. Valentine packed everything else: the clothes Guillaume brought us, the stones she carved, and even the games she never beat me at.

All I know is that today I could not stop looking at her. She gave me annoyed *whats,* and all I replied every time were empty *nothings.* She has done more for me in these last few months than I have given her credit for. Her hair is back to normal, and her beauty fully restored. Nature has paid this debt for me. With everything packed, I took a last glance at the tomb that has been our house for so long and we departed, guided in the labyrinth by a loaded Guillaume.

Valentine was right; it took many hours to reach the exit of the labyrinth. But we were lucky, and when we arrived, it was still dark enough that nobody moved around.

A stagecoach was parked near the exit. At first, I didn't pay too much attention to it, distracted by the fresh air, and fixated on the few rays of the newborn sun. As I came close, I realized the stagecoach wasn't new to us. It was the old hag's. How Guillaume had traveled to Paris and back in such a short time is still a mystery to me.

Attached at the front of the cart was an old donkey, poorly bound to a metal ring on the wall of a house nearby. I thought we were lucky nobody had stolen the cart and the animal, but on a second thought, no one would have taken the poor donkey to find themselves with such a malnourished beast on their hands. We needed it to survive only one day and one night. Just one trip, I thought.

With the sun about to come up, we became sleepy enough that we decided to spend the day in the cart. For people like us, traveling during the day would not have been the best, anyway. This must not have been Guillaume's plan—if he had any—as he had secured the donkey to the front of the cart, ready to go.

So, while Valentine carried all the trinkets inside, I helped Guillaume untie the donkey to rope it to the side of the wagon. Once done, Guillaume, as a good coachman, took his place at the helm of the cart and stood still, looking ready to guard us and our load. With him there and the sun about to rise, I went into the cart to sleep at last.

The coach had been rearranged to fit a small mattress and a few cushions. The mattress, on the floor, was fluffy and inviting. Many of the old hag's books had been amassed on one side of the cart. There also lay the bag full of stuff we had survived on during our time in the tomb.

Valentine sat on the mattress, legs crossed, even more beautiful in her nightdress. She had a book on her lap and was focused on reading it as I entered. She winced at the noise of the little door. Her eyes were full of tears.

She was reading my journal, this journal, but before my anger could rise, she dropped it on the floor.

Valentine jumped to her feet and reached me. With her arms wrapped around my neck, she kissed me full on the mouth. I kissed her back. She tasted sweet and soft, but as salty as her tears. She stopped for a second to smile at me, and I smiled back. My anger faded. Her kisses filled me with so much joy that I lifted her. Her legs wrapped around my waist as we both fell on the mattress. We slept together that night. For the first time, not as brother and sister, but as lovers do.

I was about to fall asleep with my nose in her hair when she sighed. "You know I had planned for this to happen, right?"

I smiled. She could not see me, and I could not see her, but I was sure she was smiling too.

"I had poor Guillaume go all the way to Paris and back to make this work out the way I had imagined it," she said.

At her words, I was filled with pride and responsibility. "And did it?"

She turned to face me. "No, it didn't," she said in a mockingly serious low voice.

"But why the books?" Why would she take so many for such a brief road trip?

"What about the books?"

"I mean, I get you made Guillaume fetch a mattress for us. But why the books?"

She lowered her gaze. "You know, I thought we could just run away. Me and you alone. Forget about the city and find a nice place with Guillaume helping us survive. Anyway, I changed my plan."

"Why change it? It sounded brilliant." A part of me wanted that as well. She was my best friend, my sister, now my lover. Yet, I knew far too well it wasn't what I wanted. It wasn't my destiny.

"It would never work. I would just make you sad."

"You would never—"

"You say that now, and I understand, you just had me." She pointed one finger at herself and repressed a giggle. "Trust me, I know a life in isolation is not what you want."

"But—" I stopped myself. "Yes, you are right, I guess. I'm not sure when you became the wise one, but it still remains, we don't exist in Paris. We are less than nothing."

"This is why I have a plan!" she said with a malicious smile. "But we will talk about it tomorrow."

She stayed silent for a moment, and I breathed the delightful smell of her hair. "I waited for this for a long time," she added, turning on the mattress to face me, "but even I didn't realize how much I wanted it."

"That makes two of us," was all I could muster as she kissed me again and closed her eyes to sleep. "Wait. Long time? So, you do love me after all!"

"Sleep," she said, caressing my face.

I took it as an order.

Daniel and the others were all seated on the church benches, waiting for the prince to show up. Now that the light was on, the place was a legitimate church. The seats had been placed in two sectors separated by a central corridor and were facing the enormous door that led outside. They faced a little altar and beside it stood Celeste, dressed in bulky ceremonial clothes that made her appear bigger than she was.

On both sides, the first rows were empty. Roman, Hermann, and Van Vloed had found places on the right. Daniel, Alex, and Ioan sat behind them. Hermann, more than any other, was restless and kept hitting the floor and the seat in front of him with one foot.

On the other side, Leto sat on his own. The others had little time to spend with him, and with all Alex's talk about spies, they had become unwelcoming to anyone else.

Daniel hoped the entire ceremony would only be one of Demeure's shenanigans. But abruptly, the door connecting the church to the palace opened. An overdressed Guillaume came out, rushing through the short corridor to reach Celeste's side at the altar.

Again, a door opened, but this time it was the large one behind them that led outside. Accompanied by a flurry of snow, Demeure came in, dressed in his usual suit. He wasn't alone and held a woman's hand in his right one.

The white dress reached down to her feet. A simple dress that followed the curves of her body. A wide veil rested on her head and fell to her back. A flower embroidery that moved in circles and spirals covered both the dress and the veil. The woman's dark skin and her black hair made the white of the dress stand out so much it was shining in its own light. Her green eyes pierced Daniel as she stared at him. She was a piece of a dream, his dream, nailed to a nightmare. She had the most beautiful eyes he had ever seen. Sophia's eyes.

Sophia glanced in their direction, but her eyes, wrapped in dark circles, didn't focus on anything while her head dangled left and right as she walked.

Demeure didn't look in their direction at all, but pointed straight forward at Celeste. Maybe he had decided to end this entire ordeal as fast as he could. He dragged Sophia along the aisle while she glanced, unfocused, in every direction.

Daniel tried to stand, but couldn't. As much as he struggled, his legs didn't answer his orders, and neither did his arms that kept resting on his thighs. He tried to talk and shout, but no sound came out of his open mouth.

The other guests didn't move either.

Ioan sat calmly at his left, resting his hands on the knob of the walking cane. Smoke kept rising from his hands, just to be immediately sucked back into his body.

Alex was quite the opposite. She shook her head and moved her fingers, even if barely. Tears of blood came down her eyes. She must have attempted some of her magick and failed.

More than anybody else, Roman tried to fight whatever kept them in place so much that his muscles clenched and throbbed to where it seemed as if his skin was about to explode. "How?" Roman hissed, barely audible amid his struggle.

Demeure, despite the distance, must have heard him and turned, glaring at the giant. "Thanks to you, brother Roman," he said in a hoarse voice.

Daniel knew that voice. He had heard it on the phone, and it had promised him Sophia would be safe. Hearing it again now made his beast flinch, but he couldn't do anything, bound as it was by invisible chains.

Demeure lifted his eyes off the guests and moved toward Celeste once again. When the couple arrived at the altar, Celeste stared at them, frozen in place, and glanced in the other guests' direction. The prince had to wave at her to start the ceremony.

Celeste took an ampoule from the floor near the altar. It was filled with oil and a paintbrush rested in it. With her hands still shaking, the nun drew something on the altar while glancing at Demeure. Once she was done, she waited for the prince to nod, took one candle that sat on the altar, and poured hot wax on whatever she had drawn.

Flames burst from the top of the altar, and Celeste, startled, jumped back. The red and yellow light added more shadows to those already on Demeure's tired face and on Sophia's sleepy one.

The fire burned violently, and in a few seconds, it dissipated.

Daniel's legs acted on their own, and a moment later, he stood. His face turned to watch what was happening at the altar. All the others stood too.

On the altar, drawn by the fire, had appeared two circles decorated with symbols he couldn't identify. Unable to move his head, Daniel tried to glance sideways at Alex—maybe she had a clue—but the woman could not move any better than he did, and two tiny lines of blood ran down her face. "Why?" he wanted to shout. "You were a father to me!" But his mouth didn't move.

Demeure put his own right hand on the circles and grabbed Sophia's left arm.

It was then that Sophia's eyes became wild, as if she had finally caught up with what was happening. She struggled with her arms, hit Demeure with the free one, and tried to pull away.

He was stronger and pulled her back. She cried as he forced her left hand on the altar. Nothing exceptional happened. The two of them just kept their hands on the circles for a few seconds. Then the prince took a deep breath.

Despite the lack of any clue, Daniel knew by looking at Sophia that something important had happened. It was done.

As the prince took his hand off the altar, he let her go.

Sophia screamed and sobbed so much that Celeste looked away. Daniel and the others couldn't do so, held by the invisible force keeping them still.

Demeure tapped on her head as if to stroke her hair, and she stopped screaming, reverting to her previous catatonic state. Her eyes were lost, and her open mouth drooled.

The prince made her stand on her feet and walk back along the aisle to leave the church. He had won.

As soon as Demeure was out of sight, Daniel could move his arms and legs once again.

Alex and Ioan, finally free, both sighed at the same time as they stretched.

The witch glanced at the old man and offered him a weak smile. "We are in deep trouble."

No, not another monologue from her. Not now. "You! You knew!" he yelled at Roman. "You said your friends would keep her safe." As he talked, he slapped one hand against the top of the bench that separated him from the giant.

Roman didn't reply and lowered his eyes.

"Talk!" Daniel shouted again, but Roman didn't speak.

Once again, he slammed one hand against the bench. "This is the way you want to play, huh?" This time he pushed the bench with surprising strength, so much that the bench flew and smashed against a wall. "I said, talk!"

Once again, Roman lips stayed closed.

Daniel's heart beat fast and the skin all over his body burned hot. The wolf inside him was growling. Before he could stop himself, he had already jumped on the man and pushed him with both palms against the chest.

Just like the bench, he threw Roman backward. The giant fell on another bench behind him, which gave way under his weight.

"Stop," Ioan said. "This is not the time to start a fight between us."

"He is right," Alex said.

A bitter smile spread on Daniel's face. "Really? You two agree on something? Well, I'm happy you two have found each other at the end, but this one is a traitor."

His heart kept beating faster and faster; his skin was so hot and his eyes burned so much they felt as though they might pop out of his skull. And he leaped again in Roman's direction. But Celeste, who had somehow reached the group, grabbed him by one arm.

He shook Celeste off, and she, so small, fell to the ground too.

"I'm sorry for this," Alex said, spinning one index finger in the air.

She was too slow. By the time she had moved, Daniel was already on the ground, his face pressed against the floor and one arm pointing up at an angle his shoulder should not have allowed. Leto sat on him and was holding him by the wrist.

"Nobody kills anybody here, okay?" he said, still keeping Daniel's wrist between his index finger and thumb.

Daniel slammed his free hand against the ground—his twisted shoulder and arm in pain. "Let me go!"

Leto looked away from him and straight into Alex's eyes and let go of him.

Daniel stood up and composed himself. "You can all go to hell," he said, leaving in the same direction as Demeure without looking back.

"Hot-headed," Leto said as he walked away.

"Dandy, not a good night," Alex said.

Evidence J-1541-b to the investigation I-7242—Labyrinth section
Extract from Arnaud Demeure's journal
19 January 1268

I woke up in the night to look at the sky out of the tiny window of the carriage that had been my house during the day. The woman lying next to me was still struggling at regaining her senses. The world, so different when looked at closely, was still the same as I remembered when seen from the sky above. The moon, the stars, and the sky, all still in place. His sight was not looking at us, like in the old times.

Thinking of Him, I didn't *feel* anger; I was anger, as to feel is not for me, because I am no man.

And so it kept going, and I was anger and sadness and regret and longing.

Then I turned to my companion. We had grown together, fought together, won every single battle, and survived. But something had changed between us. In looking at her, I saw a friend, a sister, a love scorching my soul. And I was not love. Instead, I was in love. And I sensed it in my tumbling heart: anger and sadness and regret and longing. All that mattered was saving her.

I was naked and weak, but with all this now inside my heart, I had a plan. I still was missing some pieces, but I knew what needed to be done.

A MESSAGE FROM A FRIEND

Daniel reached his room. He had walked at length outside of the palace, trying to understand where the prince had taken Sophia, but he could not find them, nor he could go far from the building without the box bringing him back after a few turns. As useless as the entire ordeal had been, at least it had calmed him down a bit.

He slammed the door behind him, kicked off his shoes, threw his phone on the bed, and fell facedown on the mattress. Daniel took a couple of breaths with his nose pushed on the bedsheets. They smelled like lavender. Marcel would have liked them.

Daniel startled and jumped up, sitting. He had forgotten about Marcel. He grabbed his phone, and there it was, an e-mail from his best friend.

Evidence L-1327 to the investigation I-7242
E-mail, Marcel Fontaine to Daniel Cortese
Found saved on Daniel Cortese's phone—all attachments recovered

Hey, Chief. I'm sorry I couldn't call earlier, but trust me, the moment I get my hands on that zombie bastard that stoned me, he won't know what's coming for him. Listen, I just woke up in a hospital and they wouldn't let me have access to my phone. It took me hours to convince them I wouldn't freak out if I made a call, but, finally, my charm won them over. Still your phone isn't ringing. Should I worry?

In short, the trip to investigate the guests was a minor success with the caveat they found me feverish on the beach and this has landed me under observation in a hospital.

Not sure where you keep the phone, but you better look at what I've sent you. If you wanted news on Sophia, I think this is the closest we've come to a story that makes some sense. Yet you might just be in the worst place to discover it. It is too convenient that this random lady who also was invited to the same party as you had something to do with the woman you've been searching for your entire life.

Whatever you do, even if you don't have the time to watch the videos, don't trust Aylin Van Vloed, okay? Whatever she says or does! She is bad news, and I suspect she hasn't been too kind to Sophia, so I get you'll be upset, but listen to me on this one. There is way too much we don't understand, and my instincts tell me it's better for you to stay away from that party altogether.

As usual, I've attached everything I found to this e-mail. I have little news on the others, just a little info from the Shadows.

Please, stay safe and keep your cool. And get your ass here to save me from these people before they put tubes in places I'd rather keep tubeless.

Oh, before I forget, I left a few transfusion bags for you in the fridge. Don't go through them at your usual pace, otherwise, you'll run out before I'm back, and we both know you are not good at buying this stuff at a fair price.

Fortunately, his phone had downloaded the attachment, an archive containing all the data Marcel had collected on the other guests. Daniel glanced at the folders dedicated to the others but rushed immediately to check Van Vloed's. As Marcel said, the meat was there, and his hints at a connection between Van Vloed and Sophia just didn't sound right. Inside the directory were only a few videos.

As soon as Daniel touched the play button on the first one, Marcel's face appeared on the display, blocking any view of what was behind him. He had bags under his eyes, was pale, and the bones of his face showed enough to suggest he hadn't been eating much. He had put his long hair in a ponytail and this saved him from being too shabby.

Marcel could become obsessive, but Daniel had never seen a video close-up of his obsession. He must have been skipping sleep and probably food as well, likely using Daniel's blood to keep going. It never had a good effect on him, and it was worse now that Daniel had been injecting himself with drugs from the Shadows. Still, despite the newfound scruffy look, his eyes still smiled, bright and lively, through the camera.

"Hey, Chief," said Marcel. "As I record this, I'm in the Netherlands, in a little town called Monster. I followed a trace on the invite the prince sent. Using the mail wasn't a good idea in this century, but lucky us, he might not realize it." He smiled.

"Finding the house wasn't hard, either," he said. "The host at my hotel is a nosy woman, and she was gossipy enough to tell me everything I wanted to know about the place. It's a haunted house." He nodded and grimaced as if he had just bitten a lemon. "Because, of course it is."

Daniel had to resist a smile.

"Anyway, the nosy lady told me the place is as old as the town, but it hasn't kept the same owner for long, passing from hand to hand, whenever the unfortunate owner would grow sick of pooping their pants. The place soon became unsellable, and the city decided to tear it down. When they were about to demolish it, an old descendant of the family that used to own the place came along and bought it from the town. The name is Van Vloed, of course.

"An old man no one has ever seen. They only see his grand-daughter, Aylin, our woman, coming in and out of the place at all times. She would be a looker, the host said, if it wasn't for her bookworm appearance. By the way she spoke, I think she meant that our friend is a creep."

Evidence L-0827 to the investigation I-7242
Letter, Aylin Van Vloed to Hoek-Boogaard funeral home
3 September 1666

"Aylin," your employees keep saying, "the pain will fade." With all due respect, I don't know what they are talking about. I feel no pain, and if I were to feel any, I would rather keep it to myself without having to suffer their intrusions. They might consider it unusual, but such is my request. I'm taking care of a family business, this is all. So, please, ask your people to avoid approaching me in such a way and invest both my time and theirs in managing practical matters.

I will request, if I may, all papers be dealt with at the utmost

speed. We can't ask my mother to further take part in the orga-
nization of her own son's funeral. That would be unnatural. I
understand I'm asking for further effort from you, who have
been of service to this family in every legal matter already, but I
will pay any amount required to sort this situation as quickly
and quietly as possible.

The only thing I want is to see my Sebastiaan resting in the
old house's graveyard in Griend and close a door on this as if
nothing has ever happened to this family.

Thank you for your understanding.

Aylin Van Vloed

Daniel played the second video in Aylin's directory. Marcel was
silent while on the screen appeared the shaking picture of a
house. It was a classic old two-floor with a pitched roof, ugly as
an old cat. The low fence was weathered and the gate left open.

Marcel crossed it.

The weeds inside were taller than the fence, and the skeleton
of what used to be a tree stood dangerously close to the house's
roof.

Daniel skipped the parts of the video that documented
Marcel forcing the entrance. What followed was a long section
of the video where Marcel searched the entire house, opening
and closing every door and drawer. The place was empty.
Contrary to the outside, it was almost plasticky in the perfec-
tion of its clean floors, perfectly set linens, and orderly
cupboards. And during the close-up of an empty fridge, the
video ended without any commentary.

This was the opposite of an exciting start, but the folder contained another three or four videos, so this must not have been the end of Marcel's investigation.

Daniel tapped on the third video and found himself facing Marcel eye to eye again.

"I'm recording this from an underground floor in Van Vloed's residence. I almost missed the place as the entry was hidden within the fireplace." Marcel coughed and covered his nose and mouth. "Formic acid," he said. "I paid my fair share of visits to the morgue, but this is unbearable."

He was in a corridor illuminated by neon lights. The walls were made of large bricks painted white, and most of the space was filled with boxes and boxes of syringes, needles, and plastic gloves.

He walked to an adjacent room without speaking. Here, shelves ran along the walls, full of dusty books and jars over jars filled with yellow liquid and human parts—hands, hearts, lungs, and a few newborn heads. The camera scrolled over them. Circles, like tattoos, had been carved on the specimens.

"For real?" Marcel said.

He pointed the camera at the floor, where more and more containers lay piled on each other. He coughed again and retched, and Daniel had to restrain himself from doing the same.

On a working table, beside a pair of gloves, sat three large containers filled to the brim with a yellow liquid and parts of a single victim. Everything from the neck to the waist was in the jar placed at the center. One arm floated upside down in the second jar like a grotesque art piece with part of her neck and shoulder still attached. And in the third was the head with its neck floating at the top. The curly hair and firm flesh made her seem alive, as if she were asleep, but could wake up any time.

A quick movement of the camera revealed a sink, a rusty kitchen, and a cot. Aylin must have been living down there.

Marcel moved to another room. Stacks of documents covered the floor and a tiny desk sat in a corner. While Marcel worked his way through the papers, the camera pointed at the wall. There, a genealogy tree caught Daniel's attention. At its root, the family didn't call itself Van Vloed, but Eric Van Lynden and Eva De Kock had changed their names; under them, two children, Aylin and her brother Sebastiaan.

"Oh," said Marcel as he flipped through some papers. "Many receipts from a boat rental company in Harlingen and an old letter. This Aylin really does like her boat trips. She's been going almost every day the past few weeks." He remained silent.

"Uh . . ." he said, finally swiping some papers away. "I knew I had seen something interesting! It's a note about her brother, an old transportation note for a corpse. I speak little Dutch, but it says something like *the old house's graveyard in Griend.* It's an island just outside of Harlingen. I find it curious that she has been going there so often in the last couple of weeks before the party."

A fourth video documented Marcel's trip from Monster to Harlingen and a fifth his struggles at convincing a crew of local fishermen to bring him to the island.

The sixth opened with Marcel on a beach.

"Hey, Chief," he said, almost shouting, and yet Daniel still struggled to hear him as too much wind whipped the microphone. "I'm on Griend Island. From what I've read, anything I'll find here will be ancient. The locals abandoned the island after a flood wiped out everything on it. It shouldn't be too much trouble to explore, though. The place is small. I could walk around it in an hour or two."

Contrary to what Marcel was saying, the island seemed huge

in the video. Daniel could almost taste the salt in the air and hear the noise of the grass waving on the flatland. Everything was shining, the water, the yellow grass, the sand, and they did it despite the sun being barely visible against an empty white sky. He sighed.

"According to the captain," Marcel said, walking, "there is an observation tower at the center of the island. From there, I should be able to see any remains of an old house."

At this, Marcel sped up his pace. Daniel skipped the parts of the video where Marcel crossed through the grass, and walked in silence until the point he reached and climbed the tower.

From the top, Daniel saw the entire island; a beautiful sight, but he was in no mood. Yet, before he could skip forward, Marcel yelled, "Found it!" He pointed at something blurry in the grass. "Those stones. I don't think those are there by chance."

But while Marcel marveled at a few stones, a black figure darted through the grass. Marcel saw nothing.

———

Daniel pushed play, and the last video started.

Marcel pointed at a few stones on the ground, hidden by the grass.

"This must be the perimeter of the building, I think. It has fused with the rest, but you can still see the profile of it. Over here." He pointed at a stone larger than the others. "There is an inscription."

It was true. On the stone, someone had carved a few words. *"Verrijzen zullen we, uit de vloed. Dansen zullen we, op onze graven."* Daniel had no idea what it meant, and Marcel wasn't gracious enough to translate it for him.

"As you can see, not much remains from any building, but that stone leads to a graveyard. These are gravestones, see?" He pointed the camera to show the inscriptions of names and dates. "All of them are Van Lynden. I looped around here for a while and found nothing, but then it struck me that Aylin might have played the same trick as with the fireplace. So, there it is." He pointed the camera at the ground again.

A large rectangular tombstone lay sidelong over a hole in the ground; on it, a name and two dates. "*Sebastiaan Van Vloed. 17 April 1636 - 2 September 1666.*"

"I did notice the grass was only on one side, so I pushed it, and it moved way too easily. I wanted to make sure I recorded before jumping in," Marcel said. "It smells like mold and fresh ground, but at least it doesn't stink like corpse."

The space underneath was a wide square, the size of a spacious closet. An old, rotten coffin sat at the center, but books and papers filled the floor so much Daniel could only see the top of it.

Marcel jumped in.

The room was actually larger than what it appeared from above, how much it was hard to say as the sides had been filled with more and more piles of books.

"Way too many books to go through them right now," Marcel said. "But let's see what we have here." As he spoke, he pulled open the lid of the coffin.

Nothing was inside besides a box and a letter.

"I knew it!" Marcel said and went for the box.

He extracted some keys with an address attached to them, another paper with a family tree, and a portrait. Daniel's legs jerked, and he stood up from his bed.

"What the . . ." said Marcel, zooming in.

It was just a sketch, but he was sure it was Sophia. She was much younger than he had ever seen her.

"'A memento of our fall,'" Marcel read from behind the portrait.

Another document, in Old English, was stapled behind it.

Marcel read it while showing it on camera, but Daniel read it faster as his heart beat in his throat. "'Know all men by these presents, that I, Frederick De Jong, of Talbot County and the State of Maryland do hereby acknowledge, have granted, bargained, and sold unto the said Eric Van Lynden, of Monster and the Republic of the Seven United Netherlands, one child, by the name of Elise Bakker, or Sophia, as she calls herself. For him to have and to hold the said child for life. This for the sum of thirty dollars and six shillings, current money, paid to me by the aforesaid Eric Van Lynden at and before the sealing of these presents.'"

Marcel remained silent, and Daniel was speechless too. Sophia sold as a slave. He paced around the room, his face red hot. He was about to drop the phone when Marcel spoke again.

"The letter! I almost forgot the letter." He grabbed it. "'Dear brother,'" Marcel read. He must have been skimming. Daniel could barely hear him. "'So sorry for you to wake up without me at your side . . . I will be dead already . . . world changed' . . . Wait, what?" Marcel slowed down. He was breathing harder. "'His promises have never proven empty. The moment I will enter his house, you will awake, and I will be dead already. That door will mark the start of my undoing.'

"'The thing that pains me is that you must survive this alone, but I have nobody I can trust to be your guide. There is a lot you must learn about the world and about yourself. Next to the coffin is a book. It is a history book for you to read and learn how much there is in this world for you to discover. It might be hard at first to understand it all, but I trust you can survive this. I have also left you the keys to a house and a map to find it. Make it your own.'

"'Stay out of the sun. It will make you weak. You'll be hungry with a peculiar hunger. Feed yourself with animals when the hunger rises. It will keep your sanity. When you'll feel safe enough to leave this island, wait on the beach. Anglers pass by the island every day before the sun falls—' "

A loud *thud* interrupted his voice. Another followed, and the recording stopped. The phone must have turned itself off because of the fall.

SISTERLY LOVE

Daniel paced the library where, according to the message the witch had delivered straight into his ears, he and the others were supposed to meet. His fists clenched so tightly that his knuckles had turned white. He wanted to use them against somebody's face. Until a few minutes before, it would have been Roman, but now he had someone else in mind.

The room was soaked in darkness again, illuminated only by the orange light of the fireplace and a few candles sitting on the bookshelves that ran along the walls.

And while he thought of Van Vloed, as if destiny wished to see whether he would run through with his plan, she stepped into the room. The woman, unaware of what was going through Daniel's mind, raised one hand to greet him.

"You . . ." Daniel said, "you have so much to explain!" He ran toward Van Vloed, pointing a finger at her chest.

She stepped back, raised both arms in the air, and chuckled. "Calm down, gangster. I thought you had picked Roman as your punching bag. What did I do now?"

"You can drop the act. I know you have been working with Demeure this whole time."

Van Vloed pushed Daniel's hand aside and walked away. "For God's sake, you are delusional."

"Am I? You bought her as if she were a dog," Daniel bellowed and leaped to hit the woman in the face. But as he was in midair, an invisible force pushed his entire body to the ground—every bone, every muscle weighed tons. He hit the ground so fast under his new crushing weight that his nose and mouth smashed against it. The blow had been hard enough that his nose was bleeding and his ears rang. Another mechanical sound reached his ears, like that of a fan spinning fast.

"What on earth are you two doing?" a familiar voice asked—it was Alex.

Once his body became light again, he peeked up to where the voice had come from. The witch was there, looking down at him. She pointed her left index finger at his head and kept her right hand open toward a clock on the wall that was spinning forward at a fast speed.

"Can you stop trying to punch everyone in your way?" she asked. She was talking to him. To him!

Daniel pushed himself up and clenched his fists, ready to hit her, but something within his stomach stopped him. She wasn't the enemy—Van Vloed was. "Don't you get in the middle again. Van Vloed is working with the prince."

Van Vloed and Alex exchanged looks. The witch despised Van Vloed, so Daniel expected her to side with him, but when Van Vloed shrugged, Alex sighed. "Okay, calm down and explain." Her voice was condescending.

"I can do better." Daniel took his phone, searched for the documents, and tossed the device to her.

The witch stared at the screen, her brows raising more and more as she read. "Sophia sold as a slave?" Her voice was loud and her pitch high. "And who the fuck is Eric Van Lynden?"

An odd noise came out of Van Vloed, a snort as if she had deflated. For the first time since Daniel had met her, her eyes were wide open and still. But they awoke soon enough and moved back and forth from Daniel to Alex. A smile opened on her face again as she looked up at the ceiling and replied to the question. "That would be my father's name before he changed it to Van Vloed. A great alchemist and an even greater man."

Alex walked close to Van Vloed. "Are you saying that this is all true?"

The faces sculpted on the busts of the Grigori glared at Van Vloed as much as Daniel and Alex. This somehow lifted Daniel's spirit. Also, the witch was coming his way, at last. With her on his side, Van Vloed would not have any hope of coming out of this in one piece.

"I never said that," Van Vloed noted. Her eyes, once again, swiveled from Alex to Daniel and back. "I said that Eric Van Lynden was my father's name, and I guess you can make a fair deduction that whatever document you have is telling the truth about my father buying that girlfriend of his." She waved one hand in Daniel's direction. "But I didn't say that I'm helping Demeure. I won't say the opposite either because you wouldn't believe me, anyway."

"See?" Daniel yelled. "She doesn't even deny it."

"I won't hide that I suspected you myself," said the witch, ignoring Daniel. "You've been hiding something since we arrived. I respect that; we all have. But I can't stop thinking that you are more suspicious than the others."

Van Vloed stared at Alex. She still smiled, but her face twitched as if she had to stop herself from looking elsewhere.

"I have many ways to make sure that you won't lie to me, and every single one I can think of is going to be painful. For your sake, I have to say I'm not a fine torturer. Are you game?"

Daniel studied both of them. Alex had spoken, expecting a smart answer from Van Vloed, and under other conditions, Van Vloed would have rebuffed her, but this time, she remained silent and as still as her twitching muscles allowed her.

"Good," the witch said with a dignified tone, and she pointed one palm, the bony one, at Van Vloed. The other hand dripped blood from under her fingernails. Throbbing veins surrounded her eyes. "A few rules," she said, and despite the blood and the look on her face, there was no struggle in her voice. "You lie, you puke your insides out. You piss me off, you die. Understood?"

She didn't wait for an answer. "First question. What do you have to do with Sophia?"

Van Vloed exhaled and collected herself. "I was young. I remember little of those days."

As she said so, the witch darted at her.

Van Vloed cleared her throat and slowed the pace of her words. "Let me explain. I might not remember, but Father has talked so much about his experiments, I can tell you enough. As I said, my father was an alchemist, the whole lineage was, and just like every alchemist, he was searching for one thing—"

"The philosopher's stone," intercepted Alex.

"Yes, the stone of Hermes, Moses, and Salomon was his obsession. It wasn't a stone in his mind, but a concept, a state of the spirit that allowed for miracles." Alex opened her mouth to speak, but Van Vloed talked over her. "You think of magick, but that's not it. You pay a price to do your miracles. You may use effigies and be satisfied because you don't suffer the pain of it. But someone still suffers for your greatness. What he wanted was the power to weave the world, paying no price at all."

"The Ineffable Name," Alex said. "It's just a legend."

"Not what he believed. Since I can remember, Father was familiar with the writing of the Thrice Great and his theory on the three parts of the divine," Van Vloed said and stared at the ceiling as if recalling something from memory. "One living in the sky, one dwelling in the realm of men, and a third flowing anywhere there is to flow."

"Four words to make you one with them," said the witch like

a robot. "Knowledge, Intelligence, Wisdom, and Valor, because there is no life without knowledge, no knowledge without intelligence, no use for it if not through wisdom, and no reason for it with no valor. The School fed me the same stuff for most of my life."

"He was stuck on these theories when he heard stories coming from the new continent. I must have been eight or nine, but I remember his excitement during those dinners as if it were yesterday. One of our guests talked about the slaves he had just bought. Among these, he said, was a young girl the others treated like a princess. Even in captivity, they still brought her offers. Her eyes, he said, were green as grass, which was most unusual for her people. The others called her names and told stories about the child speaking with wild animals and birds."

"Sophia," hissed Daniel.

"Surprised she was a princess for real?" Van Vloed said, giggling, but quickly regaining composure. "Father figured she might be the dweller, the Scarlet Woman. If she really was, perhaps he could achieve the stone, the name, by extracting her divinity."

"And you didn't think to tell us?" Daniel asked, his trembling hands getting closer to the woman.

Alex glared at him, and Daniel backed off. "Continue," she said, her eyes again on Van Vloed.

"You've seen her," Van Vloed said. "You don't need the eye to see the power flowing through her. And believe me, you are seeing the husk of what she was. You could almost feel a warmth, a pressure. You couldn't stop yourself from wanting her for yourself. So, Father came back from the Americas with this wonderful child. He was transfixed by her. I can never forget the mix of respect, fear, and curiosity in the way he spoke of her." As she said so, Van Vloed turned to study Daniel from head to toe. "It is going to get ugly now. Are you sure you can handle the rest?"

Before Daniel could open his mouth, Alex replied, "He'll do as I say. Please continue."

"Well then, I'm not sure how much of our alchemy they teach these days to wizards, but to make it brief, we follow simple rules. First, the greater the transmutation, the greater the pain inflicted on who wants to make it. Second, through subtraction, one can transmute everything into something purer. Following these principles, he worked day and night, not to transmute metals, but to remove the human from Sophia and seize her divine source.

"Every day, he would bring her to the brink of death but by the next, she would be on her feet. We could not see it, but he was breaking her. When she arrived, she was lively, talkative, a pleasure to have around when guests were in the house. She learned our language in a matter of days, and her mind cruised fast through our science and traditions. But years of my father's treatment broke her. Don't get me wrong, she was brilliant, almost cunning in her wits, nothing like the mumbling girl you have met, but not the joyous child she once was either.

"Yet, Father gained nothing. Her divinity stayed within her."

"How long did this go on?" Daniel asked, his fists still shaking.

"By the time she left our house, twenty years had passed."

Daniel's heart beat faster. He walked two steps away and tried to breathe off some anger. All he wanted was to see Van Vloed done and dead, but then the witch spoke.

"You did it yourself, didn't you?" Alex asked. "You took the knife from your father's hands."

Van Vloed's eyes darted from Alex to Daniel twice before she answered. "Yes, I did. Ten years after she arrived, my father had died already."

"You piece of trash!" Daniel roared and raised one hand to hit Van Vloed, but once again the witch stopped him.

"Don't make me," Alex said, and moved her bleeding hand,

drawing a circle in the air. "I don't want to harm you. You'll have time for that, but right now, I need information."

Daniel's heart beat so hard he feared it would burst out of his rib cage. Every muscle in his body was ready to rip Van Vloed into pieces, but he kept his eyes on Alex. How could she stay so calm?

"You are not telling me the whole truth," Alex said once again to Van Vloed. "You are smart and are avoiding lies, but I recognize a half-truth when I get told one. All these experiments, you continuing after your father, why were you doing all this?"

Van Vloed shook her head. "Such a waste. Just like you, so much tellur ran through her and she did nothing to stop us."

"You are avoiding my question."

Van Vloed stood in silence, once again looking back and forth from Daniel to Alex. "My brother," she said, sighing. "They say it happens to twins, one strong, the other weak. We dreamed of saving him. We gave him her purified blood, but nothing. It kept him alive, but he would not heal for good."

"How did Demeure get his hands on her?" Daniel asked.

Van Vloed shrugged. "How he found us, I don't know. He appeared at my door one day, claiming he was a colleague, a traveler interested in my father's studies. Perhaps I saw something in him, but the truth is, I'll never understand why I invited him into our house.

"As I poured his tea, he told us the story of a man. A wandering man who had to live forever, punished for tasting yet doubting the essence of God. My blood froze when he mentioned the woman in my basement, my brother's condition, and that he could use her to complete a ritual and save his life. He showed us a page from an old book with a symbol on it: a circle within a square within a triangle within another circle."

"The symbol of the stone," Alex said.

Van Vloed nodded. "Sophia, he told us, had much more

power than we needed. He could use part of her power to achieve our goal but wanted me to give him Sophia once we closed our deal. We accepted, and he told us our wish was granted."

Daniel shook his head. "And you sold her? Like that?"

"I can't say I cared about it. You might stand in front of me with your high principles, but wouldn't you have done the same to me and my brother to save the love of your life?"

Alex ignored both of them. "Continue."

Van Vloed sighed again and raised one sleeve. On her forearm, burned straight on her skin, was a circle similar to those from the tomb. "The ritual was simple. Sophia, Sebastiaan, and I had to brand ourselves with a circle. It is a siphon. It strengthens the network between us. Because of it, I could feel everything Sophia felt, and I could know when she was close. With it, Demeure broke the strands connecting me and my brother to the network. That made us immortal and made Sophia immortal too, as a side effect."

"Why would he use Sophia's power when he has enough on his own?" Daniel said.

Alex kept staring at Van Vloed and spoke. "They were guinea pigs. He wanted to try out his method to transfer power. He also needed Sophia alive until his entire plan was ready. It wasn't just a side effect. He made Sophia immortal and kept her strands intact. The School would pay anything for the secret of a ritual like that."

"But it didn't work," Daniel said, shaking his head. "Van Vloed is not connected to her. She couldn't even say Sophia was here to begin with. Her brother, too, has been dead for years!"

At this, Van Vloed's face turned grave, and she stared into Daniel's eyes. "How could you know that? Where did you find a copy of the contract in the first place?" Her mouth and tongue moved like those of an animal ready to bite.

Daniel's beast jumped in his stomach, ready for a fight.

The witch made a dull sound, as if phlegm was strangling her. "You are not the one asking questions." Her voice was raucous and the veins around her eyes throbbed. More blood dripped from her otherwise undamaged hand as she clenched the bony one in front of Van Vloed's face.

At this, Van Vloed twisted, and blood burst out of her mouth. She kneeled on the ground, puking and choking on her own blood.

It took her a minute to get back on her feet, but she wiped her mouth with the back of one hand, smiled again curtly, and patted her dress. "I shall continue, I suppose."

Alex opened her fist and nodded.

"Sophia must have broken our bond. Not too long ago, maybe just a few days. About my brother, whatever Demeure did, it worked on me, but killed him."

"If his gift works as in the stories, he couldn't have died unless one of you desired so," Alex said.

"I'm aware," Van Vloed said. She was still grinning. "And, believe me, I screamed, kicked, and punched, but it's what he said as well. Both of us must have wanted it, actually, according to the prince."

Daniel thought he glimpsed tears in Van Vloed's eyes, but it all went away as fast as it had come.

"I must have never realized how much I hated taking care of him," Van Vloed added, spitting some more blood on the floor.

"Still not the entire story," Alex said flatly.

"That's right," Daniel said. "Before coming here, she had left a message in her brother's coffin so he could find it when he would wake up. She has another deal with the prince."

Both Alex and Van Vloed turned to look at him. There was madness in Van Vloed's eyes. The witch had a puzzled look instead.

"Where did you get all this intel?" Alex asked.

Before receiving an answer, she raised a bloodstained finger in front of her mouth. "Shh! Did you hear that?"

The others looked at her without speaking.

"Someone crying," she said. "It comes from the kitchen. There is someone in there."

"Sophia," Daniel said, and he ran to the door.

Evidence L-1428 to the investigation I-7242
Letter, Roman de Polony to Azurine de Polony (never sent)
Not dated

Dear Azurine, sister,

Am I a good man?

This might be the last letter I write to you. How many before this one? I counted them at one point, but time has washed the number off my head. You know this question, *"Am I a good man?"*

I've asked it to you so many times on and off the page that I won't even try to count them.

Am I a good man? Can you be born one? Can you die one?

I ask myself this, and I can't find an answer. Yet the demon, the wolf, roars within me and grows stronger every day, every night, while I fade instead. But at every step I took since I came down that churchyard in Lyon, I asked myself, *"Is this what a good man would do?"*

Where did this lead me? To a life of killing and fighting, this is where. To a woman I could have saved had I not been so faithful in the promises of a lord that wasn't my Lord. And thus, I am close to an answer to that question, and I fear it isn't the one I want. Did I suspect it all along? Why did I keep asking if I hadn't doubted it in the first place?

If you could read this, you would laugh at what I have

become in my later years. An old man, who doubts himself like a child. For once, I have no doubts. After what I saw that man do, after all his lies poisoning my existence, I must follow the way of the sword one last time. He may crush me, but I'll regain my honor at last.

Thanks for being the silent listener of my journals, sister, for, without you, the beast roaring in my heart would have led me to disgrace.

Hoping for a life where we can talk as a family,

Roman

There was no reason to be so unfair, and Celeste, least of all, would have expected Daniel to try punching Roman.

The giant had been the one treating her with the most respect since the party, and Celeste didn't want to leave him alone in his room.

"Roman?" Celeste asked, knocking at the man's door. No answer came. "Roman, are you there? We are meeting the others to discuss a plan."

Still nothing.

"It was just a stupid argument," she said, but this time, instead of knocking, she put one hand on the handle and lowered it. The door opened. "Would you just . . ." But the man wasn't in his room. The place was as empty and poorly decorated as hers. The bed must have been tiny for a man the size of Roman. The same damp smell pervaded the air and the only source of light in the room was a candle, still lit, that sat on a desk in front of the bed. A chair lay on the ground next to the desk, tiny and made of rough dark wood. Whoever sat there had left in a hurry. She couldn't fathom how a man of Roman's size could fit in such a small chair.

Some instrument sat beside the chair on the ground, a belt with a chain. Celeste took it in her hands and studied it. What she thought were rings at first sight were tiny hooks covered in a mixture of dried and fresh blood. It was a cilice.

Celeste glanced at the floor. Drips of blood ran all the way to the door. She had stepped on one of them and stamped the wood with her bloody footprint. Roman must have freed himself from the torture device when he had left the room, and the blood must have been dripping straight from his legs. She hadn't seen a cilice in centuries. Why would Roman wear one?

Celeste put the chair back and dropped the cilice on it. As she did so, she accidentally dragged a paper that sat on the desk down to the floor. She took it and put it back, trying not to look, but couldn't resist the temptation to take a peek.

The writing was hurried and hard to decipher. Here and there the man had scratched words and rewritten sentences. It was a letter, but the opening was one Celeste would never have expected: *"Dear Azurine, sister."* Celeste looked away. Maybe she was imagining it, but as she read it again, the same words looked back at her.

Her heart pumped fast, so much she could feel it in her temples. Azurine, that was her name, one that she hadn't used in centuries. Demeure wouldn't. Not just to prove a point. Wasn't all this for her mother? But she had seen it with her own eyes, the surprises that the prince could pull out of his hat, and now she understood how Daniel must have felt.

THE RULES OF MAGICK

Daniel had already run to the kitchen by the time Alex moved. She signaled Van Vloed to walk ahead of her, but by the time they reached the door, Daniel was already in.

"What did you do?" Daniel kept repeating. "What are you doing?"

The white, bluish light filtered in from two windows and glinted off the tools hanging on the racks and the tiles on the wall.

Sophia sat at the short end of a table in the kitchen. Red spatters covered most of the table and the floor surrounding it. She had a spoon in one hand while the other covered the right half of her face. Blood flowed between her fingers and dripped onto the wood. The spoon pointed threateningly at her left eye, and Daniel, who had reached her, was trying to take it out of her hands.

Straight in front of her, on the table, was a small pile of something Alex could not identify at first. But Van Vloed, next to her, brought two fingers to her mouth, winked, and acted as if about to retch. Alex glanced again. They were eyeballs, five or six of them.

"Stop," Daniel shouted. "Why are you doing this?"

"Daniel, is it you?" Sophia asked as she stared at him. She dropped the spoon on the table, showing her face in clear sight. Her right eye socket was empty and the cheek below stained with blood. "I didn't want to see anymore. What's coming, and what they'll do. I took my sight away, but my eyes kept growing. Why are you looking at me like this? You shouldn't. You should not be looking at me like this." She tried to reach for the spoon, throwing some eyeballs on the floor.

Alex stood beside the door and watched the entire scene. Her right arm, rotten up to the shoulder, burned as if on fire, and her bones cracked menacingly at every movement. Splinters of the shattering bones pierced her perpetually healing flesh and sent sharp, intense jolts of electricity straight to her brain.

If that wasn't enough, the muscles of her left hand were twitching on their own since the spell she had to use on Van Vloed. Sure, she could have diverted the dissonance to Daniel, but he was one of the few she trusted, and Van Vloed wouldn't have survived both the enchantment and its recoil. But with Sophia in such a state, this entire situation was going south. Daniel would become useless, and Sophia, their most powerful ally, was out of her mind. Alex could patch her up again, perhaps, but what would be the consequences on whoever they'd use as an effigy?

"Poor Daniel," Ioan said next to Alex's ear. She had missed his arrival. "It must be a nightmare to him. And yeah, she is having a worse time than he is," he continued, replying to a remark she didn't have the time to think of. Was he reading her mind now? Could he do it?

"Any great idea on how to get her back together?" Alex asked.

"Great?" Ioan said. "Not sure what I have is much better than using your magick. Can you see her core soul?"

"Barely." Thousands of strands crossed Sophia's body, but

the knot in the center was almost invisible, and what was still there was faint and flaked. "She must have burned it away. I can't fix her without killing a few effigies."

"That's what I thought."

"Help her!" Daniel cried, while battling to keep Sophia still. "Stop chitchatting and help her. Aren't you two supposed to be impressive?"

"Son . . ." tried Ioan.

"Don't call me that." Daniel stopped him. "I'm not one of your children."

Ioan didn't reply but stood beside the witch, curling his lips.

"We are trying to help," Alex said. "But it's not so easy."

"Oh, is it not, Professor? Wanna lecture me now? What were you two doing while he forced her to marry him? Maybe I was distracted, but I didn't see any legend in action there, Winchester!"

Van Vloed chuckled, and Alex glanced at her, frowning.

"Where was my magick? Gone. I tried and tried. Every spell, but he didn't need to look at me to stop it."

Daniel bit his lip, glanced down at Sophia, and didn't reply.

"I know what it means to be powerless while they take someone you love away from you," Ioan said. "You might not like me right now, but I might have a way to save the one you love."

"A way?" Daniel said, wide-eyed. "Whatever it is, let's do it. Why are we wasting time?"

"Because I want to make sure you understand we will have to pay a price."

"I'm ready to do anything," Daniel said before Ioan could finish.

"We both understand, but I'm not sure Sophia would be happy about it."

Daniel peered at Sophia, who cried and struggled to reach for the spoon. "She'll understand."

Ioan sighed. "Fine, hear me out, then. Before the School of Winchester came into the picture, blood magic rituals were all immortals could do to tap into the divine waters. It's not even close to their magick, more like formulas and recipes, but it works if one follows the rites to the letter. One ritual was the blood sacrament. My brothers used it when we needed to strengthen our lines. It allowed them to share their gifts by sharing their souls and inner wolves. A matrimony of sorts."

"Ioan," Alex said, stepping in front of the old man. Daniel would not have listened to any reason, but Ioan might. "She doesn't have a soul. I don't even understand how she functions. They'll both have to live with one, and it might not be enough to keep their wolves at bay."

"You are right, as always. That is the risk I want Daniel to consider."

"I'm fine with everything," Daniel said. "Let's get it done."

"Ioan, you have seen how weak his control of the wolf is. We will lose him as well, and it might not even work."

Daniel pleaded from behind her back. "We have to try. Alex, you must understand. We have to."

Ioan remained silent. The bluish light that illuminated the room made him look even older than usual.

"Fine," Alex said. "Let's use someone else. Let it be me. I'm the one with the best control of the wolf." As she said it, she questioned herself. After all, it was her fault.

If only she hadn't asked all of them to follow through with whatever Demeure was doing, perhaps they could have saved Sophia. But why did she care so much? It must have been because they needed Daniel's and Sophia's help too. To get out of the box, they needed everybody. Why else? She was only being wise, as always.

"Noble of you," Ioan said. "But it would not work. There needs to be a preexisting bond, and those two clearly care about each other."

"What about Van Vloed then?" Alex asked.

Her words startled Van Vloed, who had been enjoying the show in silence. "Me?" she asked.

"Yes, you. You and Sophia share a bond with a spell already."

"That would work," Ioan said, nodding.

But Daniel stopped them. "No, it wouldn't. I won't let you. For God's sake, her family tortured Sophia for over twenty years, and you want to bind them together forever?"

Even Alex could not contradict him. It might have been the most convenient thing to do, but for sure, it would have been worse than death for Sophia.

"Settled," Daniel said. "What do we need to do?"

"By the book, the two sides will pour their blood and share it while a priest blesses their union. Both will have to carry offerings."

"What offerings?" Alex asked.

"The most usual would be the firstborn within their lines."

"Nice," Alex said, nodding. "Let's forget what I think about it, but I'm sure neither of them has one of those."

Ioan smiled. "I don't think it will be necessary in their case. Sophia has burned most of her soul to save Daniel. And he will do the same for her. I think both have brought enough for it to work."

"And you are positive this worked on someone who is not a Strigoi?"

Ioan's lips curled as he shook his head. "I'm quite certain of the opposite. But this is where you enter the picture." He smiled again.

Alex's mouth opened and closed, but she didn't produce a question.

"Doesn't your school pride itself on changing the rules of the game? Well, that's all you need to do here."

"What you are asking is impossible. With magick I can change how the agreement works, but you are asking me to change magick itself. It would be like trying not only to change the rules but the way we agree on the rules in the first place."

"I guess this is a no then," Ioan said.

Perhaps this is what Alex needed as well. If she pulled this off, she was sure she could also do something to overpower Demeure. "I'll give it a shot, but I can't guarantee anything."

Daniel exhaled as if he had kept his lungs full for a while and raised his sleeves. "Let's do it then. How much blood do you need?"

By the time they finished preparing the ritual, Hermann and Celeste had arrived. Roman and Leto were nowhere to be found. The nun was meeker and hollower than usual. Them filling her in about the ritual didn't improve her looks. Even Hermann's smugness had washed away, and he kept glancing at Alex, only to avert his eyes whenever she turned in his direction.

The witch hoped he didn't have any weird ideas in mind. She didn't need to deal with him too.

They had to manage with a cooking knife and a plate for soup, which they filled to the brim, as Ioan requested, with Daniel's and Sophia's blood. Sophia was so depleted by her previous feat at carving out her own eyes that she couldn't heal anymore and Alex had to use magick to treat her wounds.

Luckily, Van Vloed provided a couple of rats she had found within the walls using her gift. The thought of this nasty woman having eyes and hands everywhere somehow didn't reassure Alex. At least she could use the rats to absorb the dissonance resulting from her healing Sophia's eye and hand.

In the meantime, Ioan cut the skin of his right thumb and poured a few drops of his own blood into the mixture made of Daniel's and Sophia's. Using the side of the knife, he snapped the fingernail off the same finger and dropped it in the mixture as well. Oddly for an immortal, the wound didn't heal itself right away.

"Is something stopping you from healing?" Alex asked.

"It is an offering. It will heal only if it is accepted."

Alex leaned to look at the nail floating in the blood and shook her head in disgust. "Oh, I hate blood magic so much."

Ioan ignored her remark and drowned his wounded finger in the blood. He moved the liquid as a cook would stir a soup and spoke, almost yelling, in a language that reminded Alex of a dog barking. As he pulled the finger back out, his thumb had healed. "Offer accepted," he said. "Now the couple must drink."

While they prepared the draught, Sophia sat on her chair, and whenever Daniel wasn't too busy with the ritual, he would stay with her, stroking her hair or just talking to her—the rest of the time Celeste kept her company. Sophia was quiet, breathing with one cheek pressed against the table and drooling on its wood.

During the entire process, she followed the others as they hurried to complete the ritual as fast as possible. Alex glanced at her once or twice and wondered if they were doing her right by not letting her die. Perhaps it would have been the most respectful thing to do. She had lived many more years than she would have wanted.

Getting Sophia to drink the potion was a whole other story. The moment Daniel drank his half and Ioan offered her the bowl, she straightened on the chair and pushed the table with one hand. With the other, she tried to push the bowl away from Ioan's hands and failed only narrowly.

"No!" she screamed and stood up. She would have made it to the door if Daniel and Van Vloed, in an unusual collaboration, hadn't caught up with her and wrestled her back.

"I'm here," Daniel said in her ear in a meager attempt to

convince her that whatever this was it was for her own good. "Drink it. Would you do it for me?"

Sophia's eyes, desperate, searched for something in him first, then in the others. It wasn't clear if she was looking for an ally or for the weak link among those blocking her escape. "Please, I can't. Not again. I don't want to," she screamed. And despite Daniel and Van Vloed trying to keep her still, she kicked the table with such fury it rocked from one side to the other.

"What is she talking about?" Celeste asked, coming to help Daniel and Van Vloed.

"She is delirious," Alex said. "I'm not surprised considering everything she's been through." But she wasn't too sure herself. Sophia sounded insane by all means, but Alex couldn't wash away the idea that perhaps she was seeing something in the network, a glimpse of what was to come that no other could. And even if that wasn't the case, who were they to decide for her that she had to live? Suddenly, something heavy fell behind her. She must have been inside her own head for far too long.

"Now that is pretty interesting," she heard Van Vloed say.

She was talking to Celeste. The other didn't reply, but Sophia was now sitting back on her chair, her face looking up at the ceiling, saliva drooling from her mouth, and fast asleep.

"What did you do?" Daniel asked, pushing Van Vloed out of his way.

"She is asleep," said the nun. "I quieted her heart."

Daniel frowned, but hugged Sophia to his chest and cleaned her mouth with one sleeve. He then tried and failed to place her on the chair in an upright position and even attempted to sort her messy hair.

Alex looked away. "Shouldn't we move on?" she called without glancing at them. "I thought I was to do the hard work here."

"The witch is right, son," Ioan said, and handed the concoction over to Daniel. "It might be better if you do it, but make sure you get her to drink a couple of mouthfuls."

Daniel took the bowl from Ioan's hands, his own ones shaking, and poured some liquid into Sophia's mouth while keeping her head up and wiping the spillage off her face. A tear came down his cheeks and once again Alex had to turn away. The man had spent all his life searching for her, just so it would turn out like this?

"It should be enough," Ioan said. "The potion is doing its work. Witch, do you see the strands growing in strength? Alex?"

Alex had heard him, but something stopped her from looking away from Daniel and Sophia.

"Hey," Celeste called, touching her on one arm.

"Your time to shine," Van Vloed said to a startled Alex.

"The strands, do you see them?" Ioan was louder this time. There was a new excitement in his voice. Right then, he didn't look too different from the wizards of the School, discovering new frontiers. But for once, to her, it wasn't the right thing to do at all. All of it was so unfair. To Sophia, covered in sweat, vomit, and blood, to Daniel, who had lost her only to find her broken, and to the little girl in her dream.

But she did it, anyway. The strands carved a way to her own core soul, and she tasted once again the pleasure of the connection to the network. She was mortal again, connected to everyone and everything, ready to perform the art.

She studied Sophia. The strands connected, knotting and tightening around the woman's soul. They vibrated and linked with everything else. There were so many. Alex could not only see them but hear them and feel them on her skin. It was like music, with the sight it always was, but this time it was different.

Sophia's and Daniel's souls moved at the same rhythm, attempting to coordinate and entangle. Daniel's soul rotated, quivered, and formed arms of tellur that moved in the sea of the quintessential field to reach the last remaining ember of Sophia's soul. But as they formed, they failed at reaching the other side before Daniel's soul reabsorbed them. That was what she had to change.

Magick had always been easy for her. While the other students around her struggled, she performed miracles not even her teachers could. For the others, magick was an effort. For her it was always like a dance, or like swimming in a river's water while deflecting its currents. Not a clash of tides but flows moving and weaving through each other.

Yet this time was different. It wasn't reality she was trying to change. It was magick itself, and for once she didn't even know where to start. She tried to picture what she wanted. The strands of Daniel's soul joined Sophia's in her own mind. She sent this message through the network, to the Kia, but nothing happened.

Again and again she tried, and every time the network received her message and ignored it.

She glanced at the others, their figures hidden by the strands still floating in front of her eyes. "It doesn't work." She made sure not to look Daniel in the eyes as she spoke.

"I think I can help," Celeste said, and stepped closer to her. Nothing was meek about her for once.

"How can you?"

Celeste offered her both hands. "Your heart is not in the right place. I can fix it. Take my hands. I promise it won't hurt."

Alex's hands flinched, but stayed at her side as she studied Celeste in silence.

"Witch, what do we have to lose?" Ioan said.

Alex stared at Celeste's hands for another moment, then grabbed them in hers. A shock starting from her fingers traversed her entire body. Every light in the room shone brighter before everything around her went dark. Then a tiny light, a flame like that of a candle, lit up in the darkness. The light spoke with the voice of a man.

"Miss Dryden," Celeste said, as Alex opened her eyes. "What did you see?"

"A light," Alex said. "A voice. It said to fight because if I fight for something bigger than myself, nothing will ever make me small again."

"What does it mean?" Daniel asked.

Ioan, next to him, was frowning.

Alex focused on the network again. Perhaps the voice was right. For once, she should do what was right for someone else. For once, it wasn't about surviving, nor punishing someone, nor winning a battle, but just doing the right thing. Righting a wrong. Whoever had made the rules, whether it was the Kia, the Idea of God, or the Creators, none of them cared. They were too small, too insignificant to care.

But a few gods who were too small to care would not stop her. She closed her eyes, and with her mind, she reached a place within herself. There, shaking and spinning, was her own core soul, the thing that made her who she was. Strands departed from it in every direction, connecting her to everything else in the universe, making her mortal, but giving her access to magick.

As her thought reached it, it struggled and convulsed, breaking its precise rhythm. As a circle came to her mind, ripples appeared on its surface, which would have been that of a perfect, translucent sphere otherwise. The struggle continued until the watery surface broke and a small drop, like a tear, separated from it and vaporized into nothingness. She felt a pain she had never felt before, not even the first time she had used the circle magick. She could not fathom how Sophia had endured this over and over for years.

Once again, she sent her message up to the Kia, amplified so loud by her sacrifice, the entire network vibrated with it.

Nothing happened. It had been silly of her to hope otherwise and to waste a piece of her own soul on empty hope. But as she was about to shut her third eye, something in the surrounding network changed.

All the strands around her started shaking. Something big was coming from the unknown above. A thunderbolt of tellur came back down through the strands and struck her like lightning, and from her, it followed the network in all directions. No connection remained untouched by the storm. The entire agreement was changing, the rules were being rewritten. More than that, the network itself was changing. Strands detached and reattached elsewhere.

A buzzing sound stormed around her as this happened, but someone in that buzz, a voice, repeated something she didn't understand. She tried to focus on the voice but still couldn't grasp what it was saying. Then, slowly, every movement of the network followed the rhythm of the voice, but as soon as she blinked, her vision of the network and even the room in which she was with the others disappeared.

Under Alex's feet, not tiles anymore, but green, shiny stems of grass. A summer breeze reached her nostrils and ruffled her hair. An imperious sun shone on top of her, dominating a cloudless indigo sky. Grassy hills extended in all directions, the stems waving at the wind like a green ocean.

Someone spoke behind her. A woman, her voice like the buzzing she had heard a moment before coming to the place. She turned and behind her was a tree, a magnificent oak, so tall and old some of its branches grew not toward the sky but plummeted back down and ran over the grass. On the tree was a creature with the torso of a woman attached to the body of a spider. The woman said something, but all that came to Alex's ears was a buzz.

Three other figures stared at her from the shade of the tree. A long-legged bird with white plumage and a black face slept on the ground next to the tree. On one of the low branches sat a dog-faced baboon. Its tiny eyes studied Alex as it played with a wooden toy shaped like a crescent moon. Sitting on the grass near the tree was a little girl. She must have been around twelve, but something made her look different from any other twelve-year-old Alex had seen before.

The girl sat straight on the ground, her crossed legs hidden by a red and orange velvety dress. Her hair was white and voluminous and two serpent-shaped rings kept it together in two large braids that, like horns, sprouted from the top of her head and fell on her shoulders. At the end of each braid, she had attached two heavy-looking cylinders of gold that lay resting against her chest. A jewel, a crescent moon made of gold and sapphires, stood where the hair divided. Golden earrings covered in long feathers adorned her ears, as if she had wings on each side of her head. Her skin was shiny stone burned by the sun, her lips were plump, and her blue eyes stared straight at Alex. She was ancient beyond understanding.

Amid the noise made by the spider, the ancient girl spoke, for the first time in a language Alex understood. "I had lost hope, and yet you are here. We will write your name, but it's too early for you." As she said so, she closed her eyes, and so did the baboon and the bird.

All went dark again.

As Alex opened her eyes, she was back in the kitchen, staring at the strands of tellur floating around her. On each strand, something was forming, like letters that moved all over her own soul and flowed out from her across the entire network. She could read it, she was sure she could, but as she tried to pronounce it, her lips moved but she blabbered something that didn't sound like a word.

So, she tried again and again, but only sounds, every time different ones, came out of her mouth. It was the same the spider had muttered, and she understood what it was: her own true name.

"Alex?" Celeste asked, close to her face. "What did you just say?"

Alex jolted and stared at the young nun. "Nothing, I must have been dreaming."

In response, Celeste frowned.

"It can happen when you do complex magick," Alex added.

It was true, when doing magick, the network could sap into the magician's soul as much as the magician's identity spread through the network. Alex had seen people speaking in unknown tongues, others hallucinating, but never something this real, and it had never happened to her.

"Did it work?" Daniel asked.

Alex glanced again at Daniel and Sophia, and there it was, a full set of strands connecting their souls as they rotated and entangled.

"It did," Ioan said before she could answer, and in saying so, he smiled like a child.

Alex closed her third eye and disconnected from the network. As usual, all air departed from her lungs and a shadow of melancholy dropped over her. She was immortal again.

Her forehead was dripping, and her T-shirt was damp as well. Whatever she had done had taken a toll on her, but as she caught Daniel beaming and Sophia resting on the table, she couldn't resist breaking into a smile and raising a thumb.

Daniel jumped on her and squeezed her in a hug, sobbing too close to her ears.

At first, she thought of dodging him, but didn't. "Ahem . . ." she said, keeping both arms at her sides while Daniel wrapped them in his.

Daniel released her and stepped back. "I'm so sorry it came out like that. I just wanted to say thank you." His arms and legs were shaking.

"Not too hard after all," Alex said with dignity, and looked up at the ceiling. She pointed at his shaking limbs. "Can you keep up with your wolf?"

"I guess so," he said, shrugging.

"You must take this seriously," Ioan said. "Now you must do it for the sake of both of you. You've weakened the barrier that kept the wolf at bay so now, more than ever, you need to focus on guarding against it."

Daniel nodded without replying, as a toddler would do when dealing with a reprimanding mother.

"You are being too quiet, Witch," Hermann said, coming closer to her. "We are all still waiting for the instructions you were about to give us."

"I guess I was busy saving lives," she said, rubbed her eyes, and sighed. "But you are right, let's get back to business."

The others collected around her in a circle. Even Daniel, for the first time, left Sophia's side.

"I think I've got it at the end. Do you remember how we have one too many guests for the ritual and one less for the wedding? I couldn't understand how that would ever work, but there was only one way: the prince had a secret guest, here the whole time, invisible to our eyes. And Hermann confirmed my theory when he found his sire in Demeure's room. So, the only thing we need to find is the one guest who is not part of the ritual. There are two I suspected from the start." Alex scanned the room, and Van Vloed was nowhere to be seen. "Where is Van Vloed?"

"She was here until a minute ago," Daniel said. "But shouldn't your spell be binding her?"

"I had to put the spell down to work on you and Sophia. She can mean trouble—"

"Talking of me, Winchester?" Van Vloed asked, coming into the room. "Boy oh boy, be more trusting of the people you work with!"

Leto walked in just behind her, beaming at Alex so much his eyes were closed. With one hand he massaged his neck, while with the other he waved a salute to the room.

Alex frowned. Leto was the last person she wanted to be there, given the topic of the conversation.

"Where the hell were you?" Hermann said, getting close to Van Vloed.

Van Vloed shrugged and glanced at the others. "Just checking on the big guy. I'd rather not have a dog rampaging around. I also found this one." She nodded toward Leto.

"Roman?" Celeste said, ignoring Leto and pushing her way to Van Vloed. "Where is he? Is he all right?"

"Sister, you've gotten too attached to that dog. You really want a puppy, do you?" Van Vloed said and looked around for laughs, but no one laughed. "Anyhow, he is in the church. He has been there for hours, acting all high and mighty. He'll join us for the last battle, he said, whatever that means."

Hermann rolled his eyes and turned to Alex. "What were you saying about the ritual and your suspects?"

Alex was startled. "My suspects," she said, clearing her voice, "we'll go back to that. For now, we must find a way to get out of here, and in the meantime, we need to keep Sophia safe."

"Are you planning to use her as the prince does?" Van Vloed asked, glancing in Daniel's direction.

Daniel huffed and didn't reply. His face was pale and covered in sweat.

Alex looked at Van Vloed sideways. "Not if I can avoid it. I'd rather not channel any tellur through her with things standing as they are. For now, you all make sure you keep Sophia safe and away from Demeure. Also, someone help Roman think straight. We will need him. He might be the best option we have if it comes to a fight over who keeps Sophia."

Leto frowned, tilted his head, and stared straight at Alex. "Why is she so important, if I may ask?" he asked.

Alex bit her lip. "He went out of his way to take her hostage and marry her. He might still need her to complete his ritual, so I'd rather keep her away from him. Perhaps we can delay whatever he plans to do, at least until we have a way out."

Hearing Alex's words, Leto smiled again.

His smile made her inner wolf wince.

Alex barely heard Leto's first footstep as he moved and glimpsed only a shadow passing through the room.

In the time it took Alex to realize he had moved, Leto had crossed the whole room and was now standing behind a sleeping Sophia. "You think too much," he said. "The prince needs this woman, right? It's an easy problem to solve." As he said so, he raised Sophia's head by her hair.

Alex and Daniel both ran to reach him, but they didn't make it in time. In fact, with his free hand, Leto had grabbed Sophia's throat and ripped it off her neck. "Problem solved," he said. The throbs of blood coming out of Sophia's neck and the loud crash of her lifeless head falling and smashing against the table muffled his voice.

Daniel reached Sophia and ignored the man. "No, no, no, no," he repeated as he tried to stop the blood from flowing out with his bare hands. "Help her," Daniel said, his eyes full of tears as he stared at Alex. "Help her, please. You can, right?"

His voice shook Alex. She stayed still, stuck, looking at Leto for a few seconds. "I can't. I'm so sorry, but she is dead already." She tried to speak as flatly as she could, hoping Daniel wouldn't do anything crazy or attack Leto, otherwise he would die.

"You are lying," Daniel said. "You saved her once. Do it

again." He was shaking more than before, and he tried to stop the bleeding only to get soaked in blood. "She will help you," he said in Sophia's ears. "She is lying, and she'll come here to help you."

Celeste fell on her knees and started praying. The others, like Alex was doing, stood in silence, waiting for Leto's next move. Only Ioan didn't care about the dandy and got closer to Daniel. "She is gone, son," Ioan said, putting one hand on Daniel's shoulders. "I'm sorry, but you must let her go."

"But you can help her. I know you can. Use your blood to wake her up."

Ioan tightened his grip on Daniel's shoulder. "I can't revive the dead, and neither can the witch."

Daniel didn't answer. He hugged Sophia's hanging head to his chest, took as much air into his lungs as possible, and fell to sit on the ground, dragging Sophia's dead body with him.

Leto, towering over him, didn't flinch.

"Leave now," Ioan said to Leto, and at that moment, his wolf was as imposing, if not more so, than the dandy's.

Leto raised both hands. "Okay, I was trying to help, but if you don't want me here, I'll leave. Only make sure you call me before you make any move on the old prince."

Nobody answered.

The dandy ambled toward the door. Alex and the others kept their eyes on him the whole time. Only Celeste and Daniel ignored him. Celeste kept praying under her breath and Daniel sat on the ground, hugging Sophia's dead body.

Leto's otherwise perfect gray pinstripe suit was stained all over by speckles of Sophia's blood. On his face were no hints of emotion.

Alex barely kept her cool as he passed near her. She would have loved to punch him, but that might have been a bad idea with no preparation. Leto was fast, way too fast. And considering how quickly Sophia, an immortal, bled out once he had wounded her, he must have had some other secret up his sleeve.

So, as he had come into the room, Leto had disappeared from it again, having stolen every hope Alex had given her companions. But before she could catch a break, Daniel growled behind her. She turned, and Sophia was lying on the ground. Daniel was crouched close to her with a pool of blood at his feet. The skin on his face stretched and his jawbone was growing and elongating. Blood seeped out around his eyes.

"He is turning!" Ioan bellowed.

She could not check on the others. She tried to react, but Daniel had already leaped like a dog. As he moved, his fingers detached from his hands and dropped on the ground—talons emerged from where his knuckles had been. He leaped again. He was fast, almost as fast as Leto, and he was moving straight in her direction. Alex prepared for the impact as she stared at Daniel running toward her.

New eyes, of a golden yellow, emerged from underneath Daniel's usual gray ones. The skin on his face ripped and a thick black fur emerged from under the cuts. As he leaped a third time, he should have been upon Alex, but he missed her by at least half a meter and crashed against the wall behind her.

Daniel's shirt was ripped off his chest and his arms were overgrown. His skin was torn, and pieces of flesh fell to the ground, splashing with a disgusting noise. More fur emerged from under the remaining pieces of his old skin, still stuck to his body.

But Daniel hadn't just crashed against the wall. Both his arms and head had passed through it and opened a large hole, and his upper torso had crossed to the other side. Daniel's fangs, coming out of his new wolf-like mouth, had taken a grip of Leto's neck and his talons were piercing both the dandy's shoulders.

Leto's blood painted Daniel's fur red, but the dandy's expression remained unfazed. It took him a split second to strike back. Leto's left hand pierced Daniel in the side of his chest. The wolf whined. His entire body flinched, but he didn't release his grip. The dandy pulled out his hand, and as he did so, blood burst out of the hole he had created—once again, way too much blood for a wound on an immortal body.

"No!" Alex yelled, her body covered in flickers of lightning and flares of tellur.

Leto's arm contracted, ready to strike, but his eyes, empty and emotionless, stared straight into Alex's. He hadn't moved yet when a cloud of smoke enveloped his raised arm and a hand emerged from the smoke holding him in place. The rest of Ioan emerged from the smoke.

"Stop," he said, and there were no traces of the usual kindness in his voice.

Leto shifted his eyes to the old man and smiled, but there wasn't a hint of mockery in him. It was the grin of someone who had been taught to smile on command and did so without knowing why. "I was defending myself, old one. Shouldn't I defend myself when someone attacks me?"

"He won't attack you anymore," said the Strigoi, and touched Daniel's forehead. The wolf lost his grip and slipped to the ground, fast asleep. "Now go, and this time walk quicker."

Leto's eyes rested on the old man. The dandy sighed, scratched his head, and smiled again. "I need a cleanup, I suppose," he said as the wounds on his neck and shoulders healed. "Make sure you keep this one locked up. I wouldn't want him to harm anyone else, or worse, get himself killed." He then turned his back and walked away. "Call me when you need me," he added, waving his hand, and then he disappeared into the corridor's darkness.

Alex couldn't stop staring at Daniel, or what remained of him on the ground. She glanced at Sophia, hoping she had found peace at last. She took a deep breath and squeezed her eyes shut. Then she studied the others as they moved around the room as well. Celeste was still sitting on the ground but was looking in Daniel's direction, her mouth open and her eyes set. Hermann couldn't stay put and moved around and around, massaging his eyes and temples.

"Witch," Ioan said in a tone that suggested he might have been calling for her way too many times. He pointed at the wound on Daniel's side, from where the stream of blood hadn't stopped flowing out. "Any way you can help with this one?"

Alex moved swiftly to get closer and to check if there was anything she could do. At first, it seemed like an ordinary wound, but it wasn't healing in the way a wound on an immortal body should. As she used the eye to look at it, everything became clearer. "It won't heal. We have to use magick. Leto has changed the way the healing process works. It must be a dark gift because the same happened with Sophia."

"So, not only is he fast but he can also wound us fatally, without effort?" Hermann asked. "Just when I thought the only issue was Demeure."

Alex reached for the cross-shaped pendant. "We are two people down, so we need to get to Roman before they outplay us."

As she was about to place the jewel on the wound, Ioan caught her arm. "Are you sure you want to burn one of those?"

"I'm impressed. It's the second time you've recognized a hermetic amulet," Alex said. "I have no choice unless someone else wants a painful, long-lasting wound. It doesn't matter, anyway. The damage is not too bad, so the amulet will still hold some power. You won't believe the mess I had to go through to build this one." It was awkward to converse with a Strigoi like two old friends.

"He is right," Van Vloed said. "Why waste power on a dog? He is a liability. We should finish him before he chews on one of us."

Alex tried to catch a glimpse of their expressions. Hermann averted his eyes and Celeste didn't speak. "I don't need to remind you that you are on borrowed time, Van Vloed. I also don't think it's wise to kill each other when the prince needs sacrifices."

Ioan smiled at Alex as she turned back to Daniel. "No need to puppy-eye me, old man. It's the practical thing to do." She placed the amulet on Daniel's wound. Her cross shone with a blazing blue light, and as the light dissipated, the skin had regrown over the wound.

When Alex was done, she stood back up and cleared her throat. "I guess I don't have to tell you anymore who my second suspect was. Each of you has secrets, but I can see the patterns at this point. We are all connected somehow. Remember what Sophia said? Demeure needs a circle of sacrifices. He doesn't just need anyone. He needs people connected to each other. Demeure is building a circle like the ones from the labyrinth. Not with letters this time, but with people.

"There must be a connection between me and the Strigoi. Don't ask, but I suspect there might be something more personal than tribal rivalry, but I'm not sure what it is yet. The same thing connects my ancestry to Hermann through his sire, Valentine. We all know what connected Daniel, Sophia, and Van Vloed, and it's clear as the sky Celeste has something going on with Roman if even Van Vloed has realized it."

The nun tried to protest, but Ioan talked over her. There was excitement in his voice. "It makes sense. There must be a link between me and Roman as well. The night they attacked my castle and took my daughter away, they had a Wurdulac with them. And the very same Valentine accompanied Demeure in the old days. She came with him to my castle the night before the attack and couldn't stop staring at my Mihaela."

As they heard the child's name, Alex's and Hermann's eyes met.

"As I was saying," Alex continued, "I suspected two people. One was Van Vloed, for obvious reasons." She glanced at Van Vloed, who gave a sign of agreement with her head and smiled. "But her history with Sophia connects well with Daniel, so I discarded it. So, the only remaining one was Leto. He even tried to use his charming gift on me not once but three times, and now, after his move, I consider my suspicion confirmed."

"It's nice to hear that you have an idea of what's going on," Hermann said, "but what do we do with the ritual?"

"Nothing, we stay the course. I haven't learned enough about the ritual to understand how to stop it. I don't even get why he hasn't killed us yet, but something tells me that if it was an option, Demeure would have done it already. There are two things we can do: escape and fight back. I think we should avoid the second option, and I believe I can use those circles to open a portal stable enough to send all of us out of this place if I spend some time experimenting."

"Sure thing," Hermann said. "But what if it comes to a fight?"

"It's likely we will all die. Demeure can stop both dark gifts and traditional magick from working, but that spell I did on Sophia gave me an idea. It might not kill him, but I can make him feel some pain."

"So, what do you suggest we do, boss?" Van Vloed asked without hiding her mockery.

But Ioan replied in her stead. "Celeste will take care of Sophia. The witch said the rest already. She needs time to prepare an escape plan and a secondary plan if it comes to it. So, I guess she'll be going to her room. Hermann, you and I can go the same way and lock Daniel in his room. It's close to Alex's so if Leto or Demeure try something she will know."

Alex looked at him wide-eyed. Was he giving her orders now?

She was about to complain when Ioan spoke again. "Alex, do you agree with this plan?"

"Uh . . . sure, it all sounds sensible," Alex said. "Also, Celeste, you want to go talk with him, I know, so please take Van Vloed with you and get Roman up to speed. I will meet you all at the church once everything is ready for our departure."

"What if Leto tries something on you while you are on your own? Shall I stay with you?" Hermann asked.

"No, you shouldn't," Alex said and talked with such speed Hermann raised an eyebrow. "I mean, I need to concentrate, and I won't be able to with someone around. I have something in mind for him if he dares attack me." She nodded at Ioan. "And I've prepared something else already in case anything happens to you all in the church."

It took little to carry Daniel up the stairs, thanks to the spell Alex had done to make him weigh less so Hermann could lift him on his own. In the meantime, she and Ioan walked in silence ahead of him.

"It still feels awkward," she said as they arrived in front of her room's door. Hermann was still dragging Daniel along the corridor.

"Which part of it?" the old man asked.

"The one where someone from the School and a Strigoi work together. I thought there was some law against it." Alex smiled, but she didn't find her own joke that funny.

"I'm old enough to understand when it is time to stop fighting, and I have the habit of getting attached to the youth."

She might have looked young, she thought, but she still had half a millennium weighing on her shoulders. Regardless, it didn't seem the time for any smart remarks. She scanned the corridor to see where Hermann was at. The room was narrow and long, and the hardwood was scratched here and there, just like the white plaster on the wall. Left and right, door after door after door.

At the other end of the corridor, Hermann still struggled. She felt guilty, but released the enchantment so he would struggle a bit more.

"You said you had a daughter. Shouldn't that be impossible?"

"You thought daughters were an impossible thing?" Ioan asked and grinned, but quickly turned serious again. "I know what you mean. It should not be possible, and in fact, it wasn't easy. But she was the closest thing to a daughter one like me can have."

"I'm sorry the School took her from you," was all Alex could reply. She wanted to ask more, but somehow the words didn't come out.

"Thanks," Ioan said. A faint smile appeared on his face. "She would have liked you, my little Mihaela. She was a bit like you. Always a smart answer to anything, and a bit of a witch herself."

"A witch?"

"Well, as much as a five-year-old can be, yes. She had her sight awakened before she could speak, maybe since birth. The Strigoi Lords thought she would be our weapon to win the war. The irony is we lost her to the very war she was supposed to end."

"Awakened from birth? A witch of such power? The School hasn't seen one since . . ." She prevented herself from saying too much. The School hadn't seen one like that since her. A thought struck her, but it was so far-fetched she let it go without entertaining the idea.

"What were you saying?"

"Oh, never mind. My head gets stuck on old stories, I guess." Alex gave him a faint smile, but Ioan gave her an unconvinced look in return.

Luckily, Hermann reached them before she could further embarrass herself. "Thanks for the help," he said, stopping in front of them. He was red in the face and the yellow light of the room shone on his sweat. "Whatever you did stopped working, and it isn't like I didn't try calling you."

"You are a big guy. You'll survive," Alex said to a frowning Hermann. "Now, get Daniel to his room and lock him in."

They dragged Daniel in. At last, Alex thought, Daniel was at peace with himself, much more than he had been since the first time she had met him in the church. In a world devoid of any hope for him to be with his Sophia, it wasn't so unbelievable he would want to turn into a beast. For people like him, unable to accept the wolf as a part of them, it was often easier to become the monster itself.

The three locked the door and Alex performed a spell to bind herself to it. If someone tried to open it or even get too close to it, she would sense it. She didn't really need the spell as Daniel's door was straight in front of hers, but it felt safer this way.

"I might bring him to the School once we are done here," she said as she completed her enchantment. "Maybe there is a way to bring him back to normal." Given the way Ioan avoided her eyes, he must have known how empty her words were. "I better prepare my spells, so I'll see you as soon as I'm done."

"Actually," Hermann said. "Can I have a word?"

Alex sighed and Ioan stopped on his heels. "Sure," she said, hoping this would be short.

Hermann glanced at Ioan as if the Strigoi could understand he was being stared at. "Alone?"

Ioan chuckled. "So much youth. I'd better be on my way to the church then. Reach us when you finish, you two." He walked away.

Hermann glanced back and forth from Ioan and Alex, and as the Strigoi disappeared in the shadows, he exhaled and spoke. "She wants you to understand that none of your plans are going to work."

"She?"

Hermann avoided her eyes. "Valentine."

"Your sire? Where is she? What does she know?"

"I told you. It doesn't matter where I am, she can always reach me in my head."

"Right. Tell her I won't die without putting up a fight. Whatever she thinks she knows, she forgot that a witch of the School is in the house."

Hermann mumbled something that Alex didn't understand. His conversation with himself was stressing him, so much so that he had to clasp his own hands to stop them from moving.

Alex waited for him to complete the debate with his inner voices with more patience than she believed herself capable of.

Hermann sighed and spoke again. "I understand your pride, and you deserve to be proud," he said. His voice was different. An echo of clamoring metal came out of it. "But Arnaud is a law of the universe—a constant. One like you can't kill him."

"I've changed many of those laws myself."

A bitter smile opened on Hermann's face. "Only the ones who wear a crown, the Eldest Lords, can kill those like us. It is the shackle of eternity only the Eldest Lords and the one you call Demeure can shatter, and the shackle is a law of our Father. It has existed since before the agreement."

"You saw what I did in the kitchen."

Hermann pondered her words before speaking. "I'm not sure what you did. I wouldn't call that fluke a success against him. He has invented any magick you have ever used."

"Who are you worried about? Valentine Duchamp, or whatever your name is, are you worried for me or for him, huh? What side are you on?"

"I'm not on any side. Those like us, who wear the shackle, can't harm those like you. This also is a law of our Father. And that ritual he is preparing, unless you have given up on your own life, he will want to keep you alive. Let me talk to him. I can make him think straight and you'll all be saved. If you move on with your plans, you'll anger him more." As he said so, Hermann took a step away from Alex, ready to depart.

"I saw you talking to him in my vision. You weren't too good at it."

"You don't know what you saw," Hermann said, turning his back to her and moving another step along the corridor.

"Hey," Alex called him back. "You think it's my fault for not knowing it?"

The words had some effect on Hermann, and he stopped.

"Is the Strigoi who I think he is?" Alex asked.

Hermann sighed. "You are still too smart for your own good. It is remarkable considering how the wizards played with your mind." As he spoke, Hermann took a few steps away once again. "Make your choices wisely from now on."

Alex's stomach twitched. As she stared at Hermann's shoulders, all she could see was the shadow of Valentine. The witch's fists clenched on their own. "I'll kill you both," she muttered. "You and that bastard, I'll kill you both." But her anger went to waste as Hermann disappeared into the shadows.

The nun sensed Van Vloed's eyes on her neck. She tried to ignore the chilling sensation and kept praying over Sophia's body. The others had left her corpse on the wooden table in the kitchen, covered with a white tablecloth. The least Celeste could do at this point was to give her the Last Rites so she would rest with God.

"Do you need to do all that?" Van Vloed's voice asked from behind her.

Celeste tried to restrain herself from answering. "You don't care, do you?"

"Well, I will be wherever she is in a few hours, so I'm sorry, but no, I don't feel compelled to pity anyone." Van Vloed's voice didn't sound resigned but relieved.

"A woman is dead and one of them has turned. This isn't the way it was supposed to go," the nun said, and kept her palms against each other as she knelt by Sophia's body. She then crossed herself and stood.

Van Vloed frowned and grinned. "Did you have better expectations?"

"He never said this would turn into a massacre."

"Really? I remember you knew about me being supposed to die from the very beginning. You didn't seem to care too much about it!"

Celeste bit her lip. "It's different."

Van Vloed roared into a laugh. "Nice to hear that my departure from this world doesn't bother you."

"You chose it. He asked you, and you agreed with him it was the best for you. I tried to convince you otherwise, didn't I? So I'm not sure why you are fishing for pity now."

Van Vloed chuckled. "I didn't know I would end up fishing for pity either. You don't die every day, I guess."

"I'll say my prayers for you as well, if that's what you are asking."

Van Vloed smiled. For the first time, Celeste thought it was an honest smile. "What about your mother? Did you get her out of that American and talk to her?" Van Vloed asked.

Celeste shook her head and shrugged. "I tried, but it didn't work out the way I would have expected. She stayed hidden within him."

"So, what are you still doing here?" Van Vloed's eyes glanced from the nun to the door and back. "You are one of those things, right? Why bother with us?"

"Well, he made it pretty clear I'm a half-breed, and he cares about me only to the point my mother does. I guess I'm on the chopping block as much as the rest of these people. What about you? I've seen you helping them. Actually helping them. It was you drawing those symbols on the invites. Are you just trying to muddy the waters?"

Van Vloed made a theatrically shocked face and burst into laughter again. "Can't a woman have some fun before she dies? For all I know, if Demeure kicks the bucket, I might come out of this alive."

"And you haven't switched sides entirely because he would have just killed you on the spot. You having accepted his proposal would make it work, anyhow. Am I right?"

Van Vloed pointed her right index finger at the nun. "You are spot on. I guess that so much plotting in the shadows is making you grow into one of us."

"I don't think so. You all like to blame it on inner wolves or demons, but whatever you all have become is on you. I won't end as you did."

Van Vloed had kneeled close to the table and taken an eyeball that Sophia had thrown on the ground. She studied it, poked it with one finger, and licked it quickly. "You helped them too," Van Vloed said, and she put the eye on the table, pointing it toward Celeste. "You gave the witch some of your power. He won't be pleased."

"I didn't give her any power. I'm not sure why, but she had it in her already. All I did was help her take it out."

"Yeah, yeah," Van Vloed said, waving one hand in the air. "The witch is one thing. But you sure have taken a liking to the big man," she added with a nasty smile on her face again. "I hadn't seen that in you."

Van Vloed could think whatever she wanted, but Celeste for sure didn't want her to know what she had discovered about Roman. "Funny," Celeste said, eyeing Van Vloed and frowning. "You are a comedian. I'll take my leave now. I want to make sure I get Roman up to speed before it's too late."

Van Vloed snorted.

"Feel free to stay here," Celeste said. She was about to walk away, but then heard Van Vloed fumbling with the utensils in the kitchen. "What are you doing?" she asked, and turned around to see what Van Vloed was up to.

Van Vloed stood near the table, messing with the bowl that Ioan, Daniel, Sophia, and Alex had used for the ritual. She focused on getting some remaining liquid into a vial. "What?" Van Vloed asked as she realized she was being stared at. "I always go around with some of these," she said, and shook the bottle. "It's a quirk of my profession."

"But what on earth are you doing?"

"I'm getting some of this juice out," Van Vloed said, shrugging. "There's blood from the Scarlet Woman here, and both a Strigoi and a Winchester witch have blessed it. I bet I can concoct something powerful with this, maybe even using Sophia's power in the same way the prince does."

"Why do you have to be like this?" Celeste asked, her face hot. "You almost seemed human a second ago. I'm wasting my time. I hope I don't see you on the other side."

"Hey," Van Vloed said while screwing a cork into the bottle. "You know what? I don't need it. I'll probably be dead before I can use it, anyhow. You take it." Her left arm offered the bottle to the nun.

"Why would I want it? I don't need that kind of power."

"You don't . . ." Van Vloed laughed. "What are you talking about? Who doesn't? Have you seen this place? Your life was garbage, mine too. It is not just this room. This whole fucking planet, the entire universe was built to torture us, and you tell me you don't need power?" Her laugh was maniacal and her face furious.

"This is our playground to show our father we are worthy of his love. Justice will be given at the end for all the suffering of these innocents."

Van Vloed kept laughing, louder and louder. "Oh my God,

you keep repeating this stuff, but not even you believe it anymore. Justice, you say? My brother died and I have to die so he can live? That random crap like this happens means there is no justice. Innocent people suffer! Isn't that enough to say that innocence isn't worth it? Your entire life is a joke and you don't even understand it."

Celeste shook her head and turned away. "I've had enough. I'm going."

Van Vloed dropped the bowl on the floor. The cracking of the porcelain drove a shiver up the nun's spine, and as she stopped, Van Vloed leaped to reach her and grabbed her by one arm, the vial still in her hands.

"Leave me!" Celeste yelled.

"You take this," Van Vloed said one inch from her face. Van Vloed's breath warmed the skin of her nose. "You take it as my dying present." She then slipped the bottle into Celeste's pocket, released her arm, and smiled again. "Go now, hurry. Your lover awaits you. I'll go my way and take at least one win for myself before my unavoidable demise."

Van Vloed had gone insane, more than she had thought, but she didn't have time to mess with her now. Celeste gave her a nasty look and left the room. Outside the door was Guillaume, a mop in his right hand and a bucket in his left, ready to come into the kitchen and clean. His expression was as blank as usual. The death, the body parts, the blood, it was all normal to him. A deep sense of disgust had found a place in the nun's stomach as she walked toward the church.

Once the nun arrived in the church, she found it now looking like a real one. With all that had happened during the wedding, only now she realized Demeure had rearranged the place since their first visit.

An altar, absent when they had arrived, was now sitting a few meters from where she entered—the small door communicating with the house. She remembered herself standing behind that altar a couple of hours before and making Sophia and Demeure husband and wife.

The benches where all the others had been sitting during the ceremony were empty and the place smelled of burned wax and incense. There was no trace of the flowery flavor that burst through her brain during the ceremony.

The light of the candles was dim, much dimmer than it was during the wedding. She knew the sparking light she had seen on both previous occasions was just one of Demeure's illusions, but knowing it did nothing else beside making her notice how insufficient the few candles were at illuminating the place. Those few floating fires created oblong shadows against the walls that turned the place gloomy.

Sitting alone on one bench was Roman. The man was so big she could not believe he fit on such a tiny seat. His eyes were closed, and his hands, one wrapped in the other, touched his forehead. He didn't move or speak at all.

The nun thought at length about how to start a conversation but failed at deciding anything that made any sense. She resolved that being direct would do. "I've seen your letter," she said, reaching the altar but not moving farther. "I know who you are."

Roman didn't give any sign he had heard her speaking.

"I mean, who you are to me."

Again, nothing came from the man.

The nun moved another step forward in Roman's direction. "I've read the letters. You haven't forgotten. You kept searching for all these years," she said, but only silence came from him. "Do you even hear me?"

Roman let out a sigh and opened his eyes. "I don't know what you are talking about."

She had rushed it. Of course, he didn't understand. "Listen, I appreciate you are preparing yourself for your last fight, but there is no need."

The man's lips curled for an instant, then he let out another deep breath and closed his eyes. "Leave me alone. I don't have time for this."

"Time for this . . ." repeated Celeste under her breath. Her mouth hung open while she was thinking of what she could say to convince the man that dying there wasn't worth it. "Listen, I can get you out of here. Safe and sound and far away from Demeure. I have such power. Then we will think about the rest."

Roman opened his eyes again, his gaze piercing her. "What about the others?"

"The others? We can't carry the others. He would be too angry. But you and I, I've got at least that much power."

"Thanks," he said. "I'm not interested."

"How could you not be interested? I'm trying to save your life!" She raised her voice. Blood burned under the skin of her face.

"Why don't you ask the witch or the old man?" Roman said. "They are more useful than I am. Now, please leave."

Insane, all of them. There wasn't one of them who behaved rationally. Yet this one, this one at least, she wanted to save. He was her brother.

"Why don't I save the witch? Why not the old man, you ask? It is because of you, brother."

Roman eyes twitched, but he didn't open them, nor did he move one inch.

"My name is not Celeste Moreau. My name is Azurine." She had said it. Now Roman would understand he was in front of the sister that, for centuries, he had been searching for. A family, the same thing Celeste had searched.

Again, Roman didn't move, but breathed heavily and stayed silent for a few moments, his hands still clenched in prayer. "I know no one by that name. Leave or be quiet while I pray for my father to save my soul."

Celeste's legs trembled under her own weight. She stumbled back a couple of steps, still looking at where Roman sat. What about the letters? Did it all mean nothing to him?

She would have jumped on him, struck him until he was dead. All she wanted was to see him—no, all of them—die. Her heart still beating in her throat, she walked back enough that she hit the altar. She slid to sit on the ground.

All that spite and hate, and she couldn't even blame wolves or demons as the others did. She got up and rushed out of the door back into the house. Demeure had told her he had a point to make. He had never told her what that point was, but now, at last, she understood.

21

THE GREATEST WITCH OF ALL

Evidence S-0047 to the investigation I-7242
E-mail Attachment, Marcel Fontaine to Daniel Cortese—data
collected on Ioniță Sturdza

Name: Ioniță Sturdza
Affiliation: None
Aliases: None
Years active: Unknown
Threat Level: High
Notes: The subject is part of an ancient line of immortals. He might not click well with Miss Dryden, as their respective organizations had disagreements in the past (please see the document attached on historical notes). The Shadows alluded to some awful stories about this one. Children disappear when he is around. See the article below.

WANTED.
50,000 Fr (fifty thousand) reward for MISSING PERSONS.
FIVE CHILDREN—brothers and sisters.
Kidnapped, possibly murdered. Mysteriously disappeared.

Missing since December 1931.

Mr. and Mrs. Francis Berger of Batignolles, Paris, offer 50,000 Fr REWARD.

For any information leading to the whereabouts of the five missing children, or even only one missing child, or confirmation of the location of their dead bodies.

An assaulter killed, likely by suffocation, their parents, Raphael and Simone Berger. No bones or identification or any other marking relating to the five children were found in the victims' house. The grandparents persist in their refusal to believe the children died. No evidence or human bodies have been found in Batignolles nor in the broader area of Paris.

To all law enforcement, please be on the alert for the below five missing children who disappeared on December 25, 1931.

If you are in possession of any information regarding the five missing children named Gabriel, Adam, Ines, Juliette, and Jeanne—Berger family—please communicate with the undersigned Jean-Louis Charpentier.

Alex opened her eyes and struggled with adjusting herself to the pale light of her room. She had gotten used to the buzzing of the portal behind her and could barely hear it now.

With her hands still shaking, she took the salad bowl in front of her to find her hook-shaped pendant, her weapon of last resort. Aside from the talisman, nothing else was in the bowl. If she needed any proof that the ritual had worked, that was it. All the blood she had spilled had vanished. The old man would have said that the offering had been accepted, but she knew better.

Alex shivered as the symbols she had etched over her entire body started to disappear. She wondered whether the cold came from the copious blood loss, having burned a good chunk of her soul, or from having stayed seated still, naked, and in a half-lotus position for at least one hour. Her sore legs and abs suggested it might be the third.

At first, the jewel didn't seem changed at all, but the flow of tellur in and around it had changed. She still felt it, even without using her sight. Just like with Sophia, she had combined her own magick, the Strigoi's blood magic, and the knowledge of the circles she had found in the tomb. To think that she hadn't even known those circles existed and was now sitting at the center of one.

For the first time, she understood it all, a unified theory of magick, beyond anything she or the council had ever hypothesized. The School would hail her as a hero. Yet she didn't care about the council, the School, or any of it. Perhaps, like Sophia, she had burned away too much of her soul. All she could think about was that old man, the Strigoi, and the long chat she needed to have with him as soon as they were out of there.

As Alex was lost in this train of thought, a phone rang. She didn't recognize the ringtone. Her phone sat on the bed, no light or sound coming from it. The sound came instead from the pile of clothes she had left on the chair beside the desk. Alex stood up and almost fell back down, her legs trembling and her head spinning. It took her a second or two to regain the command of her eyes.

In the meantime, the mysterious phone kept beeping from under her sweater. Someone had a lot to say and must have been convinced that doing so with a long sequence of messages was a good idea.

Alex rummaged through the clothes, throwing some of them on the ground. At last, she found a phone in one of her sweater's pockets. She didn't recognize it at first, but then she realized it was Daniel's phone. She must have pocketed it when he had given it to her during Van Vloed's questioning.

Someone, a certain Marcel, was sending tons of messages. The witch went through the last ones. This Marcel had been writing a single word on each message to compose a sentence. *"You know I don't get bored by this shit. You better give me a sign or your phone will keep ringing all night."*

He must have been an idiot. *"Please, stop,"* she sent back.

"FUCK YOU," arrived less than a second later.

She looked at the phone in disbelief.

Another message arrived. *"I almost died to gather intel for you, and you fucking shush me?"*

Intel? Had Daniel investigated something? He knew way too much about Van Vloed, but where had he found the contract?

She closed her third eye, and once again suffered the pain and cold of detaching from the network, but at least she could now focus on the messages.

Her eyes skimmed through the e-mails. There was something there from this same Marcel guy. The e-mail had an archive attached. It contained a file—a video recording—and a bunch of folders, each named after one guest.

Alex tapped on her folder. A single file there. There wasn't much on her except that one of her aliases was the *"Bitch."* She needed to have a quick chat with the Shadows if she ever came out of this place alive.

She then browsed the other folders. First, she tapped on Ioan's, curious about its content. Once again, only a small document and photos from some old newspaper articles.

The article was followed by the grainy black and white photos of five children, all aged between four and ten years old, and a blurb describing their habits, what they loved, and peculiar signs.

Alex hoped nothing in there was true. The man sure seemed better than that. She tried again to remember Mihaela, but couldn't. She even tried using magick, but nothing. Would it be possible to ever revive a memory that was lost in the first place?

What of her parents? Were they only an illusion planted in her head? Her face was wet. "So fucked up . . ." escaped from her mouth as she wiped her cheeks with the back of one hand.

She then tapped the other names. Nothing interesting, or at least nothing that she didn't already know. She left Van Vloed for last, as she was sure, having heard what Daniel knew, that whatever she would find there would interest her, and she was right.

The witch watched Marcel's videos of his visit to Van Vloed's house and the island of Griend. As she suspected, Van Vloed must have a new deal with Demeure to resurrect her brother. While Marcel still spoke in her ears, she looked at the photographs he had sent and found a letter Van Vloed had written to her brother. There was something familiar in that handwriting. She took Hermann's phone and compared it with one photo from his visit to Demeure's room.

"You know I can feel what the package feels, and I assure you, it isn't being moved around with the level of care it deserves. I was lucky enough to identify some places it has traveled through in my dreams, and it has been in the same place for far too long. Someone, a young mortal, is taking care of it. I think he cares more about the box than about the content. Knowing what I know about your little experiment, you should take a look at this handler. He may become useful. Call me. You have my number. You better hurry before it moves again. We have already wasted enough days just because you don't like me calling you on the phone."

At first, it sounded like a bunch of nonsense, but she could swear that it was Van Vloed's writing. There was also no doubt that if someone with such a connection with Sophia existed, it must be the damn redhead.

As she thought of Van Vloed, Alex shivered and rushed to put on some clothes. Was she watching her? Van Vloed might have taken a peek, and until this moment Alex would not have cared. Even if Van Vloed had seen part of the ritual, she wouldn't have been able to understand anything. Yet the thought of Van Vloed's eyes stuck in the wall and peeking at her was revolting.

Evidence S-0076 to the investigation I-7242
Extract of a record of Strigoi lords, found in Arnaud Demeure's Palace
18 November 1531

Veles appeared again in front of the Strigoi lords. The voivodes missed his arrival. Like every time before, he came dressed as a prince from the western lands. His eyes were pale, his hair gray, and he addressed the tribes with a hoarse voice.

"My most esteemed Strigoi lords, immortal tribes, I bring you power. This in my hands is victory in wars that have yet to start." His voice was loud, and as he spoke, thunder roared in the sky outside the court. He showed a jar filled with a red, dense liquid.

The lords laughed at his words, but he didn't flinch.

"This is the blood of old, the life of the Great Ones who lived before we walked this earth. You should fear it and respect it, not mock it. And here I offer it to you for nothing, out of respect for the authority of the Strigoi lords.

"You might not believe me, but the wind of war will soon blow from the West. The wizards from the islands, who have already hunted these lands for their immortal gifts, will come back to discover your secrets. Once again, they will hunt you for your powers and nothing will stop them. When that happens, you must be ready. This blood, mixed with yours, can build a weapon that will crush your enemies."

One lord, the most respectable heir of the Sturdzas, spoke. "Even if we believed you, how can some blood ever be a weapon to us?"

"A young one among the Strigoi lords, I see. Don't you talk in your own stories about the Mechi who will come? Will they not share the blood of the Great Ones? I will tell you all how to forge it into a weapon, and maybe it will be you, youngest among the Strigoi lords, who will do it. The one who will rise above his peers.

"Mix the immortal seed of a Strigoi lord with the blood of old and seal it away to putrefy for forty days. But be careful, for the forty days must end on a night when the full moon shines in the sky. Then you must pour the mixture in the womb of a pregnant woman who has died that same night, and when you do it, you will see that the liquid will stir and move itself. For forty weeks you will leave it in the coldness of a dead womb, and every night you will feed it with the life of a man and the milk of a woman. And so, your weapon will be forged, in the crying of a newborn."

All the lords roared at the Sturdza's heir and laughed. "Take it, young one, rise above your peers."

The Sturdza alone stood in front of the others. "What do you want for it?"

But Veles vanished. Only his voice, like an echo, resounded in the air. "The day will come for me to get back the one who is mine and one more with it."

Alex slid into her jeans, put on her shoes and sweater, and secured the talismans to her bracelets. She had depleted the sphere to find Sophia. The cross had weakened with use, but she was lucky; there was still enough tellur in it that it would work another couple of times. But the hook, glowing with a white light only she could see, was her secret weapon. She held it in one hand and smiled as she fastened it to the necklace.

She hurried out into the corridor, rushing to reach the

others and leave the place with a portal she could now open at command. And once out of there, Van Vloed would have to answer a ton of questions.

Alex's heart was beating fast, like a drum ready for war. Then she caught Van Vloed, standing at the end of the corridor before the stairs. The Dutch woman was looking at her with her unnerving smile. If Van Vloed was working with Demeure, this was going to be a mess.

"What are you doing here? You should be in the church with the others."

"I saw you coming up the corridor and waited, you know, to escort you, boss."

Fuck her. Alex was sure Van Vloed had peeked into her room, and she must have also seen her using Daniel's phone. She showed Van Vloed the way. "After you, and hurry, we are wasting time."

Van Vloed nodded and took the stairs while Alex walked a couple of steps behind.

"Actually," Alex said to Van Vloed's back as they reached the floor below. "I have a few questions."

"And I suppose I don't have an option not to answer, do I?"

"You remember who puked blood last time."

Van Vloed cackled and halted. "You know what? I'm done."

"You wha—" Alex said when Van Vloed raised one hand to silence her. Something pierced the witch's left side, just above her hip. A muted scream escaped her mouth. She glanced at the wound to find that something sharp had grown out of the wall to stab her. It was yellow and smooth, perhaps a bone.

The bone retracted into the wall and she gasped for air. The wound burned as blood burst out of it. The ferrous taste of blood filled her mouth. Van Vloed must have pierced her stomach. "So, I have my answer," the witch said. Her voice was weaker than she wanted to. "You work for Demeure." And as she spoke, she covered herself in sparks of tellur.

Van Vloed rolled her eyes. "Oh boy . . . everything is so black and white with you." She wiggled her fingers and four ribs appeared on each side of the corridor, ready to hit Alex again. Another rapid flick of Van Vloed's hand, and all of them shot toward Alex's chest.

But before the bone spears could hit her, Alex had already moved away and covered the few steps that separated her from Van Vloed. Before Van Vloed reacted, Alex slapped her in the face with a hand still wrapped in discharges of tellur. Not bad for a trick she had just learned.

The power of the blow was such that Van Vloed flew against the wall. She was bleeding from her nose, but was still laughing. "Good God, Witch, that was quick. If I hadn't jumped, you would have broken my neck."

She must have moved slower than she'd wanted if Van Vloed had the time to react. The technique was still rough, but the discharge alone should have ripped Van Vloed's face off and it hadn't.

"You must wonder why my skin is still in place," Van Vloed asked as if reading her mind. "Well, screw you. I won't tell you anything!" And she burst into another high-pitched laugh, this time so maniacally that Alex thought Van Vloed was faking it.

The bones flew from the wall once again and almost hit her, but Alex jumped out of the way just in time. As she landed, though, another throb of pain came from the wound on her left side and blood burst out again. Her left leg almost gave way and it trembled under her weight. She didn't resist the urge to cover her wound.

"Oh my, oh my!" Van Vloed said. "The little alchemist might be too much to handle for the big evil witch."

"Fuck you," Alex said, and she spat some more blood on the floor. But one thing was for sure. She had underestimated Van Vloed.

"I would be polite if I were you. I've got you figured out.

That lightning you keep using, that's not magick, is it? That is one of your dark gifts, and if you use magick, you can't use that. The prince was kind enough to give me a few hints about you."

Alex glared at Van Vloed with a grim face. The Dutch woman was right, but she wasn't sure what her plan was.

"Wait," Van Vloed said. "There is more. All of this fast-moving, it's just another way to use your lightning. The dandy must have scared you a lot. I saw you in your room trying it over and over. If it wears off, you will be slow and weak."

Van Vloed knew more than she wanted. Given how fast Van Vloed moved those bones, Alex had to keep the tellur wrapping her body, but to do it she had to stay off the network which, in turn, meant no magick. If this wasn't enough, she had to be extra careful connecting to the network with such a deep wound lest the temporary mortality would kill her. Alex hoped Van Vloed didn't know about this weakness at least, as she had a good idea to buy some time for her wound to heal.

Van Vloed moved her fingers again, in sequence from the index to the thumb. In response, the bones shot one after the other from both sides. By the time Alex could glimpse them moving, her legs, short-circuited to her sensory centers, had already made her jump out of the way. She punched the wall with all the strength the tellur gave her muscles and hit the cables inside.

As she did so, she discharged so much electricity that all the lights in the corridor shone with a blinding light and exploded. Glass rained from the ceiling, refracting the light in all directions.

Van Vloed stumbled and backed off a couple of steps. She clenched her eyes and defended her face from the glass.

Alex used this opportunity to rush up the stairs. By the time she reached the top, the wound in her stomach had healed. It wasn't closed yet, but at least most of the actual damage was gone. She took a deep breath, connected to the network, and pushed herself against the door of her room.

"I'm coming!" Van Vloed called from the bottom of the stairs, her steps echoing loudly as she came up.

Alex waited for Van Vloed's head to appear from the stairs to shoot. She collected water particles from the air in a single point and froze them into a bullet of ice. She made the bullet fly with a whistle from one end of the corridor to the other to hit Van Vloed straight between the eyes. The air that had dried filled itself with a light, warm mist.

Van Vloed was pushed back a couple of steps, yet she came back up again. "A lot of pyrotechnics, but nothing more." Her right hand scratched the wall. "A one-trick pony, are you?"

Then, once again, Van Vloed closed and opened her left hand. Four ribs spurred from the wall straight in front of Alex with an ominous cracking noise. "I can see you!" Van Vloed said, closing her fist.

The bones shot out again, so fast that they seemed to fly. Alex barely managed to disconnect from the network, wrap herself in tellur, and leap away. But one bone scratched her cheek and went through her shoulder, taking a piece of flesh with it. Again, the witch screamed out.

Why had neither her gift nor her magick worked on Van Vloed? What was her trick? The same enchantments had wounded her only a few hours before.

As Alex dodged another attack, she kept thinking. Both the thunder and the ice bullet had worked on Van Vloed's hand when Alex had attached the mannequins in Sophia's hideout. Yet perhaps this was the point.

Alex had to risk it if she wanted to get out of this situation alive without using the hook pendant. She dropped her thunder and connected to the network. Van Vloed was right. She would be slower, weaker, and hopefully unknown to her opponent, mortal. Alex hoped her plan would take Van Vloed down in one go.

And so she rolled from one door arch to the other to avoid one bone that tried to reach her from the top, and in the meantime, she focused on her enchantment.

But before Alex could reach the other side, another bone emerged from the floor and impaled her through her already wounded shoulder, lifting her from the ground.

"A one-trick pony, huh?" Alex tried to shout, but her voice came out as a hiss through her teeth.

The witch clenched both fists and eyes shut and tried to forget the pain in her shoulder. The air in the corridor grew cold in an instant. Light frost formed all over the wall on Alex's left. The ice ran in a fraction of a second along the plaster until it reached Van Vloed's right hand, which she kept pressing against the wall.

Van Vloed screamed as the ice transferred from the wall all over her hand and forearm. She tried to pull her hand away from the wall, but failed on her first attempt. With her face contorted in pain, she grabbed her right arm with her left and pulled.

As she did so, the bones holding Alex in place retreated within the ceiling and floor, and the witch fell on the ground.

Van Vloed pulled again with more energy and finally detached her hand from the plaster. She screamed louder than before as the skin of her hand remained attached to the wall. Blood spattered against the plaster, instantly freezing.

Van Vloed waved her left fist. "You are a dead witch." A bone grew again from the ceiling, ready to fly at a now grinning Alex.

Alex faced Van Vloed, but could barely glimpse her in the mist. "Really? Am I dead?" She focused on the dissonance her previous enchantment had accumulated by freezing such a vast volume of air and water to near absolute zero. She followed the quintessential field, weaving the tellur that was moving in her direction, and she controlled the flow. The tellur swirled around her until, with a wave of her hands, she redirected it, swift and amplified, all against Van Vloed.

As Van Vloed lowered her fist, the bone hanging above Alex plummeted like a spear, but before it reached her, a wave of hot air flowed out of the witch, traversing the whole corridor. The recoil blew Alex back, leaving her untouched by the bone. But Van Vloed wasn't as lucky. The air flew so fast and hot it scorched the walls and reached her with such velocity it made her fly back a couple of meters until she landed with her back against the stairs.

Alex pushed herself up. Her side had healed, and her shoulder was still numb but getting better. She limped to check her work on Van Vloed. The shot of hot air had ripped off part of Van Vloed's shirt and melted the rest against her skin. Across her chest and face, her skin was charred and torn so much that it was showing the red flesh of her muscles moving below.

"Fuck you!" Alex yelled and kicked her in the ribs. "Why are you helping them?" She leaned on her.

Van Vloed didn't move. She rested on the floor, face up and panting. Every time she inhaled or exhaled, a cat hissed from inside her chest. "I couldn't die without killing you first," she said, coughing and laughing, and she raised a shaking middle finger.

"You are just a loser, not worth the years you have lived."

Van Vloed let her arm fall and clenched her fist again.

Alex caught her eyes, glancing over her shoulder. The loud noise of bones snapping and shattering arrived from behind her. She turned so fast that she almost fell on top of Van Vloed, but used her hands not to tumble on the ground.

Leto stood in front of her. In his right hand was the tip of a rib. The rest of the bone was still dangling from the ceiling. The dandy's eyes were empty, as if he wasn't keeping anything in focus, but his face turned into his usual mask. Leto smiled and waved a salute. "This was about to stab you and it looked like you needed some help!"

"I didn't," Alex said, but she wasn't sure if that was a lie or not. One thing was certain, she didn't want to deal with Leto too after this mess, and not without the others, for sure. "What are you doing here?"

"Everybody in the palace must have heard you two. It sounded like a heated debate."

Alex was ready to wrap herself in tellur again. "Let's say so. Now, please leave. I can manage on my own."

Leto sighed, shrugged, and dropped his arms. He then moved one step back without turning.

"Hey, dum-dum," Van Vloed said, coughing again. "What kind of moron are you? She knows you work for the prince, you asshole. She won't give you details of any plan if that's what you are after." Her eyes moved from Alex to Leto and back many times in a few seconds.

But before Van Vloed could add anything else, something rushed close to Alex's face and Van Vloed's head exploded, spattering blood and brain all over the witch. The tip of the rib had just flown like a projectile out of Leto's hand and straight into Van Vloed's cranium. She was dead in an instant.

"I guess that's it," Leto said.

Alex's heart pumped hard as she wrapped herself again in tellur and leaped away from the man as fast as she could. She had devised the whole trick of using her thunderbolt to move faster just for him, but never expected to have to fight him solo. Rather, she had thought of this as a way to escape and support the others in case something happened.

Alex had no time to think of countermeasures as Leto was on her again. Before she could move, Leto disappeared, but by the time a gust of air behind her neck announced where he was, the electric field around her had already detected his presence.

She tilted her head and dodged Leto, who stood between her and the wall.

The short-circuit between her brain and her limbs had worked automatically. All her muscles contracted harder and faster thanks to the electricity, so she turned and slapped him straight in the face with her withered hand covered in lightning.

Alex thought that every bone in her arm had shattered. Still a victim of her own speed, she spun on her feet and stumbled but somehow recovered by pushing herself up from the floor with her good hand.

Leto had flown a few meters down the corridor and was raising himself up as well. His left cheek was charred and a good chunk of skin was missing up to his eye. The other side of his face lacked any emotion. No anger or sign of pain of any kind. His glare was fixed on her, focused.

Now that she had put some space between herself and Leto, Alex contemplated running down the stairs, but she didn't want to offer her back to him.

He disappeared again. An instant later, he reappeared on her left side.

She jumped back and again, her left arm moved on its own, swooping in front of her to reach him.

The man moved fast, even by his own standards. He ducked, parried her fist with his right forearm, and swung it away and back.

The smell of his skin burning filled her nostrils. Yet, he had stayed in place without being blown away by the impact. At the same time, she realized that she had moved too fast and with too much force and so, thanks to him parrying, she fell fair and square on her back.

Leto's hand came down on her face, his sharp fingers moving like a blade.

Perhaps she was lucky or fast enough again, but she rolled on the ground before Leto's hand could hit her.

Having missed her, Leto's left hand had pierced the wooden floor. The bang of the wood cracking blasted in the air and the smell of wood dust filled Alex's nostrils.

The witch breathed hard, still surprised to be alive. Her left arm, already consumed by the previous magick, was bent back in the middle of her forearm, the bones protruding out. All she could see were white flashes in front of her eyes.

Leto grunted close to her as she rolled on the floor, blinded by pain, but he was struggling to get his hand out of the floor. She bounced back on her feet and tried to escape.

She couldn't go too far before Leto grabbed her by her right arm, or so she thought. Instead, the man had grabbed her bracelet with the cross. She pulled and the bracelet gave way, so she limped backward a few meters down the corridor and away from him.

No time to waste. If the man remained stuck in one place, her ice bullet would work. Alex dropped her lightning, took a deep breath, and connected to the network once again. The pain barely allowed her, but she focused on the picture in her mind: a vacuum tube connecting her right hand to the man's head. She concentrated on extracting every last drop of water from the air to form the bullet and push it in his direction using an air depression.

As Alex imagined, the network had received the order, and the engine changed the agreement to follow her will.

It was so fast that she didn't see it. The bullet flew from her to Leto in a fraction of a second and filled the room with an ominous whistle and a glimmering flash. All that followed was a bang, a flash of light, and blood spattering all over the floor and walls.

A dense fog rose because of the dissonance, as if someone had poured cold water on a hot stove. Unfortunately, this blocked her from the sight she so desperately needed. Was he dead?

She had to think and must do it fast. Why would he grab her bracelet rather than her arm? He could have known, and Demeure must have known for sure. Something told her Leto was alive and she wouldn't gamble her last talisman.

Once again, she focused on the network and took the hook-shaped pendant in one hand. A faint shimmer of light escaped her fingers, and once she opened her palm, the jewel vanished.

Alex smiled and took a deep breath. It didn't last long. As soon as the fog settled, Leto emerged from the mist just a few inches from her face. She could not even think fast enough to decide what to do, and without her lightning, her body didn't react in time to dodge.

Leto's right hand pierced Alex like a spear in the stomach and she vomited blood on the floor. The man shook her off his arm and kicked her away.

As Alex lay on the ground, her wound throbbed. It tried to close but failed. She was losing more and more blood. At first, she thought of healing herself with magick. Perhaps she could transfer the damage to the man, but even assuming she could do it, she would not be able to handle any dissonance in such a state. There must have been a simpler way.

She looked at Leto from behind her tears. The man stood there, not even a meter from her, and looked down at her. His left arm was missing. He had cut it off to escape her bullet. He was losing blood in regular bursts. The blood dropped on the floor and spattered with a horrible noise. He was pale and his face damp. This meant he hadn't used the pendant after all, and his own power was doing a good job on him too. This thought consoled her. He would be dead not too much after her.

Would he finish her now? Or would he rather let her bleed out to death?

Alex was about to accept her fate but fought against the feeling. A plan, she needed a plan.

Leto's right hand still held her bracelet with the cross jewel.

What if he didn't know what it was, after all? Or, at least, what if he didn't know how to use it? It didn't matter, anyway. She wanted to live.

She focused on the network and grasped the sphere pendant on her remaining bracelet. A simple substitution, easy enough that she could do it with a hole in her stomach.

Again, a faint light shone from her hands, and the same happened to Leto.

The man had figured it out, but it was too late. The cross was in Alex's hands already.

She hurried to get the jewel activated against her wound as the man dropped the sphere and rushed to grab the cross from her.

A blinding white light escaped her fingers a third time. It was warm and tingling in her wound—she was healing. She smiled and took as much air in as she could.

Suddenly, the man's fingers forced open her fist. The warmth left her and all at once it was rather cold instead. Her brain was telling her fingers to close, but they weren't listening. The wound and the last enchantment had left her with no strength.

Fair enough, was all she could think. It had been a good idea and perhaps, had she been more selfish, it would have been Leto on the ground, kicking the bucket. At least her selflessness had saved the hook-shaped pendant. She would not watch it happening, but those bastards would die.

A tear came from the corner of her eyes and ran down her temple onto the ground. She would never have a chat with the old man, after all. She hoped the Strigoi would understand. She closed her eyes.

"What did you do to me?" Leto asked. He was on top of her.

Alex opened her eyes again. He was all blurry, but she tried to focus on him somehow. Both his arms were back in place and his face had healed. She had done a good job with that amulet. The world had just lost its best witch.

"Answer me!" Leto bellowed, beating his chest with one fist. "What is this pain?" He was crying.

Alex closed her eyes again. All she asked was for him to stay put while she died. He still shook her by the shoulders, but it didn't matter too much. She just wanted to sleep.

"You built this thing! Tell me . . ." Leto was saying. But his voice faded away at last, and all was silence and darkness.

Then nothing, but only for a little while.

"Now is the time," another voice said. One that was both young and old at the same time. It was the ancient girl of her vision. "Open your eyes."

Alex's eyes were sore and tired, but she did as she was told. Through them, all she could see was the network, much crisper than she had ever seen it before. Every strand or node had one word written on it: her true name.

As she blinked, she lay somewhere else. The sun warmed her face while the fresh scent of grass filled her nostrils.

"Welcome home," the ancient girl said.

22

HIS SIGN IN THE SKY

Ioan had been sitting on a bench in the church for an hour at least. Roman sat still and silent beside him. "I'll be done in a minute," the giant had said as soon as Ioan had set foot in the church, but he had made no further sound since.

None of the others had showed up and the only one he had bumped into was Celeste, who was leaving the church as he arrived and looked quite distressed.

In that silence, he couldn't stop thinking of the witch, but resisted the temptation to roam too much in his worries. Daniel's turning that night had been enough for his old heart.

As Ioan was about to fall prey to his own thoughts a second time, something in the strands moved. The filaments of tellur surrounding him throbbed and shifted their places till they knotted in a single point that fluctuated brightly in front of his face.

Tempted by the shining light, he reached out with one hand and took it between his index finger and thumb. As he touched it, the light exploded in a shimmering swarm of glittering particles that floated for a few seconds and disappeared.

Something had materialized between his fingers, but before

Ioan could understand what it was, a voice spoke in his head, loud and metallic, like that of a person talking through a speaker. "Blow his ass off for me. Think of him dying and the talisman will do its job. Just try not to be in contact with it as it goes off, or you'll turn into dust. Remember, he can't kill you, and he can't use you as a sacrifice unless you want to or unless you've given up on yourselves, so use that to your advantage." It was Alex's voice, as smug as always, but also sad in a new way. Ioan's stomach twitched.

"What is that?" Roman asked. Despite his size, he had somehow moved swiftly enough that Ioan, already distracted by the enchantment, hadn't noticed him.

"The witch must have done her job," Ioan said, and moved the hooked-shaped pendant between his fingers.

"I heard it too. Do we have any hope that she is still alive?"

Ioan didn't answer and shook his head. His stomach twitched again. "We can't count on Van Vloed either, I think. If she is not here, she must be dead or on the other side. And for some reason, I think that Celeste won't come back."

Roman stayed silent for a few moments. "What about Hermann?" he asked, sitting back again. The seat squeaked under his weight.

"I left him talking with the witch. He was worried about something. I hope he is still alive, but he should have been here long ago."

Roman hummed and spoke again. "I should keep the jewel."

"Are you sure about it?" Ioan asked, but knew the answer already. He had seen enough of Roman that he disliked where the giant was going.

"The witch spoke to me too, and for a reason. I think she knows I'm the best man for the job. I have readied myself for centuries. Her message tells it all. Out of the two, I'm the one the prince can kill, anyway."

Ioan kept a grasp on the talisman. His lips curled and his jaw clenched.

"Hand it over, old man," Roman said. "You have too much to lose to be good at this."

"How do you—"

"I might be younger than you, but I recognize a restrained beast when I see one. What keeps you like that, I don't know, but I have nothing of the sort. All that keeps my beast put is the desire to kill that man, so I don't care to live after his death."

Ioan wanted to say something, but nothing meaningful came to mind.

He still held the jewel between index finger and thumb when the door connecting to the house opened with a creak. Before Ioan could react, Roman had grabbed the talisman from his hands.

The divine waters pushed against Ioan as if trying to escape the place, and moved back with so much pressure it carried all the strands along in the wave. Such a feeling could mean only one thing: Demeure had entered the room.

Roman tried to keep his beast at bay as the prince walked in silence. Two figures followed him.

Leto walked in first, as silent as the prince before him, but he wasn't himself. He was paler than usual and his right eye was twitching. He breathed hard. His hair was sweaty and he wore a pained expression. Even his suit was in disarray, with bloodstains all over and one sleeve missing.

Just a step or two behind Leto walked Guillaume, who still moved more like a gorilla than a man and risked bumping against Leto's back every time the dandy slowed his pace.

Distinct from his subordinates, Demeure had polished himself up even more than usual but kept his face somewhat down. For the little Roman could see of it, there was no sign of the prince's political cordiality in his expression.

Demeure still was the same nightmare he had set to eliminate centuries before, and the idea that the prince had plotted that as well disgusted him. The rest didn't matter. He would not forgive Demeure for having toyed with him throughout his entire existence.

The prince pulled himself to a seat on the altar and turned into the smiling nobleman Roman had seen since arriving at the palace.

As Demeure was about to speak, the door behind him opened and closed again. Celeste came in and stopped in front of the door without looking at anyone. Instead, she stared at her own feet.

Demeure sighed, and caught Roman's attention. "I guess this is it." He glanced at both Roman and Ioan. "We have the ones we need gathered here."

"Where are the others?" Ioan asked, pushing himself up against the wooden bench.

"You know the answer to that question already," Demeure said. "They sacrificed themselves for a bigger cause. Some were hard to convince, the witch most of all, but it worked out in the end."

Ioan clenched his fingers against the wood so hard that the wood creaked.

"Don't you worry, it will be easier for you two," continued Demeure.

Roman's body flinched as his inner wolf growled. "What about you?" the giant bellowed in Celeste's direction. "You work for him now?"

The nun raised her head and glared at Roman. Her eyes were bloodshot, and her fists clenched. She opened her mouth but didn't answer. Instead, she leaned against the wall and looked down again.

"Oh, right!" Demeure said. "Please don't treat her as a traitor. I'm sure she thought of betraying me quite a few times, but thanks to you she's seen reason."

Roman was breathing hard as the wolf fought to take control of his body. He needed to keep the beast restrained, at least long enough to get close to Demeure and use the witch's weapon.

The giant glanced at Ioan. The old man trembled, his fingers piercing the wood of the bench in front of him, and his face contorted in a wild expression. Had Ioan been an enemy, Roman's own wolf would have feared him. Yet the Strigoi was keeping his composure and it was perfect. If Ioan could offer him cover as he attacked, it could all work.

Roman made his move. He headed toward the central nave, keeping as slow a pace as he could. Maybe Demeure would think that he had given up. In the meantime, Roman hoped Ioan would keep the others busy.

Demeure's eyes paused on the giant. "The wolf, of course. The pup bares his teeth at his master." As he said so, he glanced at Leto.

Roman followed the prince's eyes. Leto nodded, but, for a second, remained still. Perhaps this was the occasion Roman was waiting for. The giant rushed toward the prince, trying to monitor both Demeure and Leto, but, at last, the dandy moved. He wasn't as fast as he had been before and Roman thought he had nothing of the predator that had given goosebumps even to the witch. But an instant later, there it was; the old Leto, fast and scary as always.

The giant didn't feel safe to use the talisman—he was too far from the prince and still too close to Ioan. Still, the pain in his chest was unbearable. The wolf wanted to come out, and this was the best time to let it do as it pleased.

Every muscle in Roman's body ached and his skin burned. His bones cracked loudly as they changed shape and pierced through his flesh as he rushed to the prince.

As Leto was about to jump on him, the bench slid on the floor in front of the dandy and blocked him. Ioan had pushed it, hitting Leto on one hip. A moment later, a dense smoke surrounded the dandy who coughed as if out of breath.

The wolf inside Roman missed this opportunity to attack. Instead, it planted its feet and glared at Demeure, and the prince reciprocated. More and more of the beast came out in the meantime. Its claws replaced the fingers that broke away from Roman's hands and dropped to the ground. Its teeth did the same, and Roman tasted his own blood as fangs replaced them. Finally, he was the wolf, not himself anymore.

The beast howled and growled, its skin tore itself and fur came out from underneath. But as much as the beast roared, it didn't move one more step in Demeure's direction.

The wolf must have seen it too, as Roman had at the ball hundreds of years before: death at the bottom of the prince's eyes.

Demeure sighed and as he did so, Guillaume moved. The servant let his legs go down and fell to the ground with all his weight against his back. His body cracked into pieces, making a loud noise not too different from a terracotta vase when it is smashed. Not even a second later, dust and stones emerged from the ground straight in front of Ioan.

Guillaume's body formed anew and wrapped the old man's hands and a good part of his arms within itself. As a result, the heavy smoke that had come out of Ioan to torment Leto dissipated, setting the dandy free.

Leto stood still for a while, looking at the others.

"What are you waiting for, Leto?" the prince asked in a flat voice. "If you were good enough for the witch, the wolf should be easy."

The dandy glanced at the prince and turned to face the wolf. Once again, there was an unusual numbness in his eyes, but he leaped and thrust himself against the beast, pushing one arm in front like a spear.

The wolf was fast enough to dodge it. Roman, from within the animal, didn't understand its intentions at first. The beast sidestepped the dandy and his body flew in front of it. Using this to its advantage, the beast placed one hand against Leto's chest, and with the other hand, it grabbed and pulled his thrusting forearm.

Leto's shoulder bounced back against the beast's hand, pushed by his own sheer momentum, while the arm attached to it moved forward.

The shoulder broke away from its socket with a loud crack. If he hadn't seen the dandy's arm still attached to his body, Roman would have sworn the beast had ripped it off.

"It's a Wurdulac, you child! It can fight with the strength of a beast and the brain of a man," Demeure said with a hint of annoyance in his voice.

The beast let Leto go, and the dandy stumbled back a couple of steps, holding his own shoulder in place and panting.

Leto's face was a mask. The pain had taken all the beauty from it. Then the dandy huffed, collected himself, and relaxed his shoulders, taking another deep breath.

The beast took it as an invitation and roared in his face. Before it could move, Leto had already jumped forward, and at first, Roman thought the dandy had slipped on the ground. It was too late when Roman realized what Leto was doing. With the wolf unable to react, the dandy was already between its legs, and his fingers, sharp as razors, cut the tendons behind the beast's right knee. Blood splattered onto the floor and over Leto's already dirty suit.

The wolf howled and shrieked as its right knee fell under the weight of its body.

Leto rolled on the ground to avoid the oversize monster falling on him and jumped right on the wolf with his legs against its hips. His left arm still dangled on his side, but his right one was ready to strike again as a spear pointed at the wolf's throat.

The beast was also ready to swing at the man with both arms, but Roman couldn't tell who would be faster if any of the two tried.

Before either could move, the loud sound of shattering stone broke in the air. Both the wolf and Leto turned toward the noise.

Where the sound came from, Roman expected to find Ioan struggling with Guillaume. Instead, there was a young man in a black suit covered in dust. His hair was jet-black and his figure slender, and something in him gave out a calming vibe. The young man frowned, his eyes squinting as he was patting the dust off his suit with one hand. With the other, he held a scrap of paper.

"Strigoi," roared the prince. "What did you do to Guillaume?"

The young man didn't even glance at the prince. Instead, he locked his eyes with those of the beast. "I can give you an opening, if you are still up for it," he said. He didn't move his lips, his voice sounding straight in the beast's and Roman's head.

Roman recognized the young man's voice. He was Ioan.

The rejuvenated Strigoi glanced at Leto. "Get off him, please." He stressed the words enough it sounded like an order.

The dandy moved like a puppet, stood up, and went to sit on a bench. As he reached his place, he shook his head with bewildered eyes.

"I've asked you," Demeure said, "what have you done to Guillaume?" A storm whooshed from the prince in all directions, hitting the beast's face as it was getting back up on one foot.

The prince himself, as if carried by the air, appeared a few inches from Ioan.

"The witch was right," Ioan said, still giving his back to

Demeure. "It wasn't too hard to manage once you knew what to search for." He turned, showing the paper to the prince.

"You dared!" the prince bellowed. A storm resounded in his words and the pressure of the air surrounding him grew so strong that the beast fell back on its knees.

Ioan didn't budge. A faint powdery smoke flew away from his body and floated in the air, following the currents back to him. "You need to be more careful," he said in a quiet voice. "If you keep doing this sort of thing, you will end up killing someone."

Demeure didn't reply, but pierced Ioan with his eyes.

Ioan read the paper in his hands, still squinting his eyes. "It says, 'Arnaud Demeure and Valentine Duchamp.' Where is she?" He tossed the paper over to the prince.

Demeure caught the paper. "She is close. How did you turn back into"—in search of words, the prince just waved one hand —"this?"

"The witch," Ioan said with a faint smile. "When you sent your servant to us in the labyrinth, she figured out a way to turn Guillaume's mud into my fatherland's soil."

The prince rolled his eyes. "Of course. Who else if not the witch?"

As the two spoke, unnoticed at first even by the wolf and Roman, Leto jumped in the air behind Ioan. One hand, once again, preceded him, directed at Ioan's back like a spear.

Ioan stepped to one side and Leto slid beside him, cutting with his hand only the light smoke that kept rising from Ioan's body.

As Leto landed, he bounced back at Ioan. Once again, the Strigoi moved aside just enough to dodge him. Yet again Leto landed and bounced back, and Ioan, unfazed, dodged again like a smoke-made ghost.

Leto tried and tried, panting more and moving slower at

each try but could never touch the Strigoi who wasn't even breaking a sweat.

"Boy," said the Strigoi, "you move fast, but it can't work on me. Ask your master if you don't believe me."

"Stop," Demeure said. "Just stop. He can see the future. He predicts where you'll go before you even think of moving."

Leto halted, still panting. With one hand he still pointed at Ioan, flexing his legs like those of a cat ready to jump.

"It was a delightful dance," Ioan sighed. "Your master is right, though. It's unfair on my part." He turned to Demeure, his face smug. "Speaking of my predictions, didn't I tell you centuries ago that if you stayed the course you'd end up losing everything, even yourself?"

Demeure's hands clenched. "As I told you, your powers don't work in the slightest on me. I'm still my father's son!"

"I never needed my power to see where this path you walk on would lead you."

"You will show me respect," Demeure said with a stern voice, and tightened his already clenched fist.

Ioan hugged his own abdomen and coughed. "You can't kill," he said, wiping his mouth from the blood that had dripped out of his lips. "You said it yourself, you are . . ." But, again, he bent over himself.

"That doesn't stop me from hurting you, does it?"

As Ioan struggled, Roman caught his eyes, glancing over to him. This was his signal.

Roman pushed the wolf toward the prince, but the beast didn't budge. Instead, it growled under its breath. After much pushing on Roman's part, the wolf slowly moved. It would have been simpler a few centuries before when his control over the monster was much better. The stabbing pain behind his right leg didn't make it any easier.

Despite its whining and slow moving, the prince didn't

notice the wolf approaching and neither did Leto, who seemed concerned only by Demeure's actions.

"You have been a pain since the very first time I met you," Demeure said. "Wasn't the entire purpose of your people to fight for something bigger than them? Wasn't it on your family crest? You have already given up on your life, so why are you still fighting me?"

"A pain?" Ioan said, coughing out more blood. "That boy upstairs, he thought of you as a father, and now he has turned into a wolf. That was your making. All the others are dead, maybe not by your hand, but because of you. I was a toy as well. You took away my daughter and now you want me to die when you ask me to?"

Demeure opened his hand. He was still shaking. "You understand nothing. I just granted them their wishes. Every single one of you and your obsessions, each one missing the mark, lying to yourselves. Daniel, obsessed with his love for a woman he could not have, yearning to be mortal again with her. All Daniel really wanted was to be free from the burden of the wolf, and now he finally is.

"The witch, too, with her dreams of unbounded knowledge. All she wanted was the strength to save her dad, and I made sure she had it. And you, I pity you most of all. For centuries you dreamed of spending a moment with your long-lost daughter. I gave her back to you, and you didn't even recognize her, you fool! Now you've lost her again."

Ioan fell, palms on the ground. He coughed, his mouth dry, and gulped for air. Then he spat at Demeure's feet. "Even that Valentine who accompanied you. She must have realized the monster you are and left you," Ioan said, chuckling and shaking his head.

"Don't you dare say her name!" Demeure's voice was barely audible through the thunder that resounded behind it. As he spoke, the lights in the room flickered.

The prince clenched both his fists so hard his knuckles whitened, and Ioan screamed and rolled on the floor. Demeure looked at him with burning eyes, nothing of his composed demeanor left.

It was the opportunity Roman had been waiting for. He got control of the beast and pushed it farther, closer to Demeure. The fur fell off his arms and the claws retreated, and his hands still held the jewel. One last leap, and he could reach the prince.

Before he could jump, the noise of shattering metal filled the room and another burst of air flew in all directions.

Hermann had somehow appeared out of thin air and stood now in front of Demeure, holding him by his wrists. "Killing the sons of men? Breaking the laws of our father?" he asked, his voice more solemn than usual.

"So, when you finally show up," Demeure said, freeing himself from Hermann's grasp, "you do it to defend this filth?"

"You know there is only one in this room I care about," Hermann said.

The door slammed. Where Celeste should have been standing was no one. The nun had left the room.

"And you thought of me after what? Five or six hundred years?" Demeure asked and turned his back to Hermann. "Also, your face, your voice, all of you . . . it's unsettling."

Hermann sighed. "I guess this way it would be easier for you." His voice was higher in pitch and more mellow in tone. His hair grew blond and curled, his eyes turned blue, and his body shrank by a few inches. Just like he had appeared a moment before, Hermann disappeared and, in his place, still wearing his clothes, was a woman Roman had never seen.

"I thought this party would bring back memories," Demeure said, turning to face the woman. "I never thought I'd see your face again, Valentine."

"You know it won't be for long. I made a promise."

"A promise?" Demeure asked. "What about the promise you made to me? What about staying by my side?"

"I left a second time, believing it would save you, believing it will give me back the man I loved, but I can still keep that promise. Give me that man back," she said and moved one step closer to the prince, attempting to caress his face.

Demeure stepped back. "You and this delusion . . . I'm still that man and much more than your little one was."

"You know, I thought the same about you at first, perhaps even about myself. When I and Azazel became one in the labyrinth, all its power felt like a new life. But you know how it ended, and I promised not to do it to anyone else."

"Yet I saw you over the years. You changed and changed, taking others in."

"I did. I wanted to see how they lived, what they felt. But I never merged with any of them as Azazel had done with me. I never became them. I let them live their lives. I just traveled with them, within them. To some, like my Hermann, I talked. I've been a mother to others. I wanted to understand."

Demeure pressed his hands against his face, massaging his eyes. "Understand what? Why they betrayed us? Why they had our brothers killed?"

"If you would just listen, I could make you see. Why don't you travel with me?" said the woman, holding one hand toward the prince.

He glanced at her hand. His face was tempted, but he shook his head. "No! This is not how it is meant to be. It isn't what our mother asked of us and not what our brothers would have wanted, either. We need to open the skies again."

She looked at him with a tender smile. "Little one, you lie, even when you know I've read your journal. I've seen how much you want to sacrifice."

Demeure's face changed. There was no anger in it and he didn't revert to his usual falsely kind self either. He, instead, stared at the woman like someone would stare at a spring after a race across a desert. But something broke, and fire took hold of the prince's eyes.

Roman's beast trembled and would have rushed away from Demeure had the giant not kept it in place.

"Stop!" the prince shouted, his voice like a storm. "I have one last mile to walk, and you are in my way." As he said so, a slash of light shot from below the woman's feet to the ceiling, wrapping her entire body.

"Don't you dare!" she called to him, raising one fist, but the light muffled her voice as if she were speaking from inside a bottle.

"I'll dare as much as necessary. I'm your superior in rank, and you must learn your place."

With the prince busy with the woman, and Leto still stuck watching the scene, Roman took his chance. Still half-human and half-beast, he pushed his fears away, and before he realized it, he was already jumping, jewel in hand, over the prince.

When Demeure spotted him, it was too late. Roman had already smacked the palm with the amulet against Demeure's chest.

A blinding light came out of the jewel and wrapped both Roman and Demeure. Its delicate warmth cocooned Roman, and it was so bright it dazzled him. Then, as his body burned out in the light and disappeared, all he could see were thousands of strands made of light that floated in the air. Every single filament detached itself from Demeure and immediately reattached to him somehow differently.

"You shattered his shackles. You have done a good job, my friend," the witch's voice said in his head.

He thought she was right as the white light burned his thoughts away. He had died a hero in the end.

Ioan tried to push himself back up, but his arms were shaking so much he couldn't go further than balancing on both arms and legs. Just below him was the blood he had puked. A loud whistle filled his ears, and his eyes, not yet used to experiencing light, had been blinded again by the flash. At least he could rejoice, Roman had defeated Demeure.

He tried to keep aside the good feeling and squinted his eyes to see what had happened. He might get a glimpse of the results of Roman's sacrifice. But before his eyes could get to work again, a muffled voice came to his ears.

"You see, sister," Demeure said in a hoarse voice. "Every time you turn your back on these animals, they stab you." He rose from the ground. White feathers covered the floor under his feet.

The prince was in one piece. "That witch, I knew she would be trouble. I've been lucky. Had she delivered this blow in person, I would have been dead already."

"Arnaud, it's time to stop," Valentine said from within her light-made prison. "I don't know how it is possible, but they have broken your shackles."

The prince chuckled. "Ingenious of the witch to break them. I never thought my own creation could do it. I must have been an excellent teacher to these people. Why are you gloomy?" he asked Valentine, whose eyes still pleaded with him. "All the more reason not to stop here. I might not have my shackles anymore, but I still have the soul of an angel. With the wolf gone, I only need another two sacrifices."

"Arnaud, stop it, please."

"How can I when I'm so close? Do you think I would? Look at us, shackles or not, we'll disappear. I told you already, we can't exist in this world until the sky remains closed. We will just vanish, not even die, not a sign in the sky like our brothers, nothing. I won't let you end like this."

"I never asked you to save me. I never asked you to vanish on your own while I have to keep living without your sign to pray to."

Demeure smiled. "I'm sorry, but you don't get to decide. It is a purge. Our elders were right all along. Look at these beasts. The one on the ground crawling like a worm has a list of crimes that would fill a book. Do you think the others were any better? Even Leto," Demeure said, pointing at the dandy. "My dear Leto. My child, my blade, the one I raised like a son. Isn't he just a beast too?"

Leto's body trembled as Demeure spoke. The prince didn't seem to notice, or perhaps he didn't care. Yet Leto didn't look at all like a sword, but Demeure was right, he was a beast. All the muscles of his face were set, his hands clenched into fists, and his eyes fixed on the prince.

"You see him there? Waits for an order like an obedient dog and doesn't care what the truth is. He doesn't care that everything that brought him to me as a child was one of my illusions. If I spit the truth in his face, he won't move. Even if I tell him that, by my order, he killed his own sister . . . What was her name? Violette, yes, that's right. Does he even remember her? And he didn't kill her just once, but twice. See? Despite it, he does nothing, like the spineless coward he is, he doesn't strike me!"

But as he spoke, the opposite happened. Leto shot forward, as he had done with Sophia. Ioan barely glimpsed him disappearing and reappearing at his destination. And by the time a rush of air reached the Strigoi's face, the dandy's arm had already gone through Demeure's guts.

Valentine screamed from inside her prison as the blood spattered on the ground.

Demeure rested his head on Leto's shoulders and smiled as a drop of red colored his lips. "Your emotions . . . the witch healed you. She gave you back your pain." He wrapped both hands around Leto's shoulders. "You did well, kid. You did well."

Tears came down Leto's face, and sobbing and shaking, he pulled away from the prince and looked at his own hands.

Demeure's body touched the floor and the column of light imprisoning Valentine disappeared.

"What have you done?" she yelled. The clamor of swords resounded in her voice.

Leto didn't reply. He kept staring at his hands and crying.

"Stay away from him, you animal!" She rushed to Demeure's side and pushed the dandy away. Tears ran down her cheeks. She pushed both hands against the prince's stomach to stop the bleeding, but nothing worked.

"Look at what I had to do to get your attention," Demeure said as she lifted his head in her arms.

"Don't talk, please! I can fix this."

Demeure pointed at the ceiling. "You know you can't. My sign is in the sky already. You are still just like I remember, but you must have seen so much. When did you turn into the smart one?" His voice was soft. "Will you tell me all your stories when your sign sits close to mine up there?"

Valentine nodded and tears ran down her cheeks as she stroked his hair.

"Don't you cry," Demeure said. "We've been so far away from each other. This is not too bad compared to that, not bad at all." His voice was so feeble that Ioan could barely hear him speaking. Demeure had already closed his eyes when he spoke again. "Will you promise me another thing?"

"Yes," Valentine said, drying her face with a sleeve.

He smiled. "Promise you won't turn into me."

"I promise," she said with so much struggle that her voice came out as soft as a whisper.

They both stayed silent for a while. Then he spoke again. "Say, sister, don't you love me?"

A gentle smile opened on her face as her eyes prepared to

cry again. "Never," she said, and could not stop tears from running down her cheeks.

Demeure coughed and smiled. "There has always been one thing I wanted you to say. Only one thing I wanted to hear from you, but not even as I die, you can lie to me . . ."

He fell silent. His entire body shone with a white light. An instant later, he had disappeared, and Valentine hugged nothing but air.

She sat still and stared at her lap.

Ioan had stood back up in the meantime but didn't dare to go close to her.

Leto, still in shock, stood a few inches from her.

"You," Valentine said, and the way she said it was dry and cruel. "My anger," she continued, rising from her seat. "Feel all of it."

As she spoke, Leto bent to grab his own stomach and fell to the floor.

"You will taste it all. It will rain on you and your people like the cry of a god." Her voice, once again, was the chaos of a battle.

The more she spoke, the more Leto's body bent and contorted into impossible positions as if all his bones were being crushed by an invisible hand.

The clash of swords in her voice banged so loud that Ioan had to cover his ears. "My voice—my scream—will hunt you all and find you in every dark place, in every corner of this world, everywhere you feel warm and safe, I will pursue you. This is my promise, and you can trust it because I am Azazel!"

Leto's body, now motionless, caught fire and burst into dust with a blast of flames.

"Because I am war," she said, lowering her voice and panting. "I am war, and the battlefield follows me."

Ioan caught her eyes for a second and she was as scary as the

Demeure he had known as an enemy. A moment after, she had vanished, leaving only a few falling feathers behind.

Closure to the investigation I-7242
To the hand of Horace Hastings (Interim Headmaster of the School of Winchester) only

While the investigation performed does not help us understand the nature of the paranatural events of Paris, we believe that the evidence collected demonstrates a direct connection between the activities of Mr. Demeure and the Occurrence.

Please refer to supplement S-0071 for a full report on the exploration of Provin's caves (inconclusive) and to supplement S-0073 for a report on the full swipe survey of the guests' residences. Note that Sturdza's residence was found to have been vacated ahead of our arrival.

The two subjects, Sebastiaan Van Vloed and Marcel Fontaine, associated with the guests, are in our custody and have been prepared for interrogation and memory extraction.

The parahuman entity known as "Valentine Duchamp/Azazel" is still on the loose. Given the evidence from Mr. Demeure's journals and the event in Paris, we have reasons to believe the creature has a cross-dimensional nature and can represent a global-scale threat.

Given these circumstances, we suggest scheduling an emergency hearing between the council and the founding families to initiate coordination with the other schools. This with the purpose of capturing and detaining the cross-dimensional being. As part of the hearing, we recommend officially declaring Councilor Dryden as missing-in-action and begin the process to strip Tylanus Spencer (still missing) of his honors for high treason.

23

FALLING STARS

Evidence J-1791 to the investigation I-7242
Extract from Arnaud Demeure's journal
19 August 1275

Like every other afternoon in the past few weeks, we climbed up to Saint Pierre to watch the city from above. As lively and impervious to our curse as she has always been, Renée ran and jumped and laughed through the tall grass. She was beauty, she was bliss, she was life, and she lifted our spirits like a summer breeze.

As Renée played, Valentine lay on the grass reading, and I watched the town. For once, I didn't think of war, of conquest, and neither did I think of vengeance, of salvation, or sacrifice. For once, it was heaven, and it was peace.

By the time the sun had resolved to rest, Renée was sleeping on Valentine's lap as she herself lay faceup asleep. I bent and kissed my sister, my love, on her forehead, and she replied to a question I had not asked. "Always," she said. "Always."

Ioan came back to the house. His body had yet to heal, but at least he could walk, albeit slowly.

By the time Ioan had opened the door, everything had already started turning dark for him and he could barely glimpse Celeste sitting on the floor against a wall. He took a seat next to her.

Only after a few moments of silence, Celeste spoke. "They are all gone, aren't they?"

"Yes," Ioan said, feeling his body aging again.

"I only wanted a family, you know?"

"I can understand that."

Celeste slid against the wall and stood up. "I'm so sorry for your daughter," she said and walked a couple of steps in silence. "Both of them didn't care. She didn't even speak to me once, and my brother . . . you should have seen the letter. What was he doing? Was he lying to himself?"

"You'd be surprised how many do that." Ioan sighed.

"I couldn't trust the prince, either. I hoped he would be a guide in whatever I am. But he just wanted to complete his ritual. He was only a trickster who got himself killed."

Ioan nodded. "A trickster. Not too far from what he was, I suppose. I just can't believe he would get himself killed. The way he talked to that kid, it seemed like he wanted Leto to stab him."

"Why would he thwart his own plans?"

"I don't know. People are more complicated than you expect. Yet I can't get past the idea that we could have never defeated him if he didn't want us to. I thought many times about what I'd do to see my daughter's face for just a moment, and I took the best I could out of this adventure. Maybe he did the same with his Valentine." As he spoke, Ioan rose, but his back and legs creaked under his weight.

"What do you think will happen to her? She killed a man, and I thought she couldn't do such a thing."

Ioan shrugged. "My eyes are closed," he said, tapping one cheekbone. "And I've never been able to glimpse into the future of your kind, anyway."

Celeste sighed.

"Just have faith," was all Ioan could say.

———

The morning air was still as chill in Paris as it was in Provins. Ioan shook the snow off his shoulders and put a hand against the doorknob. The freezing touch of metal reminded him of how lucky he was to have survived.

As he turned the doorknob, the wood and metal of the door creaked in a familiar way. Ioan sighed in relief. He and Celeste had to deal with the unpleasant affair of putting down Daniel's wolf before leaving Demeure's palace. That, he thought, had marked the end of a trip on which he had mixed feelings.

The house smelled like wood and the crackling of a fireplace filled the air. His skin tightened and stretched against his renewed muscles. He took the deepest breath he had taken in a few days—he was home at the end. And with being home, youth came to his body once again.

But before he could get adjusted to the warmth of the corridor, many feet rushed in his direction.

"He is back," shouted a young girl's voice. "Hurry, he is home."

His newly opened eyes weren't yet used to the light of the house and he had to squint them to see the children who had come his way. A little one had jumped on him and was hugging him at waist height. Ioan patted and stroked his hair.

A couple of blinks later, he had all of them in focus. Another three kids surrounded him. The older one stood in front, arms crossed. "You are finally back, Father," she said with a bitter voice and failed to hide any sign of relief on her face. "Weren't you supposed to stay out only one night?"

Ioan smiled. "I must have made a mistake in my evaluation."

She had turned when she was thirteen, but she liked to behave like an old wife.

"Thank you, Juliette," Ioan said to a second one who was helping him get off his coat.

"Gabriel, let Father go," said a boy, dragging the little one off Ioan's waist. "Jeanne and Juliette have both been worried sick the whole time," continued the boy, his dark eyes beaming at Ioan. "At least Juliette can handle it as a lady should."

Juliette blushed, her face wrapped in curly hair and her black eyes glittering. She indeed had looked like a lady since the very first time Ioan had taken her in. Jeanne, her older sister, who was now showing her tongue to the boy, would have been almost identical had she not grown into the modern times so fast. But as much as her brother—Adam—didn't like to admit, she was the boss whenever Ioan wasn't home.

"Aren't you supposed to predict the future?" Jeanne asked, turning back to him.

"One day you'll understand that our gift is more complicated than predicting the future, my dear," Ioan said. "Or at least for everything further than a few seconds in the future. In any case, why are you all up so early? Where is my little Ines?"

"She's in the painting room," said Jeanne. "She's been painting the entire night."

"Painting?" Ioan asked, taking off his shoes. Adam had been able at last to take the little Gabriel off him. "Has your sister been having dreams again?"

"We all have," said Jeanne. "It's been on and off every time we tried to sleep since yesterday."

"All of you?" Ioan asked again. His eyes darted from one child to the other. "All of you?" he repeated.

"Yes . . ." Jeanne said. "Dad? Is something wrong?"

Ioan had jumped to his feet again so fast that Juliette, behind him, was startled. He leaped toward Jeanne and kneeled in front of her, his eyes an inch from those of the girl and both hands on her shoulders. "What did you dream about?" he said, voice trembling. "Tell me every detail. It must be important."

"I-I don't remember," said Jeanne. "I forgot—you know that Ines is much better with the details. They forgot too. Didn't you?" she asked the others, and they nodded. "There was a voice, a woman. She kept saying that it hasn't ended yet."

"It hasn't ended? Did she say who she was?"

"She said she is a good witch," said Gabriel. "That's what she said to me, '*Papa will understand.*'"

Ioan's eyes widened, and Gabriel stared at him with an air of surprise on his face. "I need to check that painting," Ioan said. "Did Ines finish it?" But he didn't wait for an answer. Before anyone spoke, he had already darted through the corridor barefoot, the kids following him.

―――――――――

The painting room would have been immersed in darkness if not for a few rays of the sun that filtered through the window. The air was freezing. Five chairs sat in the middle of the room, each with an easel in front. Only one of them had a canvas on it and many others were stacked on the ground beside it. Drops of color covered the ground all around the occupied stand and a child was asleep on the chair in front of the canvas, her head resting on the easel's shelf.

The child's face was porcelain, wrapped in a bush of black hair, a little copy of Jeanne and Juliette. She was sleeping soundly, and someone had taken the good care to wrap her in a blanket.

"I'm sorry, Father," said Jeanne's voice behind Ioan. "I know she should be in bed by this time, but she wouldn't budge."

"You did well," Ioan said, walking toward the canvas. "And thanks for taking care of your brothers and sisters while I was away."

The light of the rising sun was enough to see the work. As usual, Ines's art was of the finest quality. On the canvas, a dark sky with gray and reddish clouds stood atop a burning city, Paris. It was impossible to mistake it for any other given the tower that stood at its center. The canvas was painted as if the painter sat on the roof of a tall building. The black silhouette of a woman was looking over the destruction.

In the painting, the tower was bent, as if melted in its middle, its tip bent to the ground. A red sun stood giant in the sky, its orange light coloring the clouds all around it. From the bottom of the sun, a straight line of red light connected it to the ground as if the sun were bleeding on the city. Feathers were falling from the sky all over the town.

And there he was now. Standing on the roof with Celeste like in the painting his daughter had left for him. "Everything will be all right," he had reassured the kids as he left the house. "Whatever happens, we will be fine. Sleep it through." But they didn't buy it. They were smarter than this, and he worried his last words to his kids would be a lie.

"You don't have to worry about them," Celeste said without turning to face him. "I wouldn't let anything bad happen to your family." Her voice was feeble and echoed, as if coming from far away. Her body immersed in the sunlight was a featureless shadow. "I made sure your eyes will stay open also when you leave your house. This way you can take even better care of them."

Ioan moved closer to the woman. "I guess I should thank you then, for today at least."

"You peeked, I know. You've seen what's behind the door I'm opening."

"I did. I must confess that I'm surprised someone like you is letting those things come into this world. Even more, I'm surprised you have managed to. How is this happening?"

"Someone like me . . ." Celeste said, shrugging, and turned to face Ioan. "You know what surprises me instead? How come you are so calm?"

"I lived a long life and I'm a prophet after all. Some apathy is the price you pay for having life spoiled for you."

Celeste grinned, but the bags under her eyes showed how tired she was. "You are a decent one. If only I had met you earlier." She sighed. "I can tell you how this all worked." She reached for something in her pockets and tossed it to Ioan.

It was a vial, dirty with blood. But before he could guess, Celeste spoke again. "Sophia and Daniel."

Ioan smiled and nodded. "A wedding vow imbued with the blood sacrament. That gave you access to Sophia's power, even after her death. That is remarkable!"

"I didn't think too much of it at the time. Van Vloed fetched some blood and forced me to pocket it. I'm not sure if she meant to plant the idea in my head, but who knows how a fool thinks."

"It shouldn't work. You would have needed seven sacrifices, and Demeure managed only five."

"He managed enough. He gathered all the ones I needed. You must have realized he didn't intend to kill Hermann. He wanted to save my mother, so she wasn't an ingredient. Sophia was another story. Once he had secured her power through the wedding, he just used her as a sacrifice."

"I see. And you weren't a sacrifice either I suppose."

"You guess right," Celeste said.

"He still missed me. I'm well and alive."

"Sure, but the ritual didn't need you by the end. Demeure

immolated himself and closed the circle. He didn't use his soul as energy in the ritual, but he had enough connections with all of you he could work well as an offer."

"And you are burning your soul as a replacement for his," Ioan said, shaking his head.

"I guess you are not a prophet for nothing. In theory, this should have been impossible for anyone aside from Demeure, because his people can't kill themselves, not even by burning their own soul. Demeure was a special one. He had the crown. He could break the shackle of eternity. But I'm a half-breed, and I don't have a shackle in the first place so I can act of my free will. It turns out that once he had opened the door, all it took was for one of his kind willing to burn their own soul for the ritual to keep going."

"And you are fine about dying . . . not even, at being consumed, just like this?"

Celeste shrugged. "I always felt the world needed some fixing, and this is how it was supposed to be. But may I ask you one last favor?"

"Yes, you can." Ioan figured what the nun was about to ask and walked in her direction.

"Will you wait with me for it to happen? We can watch the dawn coming."

The two sat on the balustrade, their legs hanging over the street hundreds of meters below. The wind blew over the empty town and everything stood still and silent. Now and then, a few rays of light, like projectiles or meteors, fell from the sky. The Great Ones, the Lords, were coming back.

At his side, Celeste's body was glowing. Ioan had seen it happen already to Demeure, but this time, it was slower. She wasn't dying. She was being consumed, fading away, used as energy in a ritual he barely understood.

"No regrets?" the old man asked.

The nun shook her head as she shone brighter and brighter. "I guess this is the end. Is it normal to be so scared?"

"Yeah, I think that's about right," Ioan said and clenched Celeste by one shoulder.

"You think He will glance into my soul before it vanishes? What will He see?"

"Don't worry about it," Ioan said. "I think you are one of the good ones."

Celeste smiled, and her light vanished as if she had never been there.

Ioan sighed as he watched the sleeping city, the bleeding sun, and the stars falling from the sky. The world, immutable for so long, was changing in front of his old eyes, and it was beautiful in its own way. Beautiful indeed.

THE END

ENJOYED A WISH TOO DARK AND KIND?

Follow me on www.mylittleblackbird.com and subscribe to the newsletter to receive monthly updates, free fiction, and other offers.

Thank you for joining Alex and the others in their struggles to stop Arnaud's ritual. I hope you enjoyed the adventure!

I am always happy to chat about my (and other people's) stories and discuss where the ideas might have come from.

If you want to chat with me, feel free to reach me at sebastiano@mytlittleblackbird.com.

ABOUT THE AUTHOR

Born and raised in Sicily, M.L. spent most of his early life inventing stories and believing he could live in them.

In high school, he spent way too much time watching B movies, playing video games, and reading everything he could get his hands on, provided it wasn't recommended by any authority figure.

M.L. spent most of his college years and adult life writing in languages only machines can understand until he decided to put some of his stories on the page.

After a few years spent in Scotland, now M.L. lives in Seattle with his wife, his cat, and a large assortment of books. When not writing, he still enjoys playing video games and explaining board game rules to his friends.

You can follow M.L. on: https://mylittleblackbird.com.

M.L. also writes as Sebastiano Merlino.

goodreads.com/mlblackbird
twitter.com/merlinoseb
instagram.com/sebastianomerlino
facebook.com/mlblackbirdauthor
pinterest.com/mahadaeva